"Bradley broadens her range with an entertaining tale of contemporary 'magick' and self-discovery that combines gothic romance, urban fantasy, and horror. With a strong heroine and a sophisticated treatment of magick, this novel offers intelligent diversion." —*Publishers Weekly*

"Bradley is a master storyteller, and her latest proves thoroughly absorbing." —*Booklist*

"Bradley's colorful compelling writing style will not disappoint her fans. But don't just give it to them. Give it to those who have enjoyed Lois Duncan . . . those who enjoy Terry Brooks's Magic Kingdom series . . . and pass it along to fans of Barbara Michaels and Victoria Holt." —*VOYA*

"It's a pleasure to see Marion Zimmer Bradley's *Ghostlight* in paperback: this haunting tale of a young woman's search for the truth about her identity will reach new audiences, combining a mystery with the deeper story of a young woman's haunting."
—*The Bookwatch* (Petaluma, California)

"Those who are fans of Mary Higgins Clark will find a rival in this [novel]." —*The Southern Pines Pilot*

"A mature, tightly controlled, and suspenseful work from an author who has produced masterful works in other genres already." —*Science Fiction Chronicle*

"*Ghostlight* finds veteran novelist Bradley at the top of her form . . . less a dark fantasy than a straightforward tale of romantic suspense *a la* Barbara Michaels. Bradley's storytelling is smooth yet relentless. Fans of Bradley's better-known tales of Arthurian lore should seek out her tales of present-day supernatural affairs. *Ghostlight* is one of her best-realized works." —*Dragon*

Ghostlight

TOR BOOKS BY
MARION ZIMMER BRADLEY

Dark Satanic
Ghostlight
The Inheritor
Witch Hill
Witchlight

Ghostlight

M A R I O N
Z I M M E R
B R A D L E Y

TOR®

A TOM DOHERTY ASSOCIATES BOOK
NEW YORK

This is a work of fiction. All the characters and events portrayed in this book are either products of the author's imagination or are used fictitiously.

GHOSTLIGHT

Copyright © 2002 by Rosemary Edghill

A Tor Book
Published by Tom Doherty Associates, LLC
175 Fifth Avenue
New York, NY 10010

www.tor.com

Tor® is a registered trademark of Tom Doherty Associates, LLC.

ISBN: 0-765-34666-4
Library of Congress Catalog Card Number: 95-20003

First edition: August 1995
First mass market edition: February 2003

Printed in the United States of America

0 9 8 7 6 5 4 3 2 1

Ghostlight

PROLOGUE

April 30, 1969, Shadowkill, New York

THE FREAK SPRING STORM BATTERED THE OLD HOUSE WITH unceasing ferocity, as if attempting to gain entry to that which went on within. Flashes of lightning burst upon the figures inside the room with staccato intensity, illuminating the scene as if for some demonic surgeon's scalpel.

It was a circular room, its only windows those that ringed the cupola above. Below those windows a ritual as old as the land upon which the house stood was being enacted. Between the lightning flashes, the candles the observers held provided the only illumination, but it was enough.

A naked woman reclined upon a draped wooden altar, her body glistening with oil. Her black hair was spread like a fan over the furs and velvets on which she lay. At her head a red-robed woman stood, her own head thrown back in ecstatic communion with the forces summoned here tonight. Her hands cupped the unclad woman's temples and she cried out words in an ancient tongue in counterpoint to the thunder.

Seven men and one woman, robed all in dark forest

green, stood at the quarter and cross-quarter points of a circle cut into the floor. Another robed figure stood just outside its barrier. Each held a beeswax candle in his hands; their chanting a sonorous antiphon to the red-robed woman's ecstatic cries. In the north and in the west, braziers filled with incense sent their perfumed smoke skyward in pearlescent columns; in the east and in the south, great crystal bowls filled with water and with flowers hummed faintly, resonating to the ecstatic chanting and the fury of the storm.

Over the sound of wind and voices, a hammering could be heard at the chamber's one entrance.

"He comes! He comes! *He comes!*" shrilled the red-robed woman.

The chanting stopped. The doors flew open.

A man stood in the doorway. His eyes were shadowed and his long blond hair flowed free. His head was crowned with silver antlers and on his brow was the golden disk of the sun. His skin gleamed with oil and shadowy painted designs. He wore nothing but an animal skin tied about his shoulders, and before him he bore, point raised, a great silver sword that gleamed in the light of the candles.

"I am the key for every lock," he intoned in a voice that held the deep organ notes of the sea. *"I am the Opener of the Way!"*

He paced slowly forward, sword upheld, until he reached the robed figure standing in the South and—lightly, lightly—touched the point of the sword to his chest. The man fell back, and the others all began to chant, their voices faster and somehow more urgent.

"The sun! Comes the sun! By Oak and Ash and Thorn, the sun! Comes the sun!"

"The sun is coming up from the South!" cried the red-robed woman. "I call thee: Abraxas, Metatron, Uranos . . ."

Her litany went on unheeded. The horned man lay his great sword down at the foot of the altar and leaned over the naked woman. The smell of ambergris, civet, and opium rising from her skin was strong enough for him to smell even through all the other perfumes. The empty wine cup was still clasped loosely in her hand.

"Katherine—are you all right?" he whispered under the sound of the chanting. He could feel the power building in him; the ritual was proceeding just as he had written it, but something here in his Temple this night was not right.

At the sound of his voice her eyes opened. Even with only candlelight to see by he could tell that the pupils were enormous with drugs.

"Come . . . the . . . Opener of the Way," she said, her voice slurred and husky.

The robed ones at the perimeter of the circle chanted in unison, their voices blending into an uprush of power that would not be denied.

"By Abbadon! Meggido! Typhon! Set!" cried the red-robed woman. "Open now, open now the Way!"

Her eyes rolled up in her head and she sank to her knees, and the horned man could feel the Powers congregate within the Temple like a rushing of wings. He drew a deep, chest-expanding breath and raised his hands to the heavens.

"Hierodule and Hierolator! Hierophex and Hierophant—" he cried out.

His voice was drowned in a crescendo of thunderclaps, blending with each other into the roar of an onrushing train. The doors, closed a moment before by one of the robed acolytes, burst open again with enough force to shatter their hinges, and an icy gale poured into the room.

"No! Don't break the Circle!" the horned man shouted, but it was futile. Panic spread like a fire through oil-soaked rags; all was screaming and chaos.

In a flash of lightning he saw the woman on the altar fall to the ground and begin vibrating spasmodically, like a puppet in the hands of a vengeful god. A crack of thunder louder than any before it seemed to split the room like an executioner's axe.

Then darkness.

Screams.

And, somewhere, a child crying.

CHAPTER ONE

WHAT IS TRUTH?

*Beholding the bright countenance
of truth in the quiet and still air
of delightful studies.*

—JOHN MILTON

NORTH OF NEW YORK CITY, ALONG THE EDGE OF THE
Hudson River, there is a small estate lying between the
railroad tracks of Metro North and the broad expanse of
the river. Its main building was once a cider mill, and the
mill—as well as the descendants of the original orchard—
still occupies the site. Brick walkways cross the gently-
rolling lawns, and there is a yearly battle between the
students and the deer for the produce of the trees.

Later buildings in the exuberantly classical Federalist
mode complete the campus, but there has been no new con-
struction on the campus for nearly a century. Its architectural conservatism makes the place so much the perfect
image of a nineteenth-century college that the Dean must
very firmly discourage the advances of several movie com-
panies every year who wish to film here, but Taghkanic
College guards its privacy—and that of its students and
faculty—in the same stern fashion it always has.

In 1714 Taghkanic College was founded to provide education to the local Indians, mostly members of the Tagh-

kanic and Lenape tribes, and to the free Blacks who had also settled in the area. Existing to this day on the terms of its original charter, Taghkanic College has never accepted one penny of government support to cover its operating costs, choosing to remain independent first from Crown and royal governor and later from the representatives of the fledgling United States.

Adherence to this policy has led, over the years, to a liberalization of its admission policies: In 1762 Taghkanic College opened its doors to "alle younge gentillmen of goode familie," and in 1816 to women, making Taghkanic one of the first institutions of higher learning in the United States to do so.

Even with such broad admission policies, Taghkanic College would not exist today save for two individuals: Margaret Beresford Bidney and Colin MacLaren.

Miss Bidney graduated Taghkanic College in the same year that the Insurrection of the Southern States turned her father's comfortable fortune into a large one. She never married, and in the last years of her life she was a disciple of William Seabrook, noted occultist.

It was perhaps inevitable that Miss Bidney's fortune should go to fund, at the college of her matriculation, what grew to become the Margaret Beresford Bidney Memorial Psychic Science Research Laboratory at Taghkanic College.

From its inception, the laboratory—or, as it came informally to be known, the Bidney Institute—was funded independently of the college through the endowment fund created by the Bidney Bequest. The trustees of the college had been attempting to claim the entire Bidney Bequest on behalf of Taghkanic College for more than fifty years and were on the verge of success when Colin MacLaren accepted an appointment as director of the Institute.

Dr. MacLaren had been known in parapsychological circles since the early fifties, frequently operating under a cloud due to his willingness to accept at face value what were dismissed by others as the ravings of charlatans and kooks. MacLaren maintained that there should be no distinction made between the fields of occultism and parapsychology when studying the paranormal, that, if anything, the occultists should have the edge, since they had been studying the unseen world for centuries and attempting to distill a scientific method of dealing with its effects. MacLaren's particular field of study was trance psychism, or mediumship, and his aggressive leadership was precisely what the moribund Bidney Institute needed.

Under his guidance, the Institute took the lead in the investigation both of psychic phenomena and its wicked stepsister, occult phenomena, and became an institution of international repute. The specter of its dissolution vanished like expended ectoplasm, and it became clear to the disappointed trustees of Taghkanic College that their rich but unwanted foster child would be around until the time when Hell froze over—an event that the staff of the Margaret Beresford Bidney Psychic Science Research Institute intended, in any event, to measure.

Truth Jourdemayne sat brooding in her tiny cubicle at the Bidney Institute in a Monday-morning stupor unleavened, as yet, by the healing power of coffee. Her short dark hair in its sensible crop looked faintly rumpled, and her white lab coat, open over a sensible cotton sweater and jeans, looked less crisp than usual. A pile of computer printouts six inches thick lay under her right elbow: Truth's work for the immediate future.

She glanced up at the clock on her wall, shoving her horn-rimmed reading glasses up on her brow as she did so. Eight forty-five, and when she'd gotten here fifteen minutes ago Meg had just been starting to fill the percolator. It was large, and old, and took its sweet time to boil; there wouldn't be coffee for a while yet. Truth sighed, and pulled the printouts over to her. Might as well get some work done while she waited.

Davy had finished the last of the runs just yesterday. It was part of an experiment Truth had designed; nothing out of the ordinary, merely an attempt to establish once and for all a statistical baseline for incidents of clairsentient perception. It was necessary work, but collecting the data to validate the experiment was a mind-numbing labor: ten individuals aged twenty to twenty-five, in good physical health, who were willing to participate in 100 double-blind machine runs of 100 Rhine cards each—and at that Truth thought her findings might be challenged on the grounds of being based upon too small a statistical sample.

But the experiment would have been impossibly unwieldy with more volunteers, even if she could have gotten them. It had taken over a year to amass the data as it was. And the preliminary work was sound enough. The experiment met all the International Society of Psychic Research guidelines: Responses were recorded electronically, symbols were chosen randomly by machine; there was no possibility that a human researcher could accidentally communicate the symbols to the subjects through body language.

Or even telepathy. It was hard enough having to design an experiment that would generate baseline statistics by which clairvoyance could be measured without having to design one that excluded other psychic talents—such as telepathy or precognition—as well. Still, Truth thought she'd managed. Since the computer in some sense already "knew" the order of all the symbols it would choose, that event lay in the past by the time the subject entered the experiment, so that any ability to see the future—assuming any of their subjects possessed such, which Truth hoped for the sake of her experiment they did not—would not be involved in guessing the symbols on the cards.

Welcome to the glamourous world of statistical parapsy-

chology, Truth thought wryly to herself, and picked up a pencil.

She'd forgotten entirely about coffee when Meg came in an hour later.

"Hello? Hibernating?"

Meg Winslow was the Parapsychology Department's secretary, short, cheerful, round, and efficient. She entered with an armful of mail and a steaming coffee cup held perilously steady with three fingers.

"I lost track of the time," Truth admitted sheepishly.

"*Lots* of lovely mail," Meg announced decisively, "and Dyl brought in some currant shortbread he made over the weekend. I saved you a piece."

Dumping the mail carefully on the desk, Meg set the cup down and dove into her jacket pocket to retrieve sugar and cream packets and a tile of shortbread wrapped in a paper napkin.

"You're spoiling me," Truth protested laughingly. This service wasn't part of Meg's job description.

"If I don't, you'll starve to death, and be buried in a pile of statistics," Meg said promptly. "I'd better get a move on—today's the start of classes, and we're sure to have a dozen lost freshmen wander in here before noon if I don't keep 'em out." Meg swept out again, carefully closing the door behind her, in obedience to Truth's preference.

As one of the nonfaculty researchers at the Bidney Institute, Truth was entitled to an office with a door, just as if she were a full professor, and she kept it shut, whether she was in the office or not. The professors whose offices flanked hers kept their doors closed only, Truth suspected, as a vacuous show of status, especially since most of them popped up and peered out at the slightest footstep from outside.

But when Truth closed her door, she meant it. Truth kept her door shut so she could keep people out. Especially now. Truth Jourdemayne hated September with a passion more often reserved for the holiday season; she hated the flocks of returning students, the bewildered new arrivals, the graduate students.

It was not so much that she disliked any individual student, she told herself unconvincingly. It was just that taken all together they were too many—too noisy, and too energetic.

Well, after all, they're just arriving, while you've been here all summer, toiling away in the vineyards of statistical analysis, Truth told herself mockingly. The Institute did not follow Taghkanic's academic year—a good thing, as they'd never get any work done—and so September was just another month for her, and not the end of a long vacation.

She sighed, and reached for her coffee—*Meg really shouldn't do things like this; if the professors notice they'll all want her to fetch and carry for them and she'll never get anything done*—and only then realized how stiff and sore her muscles were.

Tension. I really hate this place in September. A cross between a lunatic asylum and a three-ring circus—and at that, enrollment's down again. Everywhere but at good old Maggie B. There were not many places in either the United States or Europe that offered a degree program in parapsychology and the services of a first-rate research lab to boot. If not for the Bidney Institute, Taghkanic would probably have closed years ago, just another liberal-arts college caught in the money crunch.

And where would you work then? Truth took a moment to work the kinks out of her neck and shoulders before proceeding to her mail.

Most of what Meg had brought her was thick professional journals and catalogs. A book for review; another book, a publisher's blind solicitation of quotes; parapsychology textbooks mostly, but one on statistical analysis that looked interesting. A quire of letter-sized envelopes, embossed with return addresses she knew.

And one she didn't. Rouncival Press.

Frowning, she tore it open.

And tore it. And tore it, until the envelope and three sheets of heavy paper were in postage-stamp-sized tatters on her desk. Her hands shook. How could they? How *dare* they?

"*. . . since you have also chosen a career in the occult . . . valuable service . . . intimate glimpses of a great pioneer of magic . . .*"

They wanted her to write a biography of Thorne Blackburn.

Her hands were still shaking as she scooped the pieces of paper into her wastebasket. She was a scientist—she had a master's in Mathematics! Write an eulogistic biography of Thorne Blackburn? She'd rather bury him with a stake through his heart—and he was already dead.

And what was worse, he was her father.

Truth stared unseeingly at a poster of the Olana Historical Site on her cubicle wall. Thirty years ago Thorne Blackburn had been at the forefront of the occult revival that went hand-in-hand with the free love and antiwar movements of the 1960s. As sexy as Morrison, as fiery as Jagger—and as crazy as Hendrix—Blackburn had claimed to be a *hero* in the Greek sense, a half-divine son of the Shining Ones, the Celtic Old Gods. Though such declarations later became commonplace, with people claiming to be the children of everything from space aliens to earth angels, Thorne Blackburn had been the first.

He'd been the first to do a number of other things, too, from appearing on national television to conduct a ritual for his Old Gods to touring with rock bands as the opening act. Half heretic, half fraud, and all showman, Blackburn was one of the brightest lights of the occult revival during his brief, gaudy, public career.

And he'd made it pay, Truth thought angrily. While publicly he claimed to be founding an order of heroes and working magick to bring the Ancient Gods of the West into the world again and inaugurate the "New Aeon," Blackburn had somehow managed to amass the cash to buy a Hudson River mansion where he and his special followers could practice the rites of his so-called Circle of Truth in an atmosphere of free love, free drugs, and wild excess.

Among those followers had been Katherine Jourdemayne.

Truth felt the faint stirrings of a headache as she contemplated the old, familiar betrayal. Her mother had been Blackburn's "mystical concubine." Katherine had died in 1969 in one of his rituals, and Blackburn hadn't had to pay for that, either.

Because that same night—April 30, 1969—Thorne Blackburn had vanished from the face of the earth.

Truth had been raised by Katherine Jourdemayne's twin sister, Caroline, and Truth felt she had inherited much of her emotional self-sufficiency from the taciturn woman who had weathered the horrible death of her twin sister so stoically. Aunt Caroline had told Truth who her father was when she was old enough to understand, but in the seventies and early eighties it didn't seem to matter much. When the first journalist contacted her, Truth had even been surprised to discover that anyone still remembered Thorne Blackburn; he seemed to belong to the past, like LSD, the moon landing, and the Beatles. She had been courteous, though brief, telling him she had nothing to say, because her father died when she was two.

It was the last time she was ever that polite, because once the "gentlemen of the press" had found her, her life quickly became a nightmare of letters and telephone calls—and worse: visits from bizarre individuals who claimed they were followers, and in one horrible instance, the *reincarnation*—of Thorne Blackburn.

And every Halloween since she was eighteen Truth had suffered through the various calls from a particular breed of grave-robbing yellow journalist who wanted an interview with the daughter of the notorious "Satanist" Thorne Blackburn to spice up a story.

The requests from the literary lunatic fringe to write about Thorne Blackburn had fortunately diminished over the years, although they'd never quite stopped. She might even have been willing to write a book—publish or perish, after all, even for those who weren't academics on the tenure track—except that the publishers all made it very clear that they were not looking for accuracy, rather for a credulous panegyric they could pass off as gospel to their equally addled readers.

And Katherine Jourdemayne's daughter was damned if she was going to gild the reputation of a fake, a fraud, an Aquarian Age snake-oil salesman. Why couldn't all those people see what a huckster Blackburn had really been?

It was, Truth supposed, part of the reason she'd gone into parapsychology: find a way to debunk the frauds before they could hurt anyone. But sometimes she was so ashamed.

Why couldn't I be the daughter of Elvis instead? Truth thought forlornly. *Life would be easier.*

She ran a hand through her hair, still trembling with repressed emotion. Why couldn't they all realize that the only thing she wanted was never to have to think about Thorne Blackburn ever again? He haunted her life like the ghost at the feast, poised to drag her into his lunatic world of unreason.

"Hello? Anyone home? Ah, my esteemed colleague, Miss Jourdemayne." Without giving her a chance to pretend she wasn't there at all, Dylan Palmer slid in to Truth's office and closed the door.

Dylan Palmer—Dr. Palmer—*was* a tenure-track academic, a member of the teaching faculty at Taghkanic as well as a fellow of the Institute. He was a professor in the Indiana Jones mold, being tall, blond, handsome, easygoing, and occasionally heroic. Dylan's particular parapsychological interest was personality transfers and survivals—in more mundane parlance, hauntings.

"How's my favorite number-cruncher today?" he asked cheerfully.

Dylan leaned over her desk, looking more like one of the students than one of the teachers in his flannel shirt and baggy jeans. The small gold ring in his ear winked in the light.

"How was your summer project?" Truth asked.

She could feel herself withdrawing, and knew that Dylan could see it too, but Truth found his zest for life as daunting as it was exhilarating.

"Wonderful!" If Dylan was hurt by her coolness he didn't show it. "Twelve weeks in the draftiest Irish castle you ever saw—just me, three grad students, and seventy-five thousand dollars of cameras, microphones, and sensors. Oh, and the IRA."

"What?"

"Just kidding. I think that's who the locals thought we were, though—they did everything but cross themselves when we'd come into town to buy supplies." He straightened up, looking pleased with himself.

"That's just the sort of thing *you'd* think was funny," Truth said. "This isn't a game, Dylan—psychic investigation is a serious business, even if *you* treat it lightly." She heard the condescension in her voice and winced inwardly, hoping Dylan would go away before she embarrassed herself further.

"Ah, Halloween coming early this year?" Dylan asked lightly.

Truth stared at him blank-faced.

"I couldn't help but notice," Dylan said, looking downward ostentatiously. "Thorne Blackburn time again, is it?"

Truth followed the direction of his gaze, and saw a small snowstorm of torn paper around her feet. Dylan bent down gracefully and retrieved a scrap. Truth snatched at it, but to no avail. Dylan brandished it theatrically and began to declaim.

"When the frost is on the pumpkin, and Blackburn time is near/Then the ghoulies and the goblins, do jump about in fear/For Truth—"

"It isn't funny!" Truth cried furiously. She jumped to her feet and snatched the scrap of Rouncival's letter out of Dylan's hand. "Do you think I *enjoy* being reminded that

Thorne Blackburn is my father? Do you think it makes me *happy?*"

"Well it could be worse; he could still be among us. As it is, he's strictly my department. Lighten up, Truth—it isn't like Thorne's Jack the Ripper or anything. Professor MacLaren thinks he's a pretty interesting figure, actually, worth studying. Maybe you ought to consider—"

Truth felt unreasonably betrayed. Although most of the people at the Institute knew she was Thorne Blackburn's daughter—his *bastard* daughter, in fact—anyone she knew at all well knew better than to bring it up. Certainly Dylan did. Or should.

"Well, I don't have your sainted Professor MacLaren's tolerance for cheats and monsters!" she interrupted hotly. "Maybe *you* ought to consider people's feelings before marching in with your fund of good advice!"

Dylan's easy smile faded as he studied her face. "I didn't mean . . ." he began.

"You never mean anything!" Truth shot back viciously, conscious only of a desire to strike back at someone, anyone. "You're just some kind of freelance superhero, playing ghost-breaker and not caring what you do so long as it gives you a dramatic exit line and a cheap laugh. Well, I'm not laughing." She closed her hands into painful fists, willing herself not to cry.

"You're going to get awfully lonely up there on your pedestal," Dylan said softly. Before she could think of another thing to say he was gone, closing the door quietly behind him.

He killed my mother, he killed my mother, he killed my mother—

Truth sat at her desk, her eyes tightly shut against the tears she would not permit—because they were useless, because they were childish, because they would change nothing at all. Why didn't anyone understand what Thorne had done to her? He'd taken everything, *everything.* . . .

She hadn't expected Dylan of all people to take Thorne's part. She *should* have, Truth told herself. He was obviously another Thorne fan—and why not? They were two of a kind.

But even as upset as she was, Truth knew that wasn't fair. Dylan was just . . . too happy, Truth finished lamely. Dylan Palmer did not seem to ever have internalized the knowledge that life was a horrible business filled with nasty surprises, in which the best you could hope for was not to be hurt too badly.

But how could he possibly take Thorne Blackburn at face value? The man—Thorne—was a self-confessed fraud!

Truth managed a grimace of wry humor; honestly, sometimes psychic researchers were the most gullible people on earth. Every event was genuine until proven otherwise; from crop circles to Uri Geller, people like Dylan approached them with boundless credulity.

She drew a quavering breath, slowly regaining her self-control. It was just as well they did, she supposed, or else the disenchantment of discovering only fakes and coincidences year after year might be too hard to bear. She shook her head. Dylan had been a little out of line, but his bad manners hadn't warranted the response he'd gotten from her. She'd have to apologize.

I need a vacation. As her mind formed the words, Truth realized how tired she was. She'd spent the summer shepherding her project through to completion on top of her regular workload—why shouldn't she get away from Taghkanic while the first rush of fall term was going on? She could come back when it was quiet—well, as quiet as it ever got, anyway.

The phone rang.

Truth stared at it with guilty fascination. It was probably Dylan, phoning from his office to finish telling her off. But when she looked down at the phone, she realized that it was one of the outside lines that was ringing. She picked up the phone.

"Hello?"

"Truth?"

"Aunt Caroline?"

Truth felt a sluggish pulse of alarm. Caroline Jourde-mayne was a very self-contained person, and the two of them weren't really close. What could have happened that made Aunt Caroline feel she needed to call? "Is there anything wrong?" Truth asked.

"You might say that," the familiar, dryly unemotional voice said. "I'm sorry to bother you at work, Truth, but you're going to have to come home as soon as possible."

Home was the small house situated in the wilds of northern Amsterdam County over seventy miles away, where Truth's childhood had been spent and where her memories really began.

"Come home?" Truth echoed, baffled.

Aunt Caroline was not an outgoing woman; since Truth had gotten her apartment here on the Taghkanic campus, visits to Aunt Caroline had been infrequent—usually occurring around Thanksgiving, since in December the roads near the cottage were treacherous except for vehicles equipped with four-wheel-drive.

"I trust you still remember where it is?" Aunt Caroline said.

"Oh, yes, of course. But—"

"How soon can you come?" Aunt Caroline asked.

Truth frowned, juggling schedules in her mind. Fortunately she didn't have any teaching commitments to consider. She was supposed to spend a certain amount of time in the lab assisting the teaching researchers with their projects, but this early in the academic year there wasn't much of that; she could easily find someone to cover for her.

"Tomorrow," Truth said. "I'll be there tomorrow. Aunt Caroline, can't you tell me what this is about?" She could think of no secret so lurid that it could not be mentioned over the phone, and the Jourdemaynes were not a family for lurid secrets—at least, not what was left of the Jourdemaynes.

She glanced idly up at the clock on the wall as Aunt

Caroline began to explain the reason for the call, and as the distant voice continued Truth's gaze became fixed and staring, and eventually the shocked irrelevant tears began to spill down her face as Aunt Caroline continued to speak.

CHAPTER TWO

THE TRUTH OF THE MATTER

This is truth the poet sings,
That a sorrow's crown of sorrow is
remembering happier things.
—ALFRED, LORD TENNYSON

IN CONTRAST TO THE BRIGHT CLEAR PROMISE OF MONDAY, Tuesday was dark and unseasonably humid. Early that morning Truth was on the Thruway heading north to Stormlakken. There was no direct route to the town; it was a several hour drive, even under optimal conditions. She should get there a little after noon.

It was only after she was already on the road that Truth realized she hadn't smoothed over the scene she'd had with Dylan the day before. She'd been too busy arranging for her absence, and then she'd felt obligated to do some work on the project, and had let the soothing ranks of statistics drive everything else out of her mind. She knew that the longer it was before she made her apology the harder it would be, but after Aunt Caroline's news she had not wanted to risk another encounter that might open her emotional floodgates. She would not use Aunt Caroline as an excuse when she finally spoke to him, though. She would simply apologize. The Jourdemaynes were a private people, not given to explanation. Or displays of emotion.

Why don't I feel anything?

The almost commonplace beauty of the Hudson River Valley—dramatic vistas that had inspired Frederick Church and a whole school of American landscape painters—rolled by outside the car's windows, unappreciated. Dylan was fond of quoting some bit of Coleridge about a savage place, holy and enchanted. Truth had always thought that was overdramatic and fanciful—like Dylan?—but the fact was that the terrain was spectacular enough to have coaxed poetry from the souls of its phlegmatic Dutch inhabitants when they had first settled here over 300 years before. This was Sleepy Hollow Country, home and birthplace to tales of Headless Horsemen and Rip Van Winkles, bowling giants and fiddling gnomes and ghostly galleons roving the Hudson.

Truth surprised herself in the midst of this prosaic revery and found her mind engaged as if she were composing a lecture for some unknown audience, marshaling her facts. Facts had always been her way of keeping the painful world at bay. Keeping her feelings at bay.

But I don't feel anything. And I should.

Caroline Jourdemayne had been Truth's entire family from the time Truth was orphaned at the age of two. Aunt Caroline had come to Blackburn's sordid commune and taken her sister's child away, caring for Truth without a word of reproach or complaint at what must have been the fearful disarrangement of an ordered spinster life. But despite the fact that Caroline and Katherine had been identical twins, Truth had never felt the warmth for her Aunt Caroline that she assumed she would have felt for her own mother.

There was no enmity between Truth and Aunt Caroline, of course, only a rather distant and dutiful affection on Truth's part, and a scrupulous courtesy on Aunt Caroline's. If either woman thought the relationship odd, it was not something they discussed—and as Truth had grown up and away and heard the tales of her classmates' and roommates' families, she became more grateful for the careful remoteness that Aunt Caroline had preserved. If Aunt Caroline had shared her grief about her sister's murder Truth did not think she could have borne it.

But she must have felt something. Twins, especially identical twins, are supposed to be very close; the Linebaugh-Hay telepathy experiments prove—Truth broke off her train of thought, a little surprised at the clinical direction it had taken. Of course Aunt Caroline missed her sister, Katherine, just as Truth missed her mother. But there had been no one left to blame once Thorne Blackburn had vanished.

Blackburn. It always came back to him—Fortune's golden child, a man of mysterious origins who made his mark as a mountebank of mountebanks, who told everybody outrageous stories and then told them he was lying to them, a man who urged belief on his acolytes while professing no beliefs himself. A man who made promises that no man could possibly keep—but then Thorne Blackburn had never meant to keep any of his promises.

Thorne Blackburn was a spiritual con man who stole belief instead of money, and then stole the money too.

Truth jammed on her brakes, glancing guiltily into the rearview mirror at the same moment she yanked the wheel to the right. Fortunately there was no one behind her; she'd nearly missed her exit. She turned off the Thruway, and onto the patched and rutted secondary road that led toward Stormlakken. Only a little farther now.

What could she do? What could she say?

There was nothing she *could* do—Aunt Caroline had been very clear on that point. And it was Aunt Caroline who had things to say, things she did not wish to go into over the phone.

The secondary road gave way to one that was barely a lane and a half wide. Now Truth was in the foothills of the Taconic Range, and the choppy, glacier-carved terrain was a study in tall grass and scraggly bushes, scrub pine and an occasional stand of birch.

She stopped in downtown Stormlakken to get gas; it was still the same place it had been twenty years ago, and ten, and five, though the five-and-dime was boarded up now and all that was left on Main Street was a bus shelter, an auto-parts store, a branch of the Mid-Hudson Bank, and a fly-blown lunch counter. The rococo Victorian department store across from the gas station stood empty as it had for as long as Truth could remember.

A dying town; a suitable counterpart to the bleak September day. Truth was glad to go on, heading up Main Street toward the lake. Or toward what locals called the lake, although there had been no lake there for nearly three-quarters of a century.

A local water project in the early twenties—part of a plan to supply drinking water to New York City, outmoded when the Croton Reservoir was built—had drained the lake that had given the town its name and destroyed Stormlak-ken's tenuous claim to being a vacation spot. When the Thruway had gone in, the last of the vitality had drained from the town, until today it was nearly a ghost town, too far south of the tristate burgeoning of Schenectady/Albany/Troy and too far north of Poughkeepsie to be included in either area's urban sprawl.

Caroline Jourdemayne's house was a few miles outside of town, on the shore of what had once been the lake. Most of the tidy Victorian cottages that had been built upon the lake shore were long since torn down; Aunt Caroline's little house sat in isolated splendor on the sparsely-wooded hill-side looking out over the lush meadow that was the former lake bed.

Truth pulled up and parked beside Aunt Caroline's old Honda. She got out of the car. A wet dank wind was blowing across the ridge, irritating without being either cold or hot. She shrugged her purse up onto her shoulder and trudged up the steps to the house.

It took Aunt Caroline a long time to come to the door, and when she did, Truth was horrified at the changes that had already taken place in her. The black hair was limp and gray streaked, the skin pouched and yellowish, the woman herself suddenly, hideously, *old*.

"Yes," Aunt Caroline said. The skull beneath the skin grinned out, blatantly visible. "I look terrible, don't I? The doctor has given me less than a month—and it was all I could do to twist that prediction out of him. They don't like giving out facts, doctors don't."

"But when—but how?" Truth stammered. Caroline Jourdemayne turned away, walking as if her bones were made of glass. Truth followed her inside and closed the door.

The living room had the faintly out-of-touch feeling of something outside of time; the furniture was what Aunt Caroline had purchased when she was a young woman thirty years before—sleek Danish Modern bookcases and tables and chairs with cushions in olive and orange and rust, a slice of the futuristic sixties carried forward through time intact as a fly in amber.

"Cancer strikes in the best of families, I believe," Aunt Caroline said. She sat down gingerly on the sofa, wincing with the exertion. "You're looking well. How is the Institute?"

"Oh, well enough," Truth said, not wanting to talk about work. She set down her purse and jacket on the low tile-topped cocktail table next to a nondescript cardboard box of the sort used for storing personal papers.

"Can I get you anything from the kitchen?" Truth asked.

"No, but do make yourself some lunch. I imagine you haven't been eating again—as usual."

"Poor Dr. Vandemeyer is terribly embarrassed," Aunt Caroline said as Truth returned with her sandwich and tea, "but by the time I went to see him it was too late."

Truth sat down opposite her aunt on a low-slung chair and set down her teacup carefully. Now that the first shock had passed, she felt more able to deal with this sudden catastrophe. There had never been much money in the Jourdemayne family, although there was more than none; Caroline Jourdemayne, the sensible twin, had worked as a librarian for many years at the Association Library in nearby Rock Creek, but it was Grandmother Jennet's legacy that had made affordable the house and the car.

"What can I do?" Truth said simply.

"I shall stay here as long as I can. A nurse will drive down from the HMO three times a week to look in on me, but I am told that fairly soon I shall have to have someone here all the time."

"Do you want—" Truth began hesitantly.

Aunt Caroline smiled, the skin stretching tight over sharp bones. "I shall engage a professional nurse, of course. I have spoken to Mr. Branwell at the realty agency and he feels he can sell the house very quickly once—once it becomes available; the proceeds from that should more than settle the debts of my estate. What is left comes to you, of course, though I'm afraid there won't be much."

Truth shook her head slowly, trying to dispel the brisk, clinical efficiency with which Aunt Caroline tidied away her life. "I don't care about that," she said.

"No. I don't imagine you do," Aunt Caroline said, studying her closely. "But since you are to be my executor— and that soon—perhaps we could go over a few things now."

Truth felt the numb sense of impending doom that one feels in nightmares as Aunt Caroline went over the will and the other arrangements with her. Caroline Jourdemayne would be buried in the Amsterdam Rural Cemetery next to her twin. The coffin had already been purchased and the arrangements for the memorial service made with the local funeral home. Everything was ready.

All Caroline Jourdemayne had to do now was die.

"—but we could have handled all these matters by phone," Aunt Caroline went on inexorably. "There's something else."

For the first time Aunt Caroline's iron will seemed to falter. "Please—If you'd get me a glass of water—My pills . . ."

Truth fled to the kitchen for a glass of water, returning with it and the bottle of painkillers stickered all over with advisories: MAY CAUSE DROWSINESS—CONTROLLED SUBSTANCE—DO NOT OPERATE HEAVY MACHINERY WHILE TAKING THIS PRESCRIPTION. Seeing Aunt Caroline struggle with the cap, Truth opened it for her, and Aunt Caroline swallowed two of the pills. Truth frowned. She was certain the dosage was supposed to be one.

It must be very bad already. And there was nothing she could do—no way to reach out to Caroline Jourdemayne. Truth felt a sudden panicky realization that there was no time left to forge close emotional ties to her aunt. Caroline would die and Truth would be left with the guilt of selfishness.

"There. I shall be better presently, so Dr. Vandemeyer has been at pains to assure me. Now. There is another matter that we must discuss. The real reason you're here."

Truth waited, but Aunt Caroline said nothing more. Truth let her gaze drift toward the window to the stark, Andrew Wyeth–esque landscape beyond. The sky was a palette of gray on gray that seemed to cocoon the house like wet spongy flesh.

"We never did discuss . . . the past," Aunt Caroline said at last. "It's important for you to know that you're not the only one."

The only one? Truth stared at her aunt, feeling a faint alarm tinged with uncomfortable pity. What Caroline Jourdemayne had said made no sense. "I guess—" Truth began.

"I'm not quite senile yet—or drugged senseless," Aunt Caroline snapped, as if she could read Truth's mind. "But this is hard for me. For so many years I just tried to blot it all out—Thorne, and Katherine—but there are things you need to know about your family."

"My family," Truth echoed. But Aunt Caroline was her only family, and Truth found it hard to imagine anything she needed to know about Aunt Caroline.

"Your parents. Your father and mother. Thorne Blackburn most of all. You never had the chance to know him, and now . . ."

Blackburn again! Truth struggled to keep her face serene.

"I don't think there's anything you really need to tell me about Thorne Blackburn, Aunt Caroline," Truth said carefully.

"How quick you are to say that. Perhaps I should have— But there's no time now for vain regrets. You did not know him."

And never wanted to! Truth cried out silently. There was an odd tone in Aunt Caroline's voice that frightened her.

"There is a legacy . . ." Aunt Caroline's voice trailed off, and her head drooped for a moment as the narcotic relief of the pills took hold.

"Aunt Caroline?" Truth said anxiously.

The old woman roused with an effort. "I tire so easily these days; I'm still not used to it. And I shall die before I am." She grimaced, impatient with her body's failing. "There is something I have been keeping for you, some of Thorne's possessions. I know that you won't understand why; I'd hoped to wait until I could . . . But I have run out of time."

I have run out of time. That calm statement of fact roused Truth's pity as no more dramatic statement could.

"Time for what, Aunt Caroline?" Truth asked gently.

"I didn't wish to give them to you until it wouldn't—I never wanted you to hate him," Aunt Caroline said, "I just couldn't bear . . . But there is no more time. These things cannot be left around for just anyone to stumble upon once I'm dead; no matter your feelings you'll have to take them now, and I pray that—" Once more Caroline Jourdemayne broke off in the middle of a sentence, as if there were still things that could not be said. "Call it Thorne's legacy to you, and I wish you could understand what he . . . They're in a box in the bedroom—go get them. And then we must talk about the others."

What others? Truth wondered, rising to her feet. But Aunt Caroline's eyes were closed and Truth could not bear to trouble her further.

*　　*　　*

Aunt Caroline's bedroom was at the back of the house. It, too, was filled with the falsely-modern furniture that seemed to belong to a vision of some happier tomorrow. The low dresser with its close-grained teak finish—who, in those more fortunate days, had ever heard of an endangered rain forest?—the chaste double bed with the bookcase headboard and bright cotton bedspread, even the pictures on the walls could have come straight out of—

Out of 1969, Truth thought with a cold pang of realization. *It is as though Time itself stopped here when Mother died.*

She did not want to think about that, to add one more crime to the list of Blackburn's villainies. She had never before considered how the house looked, but now the knowledge was inescapable. Nothing had changed here since Aunt Caroline's twin had died. It was as if Aunt Caroline and all the house were . . . waiting.

For what?

Truth walked over to the dresser. There was a photograph on it in a silver frame—a faded head-and-shoulders shot of a dark-haired, dark-eyed woman who was the image of Caroline Jourdemayne at twenty.

But no one would keep a photo of herself on display in that way—and Caroline Jourdemayne had never in all her life worn her hair in that long, coltish tangle, or those gypsyish hoops of Mexican silver sparkling in her ears.

Mexican . . . Blackburn had taken his little coven to Mexico the summer before they'd moved into Shadow's Gate—the summer before Katherine had died.

This must be Katherine Jourdemayne.

Truth had never seen a picture of her mother. If she had thought about it at all, she'd assumed there weren't any. She picked up the frame, wondering why Aunt Caroline had never shared this with her.

As Truth moved the photo, another picture—loose, this time—slipped free from its concealment behind the frame and spiraled to the floor. Truth stooped down to pick it up.

It was a Polaroid of as ancient a vintage as the framed

photo, this time a full-figure shot of a slender, laughing, blond-haired man, his long golden hair spilling down his back as he lifted a dark-haired baby high above his head. He was shirtless and barefoot, wearing only bell-bottoms and some kind of bead necklace.

Her father.

She was entirely certain, even though there were few photos of Thorne Blackburn available today and certainly nothing like this candid shot. The one most people used was Blackburn's publicity photo that showed him in full mystic regalia.

But there was no doubt. This was him. This casual, laughing stranger was her father.

And the child must be——her.

A fury so strong it could only be hatred possessed Truth Jourdemayne's consciousness with the force of an onrushing train. How dared the man in the picture seem so normal, as if he were any young father happily playing with his infant daughter? Didn't he know what he'd done——what he was going to do?

Truth's skin crawled as though Blackburn were here with her in the room, and the fact that he had once held her tenderly in his arms seemed unforgivable. She set the photograph back on the dresser top gingerly, and set the framed picture of her mother on top of it as if she could hold down thoughts of Blackburn as easily.

Why would Aunt Caroline keep a picture like this? Truth wondered.

"I never wanted you to hate him," Aunt Caroline had *said.* An ugly suspicion was growing in the back of Truth's mind, waiting patiently but with gathering momentum for the moment it could break through into her consciousness; the prerational certainty that psychics called *clairsentience*——the ability to know what you couldn't possibly know, a perception that baffled the restraints of space and time.

Oh, knock it off! Truth told herself fiercely. Ten minutes more and she'd be seeing ghosts. *Now where's that damned whatever-it-is?*

The box was on the bed.

It was a white cardboard box—the old, heavy, glazed kind that good stores used to use—and stamped on the lid in silver was the logo of the now-defunct Lucky-Platt Department Store.

Hesitantly, Truth raised the lid. The box was filled with crisp, white tissue paper—and with more. Truth wondered what grisly legacy Thorne Blackburn could have bequeathed her.

No, not Thorne Blackburn.

"Something I have been keeping for you; some of Thorne's possessions ... These things cannot be left around for just anyone to stumble upon once I'm dead; no matter your feelings you'll have to take them now. . . . Call it Thorne's legacy to you. . . .

"I never wanted you to hate him.

"But there is no more time. . . ."

A ring, a necklace, and a book.

She picked up the ring first. Its weight almost made Truth drop it again; it was far too large for her, big enough to cover her longest finger from knuckle to knuckle. It was set with a flat oval of lapis lazuli as big as a peach pit, deeply and intricately carved with some sort of design Truth couldn't quite make out. The stone was set in what must be a full Troy ounce of yellow gold, soft enough to be pure, cast in the shape of a coiled serpent that had red-enameled letters cut into its scaly flesh and tiny winking rubies for its eyes. There were other rubies studded about the ring's bezel—not cabochons, but whole, dark red spheres like beads of blood. The ring had a Greek inscription on the inside of the band, along with a date. Both were meaningless to Truth.

The necklace was a magnificent thing: dark golden amber beads the size of walnuts, long enough to hang halfway down her torso. *It's the one he's wearing in the picture ...* A symbol dangled from it, a thick, heavy pendant of enameled gold in an eye-bewildering tangle of curves and circles and peculiar symbols. Both the ring and the necklace seemed theatrical, ceremonial, as though freighted with the weight of a vast store of purpose and intention.

Blackburn's ring. Blackburn's necklace. His legacy to her—as preserved by Aunt Caroline. For her.

Why had Aunt Caroline kept these things for her? Why had she brought her here to give them to her now?

It wasn't what she'd expected from Aunt Caroline, no, not at all. . . .

Truth realized with an unfolding sense of dismay that she'd never really known her aunt. Not what she'd expected. No. Not what a woman who blamed Thorne Blackburn for her sister's murder would have done. *"I never wanted you to hate him. . . ."* But what else could Aunt Caroline have expected?

Could she have expected anything else?

Truth closed her hands tightly over the serpentine length of the necklace, half-hoping the force would crack the amber beads. All these years she'd just assumed that Aunt Caroline was as disgusted with Blackburn as Truth was, when the reality . . .

She could see it so clearly now.

Aunt Caroline and the house had been waiting since Katherine died in 1969. Frozen in time. Waiting—

How could she ever have been so blind? It was so obvious. All you had to do was look. . . .

Waiting.

Waiting until Caroline could join Katherine in death.

Waiting until Caroline could join Thorne Blackburn.

Caroline Jourdemayne had *loved* Thorne Blackburn.

It was as if the world had suddenly tilted 180 degrees. All the unexamined facts of Truth's past, carefully buried and unquestioned, rose up as if embodying another's will and assembled themselves to form an unwelcome and bitterly plausible history.

Hadn't Caroline Jourdemayne also been at Shadow's Gate the night Katherine Jourdemayne had died and Blackburn had vanished? She had, and all these years Truth had never wondered why—but Caroline Jourdemayne couldn't have known how necessary her presence would be. She must simply have been—visiting.

Her sister and her friend.

Her *lover*?

The past suddenly seemed real, here in this room—Truth could see them all together; Katherine, trusting and helplessly fond; Caroline, skeptical and seeing danger ahead, trying to be the practical one but powerless to avert the tragedy that claimed the two people she loved most. And Thorne Blackburn.

Truth closed her eyes tightly. *No—no—no . . . This isn't true. It can't be true!*

But it made so much sense. Why keep a photograph of a man you hated? Why save his things for his daughter if you didn't think his memory was worth preserving?

Caroline had loved him.

Truth sat down slowly on the bed. Her jaws ached with the force of the denial she would not give voice to. Everything she'd ever believed had been a lie, and all this, all the rest of Caroline Jourdemayne's life, had been spent behind the veil of withdrawn nunlike asceticism that Truth had tried to pierce in vain, spent as though Caroline Jourdemayne had dedicated herself to the chaste worship of Thorne Blackburn down through all the lonely years she had spent raising his daughter.

And she'd thought it had all been done for love of Katherine, Truth mocked herself bleakly. Wrong.

She didn't love me. She loved him. Truth heard the cheated little-girl voice inside her mind and could not force it down. Aunt Caroline had loved Thorne Blackburn. Still. Now. Always. If she had hated him she would not have been there, always there—and there the one night the two of them—the three of them—had needed her most.

And when, in her teens, Truth had begun to know who he had been and to speak out against Thorne Blackburn, Aunt Caroline had never said a word.

Hoping I'd change my mind? There'll be blizzards in

Hell first, Truth thought grimly. The grief growing in her was too deep for words.

He's taken everything. He left me nothing.

Not her mother, not her mother's love—not even, in the end, her aunt's. It had all, all, all been for Thorne Blackburn, and nothing for his daughter.

Nothing. Nothing left. No time . . .

There was one more thing in the box.

A book.

She lifted it out carefully. It was about nine inches by twelve—a little larger than a modern hardcover book—and about two inches thick. There was no dust jacket, and it was bound in smooth black leather, with the sort of hubbed spine that Truth associated with the antique books in the Taghkanic College library.

But this was not an antique book—nor, as she discovered when she opened it, a printed book at all.

The title page was handwritten in black ink in a sweeping hand. It said: *Venus Afflicted: Being a Discourse on the True Rite for the Opening of the Way and Other Matters. Thorne Blackburn.*

Truth flipped through it quickly. The pages were covered with writing in a neat, modern hand, occasionally interspersed with elaborate drawings by the same hand.

It must be some kind of spellbook, Truth thought numbly. She dropped it back into the box, rubbing her hands together as if she'd touched something dirty. To foster a belief in magic in this modern day and age seemed too much to Truth like a deliberate turning away from rationalism into the dark ignorance of the past. If magic, then why not faith healing and infant sacrifice as well?

Thorne Blackburn had dedicated his life to obliterating the only weapon humankind had against the universe—the power of the mind—as if he were some demonic Quisling of unreason.

And Aunt Caroline had loved him. Had saved this—this *thing* for twenty-five years, just so she could someday present it to Truth.

As if it were a *gift*—as if it were something Truth should want.

Truth scooped the ring and the necklace back into the box and set the lid back on it. Trembling, she ran her hand through her short, sensible hairdo. Her wan, sickened face gazed back at her from the dresser mirror.

How could she face Aunt Caroline? She could not bear to seem unkind to the woman who had raised her—but how could they have any kind of rational discussion if Caroline Jourdemayne thought Thorne Blackburn and his nasty occult silliness was admirable?

There was no way.

Truth sighed deeply, suddenly exhausted. After a long moment she reluctantly picked up the box and went back into the living room.

"Aunt Caroline?"

The old woman was lying on the couch, head thrown back and eyes closed. In sleep she looked even more ghastly; looking at her, Truth could almost see the progress of the terrible disease that ate at her. At Truth's voice, Aunt Caroline roused slightly.

"Ah, there you are." Her eyes searched Truth's face hopefully. Truth knew what Aunt Caroline was hoping to see and fought to conceal her real feelings. Arguing about Blackburn now would be no kindness.

"We have to talk—about the others—" Aunt Caroline said. Her eyes fluttered closed; with a great effort of will she forced them open again. "When . . . when Katherine died there was so much confusion, so much chaos. I did all that I thought I could, but I failed the others, Truth, that's why—" her voice trailed off.

"Aunt Caroline, you're so tired," Truth said quickly. "You really should lie down and rest. Of course you haven't failed anybody. I'm sure everything's going to be fine." The hasty words rang loudly false in the room.

Aunt Caroline shook her head as if even that small motion hurt. "There were others," she said again, her voice fading.

"We can talk about them later," Truth said, cravenly hoping that later would never come.

"You must find the others. The others need you. The boy . . ." Aunt Caroline said, her voice heavy with the drug. As Truth stood watching, the older woman's eyes slowly closed again. Truth lifted her aunt's feet onto the couch and covered her with an afghan, making her as comfortable as she could. She did not wish to risk hurting Aunt Caroline further by carrying her into the bedroom, though, looking at the frail, wasted form, Truth knew she could lift her easily.

As she watched, Aunt Caroline's breathing slowed and deepened into restoring sleep. Truth picked up the pill bottle. DEMEROL, the label said. ONE EVERY SIX HOURS, AS NEEDED FOR PAIN. But Aunt Caroline had taken two. It would be hours before she awoke again.

Truth felt a keen sense of relief, and acknowledged guiltily that she was grateful not to have to listen to what her aunt had to say about events a quarter of a century in the past. Aunt Caroline was confused, that was all. There was no one to find; no one to help. Blackburn's misguided followers had scattered to the four winds, and Truth Jourdemayne certainly had no intention of aiding any of *them*, even if they needed it.

She stared around the room and, after a moment's hesitation, picked up Aunt Caroline's address book from the end table by the phone. Here, as she'd hoped, was the number of the visiting nurse who was to look in on Aunt Caroline. A quick phone call arranged for a visit in a few hours. The nurse already had a house key.

Truth scribbled a hasty note and left it on the coffee table where Aunt Caroline or the nurse would see it. Then, pausing only to retrieve her coat, purse, and the hateful box, she walked quickly from the house where Caroline Jourdemayne slept the heavy drugged sleep of the terminally ill and Katherine and Blackburn's pictures kept watch over the past.

* * *

How could she do it? The question remained unanswered
as Truth piloted her Saturn along the rutted back roads of
Stormlakken in the direction of the Thruway. She supposed
she ought to have offered to stay, but she hadn't made
arrangements to be away from the Institute for more than
the day, and she found she was reluctant to spend any more
time than she must in the house that now seemed so imbued
with Thorne Blackburn's harlequin presence.

To be entirely honest, she could not bear to stay there
now that she knew what Caroline Jourdemayne's feelings
for Thorne Blackburn were, and she could not bear to hurt
her aunt by revealing her own feelings.

From the very beginning, Truth had always respected
Aunt Caroline's mind, had patterned her maturing personality on Aunt Caroline's model. How could someone she
had always trusted to be right be so wrong about Thorne
Blackburn?

That she *was* wrong Truth had no doubt. But it wasn't
Aunt Caroline's fault. It was his. Thorne Blackburn's.
Somehow he'd managed to work his charlatan spell even
on Caroline Jourdemayne.

It wasn't fair. Unhappiness roiled Truth's stomach and
brought on the outriders of a pounding headache.

No. It was more than simply not fair. It was not right.

Truth's life, in its small way, had been dedicated to supporting Right. Sometimes it was hard to tell right from
wrong, but not this time. The faerie glamour that Blackburn
had worked over the lives of those who had known him,
overriding common sense and human decency, was *wrong*.
It had not even ended with his death; it persisted even now,
years after Blackburn was vanished and gone, continuing
to work its subtle harm.

She had to stop it.

She had to stop Blackburn, by breaking the illusion that
he'd cast, and what better way than by telling the truth—
the whole, final, *real* truth about Thorne Blackburn.

Trust cast a triumphant glance at the white box on the seat beside her. *So you left me a book, did you, Father? Well, I have a book in mind worth two of yours.*

"You're going to do *what*?" Dylan Palmer said incredulously.

"I'm going to write a biography of Thorne Blackburn," Truth repeated.

It was ten-thirty on Thursday morning. Truth sat on the edge of the desk in Dylan's office, swinging one foot back and forth while watching his reaction to her announcement.

"What are you going to call it: *'Magus Dearest'*? For heaven's sake, Truth!" Dylan peered at her as if he were not quite sure whether or not she was joking. His wheat-colored hair fell in an unruly comma over his forehead.

In contrast to Truth's efficient tidiness, Dylan's office, like its occupant, possessed a rumpled and friendly informality. Dylan's workspace was a riot of souvenirs and evidence, letters and papers and books. A number of reproduction gargoyles mounted on the walls lent a certain piquancy to the whole. There was a *Ghostbusters* movie poster on the back of the door, and another one over the desk.

"And here I thought you'd be pleased. You're the one always telling me that Blackburn's a seminal figure in twentieth-century occultism, heir to the crown of Aleister Crowley. And yet there are no books on him, his life and work. Well, now there will be," Truth said with satisfaction.

"And you're going to write it," Dylan said.

Now that her decision had been irrevocably announced, Truth felt happier and more confident than she could ever remember feeling. Finally she was in a position to take control of the nasty puzzle that was Thorne Blackburn.

"Yes, I'm going to write it. At least that way it will be of some use—and not filled with pseudo-factual accounts of trips to Venus and such-like," Truth responded. She was secretly glad to have this news to break as an excuse to talk with Dylan again; it meant that they could both pretend the incident on Monday had never happened.

"Tir na Og," Dylan said unexpectedly. "The Isle of the Blessed. Thorne claimed to go there."

Claimed to go there *and* to Venus, Truth could have told him. Since her visit to Aunt Caroline, she'd occupied spare moments glancing through *Venus Afflicted.* The name, which made the book sound so much like a warning pamphlet against venereal disease, was actually a term, Truth had found, used by astrologers when the planet Venus was being unduly influenced in an astrological chart by other planets. The person with Venus afflicted in his chart would be unlucky in his relationships with others.

Truth did not approve of astrology any more than she did of so-called real magic, but she did have to admit that astrology was slightly more harmless. She wondered why Blackburn had chosen this for his title, when it was obviously others who were unlucky in their relationship with Thorne, and not the reverse. She looked back at Dylan.

Dylan had the look of a man groping for something to say. Suddenly Truth wondered if *he* had meant to write a biography of Thorne Blackburn. This was academia, after all—publish or perish. But even if her supposition were true, she didn't waste any sympathy on Dylan's aborted project. She was much better qualified, and had access to sources Dylan didn't.

Maybe I should call it Blood Will Tell, she thought irreverently.

Had *Venus Afflicted* ever been published? She hadn't told Dylan she had a copy; it was to be the climax of her book— the thing that would ensure its publication and make it a valuable piece of scholarly research as well—and she meant to keep its inclusion a secret until the last possible moment.

"Well, frankly I don't care whether he said he went to *Tir na Og* or Cleveland," Truth said. "All I want is the *provable* facts. I've got a lot of accrued vacation coming, and I'm taking it. Three months ought to be enough time to sort out reality from fiction."

"The truth is rarely pure and never simple, so says Oscar Wilde," Dylan commented. "And what are you going to do with your truth when you find it?"

"I'm going to write it down. I don't see why people should glamorize Thorne Blackburn when they'd be appalled if they really knew the things he did."

Dylan gave her a steady look.

"Are you sure it will make a difference? Look at either of the Kennedys, at King, at Elvis. The more dirt people dish out about them, the stronger their hold becomes on the public imagination. How can you think your book will be any different?"

"I don't know," Truth had to admit. "But at least *I'll* have the whole truth." Suddenly she felt the need to convince him that what she was doing was right—and not just a petty act of vengeance. "If I wait too much longer, Dyl, the primary sources—the people who knew him—will all be dead."

"If he were alive today he'd be in his sixties," Dylan agreed. "But where are you going to start? Out in California? England?"

"Oh, no," Truth said. "I'm starting closer to home than that. I'm starting where it all really began—or ended." She took a deep breath and said the words: "I'm going to Shadow's Gate."

CHAPTER THREE

THE CIRCLE OF TRUTH

Truth, poor child, was nobody's daughter
She took off her clothes and jumped in the water
— DOROTHY L. SAYERS

IT WAS THE SECOND WEEK IN OCTOBER; PEAK SEASON FOR
the leaf color in the Hudson Valley. Oaks, maples, birch,
and poplars all turned their separate spectra of amber and
gold against a sky so blue it hurt the eyes. And Truth was
bound for Shadow's Gate.

It had been mildly surprising to discover that Blackburn
had not been responsible for the quintessentially Gothic
name of his last residence, nor had he fictionalized the
name of the nearby town in his published essays. Shadowkill was a real place, the stream from which it took its name
having been named by Dutch homesteader Elkanah Scheidow in 1641: Scheidow's Kill—*kill* being the perfectly ordinary Dutch word for "stream," appearing in Hudson
Valley place-names from Peekskill to Plattekill.

When English settlers displaced the Dutch in this area,
Scheidow's Kill became Anglicized to Shadowkill and became the name of the new English town, and *Scheidowge-
hucht*—"Scheidow's Hamlet"—became Shadow's Gate, a
name now attached only to the estate outside the little vil-

lage. Thus a spooky and theatrical taxonomy dissolved under the press of a little research into something perfectly ordinary and nonfrightening.

And damned elusive.

She'd gotten the name of the attorneys handling Blackburn's estate—and therefore the property—from the newspaper stories that covered his 1969 disappearance, but her letters and phone calls to them asking for help and information—and permission to visit the house—had gone unanswered. Still, Truth didn't think there would be any problem with just climbing over the fence and taking a walk around. And as Blackburn's daughter, even if illegitimate, she might be said to have some claim on the place.

The thought disturbed her. She didn't want anything from Blackburn, not his arcane book, not his ritual jewelry, not his—what was the phrase one of her nutcase correspondents had used? Oh, yes—not his mantle of mystic authority. Truth snorted derisively at the memory.

But she did want to see the house. She remembered nothing of the time she'd spent at Shadow's Gate; the memories of her earliest childhood. Perhaps there was something she could reclaim for herself in this journey: her history.

Almost a month had gone by while she applied for and received the leave of absence from the Institute, followed by the distasteful business of actually trying to locate some hard biographical information on Thorne Blackburn. She had spoken to Aunt Caroline on the phone a couple of times, but Aunt Caroline had not mentioned Thorne Blackburn again, or the legacy, and for that Truth was grateful.

While she'd waited for her leave to be approved, Truth collected and reviewed the material on Blackburn that she'd read when she first became aware of him, and found it was even scantier than she'd thought. There had only been the briefest of mentions in Colin Wilson's *The Occult*, and Richard Cavendish's *Man, Myth, and Magic* had little more.

When she looked at her notes after a week's hard work, they were laughably cryptic.

Thorne Blackburn, probably born circa 1939, birthplace unknown—possibly England—family unknown, early life unknown. First surfaced in New Orleans in the late 1950s, where he was doing fake voodoo rituals for the tourists— a phase of his career that hadn't lasted long—and claiming to be the Comté de Cagliostro, an eighteenth-century French con artist who'd claimed to be a thousand years old. Claims notwithstanding, Thorne had been somewhere around thirty when he died—Dylan was right; he'd be in his sixties if he were alive today.

Already well established as an occultist when he resurfaced in San Francisco in the early 1960s, Blackburn had claimed affiliation both to the Ordo Templi Orientis and the Golden Dawn. He'd made a big splash with his lectures, public rituals, and the publication of what they, in those innocent days, had called an "underground newspaper"— dedicated to Blackburn's cult, of course, and his bizarre New Age theories.

And that was that. There the story of Blackburn's life— and death—ended.

Her library request for newspaper stories on Blackburn had netted Truth a folder full of copies of microfilmed newspaper stories, none of them of much particular use beyond providing the name of the lawyer. Most of them focused on the April 1969 disappearance. Katherine Jourdemayne's death was listed as "suspected drug overdose." Police had searched for Thorne but he'd never been found; other members of the Circle had been held for a while and then released. There had been no arrests.

It was a trail a quarter of a century cold, but maybe she could unriddle it—if she visited Shadow's Gate.

Truth didn't understand where the conviction had come from that her answers were there—the estate was deserted, after all, left to rot while the miles of red tape surrounding it and its gone-but-not-definitely-dead owner reeled onward like a legal battle in a Dickens novel. If not for that,

Shadow's Gate and its hundred-acre wood would have been sold off years ago, Truth assumed. But she had to go there.

It had seemed simpler back at the Institute. Truth stared out her car's windshield in despair, at what looked like just another Dutchess County back road. She'd been driving all morning, and by now she was nearly ready to admit she was lost.

Maybe Shadow's Gate didn't really exist.

Of course it does, she rebuked herself mentally. The Bed-and-Breakfast in nearby Shadowkill, where she'd made reservations for tonight's lodging, was certainly real enough to take VISA. Truth pulled off the road at a convenient wide spot and inspected her Dutchess County map again. Shadowkill had to be around here somewhere. It wasn't just a figment of a cartographer's imagination.

Laboriously, Truth located Shadowkill on the map and then (glancing up at the road sign to make sure of her facts) State Road 43. They were about an inch apart at the best of times, and did not cross as her directions assured her they should.

Oh, I see. I should have turned back there somewhere, onto County 13. Lucky Thirteen. How appropriate.

It was just a good thing, Truth reflected to herself, that she wasn't a superstitious person.

But even a superstitious person would have been disarmed by the sight of the little town of Shadowkill, which Truth finally reached some forty minutes later.

Shadowkill was an archetypal Hudson River town, with rambling Victorian mansions grouped around a picture-perfect town park. There was a large war memorial in the center of the traffic circle, and a Main Street lined with antique stores and a number of cunning, trendy little shops, marking Shadowkill as one of the hamlets in "Sleepy Hollow Country" that obtained most of its income from tourism.

It was by now late afternoon, and it would have been reasonable for Truth to at least locate and stop in at her Bed-and-Breakfast to meet her hostess and drop off her bags, but now that she was so close to her goal she couldn't bear to stop. Shadow's Gate had loomed in her imagination for years as some sort of hideous combination of Hell House and the Bates Motel; she could not wait any longer than utterly necessary to see it as it really was and reduce it to ordinariness.

Following her directions, Truth drove up Main Street, as State 13 was now called—past shops that gave way to tidy—and costly—cottages. Then the cottages stopped, and there was about a mile where the sides of the road were edged only by running fence and grass. Then she reached the place where Main Street formed a T with Old Patent Grant Road.

Shadow's Gate was straight ahead, and the board fencing that edged Old Patent Grant Road had been removed from the area in front of the gatehouse, so that it was possible to drive right on to the property. Truth crossed the two-lane highway and pulled up into the graveled apron in front of the gatehouse. A warning quiver of alarm made the hair on her arms and neck stand up; the very air felt charged, as if before a storm.

Don't be melodramatic. It's just a house, Truth scolded herself sternly. She forced herself to look around, to gather data with a scholar's mind.

From her investigations, she knew that Shadow's Gate was an estate dating from the days when both sides of the Hudson had been studded with the palatial enclaves of the nineteenth-century robber barons. The current house, she gathered, had been built sometime after the Civil War. The gatehouse where her car now stood was a later addition—a miniature castle in itself, complete with the mammoth clock face that gave it a faint spurious resemblance to some public building. The gatehouse building formed an arch across the drive; iron gates within that arch could be closed to bar the road into the estate to the casual intruder. Truth had seen photographs of the gatehouse in the Cavendish book, and had mentally embellished that picture: the surroundings overgrown with weeds, the rusted gates padlocked shut; everything bearing a wistful aura of decay.

Unfortunately for her peace of mind, the weeds were gone, the ornamental plantings were flourishing, and the freshly-painted gates stood open to the recently regraveled drive. Shadow's Gate was very far from being a deserted relic of a ghostly past.

Someone is living here, Truth realized, and felt a muted ghost of the jealousy she had experienced at Aunt Caroline's. Shadow's Gate was *hers*—who dared . . .

"Can I help you?"

The voice belonged to the brash young man who had stepped out from behind the gatehouse. She rolled down the window and leaned out.

"I—I'm not sure. I came to look at the house," Truth said hesitantly.

"It isn't for sale," the young man said, still smiling. He was several years younger than Truth, with sun-streaked blond hair and deeply tanned skin testifying to a commitment to open-air activities.

"Oh, I don't want to buy it," Truth said quickly. "I just wanted to look at it." Some impulse of honesty made her add: "I grew up here—well, for a while. My name's Truth Jourdemayne."

By now Truth had become inured to practically every possible reaction to her admittedly-peculiar first name. This, too, was a legacy of Thorne Blackburn, but by the time she'd realized that, it had become so much her name that no amount of dislike of the giver was reason enough to change it.

"*You're* Truth Jourdemayne? *The* Truth Jourdemayne? That's great! And you're here! How did you—? Oh; I, uh, guess I ought to introduce myself. I'm Gareth. Gareth Crowther? Anyway, welcome to Shadow's Gate, Ms. Jourdemayne—I can't think of anyone who ought to be here more. Oh, boy, this is terrific—none of us knew you were coming."

Of all the possible reactions—humor, disbelief, confusion—this was one she'd never seen. Obviously her name meant something to him, but he was so innocently delighted to discover who she was that it was hard to take offense.

"But, hey! You've got to come up to the house and meet Julian," Gareth added. "It'll be great!"

"I don't think, Mr., um . . ." Truth began.

Gareth wilted visibly at this rebuff. "Call me Gareth. And—please. It won't be any trouble. Julian isn't, like, *doing* anything right now. And you could see the house. That's what you've come for, right? To see your house? Julian'll be glad to show you around."

He gazed at her so hopefully that Truth began to feel a bit guilty at refusing. Gareth was obviously a big bluff hearty puppy-dog of a man who never expected to give or receive unkindness. And she *did* want to see the house. Could the Blackburn estate possibly have been settled enough for the place to be sold? No one had any reason to tell her if it had, after all.

"Julian, I take it, is the new owner?" Truth said.

"Yeah," Gareth said. "We just moved up here a few months ago, in May."

Truth wondered a bit at that—even on such short acquaintance, Gareth Crowther somehow didn't seem a likely partner for someone who could afford a property that cost, at a *very* conservative estimate, several hundred thousand dollars.

"Go on up," he said encouragingly. "Please."

You've come such a long way; you might as well. Go on. Just take a look. The silent urging was so strong that it seemed a thing separate from herself, and still Truth hesitated.

As a parapsychologist, Truth Jourdemayne believed in the unseen world of perceptions beyond the ordinary and communications beyond speech. As a scientist, she preferred any normal explanation to a paranormal one. This niggling hunch was probably simply her own unconscious desire to lay childish bugbears to rest.

"Okay, I will," she said, deciding. "Thanks, Gareth, you've been very kind."

"Thank *you*, Ms. Jourdemayne," Gareth said, sweeping her an impish mock-bow.

"Truth," she said. His smile widened. He stepped back as her car drifted forward through the freshly-painted gates.

You could not see the main house from the gatehouse, Truth realized as she drove. She had the peculiar sense that she had just driven into a picture, or a movie—into a world that was real in a different fashion than the world she had just left, and had its own rewards and dangers.

Once you were on the estate property, the twentieth century vanished. There wasn't another house in sight; she couldn't even see the power lines she knew must be here. The gravel drive swung first left, then right as it cut through the young forest surrounding the house; the roadway was deeply ditched on both sides to carry off summer rains and winter snowmelt, and filled at the moment with drifts of leaves like golden doubloons plundered from some ghostly galleon.

Truth did her best to rein in her fancy and concentrate on the meeting ahead. Who was Julian? Why had he bought Shadow's Gate? Gareth had seemed to know who she was; how awkward was this meeting going to be?

Suddenly the wood opened out and Truth could see the house ahead. Without conscious volition, she brought her car to a stop.

Shadow's Gate was a sprawling example of nineteenth-century Hudson Valley Gothic. It bore the look of a fairy-tale castle built as a stronghold for a war in Neverland. In contrast to other Hudson River mansions constructed of native timber or imported marble, Shadow's Gate was fashioned of the local pale gray stone. Three cone-roofed towers set with long narrow windows rose up from the edges of the rambling structure, and off to one side Truth could see the geometric shape of a glass house, or conservatory, jutting outward as if it wanted nothing to do with the stone walls that supported it. The five acres or so immediately around the house was immaculately tended; across the sweep of green lawn she could see a lacy white gazebo, and high box hedges that might be a maze. Beyond those artifacts of civilization the autumn forest took possession of the landscape once more. The Shadow's Gate estate was a parcel of slightly over 100 acres.

The hundred-acre wood. Just like in Winnie-the-Pooh.

Seeing Shadow's Gate was like seeing a scene she'd thought safely buried in a children's book brought to jarring life. Truth had always been certain that she retained no memories from her early childhood, as was perfectly typical—after all, most people report having no childhood memories dating earlier than their seventh or eighth year—but it seemed, now, that she was wrong.

She knew this place. To enter its doors was to promise to keep an appointment she was more than twenty years late for.

Truth's heart slammed against her ribs at a speed suggesting panic. For only an instant the world—the car, the friendly autumn forest—was gone, and she stood naked in a place where torches made a pillared cathedral of light. She was come to judgment, but those who called her little knew what they had called to face them—

Truth shook her head, puzzled. The memory, fantasy, whatever it had been, slipped away like a dream, leaving behind it only the sense of a challenge that must be met.

"Creepy." She spoke aloud, and the last of the dream-sense vanished. The house ahead was nothing more than a stately Victorian mansion, freshly tenanted after a span of years.

"*Déjà vu*, that's what they call it," Truth told herself, slipping the car into Drive once more. *Déjà vu*, the sense of having been somewhere before. Often cited by psychics as proof of their powers, but rarely that. A complex trick of the mind, nothing more.

Nothing more.

* * *

When she pulled up in front of the house, there was a man waiting for her on the front steps.

Gareth must have phoned up from the gatehouse, Truth realized. She got out of her car reluctantly, slinging her purse up over her shoulder. The man came down the steps, moving around the car to greet her.

"Hello," he said, offering his hand. "I'm Julian Pilgrim. Welcome to Shadow's Gate, Ms. Jourdemayne."

Truth did not miss his quick assessment of her, and was suddenly glad she'd taken the trouble to dig out—and wear—one of the outfits she usually saved for professional conferences: a skirt and matching jacket in olive wild silk worn with an ivory *peau de soie* shell. The low-heeled coffee-colored pumps and matching oversized Coach bag completed the picture of an efficient, official, and *normal* person.

In the moment Julian Pilgrim took to appraise her, Truth conducted an evaluation of her own. She saw a man a few years older than she, with thick silky black hair and eyes the startling topaz blue of a Siamese cat's. His face had all the patrician arrogance of that noble breed, and his body a positively feline suppleness. He was dressed as if attending the same imaginary conference that Truth was; a jacket of subtle expensive tweed, dark slacks, a shirt with the dense, close-woven whiteness of linen open to expose his strong, brown throat. His hands were innocent of rings, and the Rolex on his left wrist was a thin, gold whisper of privilege. Looking at his hands made a faint shudder run through her body; before she could stop herself, she wondered what they would feel like touching her bare skin.

The only jarring note in this perfection was the bangle Julian Pilgrim wore upon his right wrist.

One would expect any jewelry this man wore to be elegant. The wristcuff was not. It had the dull, grainy look of pig-iron, into which, senselessly, a design in pure gold had been inlaid. She glimpsed it only a moment in her assessment; following the direction of her gaze, Julian shook his cuff down to conceal it. He wore French cuffs;

the cufflinks were flat squares of red enamel.

Their mutual assessment had taken only moments; Truth smiled, and shook the extended hand.

"I'm Truth Jourdemayne—as you know," she said. "And you're the new owner of Shadow's Gate?"

"I think of myself as a custodian only. When a man buys a three-hundred-year-old house, he must face the fact that he is only an ephemeral episode in the life of the house. But please. Do come in. Have you traveled far?" He radiated the same spellbinding fascination as one of the big cats—a tiger, perhaps—and wore his aura of charismatic masculinity like a laurel crown of triumph, seemingly unconscious of his effect on the female population at large.

"We're almost neighbors; I work at Taghkanic College, over in Amsterdam County."

Normally she would have been more specific, as, technically, Truth worked for the Bidney Institute and not for the college, but some instinct held her back from revealing too much too soon. "I didn't realize that Shadow's Gate was on the market," Truth added.

"It wasn't."

Julian gestured for her to precede him up the steps, and then brushed close to her to open the front door.

She glanced around herself, standing in the doorway. Jeweled multicolored light spilled in through the stained-glass gallery windows, threatening to carry her off again into that strange state of altered memory. She closed her eyes and looked away, stepping inside.

"I negotiated a rather delicate arrangement with the estate," Julian said, following her through the doorway. "My preemptive bid to purchase is being held in escrow, and I'm living here with some of my ... associates ... while the last details are being worked out. But am I bringing you unwelcome news? Perhaps you'd planned to live at Shadow's Gate yourself?" His deep voice was like sueded velvet, weaving a spell that had nothing to do with the house.

"I don't think so," Truth said shortly.

"I must admit I feel quite honored by a visit from Thorne Blackburn's daughter," Julian added. "Anything I can do to make your visit more enjoyable . . ."

So he did know who she was. Truth felt herself stiffening up, despite Julian's obvious charms and his apparent desire to please her. She wondered just who the dangerously-attractive Julian Pilgrim's unnamed associates were—and what sort of association it was.

"I only came to see the house," Truth said brusquely.

"And so you shall," Julian said, taking her arm. "I shall give you the grand tour."

"I expect it has been rather embarrassing for you, being Thorne Blackburn's daughter," Julian said about an hour later.

Their last stop on the grand tour had been the room Julian had called his office; a surprisingly small room tucked in beneath the grand staircase. It was filled with built-in bookcases, which were in turn filled with books—the sort that are read, not bought "by the yard" from a decorator for the look of the thing. Red silk brocade covered the walls everywhere books did not; either the original material or a cunningly-antiqued copy. There was a desk in the middle of the room with comfortable overstuffed Victorian chairs set on either side. A chinoiserie liquor cabinet in the corner and the Oriental rug on the floor completed the furnishings. Oddly enough, the room was completely without windows.

Truth looked startled at the insightful comment. Julian smiled mockingly.

"Oh, come, Ms. Jourdemayne—the look of horror that crossed your features when I merely mentioned your father's name would be clue enough to an intellect even duller than I pride myself on having that this was not a welcome subject."

Truth looked away, making a production out of choosing a seat so he would not see her blush. He'd been nothing but kindness itself for the last hour, showing her over the house and property, discoursing knowledgeably on its history—and never mentioning Thorne Blackburn once.

She ran through all the possible responses she could make. "I'm sorry if I seem rude," she said at last, settling on the most harmless. "But—"

"But you are tired of being treated as if you are not a person, with your own desires and necessities, but a sort of psychic hot line to a man you cannot even have known very well," Julian said. "And whose interests you may not even share."

Now that was a mild way of putting it.

"Yes," said Truth gratefully. She felt herself warming to Julian on a level transcending mere physical attraction, as if the unspoken camaraderie of old friendship already existed between them.

"I," said Julian, "do not ask others to share my interests— although when they do, it's an unexpected bonus." He laughed, and Truth felt herself smiling in return. "Some sherry, perhaps, Ms. Jourdemayne?"

"Yes, thank you. And please call me 'Truth,' Mr. Pilgrim."

"And you must call me Julian," he responded, going over to the cabinet atop which a crystal decanter and glasses reposed upon a silver tray as formally as in any Oxford don's study.

"Forgive me for mentioning," he went on after he had served them both with tiny delicate crystal glasses filled with the sweet, garnet-colored wine, "but of course you are aware that you are named for the Blackburn Work, are you not?"

From Julian a question that would have been annoying coming from anyone else became a matter of simple curiosity.

"I'm not very familiar with the Blackburn Work," Truth admitted cautiously.

"Children hardly ever know their parents—or what is important to their parents—and the glare of publicity turned on the Work by Blackburn's disappearance couldn't have helped. Occultists—like parapsychologists—do their best when not being hounded for a 'sound bite' for the six o'clock news."

Truth raised her eyebrows, saying nothing, and Julian chuckled at her surprise.

" 'You know my methods, Watson, now apply them,' " he quoted happily. "Anyone working in the field is familiar with the Bidney Institute, no matter which pan of the balances his soul is weighed in, and besides, how could I fail to recognize the author of *Some Preliminary Inquiries Into a Statistical Basis for Evaluating Clairaudient Perception*? I wish I had been able to come to Bern to see you deliver it; it seems we have had to wait far too long to meet."

This time there was no misinterpreting the smile or what it meant; Truth found herself flushing agreeably.

"I didn't know you were interested in parapsychology, Julian," she said. She sipped again at her sherry; its sweet-sharp taste was the physical equivalent of the October sunlight shining through the stained-glass windows in the hall outside.

"Oh, I am, but please don't be misled. My main interest is the Blackburn Work from the magician's point of view— but as Thorne himself says, we must make ourselves familiar both with the realm of scientific possibility and the range of stage illusionism in order to distinguish true magick when it occurs."

Julian settled back in his chair, and once again Truth forced away an intimate speculation of how it would feel to touch the muscles that rippled beneath the cloth.

"That seems reasonable enough," Truth said reluctantly, forcing herself to keep her mind on the matter at hand. She did not wish to argue with so charming a host, but she couldn't restrain just a small ironic jibe. "And have you seen much 'true magick,' Julian?"

"No." He smiled at her, as if inviting her to share a delicious secret, and tossed off the rest of his sherry in one draught. "But I hope to. And what brings *you* to Shadow's

Gate, Truth Jourdemayne? Surely not an interest in Hudson Valley architecture?"

He leaned forward, completely at ease, and Truth was once more reminded of a lazy jungle cat, all midnight fur and hot brilliant eyes. It was disappointing to find him apparently on the side of the Thorne-ites, but wasn't it people like Julian whom her book was meant to help?

Besides, no biographer has ever worked without discussing his subject. She would have to mention Blackburn to someone besides Dylan sooner or later.

"I am writing a biography of my father," Truth said.

Julian came bolt upright, his expression suffused with delight. "But how absolutely perfect!" he said. "You've certainly come to the right place to begin. You must stay here, of course; it will make everything so much easier for you. You knew, of course, about the collection—of course I place it entirely at your disposal—what an amazing display of synchronicity, to be sure."

"Synchronicity," Truth echoed, mystified. "What sort of a collection, Julian?" she asked, setting aside for the moment his invitation to stay.

"Why, Blackburniana—for want of a better name. You mean you *didn't* know? So much for my ego! I've been collecting for years. It's quite extensive, really: letters, tapes, mystic apparatus. Just what you'll need. I'll show you."

He stood up, offering his hand. After a moment's hesitation Truth set her hand in his. Julian's warm fingers closed over hers with a confident sense of possession, and the power that flowed through his touch made her tremble.

"I was beginning to think I'd have to write it myself, and I have no literary talent, I assure you," Julian was saying. "And there's no better way to learn about Thorne Blackburn than to write about him."

Truth stood beside Julian in an airy, spacious room that had not been included in her previous tour. Its whitewashed walls and high ceilings gave it the indefinable air of a country schoolhouse. There were no built-in bookcases here, only expanses of molded plaster and scrubbed, wide-planked oak floors. The room also contained two long library tables and several freestanding shelves and files, but the entire room was dominated by the immense oil painting hanging over the fireplace at the opposite end of the room—Thorne Blackburn in his full magickal regalia.

"It helps if you can afford to advertise in magazines and newspapers—and pay, of course. It's amazing how often cold cash is preferred to that cherished memento. But that makes me sound cynical—in truth, I was incredibly lucky to get my hands on a lot of this and I feel very—humble."

Even on such short acquaintance, Truth didn't feel that humility was something Julian Pilgrim would ever possess. One might as well wish for a diffident eagle; a submissive tiger. She shifted her gaze to the portrait, lest Julian catch her staring at him like a hero-worshiping schoolgirl with her first crush.

The figure in the portrait had bare feet and wore a flowing green robe embroidered with gold ogham runes and a wolfskin—or something meant to represent one—tied about his shoulders. The robe was belted in at the waist with a wide leather belt set with gemstones and ending in the sort of silky golden tassels that Truth associated with heavy curtains.

The figure's arms were crossed upon his chest; in one hand he held a red-and-white-striped wand topped with a golden representation of the winged Isis, and in the other, a short sword with a large *Magen David* set into its pommel and elaborate symbols engraved into its blade. Blackburn's magickal belief system—whatever it was—had a remarkably catholic taste in symbols.

A gold band supporting a solar wheel held his flowing blond hair in place, and his green gaze was directed upward. That—along with the aureole the artist had seen fit to give him—gave the figure in the picture the sappily sentimental look of a dime-store Savior.

But something was missing.

"Where's his necklace?" Truth asked. "And the ring?"

Julian shot her a look of sharp surprise. "I thought you said you weren't familiar with the Blackburn Work."

Truth said nothing, damning herself for having spoken out at all. The last thing she needed was to have Julian think that she had some secret inner knowledge of "Blackburniana" for him to tap.

After a moment, Julian shrugged. "Oh, well, my little inadequacies revealed," he said with a laugh. "The ring and the necklace *should* be there; you're right. I know they're mentioned in the literature, but as you'll note, this is hardly painted from life. I couldn't provide any photographs of either piece, so I told the artist to leave them out. Perhaps they can be added someday—if they ever turn up."

He turned his dazzling smile on her once more and Truth felt herself melting. It wasn't love, certainly, and maybe not even lust—Julian just seemed so much more *real* than anyone Truth had ever met before. She forcefully suppressed the urge to instantly hand over the necklace and ring simply for the pleasure she knew it would give Julian to have them. Whether she wanted them or not—and she didn't—all her inclination and training had created in her a profound mistrust of first impressions, seductive though they were. She would wait and see.

"At any rate, here within these four walls is nearly all that remains on Earth of Thorne Blackburn, *Magister Stella Maris*: photographs, artifacts, personal letters. The shelves contain copies of all of the books that mention him—the citations are listed in the front of each—as well as the bootleg reprints of stuff from the old *Voice of Truth*." Julian's easy gesture took in the freestanding shelves along both walls. They were filled with books, from tattered paperbacks to books echoing the gold-stamped splendor of a law library.

"You know, it's a pity he vanished the way he did," Julian continued. "The estate is so disorganized that some of those copyrights never will be untangled until the work becomes public domain sometime in the next century. But please—feel free to browse to your heart's content—and please, do consider my other offer. I would very much enjoy being your host, Truth. I flatter myself that I could even help you—perhaps more than you realize."

It was impossible to mistake the genuineness of his offer, and Truth found herself once more returning his smile.

"I really . . . I don't think . . ." Truth floundered, in spite of that. She did not know Julian—he was her father's partisan—she couldn't trust him. "This is such an amazing collection, Julian; I hardly know where to begin—it's magnificent!" she said, hoping to distract him.

"It's yours for as long as you need it." Julian folded her hand in both of his own. "Will you stay?"

"I—" Truth hesitated, and Julian, sensing her reluctance, made another offer.

"At least be my guest for dinner? The others would love to meet you—and I hope for another chance to persuade you to our cause."

Julian's steady turquoise gaze and engaging, self-deprecating smile made it impossible to evade the question, even though Truth felt, somehow, that accepting this dinner invitation would be agreeing to a whole lot more than just a meal. Once again she felt that ghostly sense of challenge.

"Very well," she said, feeling her reluctance dissolve with her assent. "I'd love to."

"That much is settled then."

Truth was about to ask what time she should return, but Julian forestalled her once again.

"May I leave you here for a while? I'd much prefer your company to what I ought to be doing, but there are some calls to California that I really must make. I hope you can amuse yourself here?"

Truth nodded. Julian continued, making his way toward the door. "I'm so glad you're staying; I'll tell Irene." He pronounced the name in English fashion, giving it three syllables and a long "e" on the end: *I-ree-nee*. "She does me the favor of supervising our domestic arrangements, and

I'd be lost without her. I'll be back as soon as I may, but feel free to ask Irene or any of the others for anything you need."

"Of course," Truth said, slightly dazzled.

The afternoon sun, beating in through the high, uncurtained windows, bathed Julian in orient splendor, granting him a genuine halo in counterpoint to the painting's trumpery one. He looked like what he was—a powerful, important man. A man who would do great things—and who seemed already to believe that she would help him do them. He opened the door to leave.

"Julian," Truth asked with sudden urgency, "What do *you* think happened to him? Blackburn, I mean. He can't just have up and vanished." *Can be?* a part of her mind added in new uncertainty.

Julian paused.

"I think—I think he found what he sought, or nearly so. No frontier can be explored without risk—and magick is no game for amateurs."

He turned and walked from the room, closing the high double doors behind him as if furling an angel's wings.

CHAPTER FOUR

TO SEEK THE TRUTH

*We owe respect to the living; to the dead we
owe only truth.*

—VOLTAIRE

TRUTH SAT DOWN AT ONE OF THE LONG LIBRARY TABLES.
Now that Julian was gone, taking his energizing aura of
glamour with him, she felt suddenly weary. It had been a
long day, and a long drive on top of it, and now she's
agreed to have dinner with an entire mansion full of—

*Never mind "magick or not"—the real question should
be: "Fruitcake or not"?* Truth told herself derisively. On
almost any other occasion, the subject under review would
be Thorne Blackburn. Today it was the far more immediate
Julian Pilgrim. The undeniably handsome, charming, and
fascinating Julian Pilgrim.

She picked up her purse from the floor and opened it,
removing a thick notebook and a tiny tape recorder, ready
for the business of note-taking. But at the moment, Truth's
mind was elsewhere.

Magick? Or . . . not?

Always before, Truth had felt comfortable with her
sweeping dismissal of magick as an intentionally fraudulent
sort of psychic shell game. It was easy enough to do so:

She'd never met a really admirable person who professed to believe in it. But now there was Julian, who spoke of magick with the same calm acceptance that Truth's colleagues at Taghkanic spoke of Chaucer and submolecular physics.

He was wrong, of course, Truth decided, sighing regretfully. A belief in magick had informed the great minds of the Renaissance from Francis Bacon to Isaac Newton, but that didn't make them right. But at least Julian was in good company with his delusions.

But they were only that, and as impossible of proof as any other matter based on faith. Which, as Mark Twain had once remarked, consisted of believing "what you know ain't so."

Truth sighed, leaning her chin on her hand and gazing out the window like a dazzled ingenue, letting her mind play for a moment with the enticing fantasy of living here at Shadow's Gate while she researched her book—and weaned Julian Pilgrim away from his logical fallacies.

With regret, she dismissed the notion. Julian was not her concern, she told herself firmly. He was unlikely to give up his beliefs just on her say-so, and she ought to be grateful for them anyway; with whatever motivation, he had amassed a fine collection of precisely what she needed and was willing to let her use it to write her book.

So she should stop daydreaming about how it would be to kiss a man she'd met for the first time less than two hours before and do something to justify her presence here.

She stood up, taking the tape recorder with her, and began to explore the trove that Julian had so magnanimously thrown open to her.

Here, in glass cases along the walls, were most of the objects she'd seen in the portrait, plus others.

"A shallow bowl, looks like—obsidian? Didn't Dylan show me something like that last year? A *scrying glass*, I think he said. I wish he were here now. I don't think I have a hope of understanding most of this stuff without a background in magick. Let's see, some things that look like silver hat pins, a small sickle . . . copper? Looks sharp. I've got to get a camera in here and photograph this stuff. And several daggers: One has a black hilt with about a six-inch blade. . . ."

She continued to dictate into the machine as she studied the objects in the glass cases beneath the windows: the daggers, with black and white and red hilts, the solar crown from the portrait—and here a matching lunar one, all in white silver. Only the fear of somehow offending Julian kept her from opening the case and picking it up; her forehead tingled as if anticipating the crown's cool weight.

It's been a long day, Truth repeated reassuringly to herself. She rubbed her forehead, blotting the sensation away, and forced herself to continue taking notes.

"I wonder who wore these? Is there an actual full description of the Blackburn Work anywhere, I wonder? Julian seems to think it's something real—well, as real as magick ever gets."

It was difficult, looking at the tools, to remember that they were simply items in an expensive and delusive form of theater. The objects seemed filled with such purpose—as if they knew they had once been used and looked forward to the day when they would be used again.

Truth turned away, barely able to repress a pang of unease. The things this room contained were nothing like the trappings of Wicca, the faddish Earth Religion that had been in vogue among the Taghkanic kids a few seasons back. One of Truth's test subjects had been a self-proclaimed "Wiccan High Priestess," and Truth had been forced to endure a number of lectures and demonstrations of the power of Wicca in order to get Sally to run the test series Truth had wanted. At the time, Wicca had struck her as essentially harmless, if silly—and Sally's results hadn't been any better than the statistical norm, either, for all her claims of "working magick" to influence them.

These things were different. When she closed her eyes, she could still see them.

You're just tired. And Dylan could give you a dozen ex-

*planations for this phenomenon without stopping to think—
or mentioning magick.*

Resolutely, Truth turned to the bookshelves. The Cav-
endishes and the Wilson were there, as well as a number
of books by Blackburn's predecessor in the Trickster tra-
dition, the Great Beast, Aleister Crowley. Truth frowned
slightly. This was supposed to be a collection of Blackburniana, and Crowley had died in 1947; what could he have
had to say about Blackburn? She picked up the nearest
volume, *Gems From The Equinox*, and flipped it open.

To my faithful serpent's tooth, Thorne Blackburn, it
said, and was signed in a looping scrawl spangled about
with symbols. *Serpent's tooth?* Truth wondered. Then she
remembered—it was a quote from the Bible: *"How sharper
than a serpent's tooth is an ungrateful child."*

Had Blackburn been an ungrateful child? And if so, to
whom? He could have been no more than eight years old
when the book had been signed to him, assuming the signature was genuine.

"Seems to have known Aleister Crowley rather well, if
inscription is any clue," she told her tape recorder. "But
from where? Wasn't Crowley English?" A thought startled
her to laughter. "Was Blackburn American?" Her sources
had seemed to indicate he might be English—but in that
case, why come to America for the Blackburn Work?

Perhaps Julian would know.

She quickly checked through the other books on the
shelves; it appeared that a good portion of them had come
from Blackburn's personal library, which was the reason
for their inclusion here. Truth rattled off their titles into her
tape recorder for later checking.

"*The Magus*, Francis Barrett; *The Sacred-Magic of Abra-
Melin the Mage*, MacGregor Mathers, editor; *The River
Where the Ghosts Walk*—"

A couple of large, gray boxes proved to contain
archivally-stored copies of Blackburn's newspaper, *The
Voice of Truth*. Truth looked through a couple of them—
the newsprint was already yellow and flaky with age—but

found the combination of esoteric content and whimsical typesetting difficult to follow.

What did shine through was the aura of hope that had suffused those enchanted years just before her birth, when everything was thought to be possible, and the Four Horsemen of Disease, War, Hunger, and Death could be stopped forever.

Now the world knew better. There would always be newer and more frightful plagues, fiercer and more unjust wars, and people starving to death on the sidewalks of the richest nation on earth.

Truth shook her head, dispelling those morbid thoughts. Parlor philosophy would gain her nothing—and despite all he'd said, this might be her only chance for a look at Julian's trove. Collectors were a notoriously fickle lot; if she didn't share his view of Blackburn's greatness—and she didn't—he might change his mind about allowing her access at any moment.

The file cabinets were next. Truth opened the first drawer and realized with a sense of defeat that here was simply too much information to sort through and process in the little time she had. She closed the drawer and opened another almost at random. A jumble of blank manila file folders in unlabeled dark green hanging files met her gaze.

"Oh, my God," Truth said in despair. "How can anyone ever find anything with a filing system like this?"

She stopped and wound the tape back to erase that last comment, then pulled a folder out of the jumble in the drawer. It was filled with about fifty sheets of 8½-by-11-inch paper in various colors, all handwritten on in purple felt-tip pen in an even, Spencerian script.

For all its antique penmanship, the materials themselves were very modern—this was no artifact produced in Blackburn's lifetime, but something from the last year or so, Truth judged. What possible connection could it have with Thorne Blackburn—unless, of course, it was Julian's own attempt at the start of a biography?

She turned so that the sunlight from the tall windows

that flanked the fireplace and that ridiculously hagiograph-
ical picture fell on the pages, and began to read through
the contents of the folder, being very careful not to get the
pages out of order.

It was not a biography.

At first Truth thought that what she was looking at was
a play—if they could do it for Evita Perón, then why not
for Thorne Blackburn?—with stage business, entrances and
exits, and speaking parts for the "Hierolator" and the "Hierophex" and a number of other vaguely Roman Catholic—
sounding things. What was an "Hierolator"? Truth wondered. *Hieros* was Greek for sacred, of course, and the *lator*
suffix meant worshiper. Thinking along those lines, Hierophex would be "sacred creator" or "sacred builder."

Sacred worshiper? Sacred builder? It seemed to make no
sense. Truth read onward, willing herself to understand.
The script kept stopping and starting up again, with the
words and actions in a slightly different order, until Truth
finally realized what she was looking at.

It was not a play.

It was a draft of one of the rituals in *Venus Afflicted*.

But this was ridiculous. You produced the rough drafts,
then the finished book. You did not produce the finished
book—which was in her suitcase in the trunk of her car at
this very moment—and then, thirty years later, settle down
to produce the rough draft.

Unless it wasn't a rough draft, but a . . . reconstruction?

No. Surely *Venus Afflicted* had been published in
Thorne's lifetime? It *must* have been—and no matter how
small the edition, Truth was sure Julian would have a copy.

She set down the file folder carefully on the table and
returned to the shelved books. Every work on Thorne, Julian had said, and a number from his personal library besides. Even the bootlegged English version of parts of *The
Voice of Truth*.

But there was nothing here about the Opening of the
Way, the purported subject of *Venus Afflicted*.

And if it existed anywhere on earth in any form other

than as that book in her possession, Julian would have it here. And he did not have it here.

Truth felt a sudden thrill of scholarly excitement; even if *Venus Afflicted* was complete claptrap, she had the only copy. It had never been published—but she would publish it: *Venus Afflicted*, the spellbook that Blackburn considered the capstone of his work.

"But—" she said aloud. The capstone of his work? She didn't know that—how *could* she know that; she didn't know what the Blackburn Work *was*!

The world reeled, and she was back in that cool, directionless place surrounded by pillars of light, the place of the Word that made the worlds. . . .

Truth clutched at the table with a sudden need for support. A chill immobility seemed to be sliding over her skin, taking possession of her senses, luring her into that other reality. Unnoticed, the folder of papers fell to the floor, hissing as they slid free in a fan-shaped jumble. Suddenly a sharp bang jolted her back to her senses—the tape recorder had slipped from her hand and crashed to the floor. The little door in the side popped open on impact, and the cassette went skittering across the floor.

Grumbling to herself, the spell broken, Truth stooped down to retrieve both cassette recorder and papers. A quick check assured her that nothing was damaged—although the papers were now out of order. She didn't think it would matter too much, all things considered.

That's what you get for a glass of sherry on an empty stomach—and no lunch besides, Truth scolded herself. She'd meant to stop for lunch in Shadowkill, but she'd been so eager to see Shadow's Gate that she'd forgotten all about it until now.

She glanced at her watch. Four o'clock. She didn't know what time dinner was at Shadow's Gate, but she was sure it wasn't for a while yet. She thought she'd take a walk around outside; not only was this local shrine to her dear departed father beginning to get on her nerves, but there was no way she could even begin to process the wealth of material it contained in a day or even a week. She could probably get as much done by just interviewing Julian about Thorne Blackburn—now *there* was a dangerously attractive thought. . . .

She was loading her tape recorder and unused notebook back into her purse when there was a flurry of tapping upon the double doors. Before she could reach them, much less open them, one of the doors burst inward, bringing with it a bustling white-haired woman draped in shawls and carrying a large tole-work tray.

The woman set it down on the nearest available surface with a rattle and clunk—Truth saw that the tray held a dark blue teapot and a round, golden cake drizzled with glistening white fondant icing. Truth felt a reflexive clutch of craving.

"He's a dear boy, but I swear by the Rood, he hasn't a brain in his head! I told him, see if I didn't, that you'd be wanting your tea, coming in the middle of the day as you did, and he'd have it that you wanted to be left alone—but if you weren't this instant about to set off in search of a nice cuppa, my name isn't Irene Avalon!" the intruder said, flashing Truth a cheery smile.

Irene Avalon was a woman well into her sixth decade. She wore a voluminous caftan in a swirling purple print, and a fringed shawl in a clashing pattern hung from her elbows. Delicate wire-rimmed half-glasses were secured about her neck with a chain and lay, for the moment, upon her ample bosom, and she was wearing a glorious amber necklace in a dark cherry color. Age had turned her hair silvery white; it was coiled on the crown of her head and restrained by hairpins into an untidy knot. She was not a tall woman; Irene stood a few inches shorter than Truth, with the plump softness to her figure that sometimes comes with age. She looked, in short, the perfect figure of anyone's dotty Spiritualist aunt in any of a number of British farces.

"Well, my girl? It's been a long time, I'll grant you that,

but no word of greeting for your old Aunt Irene?" And in fact, Irene had the lingering trace of an English accent in her actress-perfect diction.

As she spoke, Irene removed items from the tray onto the table: two delicate cups of blue and white china and their matching saucers; sugar and cream in quaint Staffordshire bowl and pitcher, stiff white napkins of starched linen damask and ornate silver spoons.

"I think—" Truth began, but the words wouldn't come. *I think you must be mistaken; I don't know you* she'd been about to say, but she felt, somehow, that wasn't quite true.

I haven't been here three hours yet and this place is getting to me, Truth thought in facetious despair. But the woman was nearly familiar, like something from a half-glimpsed dream.

"I'm not quite sure . . ." Truth said hesitantly.

"Well, and you only a toddler—how should you remember me? And after—oh, that was a horrible time, horrible, and I don't blame Caroline at all for wanting to make a clean break of it, but still—oh, never mind that," Irene said, admonishing herself. "You've come back now and that's what matters. But then, I knew you would, once Julian began the Work again—Oh, dear girl, I remember standing with you in this very room; you were in diapers then, and probably don't remember. But do have some tea," Irene said, halting her flow of reminiscence with an effort.

"Thank you," said Truth, since there didn't seem to be much else to say in the face of such effusive friendliness. Her desire to leave was gone; the room could not manage to seem menacing, now that Irene was in it.

Truth seated herself at the table again, and was rewarded with a steaming cup of dark-steeped tea and a generous wedge of red-golden cake. She managed to restrain herself far enough to lighten her tea with a liberal dollop of cream before taking a bite of the cake. The complex resonant flavor of scratch-baking exploded in her mouth; sweet and tart and spicy all at once.

"This is wonderful," Truth said, swallowing hastily.

"It was your father's favorite," Irene said serenely, unaware of the reaction her simple statement caused. "Bergamot, whole oranges, and just the tiniest hint of *pure* frankincense, powdered—oh, my dear, you look so much like our poor Katherine; it's simply heartbreaking! You must be quite the grown girl now; goodness me, it's—what?—twenty-five years and more since we were all here together at Shadow's Gate last! But now you've come, just as the Master prophesied, and we'll complete the Work at last!"

Truth sipped her tea and looked longingly at the cake on her plate—why did the simple statement that it was Blackburn's favorite turn it to ashes in her mouth? She couldn't give up the entire material world just because he'd once inhabited it!

"The work?" Truth asked, hoping to distract herself.

"The Blackburn Work," Irene assented, taking another bite of cake. "But my dear—you're not eating!"

Strangely unwilling to hurt the feelings of the older woman, Truth took another bite of the cake, and felt her foolish aversion to it melt away as if it were the citrus spun-sugar of the icing.

"Of course we are beginning the Master's Work again, now that we have nearly all we need." Irene resumed her chatter as soon as Truth began eating. "We were at an impasse—I was great once, I can say this now without either false modesty or pride, but Those Beyond have thought it meet and fit that my powers dwindle to nearly nothing—oh, I know it happens to nearly all of us whose powers are the gift of Nature rather than the Art, but I was convinced that I, Irene Avalon, would be spared!" Irene said with a self-deprecating laugh.

"At an impasse? Why?" Truth asked. *And what* was *"the Blackburn Work"—really?* she added silently, willing an answer from the woman seated opposite her.

Irene stared at her, startled, then smiled. "Oh, you are so much like Katherine that I forget what a neophyte upon the

Path you are! The Work needs a medium, my dear—one whose gift is to act as a conduit between the other world and this one." For a moment some memory seemed to dim her smile, then it passed like a cloud from the face of the sun.

Truth stopped herself on the point of telling Irene that she knew very well what a medium was, since the Bidney Institute worked with several—and that she certainly didn't believe in the spirits some of them claimed to conjure.

"I see," she said instead.

"Oh, you do not," Irene contradicted fondly, patting Truth's hand. "But you will. At any rate, when Julian gathered us all back together—well, gathered me, at any rate; the others, alas, all came to the Work after our dear Master had seen fit to leave us for a while—he hoped to begin the Work at once, but as I told you, I am not the woman I was when I worked as Thorne's Hierophex. Fortunately he found Light, and I was able to train her."

"Julian found the light?" Truth floundered. She hadn't heard so many bizarre pseudo-technical terms flung about so casually since the last time she'd unwarily listened to a conversation between two deconstructionalists in Taghkanic's English department.

"Oh, no, Truth dear. Julian found *Light*—she's a dear girl; you'll meet her at dinner tonight—and now our Circle has an Hierophex again. And we have an Hierolater—the Sacred Concubine, you know—too: Our preparations for resuming the Work are nearly complete."

Irene smiled proudly, and something deep inside Truth flinched away from the hope and trust in those calm blue eyes. She could not bear to say the words that would seem to agree with Irene's beliefs, but just as surely she could not bear to present her own in the face of that kindly fondness.

Truth felt a hard hot pain in her throat—because of Blackburn, she told herself, Blackburn who had made good people love him and then had run away.

"Tell me more about the Work," Truth said, managing to keep her voice steady.

"Oh, well, of course you could read about it," Irene said, obviously itching to unburden herself, "but I could just tell you a little, shall I? It's the Great Work—attuning ourselves to the New Aeon and then Opening the Way for the *sidhevalkirie*; the Spirits of the New Aeon who will ride forth into the World of Men to guide them on the Path. Which works out just fine, Truth dear, except that my old memory isn't quite what it once was, you know—and I did only see the entire ritual once," Irene protested amiably. "As you know, of course, the Hierophex is not actually *present* during the ritual itself, but in a trance state."

"Ah?" said Truth inquiringly. She knew no such thing, but she did know how to fish for information. The cake was long gone, and now Truth drained her teacup. Irene beamed approval and poured it full again. Truth added more cream, promising to do dietary penance later.

The odd feeling of *doubleness*—of being herself, but also some *other* who knew things Truth Jourdemayne could not—was entirely gone: Nothing fey could survive in Irene's motherly down-to-earth presence. But, Truth had to admit, Irene had certainly raised up more questions than she'd answered.

"So of course, being . . . absent . . . you won't be able to help Julian reconstruct . . ." Truth let the sentence trail off invitingly.

"The Opening of the Way," Irene confirmed without hesitation. "I'm doing the best I can, and of course the first nine Stations are a matter of public record, but without *Venus Afflicted* I don't know if we'll ever have the whole rite back again."

The watch on Truth's wrist said five-thirty, and she was alone in an upstairs bedroom at Shadow's Gate. It was a lovely, old-fangled, blue-wallpapered room that peered out over the back terrace and lawn into the spreading twilight forest beyond. Antique Tiffany-glass sconces burned on the walls, diffusing a lovely pastel light and giving the room a golden *fin de siècle* glow, as if at any moment it might vanish, like Brigadoon, into another age.

Irene had been fiercely incensed at Julian's cavalier treatment of his guest, displaying a motherly indignation that made Truth smile inwardly. Once Truth had told her that she'd been on the road since six this morning and gone without lunch into the bargain, Irene'd made Truth give her the keys to the Saturn and sent Gareth out to retrieve Truth's suitcase, then had shown her up to this room so that Truth could "wash up a bit and have a nice lie-down" before dinner, which would be served around seven-thirty. Truth had jumped at the opportunity to change her travel-crumpled suit for something a little more suited to what promised to be a fairly fancy—and fraught—formal dinner.

She ran her hand through her sensibly-short dark hair until it stood up in rumpled, spiky dishevelment, then sat down suddenly on the bed and regarded her reflection in the antique maple cheval-glass that stood in the corner. A dark-haired woman in her late twenties, dressed in an ecru-colored slip and dark nylons, stared back belligerently.

She'd taken off her traveling suit and hung it on the back of the door to the connecting bathroom with the hangers she'd found in the closet, in the hope that some of the wrinkles would hang out of the thing; silk was supposed to be accommodating. Her suitcase and travel case—all she thought she would need for the short stay she had contemplated in Shadowkill, New York—stood like silent sentinels of high-impact burgundy plastic beside the bed, awaiting her pleasure.

What am I doing here? Truth asked herself helplessly. She felt the same outsider's embarrassment she'd feel if she'd been caught sneaking into a mosque. Irene Avalon was a sincere believer—

Sincerely deluded, a nasty little inner voice corrected.

—in Thorne Blackburn and his whatever-it-was. Julian
Pilgrim was—

A treacherous heat rose into Truth's cheeks as she contemplated Julian. What Julian was, was exciting, as nothing
in her carefully regulated and measured life had ever been
nor was ever going to be. He wore an aura of romance and
danger like a magician's cloak.

True enough, the inner voice admitted grudgingly.

But she recoiled from what else was almost certainly
true. She didn't want to think of Julian as a magician committed to the Blackburn Work.

*. . . Even though he's obviously bankrolling it, eh, Truth
my rationalist dear? How about some truth in advertising,
little namesake? It's all right for a dotty harmless old lady
to believe in magick, but you'd much rather that this knight
in shining shadows be morally impeccable—*

Truth expelled her pent-up breath in a huff of exasperation. Julian's beliefs didn't matter to her, because Julian
didn't matter to her.

Liar.

"Oh, all right!" Truth said under her breath. Julian
was as attractive as something out of a romance novel—
witty, handsome, delightfully mysterious, unattainable, or
almost—

And he wasn't getting *Venus Afflicted* out of her if she
had anything to say about it, Truth swore.

Once the definite decision—a vow, nearly—was made,
Truth felt a great burden lift from her shoulders, as if Something had been waiting to hear her decision. She was only
lucky she hadn't mentioned its presence to Julian when
they'd talked; it was easy enough to conceal something that
no one was looking for, and she intended to conceal the
only copy of Blackburn's spellbook no matter what. The
new improved Circle was not going to get its hands on . . .
what?

Well, whatever *Venus Afflicted* was, they weren't getting it.

The relief Truth felt convinced her that this was the right thing to do: She didn't know all the details of how and why and who, but she knew that Julian Pilgrim could not be allowed to get his hands on the final ritual for "opening the way"—whatever it was.

Why not? a sly inner voice asked. *If it's all nonsense and mummery, what does it matter what mumbo jumbo he does here? You don't even have to give him the original—just take it down to the town and make a copy and give him that. He'd be grateful. He might even be very grateful. . . .*

This sneaky new direction for her thoughts was too much. Truth bounced to her feet and swept up the suitcase, spreading it open on the bed, banishing this particular line of introspection. Her reflection echoed her in the window's glass, and Truth took a moment to pull the shade and draw the long white lace curtains shut, shutting out the twilight.

What could she wear to dinner? She looked at the sensible sweaters, the practical cotton pajamas, the businesslike chinos and blouses and skirts that she'd packed, and sagged despairingly. There was nothing here that would make her fit into Julian's world—even as a guest. Nothing, except—

She picked up the item and shook it out, holding it up high so it wouldn't touch the floor.

She wasn't quite sure why she'd packed it; when she'd made her choices of what to bring she hadn't contemplated any occasion for which it would be suitable. In fact, to be perfectly honest, it wasn't the sort of thing she bought for any occasion; she didn't know why she had it at all.

Bought by my evil twin, obviously, Truth reflected with an amused quirk to her mouth.

It was a princess-line dinner dress in delicate midnight blue wool jersey, simple, elegant, and regal. With its long sleeves and jewel neck, it was far too fancy and formal for any affair that Truth Jourdemayne, psychic research statistician, would ever attend.

But it was just right for dinner at Shadow's Gate.

A quick sponge bath, a splash of the lavender cologne she favored, and Truth was ready to dress. She pulled the dress on over her head, cursing the long zipper up the back—why weren't women's clothes designed so that women could dress themselves? she wondered for the hundredth time—and regarded herself in the cheval-glass.

A stranger stared back, a mocking light of challenge in her dark eyes. Did she, in fact, resemble her mother that much? Was this what Katherine Jourdemayne had looked like? Truth wondered, though the question probed the psychic sore spot where all Truth's unanswered questions about the mother she had never known had festered. Truth stared at the reflection curiously, willing it to give up the secrets of another woman's past. Katherine Jourdemayne? It was easy enough for Irene Avalon to say so, but Irene hadn't seen Katherine since they were both young women; it would be easy to be carried away by the emotion of the moment.

But Irene Avalon had not been only Katherine's friend. She had been the friend of both Truth's parents, and Truth at last surrendered to the need to know about them—about her mother, and, yes, even about her father. If she did not ask her questions soon, the people she could ask would have passed from the world and left her questions forever unanswered.

She would not let that happen.

Truth inclined her head graciously to the stranger in the mirror, and then slipped her feet into her black pumps. A few quick primpings with her hair and makeup, and she was ready.

Or almost. As it was now, the dress looked almost formidably severe. She needed some jewelry to bring the outfit to life, but Truth didn't have much in the way of trendy, expensive, and frivolous fashion accessories. Other than a few pair of "good" earrings and a short gold chain, Truth owned no jewelry at all.

In her earlier search for something to wear she had nearly

emptied her suitcase. All that was left in it now was her bathrobe and the item it was wrapped around—*Venus Afflicted*. Now she turned to the traveling case she had also brought—that squarish boxy article that had once held a lady's elaborate toilette—and in the modern day, proved so useful for the transport of the small yet fragile articles that a woman still traveled with.

She opened it and lifted out the top tray. There, inside, tucked into a jewelry roll, were the necklace and ring that Aunt Caroline had given her: Thorne Blackburn's necklace and ring. Perhaps . . . ?

The ring was obviously impossible; it slid off every finger she tried it on, and even if she had been able to make it fit, it would have weighted down her hand as much as if she were carrying a dumbbell. Not the thing for a dinner party. She dropped it back into the little satin pouch and picked up the necklace.

Even such an amateur of gemology as Truth could tell that the amber beads were of a much finer quality than those in Irene's necklace. The necklace rested on her palms, light as a soap bubble. The ancient Greeks had called this substance *electrum*, and said it was no less than fossilized lightning, dropped from heaven by Zeus's careless thunderbolts. The Greeks had called it so because true amber, Truth knew, would hold an electrical charge; properly magnetized, the beads would draw threads and pieces of paper to stick to them, and even give off a weird bluish glow in the dark. As Truth ran the beads through her hands they seemed almost to glow without electricity, gathering all the light in the room to radiate it with an intense citrine radiance.

She dropped the necklace over her head: The ornate enameled golden pendant swung free, then dropped into place below her heart with the soft heavy force of a love-pat. Against the dark fabric, the stones that had once been the life blood of a tree burned with even brighter fire, giving her the look of a warrior priestess readying herself for battle.

No, Truth decided reluctantly, gazing at her reflection. It was beautiful, but it wouldn't be at all appropriate—not to mention the questions it would raise. With hesitant regret, she removed Blackburn's necklace and stowed it back in the train case with the ring. A long silk scarf, knotted loosely about her throat, provided a poor—but adequate—substitute.

I guess they'll have to take me just as I am. Truth looked at her watch. Seven o'clock. Half an hour before the time Irene said they would all be gathering for dinner, and in all likelihood the evening would not be over until ten or later. Truth was glad she'd asked Irene to call the Bed-and-Breakfast for her and tell them she was already in town and would be arriving later tonight—she'd hate to get there and find out some stranger had ransomed her bed right out from under her.

Anyway, she might as well go down now.

She took a step toward the door and hesitated, then turned back. She'd left the contents of her suitcase scattered all over her bed—including *Venus Afflicted*. What if someone came in?

She frowned, standing over the suitcase with a handful of sweaters. What if someone *did* come in—not that they ought to—and went through her suitcase, which was far beyond the pale of good manners but might still happen? She didn't have the key to her suitcase, and she supposed the lock wouldn't stop someone who was really determined anyway.

She frowned, considering for a moment, then removed *Venus Afflicted* from inside the bundle of her robe. She should just put it somewhere—for safekeeping.

Where?

After a bit of thought, Truth slid the book between the mattress and the box spring, up near the head of the bed where a certain additional elevation of the mattress wouldn't be noticed on a casual inspection. She smoothed the candlewick cover down again and dumped her clothes loosely back into the suitcase.

In the doorway she stopped and took one last survey of the room. Everything looked perfectly innocent.

Aunt Caroline always used to say: If something looks too good to be true, it probably is. Truth smiled, and squared her shoulders, and went down the stairs.

CHAPTER FIVE

TRUTH AMONG SHADOWS

Through the unheeding many he did move,
A splendour among shadows, a bright blot
Upon this gloomy scene, a Spirit that strove
For truth, and like the Preacher found it not.
——PERCY BYSSHE SHELLEY

WHEN SHE REACHED THE TOP OF THE STAIRS, TRUTH SAW
that Julian was waiting for her on the landing. At the sight
of him, Truth was glad she'd yielded to some martial impulse and dressed for dinner; Julian had shed his country-
squire tweeds for what looked like an Armani suit in
midnight silk. He smiled when he saw her.

"Ah, Truth. I was just coming to see if you were ready.
We're assembled in the parlor for preprandial sherry. Not
that we're usually so formal—it's in your honor, you might
say."

His gaze rested on her with obvious male approval, and
Truth felt the heat rise in her cheeks again. What was it
about the master of Shadow's Gate that flustered her so?
This wasn't at all like her; she was always so cool and self-
possessed, a creature of the mind, ruled by the mind and
wary of emotional entrapment. No flighty Gothic heroine
she!

She came down the last few steps and Julian offered her

his arm. Reluctantly Truth cudgeled her slothful brain into gear.

"Who will I be meeting tonight, Julian?" She heard the faint quiver of nervousness in her voice and winced, but she couldn't help herself. The thought of meeting a large group of people—let alone people who were obsessed with Thorne Blackburn—filled her with reflexive dread.

He offered her his arm and she took it. The faint, elusive scent of male cologne filled her nostrils, and for a moment before she dismissed the frivolous thought Truth fancied she could feel the thrill of some electrical pulse where her fingers rested on the warm solidity of his arm. They started down the rest of the stairs together.

"I won't fling you into the lion's den alone, Truth," Julian said with lightly mocking reproof. "But you'll be meeting the rest of our Circle this evening, at least those I've been able to gather so far. The Work requires a Circle of thirteen to do it properly, but it can be managed with fewer."

And are you managing it? Truth wanted to ask, but they had arrived.

Like most Victorian mansions, Shadow's Gate had a certain bilateral symmetry to it, including matching parlors on either side of the entry hall. Truth had been in one of them—the Blackburn museum—for several hours today. Now she entered its counterpart.

Nothing could have been more different. Though many of the rooms at Shadow's Gate held what must be the original furniture, it was plain that Julian had not in any sense created a museum-mansion where the clock was stopped in 1895. The walls of this parlor were a dark shade of Paris green, a color picked up in the brocade curtains and the exquisite Oriental carpets underfoot. But the long sectional couch was entirely modern, its sleek Italian lines upholstered in butter-soft oyster-colored leather, and the tables were modern constructions of glass-topped bronze.

Truth was no sheltered simpleton—no one who had any

connection with a college's incessant quest for money could be that innocent of how the world worked—and the sheer amount of money a room furnished in this fashion represented was like a warning flag. The rich, as F. Scott Fitzgerald once said, are different from you and me, and in Truth's experience, that difference meant the ruthless disregard for the consequences to others of one's actions that only the sheer power of wealth could make possible.

She managed to gather a confused impression of half-a-dozen assorted people standing as if waiting for her before Julian's hand upon her waist propelled her gently into the room.

Thrown to the lions . . .

"Ladies and gentlemen," Julian said. "It is my great honor to present the daughter of Thorne Blackburn—Truth Jourdemayne."

Truth flushed exasperatedly. Why had Julian . . . ?

"Should we applaud?" a male voice drawled. Its owner came forward, glass in hand. He wore a dark vest with his tweed jacket and old school tie, and Truth instantly if unconsciously pegged him as a down-at-heel professor—the man had the moon-pale skin and hollow eyes of one who spent his waking hours indoors in dusty archives poring over obscure texts. He seemed to be somewhere in his forties, his hair dark and in need of cutting. His eyes were gray, and he had the look of an irritated falcon.

"No offense, dear lady," he added, with a mock bow in her direction. Truth found herself smiling in sheer relief at the familiarity—just like any boring faculty tea, at least so far.

"Oh for God's sake, Ellis," Julian muttered. "Truth, allow me to present Ellis Gardner, much as I'd rather not at the moment. He isn't usually this bad. Ellis, can't you—"

"My dear Hierodule, it is only the sherry that makes me tolerable at all," Gardner said mockingly. He took Truth by the hand and drew her away from Julian's side. Though he did smell strongly of sherry, and from Julian's comments probably was a frequent overindulger, both Ellis's speech and gait were steady as he conducted Truth about the room and its inhabitants.

"Allow me to introduce the rest of our merry band of seekers after truth. The founder of the feast you already know"—this with an ironic nod toward Julian, whose face was studiously blank—"and our dear Mrs. Avalon, who deserves better."

Irene was dazzling in a caftan of bright gold lamé and several additional necklaces and bangle bracelets. Her eyes were heavily made up for evening, painted in a highly theatrical Egyptian style, with long, black tails of kohl wrapping around her temples and the area from lid to brow painted a jewellike turquoise blue. Her face looked like a painted mask, out of which the motherly sensible woman Truth had met this afternoon gazed.

"Ellis, do be a good boy," she urged.

"And this is Gareth Crowther, of whom you have also had the dubious pleasure. Gareth is our rude mechanical," Ellis said.

"Knock it off, Ellis," Gareth said without heat. He was wearing a pearl-buttoned denim shirt and his hands were almost painfully clean after the grease Truth had seen on them at the gatehouse. "Glad you're staying, Truth," he said.

Truth opened her mouth to correct his misapprehension— hoping Julian did not share it—when Ellis spoke again, turning to gesture at someone on the far side of the room.

"Mr. Crowther worships from afar at *this* shrine," Ellis said in the orotund tones of a tour-bus operator, "our *soi-disant* Hierolator, the lovely and attractively-packaged Fiona, known as Miss Cabot to her friends—"

Truth's gaze followed Ellis's gesture, to where a young, heavily made up woman whose flaming red hair cascaded down her back stood within a pool of halogen illumination as if within a theatrical spotlight.

Fiona Cabot wore a long-sleeved dress of tie-dyed panné velvet that was both short and tight, hugging her sleek yet opulent body as snugly as a dancer's leotard. A shadow of lace trim showed at the edge of the low-cut neckline, and she wore a wide black velvet ribbon tied around her throat. She smiled chillily at Truth, the salute of equals across an arena.

"One dares not get too close," Ellis continued smoothly, as *Hamadryad orientalis*—the king cobra—can spit poison a distance of several yards."

Fiona's chin came up sharply and she glared murderously at Ellis momentarily before setting her glass down sharply on the nearest flat surface. She crossed to Julian with quick angry steps, and Truth thought unkindly that if she were really the cat she seemed her tail would be fluffed out and lashing.

"*Dar*ling Julian," Fiona said in gritted-teeth accents, wreathing her arm through his and leaning coquettishly against him. "Do we have to put up with this again?" The stiletto heels she wore made her nearly his height.

Truth felt an unreasonable spasm of jealousy—but on the basis of Ellis's introduction she stole a glance at Gareth's face, and saw her own jealousy refined to fever pitch and blazing nakedly from his eyes.

Gardner's right about one thing: Gareth's in love with Fiona. And I'll bet she knows it, the bitch, Truth mused to herself. Her distaste for the situation she found herself in increased.

"Ellis, that's enough," Julian said curtly.

Some power thrilled out across invisible lines of command; Truth felt Ellis resist it for an instant and then succumb.

"Oh, very well," the older man said. "The rest of our bear-garden, then—briefly." He took a firmer grip on Truth's arm—almost for support, she thought, although he hadn't needed it a moment ago.

"Donner Murray." A brown-haired, brown-eyed man of about Truth's age, wearing a gray corduroy jacket and no tie. He smiled at Truth—civilly, a little distant—and raised his glass in silent salute.

"Caradoc Buckland."

"Pleasure to meet you."

Caradoc had dark brown hair cut fashionably short. A large gold ring glinted in one ear, and he wore a massive gold signet on his right hand. He was dressed more fashionably than Donner, in a pale designer suit worn with a dark collarless shirt.

"Hereward Farrar."

By now Truth's head was spinning with this catalog of peculiar persons to which she must somehow remember to attach the right equally-odd names, but Farrar was one she'd have no trouble remembering. His gray eyes were so pale they were nearly silver, and his red hair—darker than Fiona's—was long in the style of a generation before. He smiled his faint wolf-smile at her, as impersonal as a forest predator's. Here was one who stood apart and did not give his fealty lightly. She was conscious of his swift appraisal returning her own before he smiled.

"Ready to run screaming into the night yet, Truth?" Hereward asked.

"Not yet," Truth answered.

"Your sherry, Truth," Julian said, stepping away from Fiona and taking back firm control of the situation. He handed Truth the small, delicate-stemmed glass and took the opportunity to detach her from Ellis. Fiona hesitated and then decided to make the best of it, turning away to engage Donner in conversation.

"I'm afraid that Ellis has a rather difficult sense of humor," Julian said, drawing Truth to one side. Was it her imagination, or was the smile Julian gave her warmer than the one he reserved for Fiona?

Truth sipped at her drink before replying. It was an excellent sherry; if tastes here ran to blood-sports before dinner, at least there were compensations.

"Oh, I'm hardly made of spun-sugar," she replied. "And none of those witty comments were directed at me, after all."

"I just don't want you to think badly of us," Julian said simply. He was about to say more, but Irene interrupted him, crossing to him from the doorway with a look of worry on her face.

"Julian." Truth remembered that Irene had left the room just after being noted in Ellis's catalog. "Have you seen Light?"

"In her room?" Julian said, half-questioning.

"I've just been; she isn't there. Oh, Julian, if she's wandered off again—"

Watching Irene's face, Truth could see honest concern and worry reflected there. Earlier Irene'd spoken of Light as a full partner in the Blackburn Work, but now she was acting as if Light were a wayward child.

"I'll send someone to look around," Julian said. "She may have gone outside without anyone seeing. Gareth—?"

"There's no need for that. She's here now," a deep voice said.

A man and a woman stood in the doorway.

That must be Light, Truth thought inconsequentially.

The woman was slender, almost frail. She wore a tunic and wide trousers in a silky pale material. Truth was too far away to see her eyes, but the brighter light of the hall haloed the girl's long silver hair with an almost unearthly radiance.

Unearthly. That's for sure. She looks almost like the Hollywood version of a psychic.

Truth's exposure to mediums was fairly limited, as what the Institute jokingly called their care and feeding fell more within Dylan's sphere, or even Professor MacLaren's. What Truth knew was more or less what everyone knew: a medium was a natural psychic, sensitive to the emanations of what some of the more old-fashioned among them still called "The Spirit World"; one who, when in trance, served as a conduit for other entities to communicate with the living world. *Or seemed to*, Truth reminded herself with the habit of a professional skeptic. Dylan's psychics located ghosts for him in the haunted houses that were his pet projects, but Light—an odd name, but no stranger than Truth's, or, in fact, anyone's here—seemed almost to be a spirit herself.

"Julian!" Light ran to him with a childish openness and flung her arms around him, hugging him tightly. "I'm sorry I went out, but saw them again—the red stag and the white mare—and I—"

"And now you must greet our guest, Light," Julian said with fond firmness. He placed a hand on Light's head and looked up at Truth. "Light is our psychic, and sometimes gets . . . easily distracted. Don't you, little one?" he said indulgently.

Light shook her head violently. Her voice and gestures were those of a much younger woman, and Truth felt a sudden pang of protectiveness. She had no sense that Light was mentally impaired, but it was obvious that she was unequipped to deal with the modern world unaided.

"I was not distracted!" Light protested, still taking no notice of Truth. "I was following the red stag. The red stag and the white mare; the gray wolf and the black dog; red and gray and black and white, the four wardens of the Gate," she singsonged excitedly.

"But you must not follow them into the wood, child. Though they mean you no harm, there are other dangers in the wood," said the man who had entered with her.

He was easily two inches taller than Julian, with curly black hair that shone blue where the light hit it. The deep voice was faintly foreign, with a lingering trace of an accent Truth couldn't quite place. She looked up, into his eyes.

Falling, and in place of the Light and the Word was darkness and the fire eternal—

With an effort, Truth dragged herself out of . . . what?

"Hello, I'm Truth Jourdemayne," she said, almost as if daring him to contradict her. Feeling oddly formal, she held out her hand.

He took it, bowing over it in an equally formal fashion. Truth forced herself not to recoil at the touch. Power blazed through his skin; her hand tingled harshly, and surreal images exploded behind her eyes like fireworks. Why was *he* here—and what was he doing in this disguise? These were not his clothes—this was not his place!

"And the last of our band appears. Truth, this is Michael—"

"—Archangel," the tall man finished, releasing her hand and looking into her eyes once more. The brief hallucination vanished, and Truth saw that Michael Archangel's eyes were black, the division between iris and pupil nearly invisible, and his skin was the clear pale olive of a Renaissance icon's.

"It would be less unusual rendered in my native Greek," he continued, "but it was Anglicized so long ago that it does not seem worth the trouble to change it back."

Truth stared at him and then at her fingers. They looked normal—why had they tingled with that ascetic fire? And where had that alien certainty come from? She'd never seen this man before in her life!

"The Archangel Michael, captain of the armies of God," Julian said mockingly. There seemed to be an edge to his bantering now that Truth didn't remember hearing before.

"Who will put down the Serpent in the last days, and cast him utterly into the Abyss for all time," Michael agreed, as if finishing some sort of catechism.

"But meanwhile, doing research in our collection," Julian said smoothly. He disentangled Light from himself and gave her a gentle push in Irene's direction. "Run along and find Irene, sweetheart. She'll get you something to drink."

Light smiled at them sunnily, including Truth in this silent welcome, before turning away.

"If you'll excuse me," Michael said, strolling after Light.

Julian watched them go, a faint preoccupation on his face.

He doesn't like Michael and Light being together, Truth thought with that new unreasonable certainty. *Why?* She forced herself to disregard this intuition; it would be so easy to convince herself that this inner voice was always right— and that was where delusions of great occult power came from.

"Who *is* he, Julian?" Truth asked, knowing the question sounded juvenile and still unable to keep from asking it.

"An old school chum of mine, actually. Not what I suppose you'd call a believer; he's using my collection to do some research work of his own," Julian said. "But not a skeptic, either. Michael's allegiance remains . . . uncommitted."

Truth and Julian were still standing more or less in the middle of the parlor. The others had scattered into comfort: Hereward was sitting on the oyster sofa talking to Fiona, who was perched on its arm, her hemline riding perilously high. Ellis, as was only to be expected, was standing near the sherry decanter, his glass full once more.

Gareth, surprisingly enough, had gone over to join Michael and Light. One of the other men—Donner or Caradoc, she wasn't quite sure—was explaining something to Irene with expansive gestures; the other was seated at the opposite end of the couch.

An ordinary family gathering—if you happen to be the Addams Family, Truth thought unfairly. She wondered who all these people *were*, really, and how Julian had gathered them all together. Surely people weren't named things like 'Hereward' and 'Caradoc' in this day and age.

If I were practicing magick, I'd probably want an alias too, Truth thought reasonably, and turned her thoughts back to Julian.

"What do you think of the Blackburn collection, now that you've had a chance to look it over?"

"I've barely begun," Truth protested, "but I can already see that it will take me weeks to really get a handle on what you have there." *That, and a native guide.* "Just how valuable is your collection without a copy of *Venus Afflicted*?" she asked boldly. "Irene told me about it this afternoon," Truth added, noting Julian's look of surprise.

He took a moment to choose his words before he spoke. "A complete collection is always more valuable than an incomplete one, of course. My collection is reasonably representational, allowing for the fact that magickal records and artifacts have always been simultaneously considered deeply confidential and highly ephemeral, so that most collections simply vanish upon their collector's death."

"But—?" prompted Truth, who knew she hadn't heard an answer yet.

"I would give my immortal soul to hold *Venus Afflicted* in my hands," Julian told her flatly. "Assuming I believed I possessed one," he added, to lighten the moment.

Truth was fortunately saved from any need to reply by the chiming of a small bell.

"Dinner," Gareth said, his voice echoing Truth's feeling of relief.

The dining room of Shadow's Gate more than lived up to the rest of the house's Rockefeller-era opulence. It could easily have accommodated a table twice the length of the one that was there, and as it was, the eleven diners had ample space to spread out along its white-damasked length.

Above, two enormous Waterford crystal chandeliers filled the room with sparking light. The floor's opulent parquetry was covered by an immense Aubusson carpet in cream tones, and a brace of dazzlingly ornate silver candelabrum stood ready to light on the marble-topped ebonywood sideboard along with a number of single silver candlesticks.

The room was half-paneled in the style of a bygone age, and from the wainscoting to the ceiling the walls were covered in a golden silk brocade. An arched set of double doors led out into the house's central space, and two smaller doors led to the kitchen and the butler's pantry.

Julian went to the head of the table and gestured to the foot.

"As our guest of honor, the place of honor is yours," Julian said to Truth, gesturing to the foot of the table.

"Oh, I couldn't. Really," Truth said, hesitating in the doorway.

"Julian, really!" Fiona cooed in falsely-honeyed tones.

"You'll make her feel quite conspicuous." Fiona slithered into the seat at the foot of the table with an alacrity that suggested it wasn't her usual place, and shot a look of defiant triumph at Truth.

Truth sensed a sudden tension in the room, like a whip-crack of distant thunder, but Julian said nothing, merely drew out the chair at his right.

"Here, then," he said, smiling. "So I can monopolize your conversation throughout the meal."

The others all settled into new places around the table. Truth was amused to find that Ellis Gardner then seated himself on her right, obviously glad of a fresh ear for his tattle. Truth wondered if it was a good idea to cultivate him: On the one hand, you learned everyone's secrets—a version of them, anyway—but on the other hand, most other people wouldn't talk freely to you once word got out that you were companioning a scandalmonger.

Scandalmonger. Now there's an old-fashioned word! Wonder where that came from?

Michael graciously allowed Irene to take the seat on Julian's left before settling himself next to her with Light on his other side. Truth, gazing across the table into Michael's midnight eyes, had the feeling that more was going on here than a dinnertime game of musical chairs, but brushed the thought aside. It was nothing to do with her, after all.

The soup course was passed, and Truth thought longingly of her room at the Shadowkill Bed-and-Breakfast, far from all these passions and factions and seething hidden agendas. Once there, only see if she ever came back to Shadow's Gate!

But you'll have to. Your work here isn't finished yet, an inner voice reminded her.

The thought checked her as if it had erected a physical barrier. It was true. She'd barely even begun to outline her biography of Thorne Blackburn, and she already knew that most of the material she needed to write it was here in Julian's collection. Julian's collection, Irene's memories . . .

She glanced across the table to where Light sat between

Michael and Gareth. Light looked up when she felt Truth's eyes on her, and smiled shyly before ducking her head again. Truth felt an answering smile tug at her own mouth. And while she was meddling, she'd better also find out from Irene just what Light's position was in this odd extended household, and if Light were being . . . exploited in any way.

"Some wine, Truth?"

She was roused from her list-making reverie by Julian's question. She nodded, and he poured her glass full of a sparkling straw-colored vintage.

"I am not one of those who believes the path to power lies in denial and asceticism," he said, smiling at her. "Certainly there are occasions upon which fasting and petition are appropriate, and then I employ them, but how much more true is it that we must understand what range of information our senses can provide if we are to fully master them?"

"You know I understand very little of your . . . practices," Truth said frankly. After the sherry, she wasn't sure she wanted another glass of wine immediately, but everyone else at the table, even Light, was drinking, and besides, she'd have a full meal to offset its effects. "Is that what Blackburn believed?" She raised her glass and sipped.

"In this as in all things, you behold me his pupil," Julian said, smiling.

"*I'd* like some wine, too, Julian," Fiona said, raising her glass meaningfully. Hereward, laughter in his eyes but his face as irreproachably blank as a butler's, poured her glass full from the second bottle at the foot of the table.

"Not that Julian hasn't found some improvements to make to the Master's Work," Irene said cheerily, interrupting Fiona as if she hadn't heard her.

"If the Work is to succeed, we can't regard it as some sort of received truth, to be trifled with only at our peril. The Wheel turns," Julian said.

"And Julian," Ellis said *sotto voce* in Truth's ear, "intends to be on top of it no matter how much it turns."

Truth glanced toward him, an automatic social smile on her face. It was an impression of Julian she'd already collected for herself, but knowing that about him only seemed to make him more exciting.

What was Shadow's Gate turning her into?

Dinner was a long and lavish affair, though its accoutrements fell short of the hordes of liveried footmen that the dining room seemed to call for. The food was expertly prepared and its presentation worthy of a four-star restaurant, but in the modern day, throngs of convenient servants such as peopled the Gothic novel were not so easily come by. The cook and one assistant brought the food to the table, after which the diners served themselves.

The talk—and the wine—flowed freely, conversation ranging from such homely topics as possible future difficulties with the property's well to the latest movies. It was a warm easy camaraderie that made Truth feel like an accepted member of the group.

The only faintly sour note was Fiona's continuing dislike, but that was easily understood. Fiona's attraction to Julian was obvious—even if it didn't seem to be mutual.

It was just like a Shakespeare comedy, Truth mused to herself. She wondered if the tangled affections at Shadow's Gate would sort out as easily and neatly as the ending of an Elizabethan play, with all these various sets of mismatched lovers finding their proper mates. Meanwhile, Gareth loved Fiona, Fiona loved Julian. . . .

And who did Julian love? Light?

No, Truth decided upon careful consideration. Julian's feelings for Light were not those of a would-be lover. She glanced across the table to where Michael was deep in a soft-pitched conversation with the silver-haired girl. Maybe it was Michael who loved Light; oddly, Truth had the feeling that Julian disapproved of that relationship. Why, if he didn't want to take Michael's place? Surely, if he disliked

Michael Archangel so much, he would not have him as a guest in his home.

The cook and his assistant came in again just as the last diners were finishing—Truth, who had been watching for it, saw Julian surreptitiously push a button with his foot—and began to clear away. When Truth saw Gareth and Donner get up to help she started to rise also, and was stopped by Julian's hand on her arm.

"Rank hath its privileges," he said. "Hoskins likes to leave as soon as the dessert course is ready, so we tend to give him a hand. But it's out of the question to ask an honored guest to work."

"Dessert?" said Truth weakly. She couldn't remember the last time she'd eaten this much: clear soup, roast beef and roast potatoes, vegetables glazed and poached and broiled, and half a dozen different hot breads had only been the beginning.

In a few moments the table was cleared and Hoskins's assistant came out wheeling a cart that held new glasses, plates, and silver. Behind Davies came Hoskins himself, carrying a huge tray that proved to contain several different kinds of pastry.

"Irene told me you have reservations at a place in town. Now that you've had a chance to assess the collection, do you think I might persuade you to stay here instead?" Julian asked as the tray was being carried around.

Truth hesitated. In her experience, so generous an offer rarely came without strings, even though she hadn't seen any yet. And despite the convenience of such an arrangement, and the enticing proximity of Julian Pilgrim, Truth still felt that Shadow's Gate was somehow a challenge to her that she wanted to assess before accepting. It would be easier to think the matter over somewhere outside the overwhelming presence of the house.

"While I don't think I could do my book without what you've gathered here," she began, tactfully.

"Then it's settled," Julian said. "You'll—"

Whatever he was about to say was drowned out by a

whip-crack of thunder. The lights gave a moth-wing flutter.

"Here we go again," said Gareth, slipping back into his seat.

"What he means is," Hereward said, reaching for his own dessert as the tray passed him, "is that sitting in the Storm King's backyard, you've got to expect the occasional storm."

"I just wish it *were* occasional," Caradoc said. "At least the power failures provide good practice at getting around by candlelight."

The tray was presented to Truth. Urged on by Julian, she selected a poached pear, which seemed to be the least caloric of the offerings.

"Do you lose power often?" Truth asked. Storm King, she recalled, was the name of one of the local mountain peaks.

"Usually just a matter of flipping a circuit breaker," Caradoc said, "which is our resident technojunkie's purview"— Gareth bowed where he sat, grinning—"but sometimes the whole area goes."

"If you can't see the lights down in Shadowkill when you look out the third-floor window, give up," Gareth said. "It means the power's out all over Shadowkill Township and probably northern Dutchess County as well."

Light giggled, a silvery, elfin sound. "I like storms," she confided shyly. Truth smiled back.

"So do—" she began, but broke off as the lights flickered again to the accompaniment. Truth put down her fork.

"I've really enjoyed the evening, but I think if it's going to storm I'd really better get going," Truth said firmly. She'd have enough trouble finding the Bed-and-Breakfast in the dark without having to find it in the dark during a storm.

"But Truth! Surely you're staying?" Irene said incredulously.

"There's plenty of room," Gareth added.

"I was hoping you'd accept my invitation to write your book here," Julian said, "but even if you will not, surely a night's hospitality would not be too much? I'd hate to send someone out to find an unfamiliar destination in weather like this."

"He's right. You wouldn't send a knight out on a dog like this," Caradoc said, smiling his crooked smile.

At that moment the lights went completely out, and there was a deafening slap of thunder, followed by a spatter of raindrops flung like pebbles at the dining room windows. After a moment's pause there was laughter and scattered applause, led by Julian.

"You see, Truth, the Old Gods smile on our wish that you remain," Julian said out of the darkness. There was a scuffling and a scrambling, and then Truth heard the sound of a match being struck.

By the light of both candelabra—some two dozen candles—the dining room was surprisingly bright.

"The lights are *all* out," Light said, marvelingly.

"Who wants to go check?" Gareth asked.

"You do," Donner told him, crossing to the sideboard and handing Gareth a single candlestick. Grinning in good-natured defeat, Gareth lit the candle from one of the candelabra and walked out, shielding the flame with his free hand.

"More wine?" Ellis asked, filling his own glass. Truth shook her head and he shrugged.

"Why doesn't he use a flashlight?" Truth asked Julian.

"Batteries have a way of going dead at Shadow's Gate," Julian said. "It's easier to use candles than to struggle with them. I'm afraid that your watch's battery will require replacing rather soon as well."

Well, that's something I can check, Truth thought determinedly.

"I think you would be wise to accept Julian's invitation," Michael said to Truth. "Your luggage is already inside, is it not?"

"Yes. Certainly," Truth said. It was an odd question, though—why had Michael thought she'd come with luggage?—and Michael had been one of the last to appear in the parlor tonight. Had his absence been spent searching her room?

Any more paranoia and you're going to start believing in UFOs and assassination conspiracies too, Truth scolded herself.

"Let's call it settled," Julian said firmly. "I can't possibly let you leave tonight; it would be far too dangerous. Irene, dear, I think the coffee must have brewed, but you'd probably better use a thermal carafe instead of the silver tonight to keep it warm."

"Just like old times," Irene said happily, going off to the kitchen in a swirl of candlelit spangles.

"I'll help," Truth said, jumping up this time before Julian could stop her.

Irene had brought only a single candlestick into the kitchen, and in the leaping shadows of its wavering flame the kitchen was a spooky place. The storm had worsened in the few moments it had taken Truth to cross the room, and the howling wind flung rain at the kitchen windows with force enough to make the panes rattle in their casements. The sound made Truth think better of her determination to leave. Julian was right; this was no night to try to find a place she'd never been before, and it *had* been a long day.

"It's a wild night," Irene said happily. "Thorne used to do his best work on nights like this—when the Wild Hunt rode." She bustled about the kitchen with the ease of long familiarity, taking down a pair of thermal carafes from the cupboard and decanting the coffee from the silent chrome percolator into them. "Oh, I do miss him. And it's no night to be out on the road if you don't have to," she added, changing the subject to practical matters with what Truth was learning was Irene's customary quickness.

"Irene," Truth said. "That girl—Light—where did she come from?"

"Oh, Julian found her. When he got Shadow's Gate back last year—it's almost a year this month that he sent for me—he did one of the minor Workings, and here she was."

Drat Irene's fuzzy occultism, providing a magickal explanation for everything, Truth thought with annoyance.

"Yes," she said patiently. "But where did she *come* from?"

"I think she must have been in hospital somewhere," Irene said vaguely, stacking cups and saucers on another tray. "She hasn't any family, poor dear, and sometimes those with the greatest Gifts are the least able to deal with Malkut—the Sphere of Manifestation."

Or with the real world, either, Truth added mentally. It was odd, though—if Light really didn't have any family, how had Julian gotten her out of the institution?

Assuming she'd really been in one, Truth added conscientiously.

"But now that you're staying, we'll have plenty of time to chat," Irene added in her brisk English fashion. "Do take these out to the dining room for me, there's a dear," she said, handing Truth a tray full of coffee cups.

"It's all black, as far as the river—phone's out too," Gareth announced with satisfaction as Truth reached the dining room. "I took a look outside," he added—unnecessarily, as his hair and shirt were plastered to his skin as if he'd been standing under a showerhead. "It's really wild. A good night for—things," he finished stifledly, with a glance at Truth.

Truth carefully set down her tray, and Michael rose from his seat to help hand its contents around. He seemed to be studying her as if seeking the answer to a question. Truth smiled automatically. Irene followed Truth out of the kitchen, sans candlestick, to set the carafes on the table.

"There's a bit more in the kitchen," she said, "getting cold."

"We'll be wanting it," Hereward said. "Even if it's cold. Long night tonight, eh, Julian?"

Julian smiled anticipatorily. "You're welcome to join us,

Truth," he said. "As an observer, or . . . what you will."

Truth recoiled inwardly, finally realizing what the hints and the sideways looks were about. Julian meant to do magick tonight—from her reading of *Venus Afflicted* she'd gathered the hazy impression that Blackburn preferred his rites to be enacted during storms.

As a scientist and psychic researcher, Truth felt she should be able to regard any peculiar manifestation with perfect calm, and she certainly didn't believe in magick, but the thought of being anywhere near a Blackburn-style magickal rite filled her with suffocating dread.

He killed my mother. Here, in this house, on a night like this. He killed her—

"Truth?"

Julian touched her arm and she startled and gasped, slopping coffee onto her hands and the tablecloth and then flinching at the touch of the hot liquid. She stared at him wide-eyed, heart racing.

"Are you all right?" he demanded.

She set her cup back in its saucer and swabbed at her hands. Fortunately, she didn't seem to be badly burned; the tablecloth had taken the worst of it. "I'm sorry, Julian. I hope the stains will come out; I don't know where my mind was. . . ."

"It's all right," he soothed. "This house can have that sort of effect on people, especially during a storm."

"Thanks," Truth said, not quite knowing what she meant.

No one else seemed to be paying attention to the small accident. She sipped at the coffee left in her cup. She had loaded it with cream and sugar in hopes that between the caffeine and the sugar she could stay awake. The day's events, on top of the long drive, had caught up with her, and the candlelit dimness served only to underscore how tired she felt.

"There are a number of observances—the Smoothing of the Path—that precede the Opening of the Way," Julian amplified, "and night is a good time for them. It's a time when the psychic interference, both of sunlight and of waking minds, is minimized."

Truth found herself nodding in reluctant agreement. Most of her "professional" psychics—those who believed in and acknowledged their psychic powers—felt that their Sixth Sense was strongest during the night hours.

But to participate in one of Blackburn's rituals . . . ?

Julian was watching her, obviously awaiting her response.

No! some inward part of her mind screamed.

"Uh, I really don't think—I'm really tired; perhaps some other time," Truth floundered.

"I look forward to it," Julian said, smiling with intimate meaningfulness.

"I'll just go make sure everything's ready for Truth in her room, and then pop off down to the Temple, shall I?" Irene said. "I'll say good night now, dear."

Irene got up from her place and came around to where Truth sat, leaning over to kiss her upon the cheek. Truth reached up and patted the beringed hand resting on her shoulder, biting back a sudden upwelling of tears. She was tired, that was all. That explained everything. Everything.

"Good night, Aunt Irene," she said aloud.

Irene Avalon walked from the room bearing a candlestick before her like a flaming sword.

"Are you feeling strong enough to work tonight, dear?" Julian asked Light.

"Oh, yes!" Light responded.

Truth glanced at her. There was no doubt of Light's sincerity; her eyes sparkled in the candle flame and her delighted smile was entirely genuine.

"But won't you come too, Michael?" Light asked plaintively, turning to him. "You never do."

"And I never will," Michael Archangel told her kindly. "Each tailor to his own last." He got to his feet.

"And each cat to his own rat," Julian said. "We'll leave Michael to find the truth in his own fashion, and hope we can encourage our Truth to join us," he finished punningly.

Michael acknowledged the remark with a bow and a slight smile and left the room. He didn't bother to take a candle.

Oh, well, I suppose he's been here long enough to know the house. Truth drained her coffee cup and stood. She could sense an undercurrent of anticipation among the remaining people at the table, an eagerness to be on about their business, or, rather, Thorne Blackburn's business.

"I'll say good night," she said. "It's been a pleasure to meet all of you." *But not much of one, all things considered.*

"I'll light your way," Ellis said, walking to the sideboard for another candlestick and lighting it from one of the ones burning upon the table. It seemed that the display Truth had thought only for show was entirely practical after all.

Not having a strong enough aversion to Ellis's company to make a scene, Truth followed him out. As she left the room, she could already see the other five drawing together in secret council.

Just like in some kids' club with passwords and secret decoder rings, Truth scoffed to herself through a faint tinge of jealousy. It was never pleasurable to be excluded from something, even if it was something you didn't really want to belong to.

Truth kept a tight rein on her imagination as she went up the wide stairs with Ellis. The candle flame seemed to conjure dancing animal shapes out of every corner, and despite the fact that she *knew* they were illusions, she flinched each time one seemed to spring.

Ellis, too, was wary, walking as if these imaginary dangers were real, and Truth's unease fed on his. She was very glad when they reached the door of the room Irene had given her earlier to rest in. The door swung inward at her touch, and Truth could see that Irene had indeed been here, turning down the bed and leaving a candle in a glass chimney burning on the bedside table.

Ellis stepped back for her to enter. The candlelight cast the curves and hollows of his face into sharp relief, making it a Mephistophelean mask. As he turned to go, Ellis hesitated.

"This is an old house, and so old advice seems best. Believe only half of what you see, and nothing of what you hear."

Before Truth could frame a suitable rejoinder to this, he turned away and left her standing there.

As soon as the door closed Truth lifted the mattress. *Venus Afflicted* was there, just as she'd left it. She felt obscurely relieved, as though there were danger all around her which she was avoiding merely by dumb luck. After a moment's hesitation, she lowered the mattress again, leaving the book where it was.

A gust of rain struck the window with a faint drumroll, followed by the flash-and-flash-again of two lightning strikes nearly on top of each other.

Truth winced, hoping the storm wouldn't keep her awake all night. Though the Hudson River Valley was famed as a mother of storms, there were usually more of them in the summer than in the fall. There'd be precious little fall color this year if the storm blew all the leaves off the trees now.

By the light of her single candle, Truth made ready for bed, hanging the blue dress up neatly in the empty closet. She tried to review the day's events and put them in some sort of mental order, but every time she tried they went spinning out of her grasp. Should she stay at Shadow's Gate as Julian seemed to expect? It would make her research easier—and though she wished now she'd never considered writing a book about Thorne Blackburn, she'd told so many people of her plans that she'd look very foolish backing out on them now.

She hated to look foolish, no matter how many times she told herself that other people's opinions didn't matter. And she certainly wasn't going to give up her project on the basis of nothing more than some sort of anxiety attack!

Such ringing declarations were all very well, but how

closely should she ally herself with this new Circle of Truth? To do so might be to destroy her credibility as a serious researcher; on the other hand, information on them would be a valuable sidelight to Blackburn's bio, but then again—

A jaw-stretching yawn reminded Truth that she was in no shape to consider these matters now. Everything would seem clearer after a good night's sleep, anyway.

Truth slid into her borrowed bed and blew out the candle.

Some unknown time later Truth wrenched herself to wakefulness from a vivid dream of water. Welling up from the earth, falling from the sky ... Random scraps of dreamed conversation skirled through her mind: *"Come thou elemental prince, Undine, creature of water: Thou who was before the world was made—"*

But the dream was not what had wakened her. Truth stared into the darkness, every sense straining to the utmost to discover what it was that had roused her. The rain had stopped, and a scent that managed to be sharp and cloying at the same time filled the silent room, making her throat dry and ticklish.

Incense, Truth realized. *It must be coming up through the vent from somewhere else in the house.* Hadn't Irene mentioned there being a temple on the premises?

That she could smell the incense in her room meant that there had to be a vent connecting the two—somewhere. Maybe she could close the one in here before the incense smell permeated every article of clothing she'd brought.

If there were matches with the candle her touch-search of the area around it failed to find them, but by that time her eyes had adjusted enough to discern a faint glow coming from the wall near the floor—the vent opening she sought.

Now to close it. Truth climbed out of bed and went over toward it. Just as she had thought, the scent of incense was strongest here, making her eyes water with its intensity. She crouched down on her heels, running her hands over the metalwork to see if she could close it.

"Get *out*!" The voice was loud: masculine, angry—and inches from her face.

Truth flung herself backward in reflex, stifling the scream that threatened to burst from between her tightly clenched teeth. She scrabbled away from the wall on heels and elbows, conscious only of a desire to put as much distance between herself and the voice as she could.

She cracked her head painfully against the bed frame, and the sudden pain shocked her into rationality, although it did little to stop the racing of her heart.

There was no one behind the grate.

The voice had not been talking to her.

It was only a freak of the house's acoustics, carrying a voice from elsewhere into her ears.

There was no one there—*no one*!

She believed that, Truth told herself. But after she scrambled back into bed, clutching the covers up to her chin, she lay awake, stiff and trembling in the darkness, until the sky turned gray with dawn.

CHAPTER SIX

THE MIRROR OF TRUTH

Most true it is that I have look'd on truth
Askance and strangely; but, by all above,
These blenches gave my heart another youth,
And worse essays prov'd thee my best of
love.

—WILLIAM SHAKESPEARE

THE NEXT TIME TRUTH AWOKE THE SUN WAS HIGH IN THE sky. She stretched creakily, wondering why she was so stiff. Suddenly memory of the events of the previous night clicked into place; she glanced around and located the vent she had crouched beside. It looked harmless in the morning light, its white-painted grille nothing more than the covering for a duct of the kind that abounded in these old houses. Harmless.

Had it only been her imagination? A dream perhaps, brought on by the rich food and strange surroundings? Truth got out of bed and crossed to the window, looking out. The day was crystalline, blue and untroubled, and the only evidence of last night's storm was the new patterns of wet autumn leaves blown in drifts across the lawn.

She glanced at the watch on her wrist and groaned. Ten-thirty! She'd hoped to catch Julian this morning at breakfast and settle matters between them. Even though she hadn't quite made up her mind to accept his offer to stay at

Shadow's Gate, at least she could have worked out some kind of schedule for her use of the collection.

On the other hand, one of the others might be able to tell her where he was, and whether he was busy. She dressed hurriedly in an olive cotton sweater and khaki skirt, and gazed in dismay around the room's disorder. It seemed that every item in suitcase and train case both had been unpacked and left strewn around the room. How had she managed to make such a mess in just one night?

Well, she could just take care of it later. After she saw Julian.

She stepped out into the hall and headed downstairs. On her tour of the house yesterday afternoon she had seen no other arrangements, so she assumed that breakfast would also be served in the dining room. At least that would be the place to start looking. She wondered why Irene or Ellis hadn't mentioned a time for breakfast last night; she could have set her alarm, something she ought to have done anyway.

Several minutes later Truth was staring at an unfamiliar hallway in puzzlement. The wallpaper was dark cream with a pattern of flowers in blue, completely unlike the blue-and-white stripe in the hall outside her own room. She didn't recall seeing it on yesterday's tour, either. She ran her fingers lightly over the wall; the covering beneath her fingers shifted and crackled, as if it were old and dry; neglected as nothing else she had seen in Shadow's Gate had been.

How had she gotten here? The path from her room to the stairs was very straightforward: down to the end of the hall, turn right, and the stairs were at the end. The picture of the dark oak newel posts carved with acanthus leaves was sharp in her mind.

The stairs had to be around here somewhere.

She backtracked, feeling certain she should be able to at least find her room again, and instead found herself faced with a narrow, unfamiliar flight of stairs going *up*.

This is ridiculous. I was up and down that front staircase twice last night—and I haven't taken any stairs this morning. Truth frowned. Julian had certainly hinted heavily enough that Shadow's Gate was haunted, and this kind of spatial disorientation was a common "symptom" of the kind of paranormal events associated with so-called haunted houses.

Of course, getting lost might also simply be the result of a combination of too little sleep and too much incense—assuming she hadn't dreamed it. But no, her room had still smelled faintly of incense when she'd awakened this morning. For a moment Truth's mind flicked back to that disembodied voice of the night before. Had it really happened—and if so, was it an indication of a haunting?

Even allowing for the voice being natural instead of supernatural, it presented a pretty puzzle. Who had been speaking and who had been being told to get out? She didn't think the speaker had been either Julian or Michael, and she hadn't heard the other men talk enough to be certain about identifying their voices.

By a determined counting of steps and turns, Truth regained first the familiarly-patterned wallpaper and then her own bedroom door.

She looked back the way she had come. The hall looked "normal" up to the turn—and at the moment, Truth wasn't willing to go and check what might lay beyond. She stood with her back to her door for a moment, consciously calling up a picture in her mind of the route to the stairs before setting off again. This time she found them easily—the only mystery was how she'd managed to miss them in the first place.

As she started down she glanced again at her watch and felt a sick pang of alarm lance through her.

The watch's hands registered eleven o'clock, and the steady motion of the second hand testified to the fact that her battery, at least, was still working.

Only she'd left her room at about eleven, and she'd been

wandering through the halls looking for the stairs for at least twenty minutes.

How could it still be eleven o'clock?

By the time she reached the dining room Truth had pushed this latest disturbing addition to her steadily growing list of questions to the back of her mind. She couldn't come up with answers to these puzzles alone—and it was starting to become disturbingly apparent that no one here in Shadow's Gate would have any answers to give her that didn't involve the intercession of Thorne Blackburn.

Oddly enough there was no scent of incense anywhere on the ground floor, although almost certainly the Temple must be here. She wondered exactly where the Temple was, and thought with a traitorous flutter in the pit of her stomach that undoubtedly it wouldn't be at all difficult to get Julian to show it to her.

The doors to the dining room were open; when she glanced through them she was surprised to see Ellis Gardner, presiding over the deserted table like a reigning monarch. He smiled when he saw her.

"Well, my dear, you're up early. Come, have some coffee—the power came back on sometime in the early hours and Mr. Hoskins has provided us with the necessities. We're less formal than at dinner, you will note."

He gestured to the basket of rolls and the thermal carafe on the table. On the sideboard, the silver candelabra of the night before had been replaced by stacked cups waiting, hotel-style, for use.

"There's no need to be quite so offensive," Truth said, selecting a cup from the sideboard. "I know it's after eleven, but I overslept."

Somehow, the small inward voice commented.

Ellis's eyes opened wide in genuine surprise. "My dear girl—or should it be 'woman' in these decadent days?—I meant it in all sincerity," he protested. "I didn't expect to see anyone else for hours yet. Between Julian's all-night rituals and Michael's all-night prayers, there's usually not a creature stirring here before two in the afternoon."

"Prayers?" Truth asked, sitting down within reach of the coffee. Praying seemed an odd occupation for a magician.

"Oh yes, indeed," Ellis said with relish. "Our fallen Archangel is not what he seems—but then, the Roman collar is a trifle archaic, fashionwise, and does tend to put people off, so its omission should come as no surprise." Ellis pushed the carafe toward her.

"You're saying he's a priest," Truth said. She picked up the pot and poured, and the rich fragrance of freshly ground and freshly brewed Jamaican Blue Mountain coffee surrounded her. She inhaled deeply.

"A lay brother, merely," Ellis said with arch courteousness, "serving in some humble capacity with the Congregation for the Doctrine of the Faith—or, as it was formerly known, the Holy Office of the Question."

"Michael's a member of the Inquisition?" Truth said incredulously, once she'd sorted out what Ellis had said. "You've got to be kidding!" She'd never seen anyone who looked less like a priest—or an Inquisitor.

"If I must, I must," Ellis said dismissively. "But you might ask him sometime who he is, and what he's doing in Julian's library. Oh, and you might ask why he and Julian have concocted that silly cover story between them."

Ellis had the look of one who wanted to be badgered into giving up his secrets, and though Truth wasn't certain that she had the stamina for it this morning, under the tonic influence of coffee she decided to take a stab at it.

"Okay, Ellis, I'll bite: What cover story?"

Ellis paused to sip at his coffee—or, judging from the smell, coffee and brandy. She remembered what Julian had said last night about Ellis's drinking. Apparently it was both heavy and chronic.

"That Michael and Julian are old friends. They aren't, you know. I've known Julian longer than anyone here, and I can swear to that," Ellis said.

" 'And why are you telling all this to me, a traveling

musician'?" Truth asked, quoting W. S. Gilbert to good purpose.

" 'I spend my time walking up and down in the world, seeing what mischief I may perform,' " Ellis responded, capping her quotation with one of his own. "And as you're Thorne's daughter, I felt you ought not to operate under so much of a handicap."

While she was no more resigned to that relationship, Truth was certainly becoming more desensitized to it through these constant reminders of it by everyone she met.

"Did you know Thorne Blackburn?" she asked. She wondered what imp of perversity possessed her to act so against her own deepest desires. She certainly didn't want to hear about Blackburn over morning coffee.

And she was pretty sure the answer would be no, anyway—Ellis looked to be in his forties, not old enough to know a man who had died twenty-six years before.

"I met him once," Ellis answered, surprisingly. "Nineteen sixty-seven; I was seventeen. The Glass Key opened for him on the East Coast leg of the Universal Mystery Tour."

The Universal Mystery Tour had been Thorne Blackburn's melding of music and magic; six weeks of barely-controlled chaos; Blackburn's last big public display before vanishing into the wilds of Upstate New York.

"So you're an ex-rock'n'roll star?" Truth asked, trying for a light touch. It was hard to believe, looking at Ellis's tweedy professorial bearing.

"Every man and every woman is a star," Ellis said, "As Nietzsche didn't precisely say. I was their drummer; in fact, I think there are some pictures of Glass Key in the collection—Thorne used to photograph everything, and Julian found several albums full of old photographs here when we moved in."

Ellis's face was wistful, looking back to a time that had held more of joy and meaning than the present did.

"Ellis, why are you here?" Truth asked intently.

He blinked, focusing on her once more. "Where else should I be? The heart has its reasons." He gestured, waving the question away. "But you'll be wanting to go about your father's business. A word of advice first, if I may."

Truth, struck spellbound by the change in his manner, nodded assent.

"First, remember that the old saying 'The enemy of my enemy is my friend' is not so very often true. Beware our friend Michael: Ultimate goodness has so little in common with humanity that it might as well be its opposite."

"And second?" asked Truth, with what she felt was admirable composure.

"When dealing with that which you do not understand, to thine own self be true. Honesty is the best policy, so remember that you are human, dear Truth—or nearly so."

Ellis moved with the expert grace of the veteran actor, and so he had crossed the room before Truth realized he was moving. The closing of the dining room door behind him followed so neatly on the end of his exit speech that it took Truth a moment to realize what he'd said.

"Remember you're human, or nearly so?" What the hell is that supposed to mean?

It was, she supposed peevishly, another piece of the great Blackburn riddle. Everyone here must have some sort of connection to Blackburn, even though Julian, Gareth, Donner, Caradoc, and Hereward—and, to be fair, Fiona—could only have been children when Blackburn had been alive.

And, dammit, she hadn't had a chance to ask him about Julian.

She brooded through a roll and a second cup of hot coffee, filing Ellis's cryptic and unbelievable revelations and warnings about Michael in the same mental folder as all the peculiar things that had happened to her since she got here.

If they'd really happened. If she weren't just having some kind of causeless breakdown.

She lingered as long as she could bear to but no one came to join her. The only sounds anywhere were the faint clinks and thumpings of food preparation coming from the kitchen, and she was forced to the conclusion that Ellis was at least being accurate about the household's nocturnal habits. Julian was probably still in his bed. The entry hall and the stairs above held nothing but silence when Truth made her cautious way from the dining room to the room housing the Blackburn collection.

The wide, spacious room looked inviting with the late-morning sun streaming in through the high, uncurtained windows. Truth set down her coffee cup carefully, out of the way of anything made of paper, and resumed exploring the material.

Odd. Both Julian and Ellis said that Michael was doing research here at Shadow's Gate, but this isn't an exhaustive collection on anything but Thorne Blackburn, and Michael doesn't seem to be researching him—and if Ellis were telling the truth about Michael being a, a "lay brother," Michael would have access to the Vatican Library, wouldn't he? And the Vatican has the largest collection of books on sorcery in the world.

She filed one more thing away to brood about later; at the moment her business was backtrailing Thorne Blackburn. Ellis had said there were pictures here, and Truth hoped they would tell her more than the confusing papers she'd stumbled across yesterday. They said one picture was worth a thousand words, after all.

Her heart beat fast with the sheer reaction of at last confronting the enigmatic spirit that had overshadowed her young adulthood. She was repelled by everything Thorne Blackburn seemed to stand for, but, approaching him with a scholar's discipline, she found she could consider even Thorne Blackburn with a certain detachment.

The collection that Julian had amassed was even more complete than she had thought the day before. As she browsed through the shelves and drawers, making mental notes on what areas to tackle in-depth first, she found numerous testaments to Julian's encyclopedic thoroughness.

A number of record albums—their reason for inclusion

uncertain, except for the one by Glass Key that had a photograph on it of a very young Ellis Gardner behind a psychedelically painted drum set.

Several videocassettes carefully labeled as copies of Blackburn's media appearances, including his infamous Johnny Carson guest shot and the segment of *The Ed Sullivan Show* that only the live studio audience had gotten to see. There was a rumor that Blackburn had been on *The Dating Game*, as well.

A VCR stood ready in case she wanted to run any of these, and despite her self-control and best intentions, Truth felt the hair on her arms and neck stand up straight at the prospect of confronting a moving, talking image of Thorne Blackburn.

Grow up! Truth scolded herself. A picture couldn't hurt her, and she'd have to delve more deeply than this into Blackburn's life if she meant to debunk him thoroughly. She'd run the tapes later, just to get them out of the way. Right now she had another goal in mind.

After a little more searching she found them: five thick, old-fashioned photo albums, slightly battered and carrying a psychic aura of dust for all that they were newly clean.

They were stored archivally, lying on their sides on a wide bottom shelf, and Truth picked them up one by one and toted them over to the table. Set side by side, the five volumes nearly covered the surface of the long table. She pulled the nearest one closer to her and lifted the cover.

The album's pages gave off the sweet, musty smell of a long-shelved book as she opened it. These must be the original albums that Julian had found in the attic; these pictures ought to be removed, cataloged, copied, and conservation-mounted to protect them further.

Carefully she lifted the cover page. The pages were a rough, creamy oak-tag paper, and the pictures—some black-and-white, some color—were held down with small paper corners, or in some cases, yellowed and disintegrating Scotch tape. Some of the pictures had writing of their same ancient vintage beneath them in a slapdash, unfamiliar hand. Blackburn's?

Kate in the Hashbury, one entry said cryptically, beneath a faded color picture of a laughing, dark-haired girl in an ankle-length, high-waisted dress and braided headband. Truth could see a slice of a white Victorian house in the background, an American flag hanging in an upper window. The girl wore tiny, square, wire-rimmed glasses with pink lenses, and a peace symbol flashed among the love beads around her neck. Across a quarter of a century she smiled into the lens of an unknown photographer, her hand raised in a "V" sign. A peace sign, Truth remembered, dredging up the fact from some well of antique trivia. *Kate in the Hasbury. Haight-Ashbury. San Francisco.*

Kate. *Katherine.*

Mommy. Truth's lips moved soundlessly over the word. With a careful fingertip she touched the image. This was Katherine Jourdemayne, and if Truth could somehow step into the picture she would stand face to face with a girl younger than she was, a girl who believed that love and magick could change the world.

She glanced at the other pictures on the page. All of them seemed to be taken in San Francisco sometime in the early middle sixties. One of them looked as if it might be Irene as she'd been then, the sagging lines of age erased, the white hair darkened to a flaming red.

Another photo that caught her eye was a picture of a man and woman, surprisingly respectable considering the company their photo was in. If Blackburn had taken these he must have known them, but who were they? She studied the picture more closely, finding something elusively familiar in the image. The man was somewhere in early middle age, Truth guessed, dressed in a faintly archaic sport coat and slacks. He looked vaguely Scots, with a high square forehead and a firm chin. Even in the faded picture his eyes were a piercing pale blue, and his bulldog stubbornness seemed an essential part of what he was.

The woman beside him was nearly as tall as he—

uncommonly tall for a woman—with gray eyes and wavy pale hair. She reminded Truth oddly of Light, though the two women looked nothing alike, and the woman in the picture had the sort of face that is good rather than pretty. She wore a neat dress and hat, the counterpoint to the tall man's respectable clothing. After a moment Truth could make out a caption, written in faint pencil: *Colin and Claire—the loyal opposition—Golden Gate Park, 1966.*

Colin MacLaren and Claire Moffat. Truth's fingers itched to remove the photo and take it away with her, while her scholar's instincts kept her from doing so. Here was proof that Professor MacLaren had known Thorne Blackburn.

But it's not exactly a capital crime, is it? Truth thought through her rising excitement. *I wonder if Julian will let me get any of these pictures copied? A book's better with pictures. And I wonder if I could get an interview with Professor MacLaren. I know he retired from the Institute several years ago. I wonder where he is now? Dylan would know.*

Thinking about Dylan made her feel oddly guilty, as if she'd done Dylan Palmer some treacherous harm. Truth examined her conscience scrupulously and couldn't think of any; it was true they hadn't parted on the best of terms, but that was no reason for this sudden pang of conscience.

Displacement. That's what the headshrinkers call it. You're worried about something, so you pretend you're worried about something else. Simple.

Truth gnawed her lip, wondering if she should give Dylan a call anyway.

And tell him what?

Sighing, Truth went back to the photos. Most of the pictures in this first book were captioned, but some were not. There was a picture of a deaccessioned schoolbus with the words MYSTERY SCHOOLBUS painted on the side and a group of people standing in front of it, Irene and Katherine among them. Katherine wore bell-bottomed jeans and a chambray shirt tied snugly beneath her breasts, and was smiling radiantly at the photographer. Thorne Blackburn. Always the photographer, never the image, as if he'd keep his secrets even from film.

She flipped through more quickly now, hunting fruitlessly for a picture of Blackburn. Near the end she was stopped momentarily by a studio portrait of a man in a cowboy outfit straight from a Wild West show—except for the alchemical symbols embroidered on his shirt and the stars and moons painted on his black Stetson.

The note under the picture said merely *Tex Arcana*, leaving Truth to wonder who—or what—he was. Or had been. But the past kept its secrets. She slid the first album away and drew another one toward her.

Blackburn at last.

On the first page there was a picture of Katherine heavily pregnant, standing next to Thorne Blackburn in an anonymous living room somewhere. He looked almost bashful, ducking his head and turning away as if he didn't want to be photographed. And young—immortal now, as only those who had eaten the apples of Avalon could be. Forever young.

Truth waited for the flare of self-righteous indignation that the sight of Blackburn always brought her, but now she felt only weary pain. The people in those photos, they'd all been so innocent then. No one had ever done anything like what they were doing before; how could they know how it would end—in ruins, in flames, in lies and broken promises? Had Blackburn even known—really?

She turned the page.

Truth had to smile at the pictures of Blackburn's acolytes in their lurid costumes; they looked like a cross between an Odd Fellows convention and a showing of *The Rocky Horror Picture Show*. If they were supposed to be either inspiring or intimidating, they failed miserably. She wondered what *they* had thought their robes made them look like.

Truth reached the end of the album, and hunted through the other three until she found one with pictures from the time in Mexico. The album had several blank pages, several places where photos had been removed, leaving darker rectangles behind. She wondered why—and when.

Many of the pictures were faded with time or overexposed into illegibility, many were ciphers—uncaptioned, of people she didn't know. But others were more forthcoming, telling their stories across the years.

The Mystery Schoolbus, battered now, serving as backdrop to a crude camp.

Photos of rural Mexico, such as any tourist might take.

Photos of Katherine—and of Aunt Caroline, her dark hair cut sensibly short, standing next to her twin. Each of the women held one hand of a diapered child about a year old, supporting its first unsteady steps.

Supporting *her*.

Truth tried to summon up some interior resonance to the images she saw; some proof within herself that the infant in the pictures was her, and that these experiences were a part of her life. But no emotion would come; there could be no faith, only intellectual belief. She had the maddening sense of a riddle whose solution would explain her life and give it meaning, but the solution was just out of reach.

Truth shook her head. There were no answers in the past. Aunt Caroline had told her that often enough.

But Aunt Caroline had been telling her that for reasons of her own, Truth realized suddenly.

There comes an unsettling time in most children's lives when they must acknowledge that those who have raised them are as human, fallible, and mortal as they themselves. For the first time Truth thought—*really* thought—about Aunt Caroline as a woman Truth's own age or even younger, and wondered what that woman must have been like.

She had been a friend to Thorne Blackburn—the pictures were the final proof—if not a member of his Circle. She had been *here* at Shadow's Gate the night her sister died and Blackburn vanished.

Vanished. Every newspaper report had said so; the police

had searched for him for weeks after Katherine's death. But Blackburn had vanished.

And gone where?

Truth shook her head, as if imagination were an unruly horse that had balked at the jump. She didn't know where he'd gone. And at the same time, what Aunt Caroline had said the last time Truth saw her came back to haunt her:

"The others. You must find the others."

She turned the pages slowly, frowning meditatively.

What others?

She'd assumed at the time that Aunt Caroline had meant the other members of the old Circle of Truth—or at least their families. The newspaper stories had called Shadow's Gate a "hippie commune," and mentioned children, though no names had been mentioned. And any "children" who had been here in 1969 would be her age or older today—hardly in need of finding.

But even if that had been what Aunt Caroline had meant, Julian seemed to be taking care of that with his ingathering.

"It's important for you to know you're not the only one. I failed the others—"

Aunt Caroline was a sick woman: dying, heavily medicated. . . .

Truth stopped at a photo that had been blown up to cover the entire page. Unlike the others it seemed to be glued down, the edges curling away from the adhesive. The backdrop was familiar—the photo was taken on the front lawn of Shadow's Gate—and it must have been taken professionally, because Blackburn was in it.

Twenty people, looking oddly like a graduating class of wizards in their long robes. Blackburn's Circle of Truth. She picked out Blackburn and Irene; herself, holding Irene's hand with one childish fist and clasping a stuffed monkey to her chest with the other; Katherine in a white robe; and Caroline beside her in street clothes, holding a baby.

Not her baby. Caroline had never had children. And not her sister's, either—Truth was elsewhere in the picture.

Not just other children—*Blackburn's* other children. That was what Aunt Caroline had meant—that Truth Jourdemayne wasn't the only child of Thorne Blackburn.

There were others.

The right side of the picture was torn away, the edge still sharp and white. *As if it were torn recently. Why?*

All Truth's anxious study of the image could not produce any more children than her two-year-old self and the months-old infant, but Aunt Caroline had said "children." Not just the children of Blackburn's followers mentioned so peripherally in the newspapers, but Truth's half-brothers and-sisters.

"The others. You must find the others."

It was an effort not to imagine lost children, but this picture had been taken twenty-six years ago; even the baby pictured here would be a young woman now.

Or man. Why do I think it's a little girl? It could be either.

Caroline Jourdemayne would know.

Truth stood up, closing the album. There had to be a phone in Julian's office. She'd call her aunt right now and ask the questions—and hear the answers—that she dreaded.

She had stepped away from the table when the door opened.

"Well. I thought I'd find you here," Fiona Cabot said triumphantly.

Even in the unforgiving noontide light Fiona Cabot did not look old, but the sunlight disclosed the marks of dissipation and overindulgence beneath the heavy, carefully-applied makeup. Her hair, which owed more to henna than to nature, spilled over her bare shoulders; Fiona's off-the-shoulder leotard and designer jeans left precious little to the imagination.

"Good morning," Truth responded, uncomfortably conscious of what a drab conventional figure she presented next to Fiona's outlaw flamboyance.

"Dug up any good dirt lately?" Fiona purred, edging closer to the table on which the albums lay. Irrationally,

Truth felt the urge to protect the photographs from her, although the plain truth of the matter was that Fiona had as much right as Truth and maybe more to dispose of them.

Fiona flipped open the nearest book. "You were such a beautiful baby," she cooed, the implication being that Truth had not lived up to her early promise.

"Was there something you wanted?" Truth asked with frigidly correct politeness. Each word was bitten off with the frozen crack of a bough breaking in winter.

Fiona slammed the album shut with a carelessness that made Truth wince inwardly.

"I just wanted to let you know: You may come waltzing in here flaunting your illustrious parentage and thinking that Julian and the whole Circle will fall into your hands, but they won't." Fiona had moved closer to Truth with every word, until now she was standing far too close. Truth recoiled, having a subliminal flash of something thin and rat-like with long needle teeth.

"Yes, that's right," Fiona crooned. "You've come to it too late—*my* powers are honed, and what you need to know you'll never have time to learn. Julian deserves his true mate—and that's something you'll never be!" Fiona's blazing green eyes burned into Truth's, until Truth was afraid that Fiona meant to attack her physically.

"Of course, I don't think she'll ever be a toaster oven either, but I don't think it bothers her much," a male voice drawled.

Truth jerked in involuntary surprise, and Fiona jumped back, turning toward the sound.

Hereward Farrar stood leaning in the doorway, smiling dangerously at Fiona.

"It's all right," he told her with spurious compassion. "Redheads are supposed to be jealous. Too bad you don't come by the color naturally," Hereward said.

Fiona glared murderously at him—and then back at Truth, who was regarding her inadvertent rescuer with relief. Truth could tell when the other woman decided to cut her losses; Fiona stalked from the room, slamming open the other half of the double door and sailing past Hereward as if he wasn't there.

"She's got all the occult power of a coffee filter," Hereward told Truth confidingly, "so don't worry. It's hard to get women for the Work, though, so in some sense you have to take what you can. get," he added. "Most of the ones who are interested are attitude cases of one kind or another, unfortunately."

"As the men, I suppose, are not," Truth commented caustically, still irritated about the morning's earlier conversation with Ellis. "Thanks for the timely intervention, Hereward; Fiona seems to have gotten some wrong ideas about things."

"She thinks she's got some kind of claim on Julian. She's his Hierolator, that's all. Monogamy and the enslavement of women by marriage are both things that have no place in the Blackburn Work," Hereward added.

Every time I start to think these people are going to talk sense, they start babbling nonsense.

"Well, thanks anyway," Truth said awkwardly. What with Ellis, the revelation of the pictures, and the encounter with Fiona, all Truth wanted was to get away and think.

"Sure," Hereward said. There was another pause, as if Hereward were waiting for her to say something more. She didn't, and he shrugged, turned away, and left.

Truth resisted the temptation to see if the library doors would lock. She compromised by leaning against them for a moment, and found her heart racing as if she'd been running.

Oh, get a grip. They can't kill you. They can't even hurt you, Truth scolded herself. But suddenly she felt an almost desperate need to get away, a need that forced her out of the library, after first making her peer around the edge of the half-opened door to see that no other members of Julian's Circle lay in wait.

*   *   *

She reached her room without difficulty, only remembering after she'd gained its refuge that Shadow's Gate was apt to play nasty tricks on those who tried to navigate its corridors. She closed the door and turned around.

Someone had been here. The anxiety that Truth had felt downstairs sharpened. She ran over to the bed and yanked up the mattress.

Venus Afflicted was still there.

Truth stared at it, realizing that the cliché "giddy with relief" was nothing more than a literal description. She took a deep breath, and shoved the grimoire a little farther in before lowering the mattress. The lump of book was almost unnoticeable as Truth smoothed the candlewick coverlet back into place. The reverse of "The Purloined Letter" method; as long as no one thought to look for it, it was safe here.

She looked around. The room was not as she had left it. Now her suitcase was set up on a stand, and the clothing she'd left lying around was set neatly back inside it. Irene. It must be. She could not imagine Fiona doing something so considerate, nor—for other reasons—did she think this was the work of any of the men she'd met last night.

There was a folded sheet of paper lying on the smooth coverlet of the newly-made bed. Truth picked it up; it was a sheet of good stationery, covered with firm italic writing in black ink.

My dear Truth (she read) *I hope that you have had the chance to meditate upon the collection and the company and to decide that the one is valuable and the other harmless. I found you gone when I came by this morning and thought I'd rather leave you a note than take the chance of interrupting your studies. If you need me, I'll probably be in my office, and I look forward to talking to you soon. Julian.*

Truth bit her lip in indecision. She needed to talk to Julian about using the collection; she needed to decide whether to stay here or in town. But the thought of staying here long enough to do either of those things made her hands tremble with the need to get *out*.

She barely suppressed a scream when she heard the sound of a knock at her door.

"Truth?" a low voice called. Michael.

Truth recoiled, a vivid tactile memory of last night racing over her skin. She was drawn to Michael, but as the moth is drawn to the candle flame—and after Ellis's disclosure this morning she wasn't sure how she could face him without blurting out a bunch of crazy accusations. For that matter, she couldn't bear to face anyone right now.

The tapping came again as she stood frozen in the middle of the room, praying he wouldn't try the unlocked door. But Michael Archangel was a gentleman, and a moment later she heard his footsteps walking away.

When she was sure he wouldn't hear, she bounded over to the door and quickly locked it. Feeling safer now— though how could Michael threaten her?—Truth drew a deep breath.

She needed to get out—out of this house where all these forceful personalities pressed in on her so stiflingly. What had seemed so reasonable in the sunlit library seemed more impossible by the moment, and all Truth could think of was flight.

Truth drew a deep breath. She was honest enough to admit that she was teetering on the edge of panic at this very moment. But that honesty raised more questions than it answered, because she could not think of any explicit reason for her fear.

The voice last night? A dream or maybe an echo from somewhere else in the house. Either way, not an immediate threat.

The misdirection on her way to breakfast? More interesting than anything else, actually; she knew enough from listening to Dylan to know that "hauntings" fed on the emotions of their victims, and if one could remain detached, a haunting could not harm.

Fiona? The conversation had been unpleasant, surely, but nothing more than that.

Michael? Was it the thought of seeing Michael again that was driving her to panic?

No. Yes. She didn't know. All she knew was that she had to get out of here—get out of this house—before something dreadful happened.

She had to go down to Shadowkill; she had to call her aunt; she had to keep *Venus Afflicted* safe. Clutching her purse to her as if it were a baby, Truth eased open the door of her room and looked anxiously out.

CHAPTER SEVEN

THE SONG OF TRUTH

I held it truth, with him who sings
To one clear harp in divers tones,
That men may rise on stepping-stones
Of their dead selves to higher things.
—ALFRED, LORD TENNYSON

SUCH HIGH GOTHIC TERRORS SEEMED TO BELONG TO AN-other universe the moment Truth started her car down the drive. The noon sunlight sparkled on the rainwashed woods, and Shadow's Gate seemed as harmless and som-nolent as some lath-and-plaster Sleeping Beauty's Castle in a California amusement park.

She'd seen no one on her way out of the house. No one stopped her at the gatehouse, and in fact the scrolled iron gates stood open, so she did not even have to stop and open them herself. Once she'd crossed Old Patent Grant Road and was heading down County 13 toward Shadowkill, the last of her anxiety vanished like a bad dream.

She still wasn't certain why she felt that concealment of the grimoire was so necessary, but it was the only thing she *was* still certain of. Possibly Blackburn hadn't been entirely a criminal fraud—Truth wasn't willing to commit herself on that one—but even if you believed that every ridiculous claim he made was the literal truth, should mere mortals be given the power to storm heaven's gates? Or to think they could?

She spared a moment to try to imagine Gareth wearing the fantastic ritual robes she'd seen in the pictures, but even imagination failed. Gareth seemed far too normal.

But that's the thing. Normal people get caught up in this magickal dream-world. Why?

No answer was forthcoming, and Truth reached the village of Shadowkill. The little Hudson River town was vivid in the crystal-clear autumn air, and Truth, now calm, decided to tackle her chores in order and drove to the Bed-and-Breakfast she'd been supposed to stay at last night.

"Oh . . . hello. Are you from the insurance?" The woman who had come to the door in answer to Truth's knock was wearing a stained sweatshirt and equally grubby sweatpants, carrying a mop in one hand and a sponge in the other. She looked harried.

"Um, no. I'm Truth Jourdemayne. Mrs. Lindholm?"

"Oh, my God," Mary Lindholm said. She hesitated, biting her lip. "Well—come in." She held open the screen door.

Truth stepped into the foyer and instantly saw what was behind Mrs. Lindholm's reluctance.

"What . . . happened?" she said, stunned.

"What didn't?" Mrs. Lindholm said bitterly. "Part of the roof blew off, the water heater exploded, the pipes burst—God alone knows why, at this time of year—and—well, see for yourself." She gestured sweepingly. "It's a good thing you weren't here last night—you might have drowned."

The walls bore a high-tide mark as of a great outrushing of water. The wallpaper was crinkled and bowed, obviously soaked through, and the ceiling was soggy, cracked, and seemed to sag downward.

"So if you want your room . . ." Mrs. Lindholm said helplessly.

"Um, no," Truth said. "In fact, I came to apologize for wimping out on you at the last moment, but some friends have invited me to stay, and—" She listened to herself spouting this plausible half-truth with a sort of detached amazement. She hadn't come here meaning to say anything of the sort—and while, after seeing the water damage here at Mary Lindholm's, she knew she couldn't possibly stay here, there was always the prospect of another B-and-B in the area, or even a chain hotel.

Mrs. Lindholm gave her a weary smile. "Actually, I'm glad you didn't show up last night, all things considered. And if you see an insurance adjuster out there anywhere, send him up, will you?"

"Sure," Truth said, bidding Mrs. Lindholm a grateful farewell.

It was only after she was in her car and driving away that she remembered her dream of the night before: *"Come thou elemental prince, Undine, creature of water—"*

Coincidence, Truth told herself firmly. *It was raining outside—why shouldn't you dream of rain?* The faint nagging feeling that there must be some connection between her dream and the condition of Mary Lindholm's Shadowkill Bed-and-Breakfast was easy to dismiss; science was a great believer in coincidence.

She parked in the public parking located in the center of town and set off on foot. The October sun, unseasonably strong, was a welcome warmth on her shoulders, and the brightly-decked shops on every side gave a welcome respite from the problems plaguing her.

A rumbling in her stomach reminded her that coffee and bread at eleven wasn't much in the way of either breakfast *or* lunch. Truth stopped at a sidewalk deli and bought a salad and coffee. Sitting at one of the outside tables provided for customers, she caught sight of a green-and-white sign that told her what her next stop must be.

*   *   *

The Shadowkill Public Library was housed in a turn-of-the-century building that had the grandiose architectural ornament common to public buildings of that period. Since Shadowkill was a rich township, its library did not suffer the cheeseparing and overcrowding common to area libraries—a new modern wing in bland limestone angled off at the back, and the interior of the older building was beautifully kept.

"Excuse me, is there a public phone here?" Truth asked the librarian at the information desk.

The librarian pointed, and Truth detoured to an alcove where a bank of public phones stood. It took several minutes of juggling purse, wallet, and phone card before she managed to put her call through.

"Hi, this is Janine," an unfamiliar voice said brightly.

"I'm sorry; I must have dialed the wrong number," Truth said.

"Were you trying to reach Caroline Jourdemayne?" the voice asked carefully.

Truth felt a sinking sensation. "Yes."

"She's asleep right now," Janine said. Truth took a deep breath of relief. "If you want to call back after four, she should be awake then. I'm Janine Vaughan, Ms. Jourdemayne's aide."

"I'm Truth Jourdemayne," Truth said. "Is she—"

"Oh, you're her *niece*!" Janine said excitedly. Truth felt privately that nobody could possibly be that pleased about everything, but it was probably a defense mechanism against working with terminal patients all the time.

"How is she?" Truth asked.

"Oh, about the same," Janine said, her tone flattening a little. "She's still pretty alert. Dr. Vandemeyer doesn't think he'll have to move her to the hospital just yet."

"Well, that's good," Truth said. What else was there to say? "I'll call her back later."

"Shall I tell her you called?" Janine asked animatedly.

"No," Truth said. "I don't want her to worry when everything's fine. I'll call her back."

"After four," Janine said.

Truth hung up the phone and walked slowly back to the information desk.

Her first impulse had been to run to Aunt Caroline for information, but now she saw that she should think carefully before acting on impulse. Aunt Caroline was frail, dying, her mind possibly clouded by drugs. Truth would have to frame any questions she posed in a manner that wouldn't cause Aunt Caroline to be unnecessarily upset.

Whatever way that might be, Truth thought with a glint of black humor. What *was* the tactful way to open a discussion about the number and current location of Thorne Blackburn's bastard children?

"Excuse me," Truth said, returning to the pleasant woman at the desk. "Do you have a local history collection?"

A few minutes later Truth sat at a small table in a long room on the second floor of the library. Folders full of dusty newspaper clippings were piled high at her elbow.

"That's everything we have in the clipping files on Thorne Blackburn and Shadow's Gate. Don't mix up the files," local history librarian Laurel Villanova said.

"I won't," Truth promised. "There's just one more thing. Would you have anything on the . . ."—she cudgeled her memory for the name—"on the old Elkanah Scheidow patent grant?"

"Oh, you want the early history material." Laurel's brow cleared. "I think there are a couple of books in the noncirculating collection. Let me go check."

Laurel left. Truth paged through the file on Blackburn's life as reported by *The Shadowkill Times-Reporter*, *The Poughkeepsie Journal*, *The Albany Times*, and other area papers. There wasn't anything much that she hadn't seen before: Blackburn had resided in Shadowkill for about eighteen months, during which time he'd fought constantly with the town council and had minor skirmishes with the

Dutchess County Sheriff's Department. She put the wad of clippings dealing with her mother's death back into the folder unread. There might be more about Blackburn's children in them, but there would be time enough to face them later. After all, she had waited more than a quarter of a century already.

The second file, the one on Shadow's Gate itself, was more interesting. The earliest clippings were dark brown and flaked when she touched them. The paper had been called *The Shadowkill Times Eagle* then, and the earliest clipping in the folder dated back to 1934.

"Here you are," Laurel said, coming back with three books. "This should give you what you need."

"Thanks," Truth said, handing back the file on Blackburn. She settled down with the remaining folder and the books and began to read, taking notes as she did so.

A few hours later Truth looked up from her note-taking, working the cricks out of stiff shoulders and back. She'd found what, subconsciously, she'd hoped and expected to find, and wondered what she ought to do next.

The house called Shadow's Gate that she'd stayed in last night had been built, as she'd thought, out of an excess of High Victorian Gothicism in 1882—the same year, oddly enough, as the gunfight at the O.K. Corral which signified the end of the Wild West. It was the fourth building on the site, the first being Scheidow's own 1648 house and trading post, of which only engravings survived. Those pictures showed a typical seventeenth-century Dutch frontier home, built of mortar and local stone, small, low-roofed, and narrow-windowed.

The second house on the site of Scheidow's *gehucht*, or hamlet, had been built in 1714 and also survived only in pictures—the British had burned it to the ground during the Revolutionary War, sometime in the 1770s.

Of the building which must have occupied the site for

some part of the next hundred years she found no record
at all.

It would have been easy to dismiss the sources that spoke
of the current building as the *fourth* house, not the third,
save that there were so many of them—and if there really
had been no house here for over a century, why did every
source on the 1882 house speak of it as a *re*building of
Shadow's Gate? Surely the name would not have survived
so long, attached to an empty field?

For that matter, *when* in this period had the name of the
early town been Anglicized and transferred to the house?
The Scheidows—variously spelled—had certainly remained
in the area. In fact, the Schydows, Skydoes, Cheidows,
Cheddowes, Shaddows, and Shatterses—names culled from
the Shadowkill genealogy the librarian had brought, still
filled several columns of the local phone book and continued
as an active presence in local affairs.

Most of the information Truth had came from one book:
A History of the Early Days of Scheidow's Kill, written by
Matthew Cheddow, descendant, and privately published in
1923. Matthew had been living in Shadow's Gate at the
time, and in the rambling fashion of amateur historians, had
included a chapter on his house. She went back and looked
at it again. Yes, there it was:

> *Incorporating what he could of the original foun-*
> *dation, the builder began work on this, the fourth*
> *house to grace Ancestor Scheidow's lovely rural*
> *coign, in 1878.*

She scanned a few paragraphs more and found something
else.

> *The underground stream, whose spring had proved*
> *so beneficial to early settlers but whose chthonic wa-*
> *ters had proved so challenging to previous builders,*
> *was carefully reinforced with a sub-basement before*
> *building began once more on Elkanah Scheidow's*

original site. The spring was incorporated into the design of the house.

How? Truth wondered. She turned back to her other source: *Hudson Colonial Days, With a Brief History of the Scheidow and von Rosenroth Patent Grants,* and took another look at the original map of the area. Yes, there was a spring indicated, just about where the modern house stood. Each house had been built near—or over—that spring.

That meant that Shadow's Gate was built over an underground stream.

In some way that parapsychological researchers were only just beginning to understand, most psychic manifestations involved some aspect of magnetism—from dowsing, which seemed to relate to the ability to sense almost infinitesimal changes in the Earth's magnetic field, to psychokinetic—poltergeist—activity, which generated a magnetic field strong enough to stop watches and blank recording tape at the same time it flung chairs and dishes through the air. Dylan even claimed you could magnetize ghosts, although Truth wasn't quite sure how you could test a hypothesis like that.

But she did know that in a significant proportion of all cases of haunted houses, it was found that the houses had been built over underground streams, springs, or covered wells. There was something about water that either unlocked the forces of the Sixth Sense or drove people crazy. Truth wasn't sure which.

But she thought she had the answer to part of the riddle of Thorne Blackburn.

It wasn't that he was a great magician with the occult powers he claimed.

It was that he'd bought a haunted house.

It was not an hypothesis that would commend itself to everyone, Truth supposed, but parapsychology was her field, and she'd far rather spend her time trying to map paranormal activities than to—

Invoke undines, the elemental spirits of water?

Truth pushed the thought away. Maybe Julian had been doing just that—in *Venus Afflicted*, as she had reason to know, the first four of the ten rituals were called "Crowning the Elemental Kings"—but even if he had done that ritual it didn't mean that an actual Elemental had objectively gone and destroyed Mary Lindholm's house.

But it was awfully convenient, wasn't it? Because now you're going to have to ask Julian if you can accept his kind offer after all—and stay at Shadow's Gate.

That was ridiculous.

She didn't have to.

She *wanted* to.

Truth separated her notes from the books and clippings, and went to find the local history librarian.

Laurel Villanova was carefully paging through a back issue of the *Times Eagle* when Truth approached.

"Done already?" she asked.

"For today," Truth said. "I might want this material again later in the week, though."

"I'll keep it out for you, then," the librarian promised. "Is there anything else you'll need?"

"I'll let you know," Truth said. "I don't really know myself, yet."

"Well, if there's anything I can do," Laurel said, rising to let Truth out of the office.

Truth realized that she had only the foggiest idea of the time as she stood on the library steps. Though sunset was hours away yet, the air held the clear, water-glass promise of twilight. She stuffed the day's notes willy-nilly into her shoulder bag and headed for the car at a rapid pace, as eager to get back to Shadow's Gate as she had been to leave it earlier. Julian must think she'd fallen off the face of the earth.

She reclaimed her car without too much trouble—it was silly, really, to drive when the center of town was two miles, at most, from the house. She'd know better next time.

She drove in through the gatehouse—Gareth waved— and on up to the house. Parking the car next to a white Volvo station wagon and a black BMW she suspected of belonging to Julian, she locked her Saturn carefully before skipping up the steps to the house. On an impulse, she tried the door before ringing the bell, and found it unlocked. She stepped inside.

"Truth. A word with you, if I may?"

Michael. With the sound of his voice all the psychic weight of the house descended on her again, and the serenity that her afternoon in Shadowkill had lent Truth vanished in a seething rush of apprehension.

She turned around. Michael Archangel stood in the hall, grave and cool and formal as she had always seen him, but once again she had the quick fearful vision of a panther chained by lightnings.

"Certainly." What else could she say? *"By the way, I hear you're a member of the Inquisition; turned any good thumbscrews lately?"* He'd think she'd lost her mind.

"Why don't we go out to the garden?" Michael said.

He led her out a side door onto a tiny terrace tucked into a corner of the house. It had a bench, table, and chairs on it, and looked like a lovely place to linger when the weather was warmer, but the setting sun cast it in shadow now, and Truth shivered just a bit.

"It will be warmer in the sun," Michael promised, leading her down the steps.

Here, directly behind the house, something remained of the formal gardens that must have surrounded the fourth Shadow's Gate in its heyday. Flagged walkways were edged with rosebushes and flower beds settling now for their yearly sleep. To the right, across a perfect expanse of green now raked clear of the storm's detritus, the severe geometric shape of what Truth knew from her researches to be a labyrinth created of boxwood hedges formed a smooth, dark green wall. One of the paths led in that direction, and Michael followed it.

"You seem somewhat more reconciled to us than you did last night," Michael said.

"Do I?" said Truth. *I suppose familiarity breeds contempt.*

"Julian says that you are a scientist. A parapsychologist." Michael rolled the word around in his mouth as though he'd never heard it before.

"My specialty is statistical parapsychology; you could say I've specialized in learning to see what's there." *And nothing else.*

"Yet those who are the most rigorous in their examination of the merely physical world miss much: the beauty of a poem, the song of a lark—"

"If I can file the poem and record the lark I'll settle for not appreciating them," Truth said curtly. "My field is facts. How long have you known Julian?" she asked, moving to the attack.

"Oh, quite some time," Michael said easily. "He has accomplished a great deal in a very short time—and wishes to do more. He is a man of great power."

"Occult power, you mean?" Truth asked, fencing for a way to turn the question around to Michael.

"Why should I praise him according to the standards of a system in whose existence you refuse to believe?" Michael said, smiling.

"But in which you believe?" Truth asked.

Michael smiled. "If I said yes, you would discount everything else I have to say."

"Which is?" The question bordered on rudeness and Truth was sorry for it, but the last thing she wanted just now was another round of ritual-cloak-and-sacred-dagger.

"Often we find ourselves determined to know things when to know nothing would be the wiser and happier course—not only for ourselves, but for those around us," Michael began. "It is not that learning is, in and of itself, wrong, but—"

"But there are things that Man was not meant to know?" Truth shot back.

"Would you give a baby a loaded gun?" Michael said quietly. Truth was stung to silence by the image he'd presented, and Michael continued. "No. No one would. But a grown man may handle a gun safely, although the potential for abuse and sorrow is still enormous. If I tell you that there are things which exist, which have existed from the creation of the world, things that Man may someday wield, but which his wisdom is not yet great enough to bear—"

"I don't think you—or any other person—has a right to draw the line between things that can be studied and things that can't. There is nothing which cannot be studied."

Michael smiled. "There speaks the voice of Science."

They had reached the edge of the maze. Truth stopped, and looked back toward the house, but if anyone was watching them from its various windows she could not see them.

"I don't think that happiness is more important than knowledge. And I don't believe in magick," Truth said flatly.

"If you do not believe in magick—in the supernatural— how can you believe in evil?" Michael's voice came from behind her.

Shadow's Gate cast long slanting rays of darkness across the lawn. Truth took a deep breath and counted to ten before she spoke. How could a mere two miles' drive in her car make so much difference to how she felt? She'd be seeing ghosts and fairies next.

"I do not wish to disparage your beliefs," she said, turning to face Michael, "but in my book, the only evil in the world comes from what people do to other people and there isn't a damn thing supernatural about it. There is no such thing as magick—there are only natural laws that we don't yet fully understand."

"And if I told you that such a thing—magick—exists outside your laws?"

"Then—I'm sorry—but I would have to tell you to have a nice day. I don't share your beliefs."

"And so you will stay to learn that of which you would have been happier to remain in ignorance. For I tell you this and truly: If magick is evil, there is evil here. And sorrow."

Truth opened her mouth—and closed it, firmly. "I have to go now. I guess I'll see you at dinner, Michael?" she said with determined diplomacy.

"Of course," he said with grave courtesy.

She turned to go back to the house.

"And, Truth?"

She stopped.

"Have a nice day," Michael said without a trace of humor.

Truth reached the house minutes later in a state of simmering fury that her colleagues at the Bidney Institute had long since learned to recognize and walk softly around.

How *dare* he make fun of her? Lead her on, force her to listen to all sorts of stupid mystic psychobabble, spout clichés too tired even for "B" movies, and then, when she tried to be polite, twist her own words and use them to mock her! She would *not* be mocked—how dare he raise his eyes to such as she was. . . .

She lunged up the stairs and twisted savagely at the knob of the terrace door. It opened and she passed into the house, coming within a hair's breadth of slamming the door behind her.

He was going to be sorry. Was he trying to make her leave Shadow's Gate? She'd take out a long lease. Were there things Man was not meant to know? Lead her to them. So you shouldn't give a baby a loaded gun? She'd give it a bazooka. She'd—

"Truth. There you are," Julian said warmly. He crossed the foyer and took both her hands in his. "You're so flushed. Have you been running?"

Her raging arrogance vanished like a popped bubble at the warm touch of Julian's hands, and for a moment she was dizzy with the suddenness of the change. What had she been thinking?

Or was the question, *who* had been thinking?

"Only running around in circles," she said to Julian, with an unforced smile. "I'm sorry to have missed you earlier, but I had to go down into town for something and I just got back."

"Will you be staying, then?" Julian asked. He was still holding her hands, his fingers moving slightly, stroking her wrists.

No! Truth cried mentally. Not when something in this house seemed to turn her into a madwoman each time she crossed its threshold!

"Well, as a matter of fact, I was going to ask you if I could—if the offer was still open," Truth heard herself say. "I know it's—"

"Wonderful," Julian finished firmly. "The others will be delighted—especially Fiona. She was just telling me how much she likes you."

I just bet, Truth thought. But her decision was made. And even if it wasn't the one she'd meant to make, she was curiously reluctant to change her mind now. "So—great. I'll spend the next week—probably the next month—going over what you have on Blackburn and getting my notes in order. Damn—I should have brought my notebook computer with me."

"I'm afraid it wouldn't work very well here," Julian said. "The power supply, as I told you, is very irregular, and batteries lose their charge too fast to be of any real use. I can loan you a manual typewriter, if you like, and we do have a copier—you may make copies of anything you like, as long as the electric is working."

He was still holding her hands, and tension of another sort was growing in her, driving out the confusion and anger with a warmer and purely mundane emotion. Her fingers curled in Julian's, and she felt suddenly shy.

"Great," Truth said. She'd taken notes by hand all through school; it wouldn't be that hard to go back to it for a while. And she'd ask Meg to send her computer anyway, just in case.

"And stay as long as you like," Julian went on warmly. "It cannot have escaped your notice that my—resources— are not easily taxed. I would be honored to provide any help I can to your work."

"Thank you," Truth said. She hesitated, reluctantly pulling her hands free of his. "Julian, you know I'm not a— that I don't believe the things you do about the nature of reality. I don't intend to pull any punches. Whatever I find out about Blackburn I'm going to write about—even if it isn't very flattering."

Julian's smile grew warmer yet. He put an arm around Truth's shoulders and began to walk toward the stairs. "Publish and be damned, as Wellington once said—or would 'Tell the truth and shame the Devil' be more *apropos*? Neither Thorne nor I has anything to fear from the honest truth, Truth. And I've never believed that the cure for the world's ills is a coat of whitewash."

Truth let out a deep sigh of relief. Though Julian might be a sincere believer, it seemed he was willing to let others possess beliefs of their own.

"Is there anything I can get you right now?" he asked.

Belatedly, Truth remembered her intention to call Aunt Caroline. "Is there a phone I can use?" she asked.

"This way."

"Unfortunately, the only phone is in here. We don't bother to carry cellphones; the reception inside the gates isn't very good—to put it mildly—and the house tends to be rather hard on electronic equipment in general," Julian said, leading the way into his office. "A land-line is our most reliable form of communtication with the outside." He crossed to the desk, picked the phone up, and listened.

"—and as you can see, 'reliable' is a relative term," he said ruefully, holding the receiver out to her.

Truth took the receiver and held it to her ear. Nothing. She reached over and jiggled the connect button. Nothing.

"It's out," she said, half-questioningly.

"It often is, after a storm," Julian said. "I'll send Caradoc into Shadowkill to call tomorrow morning if it isn't back up by then, but the phone company is usually pretty good about restoring service quickly." He shrugged. "I can run you back down there right now, if you like. Was it an important call?"

"No, not really," Truth said, hesitating. She put the receiver back in its cradle. "I'll try tomorrow."

"That's all right, then. Look, Truth—"

Truth glanced up at him, alerted by the new note in his voice.

"I know that you don't believe in the Blackburn Work— and believe me, I have no intention of proselytizing—but I know that you must be something of a trained observer. Have you ever had any experience working with mediums?" Julian asked.

"Yes, a little," Truth admitted.

"Well this evening the others are going to be engaged in meditation exercises. It's a fast day for the *Practicuses*— our "entry-level" people, you might say—but every one of the rank of *Adeptus Minor* or above is exempt, which is, at the moment, only me, Irene, and Light, and of course you and Michael don't adhere to our disciplines. Anyway, I thought I'd hypnotize Light and try her on a little psychometry. I'd be very pleased to have you observe."

"Hypnosis?" queried Truth doubtfully. Psychometry, she knew, was the attempt to discover information about an object—or its owner—by psychic means, but the Institute had never been able to come up with a test for it that didn't exclude the possibility of simple telepathy instead.

Julian grinned at her. "Oh, don't worry. I'm a licensed hypnotherapist, as a matter of fact. Hypnotism can be, if not quite dangerous, then at least unpleasant in the wrong hands. I'd never do anything to hurt Light."

"No. I know you wouldn't," Truth said. "And I'd—I'd

like to watch your ritual, Julian," she added shyly.

"Not a ritual, Truth," Julian corrected her gently. "Our rituals involve magick, and I would as soon expose you to them unprepared as I would allow the village idiot to hypnotize Light. Tonight is merely a *practice*, shall we say. In the nature of an experiment."

The evening meal was much less elaborate and formal than the one the night before had been, and with only Light, Michael, Julian, and Irene there Truth had the chance to spend more time with Light.

The previous evening the girl had seemed nearly simpleminded, babbling on about visions in the woods. Tonight she merely seemed shy, spooning up her soup and buttering her roll with the deft physical economy of the blind, though Truth knew that she could see very well. It was nearly as if she saw what was not here—or perhaps, more accurately, more than what was here.

"I suppose it must be very interesting—to go to college, and see all those people who come from everywhere," Light said softly to Truth.

"Haven't you been to college?" Truth asked, surprised.

To her distress, Light flushed, the pinkness visibly marking her pale skin. "No," Light said, softer still. "I've never been to school."

"But—" Truth said, faltering.

"There are more ways to learn than by attending a school," Michael said, dividing the gentle rebuke between the two of them. "If you can read, there is no worldly wisdom that cannot be gathered from the pages of a book."

Light cast a glance of appeal toward Truth, and Truth wondered in that moment whether Light could read, either.

"And if you can't read," Truth said, making certain it sounded as if she were making a light joke, "you can learn that to start with, and study everything else by mail."

Light looked relieved, but it was Julian's smile of warm approval that Truth cherished more. She pulled him aside for a moment, in the exodus that followed dinner, to question him.

"Can Light read?" Truth asked him without preamble.

"Actually," Julian said, "I'm not sure. She has a remarkable aural memory, though; anything she's heard once she can remember forever. But she doesn't respond at all well to direct questions—as I'm sure you'll discover."

"Where did you find her?" Truth nerved herself to ask.

"In a place she is much better away from. Call it psychic sensitivity if you will, or dress it up in psychiatric mumbo-jumbo: The fact remains that Light is . . . fragile. Six months ago she could not bear to be in the company of even as many people as she was last night, but I think she's lonely too. Certainly it can be isolating to see the world in a different way than others do. She seems to have taken to you, though, and I hope you'll be kind to her."

"It's easy to be kind to Light," Truth said honestly, and it was true, even though she found her instant partisanship of the young silver-haired psychic somewhat unsettling. Slow to love and slower to trust, Truth had always been very self-contained. She had always tried to need no one, uncertain of her ability to give anything in return for another's affections. Now that was about to change; Truth felt as if everything in her life was changing at once.

"Good," Julian said. "Now, if you'll come with me, I'll show you something that few people have ever seen."

In 1969, in the aftermath of Katherine Jourdemayne's death and Thorne Blackburn's disappearance, Blackburn's antics received more publicity than possibly even he could have wished. Pictures of Shadow's Gate were spread across every front page in America, and a color spread even made that week's issue of *Time*. But amid all the publicity, the actual site of the murder had never been photographed—at least not any photos that had survived.

Julian led Truth down a narrow hallway with many steps up and down, until they stopped in front of a pair of tall oak doors that Truth remembered passing on her tour of the house yesterday. Ornamented in the style of their day, both the doors and the door frame were carved with acanthus-leaf motifs, and the lock plates and doorknobs were marked with a relief of a wavy-rayed sun.

"Where are we?" Truth asked, confused.

"This is the true center of the house. You can't really tell from the outside—it's quite a cunning bit of *trompe l'oeil* architecture—but Shadow's Gate is built in a hollow square. Around this."

He stepped forward and opened the door. Truth walked in past him and looked up.

This strange central folly to Shadow's Gate was a circular room nearly thirty feet across and almost twice that in height. There were three narrow archways set opposite the doors, each a little taller than the doors they had come in through and curtained, now, with thick black velvet. The ceiling itself was domed and ribbed, painted with a representation of the Zodiac, the allegorical figures wearing the bright stars of their constellation-namesakes like jewels. Below the dome, a band of windows circled the room. Each window could be opened separately, and in the center of each was set a shield-shape of colored glass, etched with an image it was too dark to see.

Below the windows the ornately-ornamented carved oaken panels swept to the floor without a break. Truth was surprised to see light fixtures ringing the room, but their ornate antiquity told her that the first illuminating agent in this room had been gaslight.

Between the light fixtures were enormous Egyptian statues—painted board, Truth realized after a moment, but at first glance the twelve-foot-high figures looked real. She wasn't Egyptologist enough to recognize them, but there was a woman with a lion's head and one with the head of a cow, a man with an ibis's head and one with the head of a dog—or a jackal? Between them were hung banners in red, white, black, and gray. There were figures on the banners, but Truth couldn't quite make them out.

What had Light been saying the night before? *"The red stag and the white mare; the gray wolf and the black dog; red and gray and black and white, the four wardens of the Gate."*

Again Truth had the faintly-embarrassed sense of being caught eavesdropping, as a child might who wandered into a conversation adults held among themselves.

As if her eyes were drawn downward by the dangling banners, Truth found herself staring at the floor. It was a work of art, if a little dizzying: Tiles of black and white marble, each twelve inches square, marched across the room in chessboard perfection. Their geometry was overlaid with an elaborate figure of circles and signs in golden marble; between the inner circle and the outer were circular tiles of a dull red stone, each inlaid with some brightly-glinting symbol.

Truth's eyes were drawn back to the star shape that filled the inner circle. It had seven points—no, nine. . . .

"Thorne had the floor redone as you see it when he bought Shadow's Gate. It's the only change he made to this room, other than the decorations around the walls."

Truth jumped. She'd almost forgotten Julian was with her.

"You mean the original builder *built* it this way?" she said with faint outrage.

"Why not?" Julian shrugged. "Everything was less expensive then. The Spiritualism vogue was in full swing. They may have held séances here. It may have been the house's ballroom. Who knows?"

Blackburn had known. Truth was sure of it.

"Well," Truth said. "What do we do now?"

"First," said Julian, "I set the stage."

There was furniture in the room—difficult to notice in the first shock of seeing the central Gothic folly of Shadow's Gate. Julian went to the side of the room and came back with two plain wooden side chairs, a stool, and a jarringly modern floor lamp.

"Of course, when we do ritual the place looks different.

You're welcome to see how it looks, sometime before we work. The rest of the time, the Altar and all of the Weapons remain in storage. One of the advantages to an old house is that there's always enough closets; do you know this place has thirty-seven rooms? And you sit here," he finished, setting one of the chairs beside Truth.

She sat down, feeling uncommonly meek. Julian switched on the floor lamp—the extension cord it plugged into curled across the floor like an abandoned licorice whip before vanishing beneath the curtains of one of the alcoves—and then crossed to the panel of switches beside the door. He pressed the black, pearl-crowned buttons one by one until all the sconces were dark and the only illumination came from the tiny halogen bulb of the lamp on the floor.

Truth felt as though she'd been plunged into a cave, or to the bottom of the sea. Suddenly she felt pressure, as if the vast volumes of empty space surrounding her had a palpable weight. The darkness was pressing her down, like ells of smoky velvet. Her heart thudded faster.

She took a deep breath and began counting her heartbeat, seeking calm. On some preverbal level she knew that Julian was perfectly at ease here, but strangely the knowledge brought her no comfort.

There was a rustling off in the darkness, and a pale shape moved forward, but before anything as clean as fear could penetrate the oppression that gripped her, Truth saw that it was Light.

The young medium was wearing a simple floor-length white robe. The sleeves were straight and narrow and came down over Light's hands. It was not sashed, nor did it have fastenings of any sort, going on over her head by means of a simple neck slit. Her face was still and composed as she seated herself on the chair, and Truth saw for the first time that the lamp was adjusted so that its illumination would not reach Light's face.

"You know what I'm going to do tonight?" Julian asked her, his voice low and soothing.

"You're going to hypnotize me, just like you did before," Light responded.

"That's right. And when I've done that, I'm going to give you some things to hold. I want you to tell me stories about them."

"What kind of stories?" Light's voice was sleepily curious, already remote although Julian had not yet begun inducing the trance state.

"Any kind you like," he said kindly.

Julian drew an object from his pocket: an egg-shaped piece of quartz, Truth saw, with a long chain attached to it by a band of silver about its middle. It must be faceted too: it flashed as he held it in the light. Truth could see the iron band of the bracelet he wore as the dark sleeve of his jacket fell back.

"Watch the light," Julian said softly. "You're in a room with a staircase leading down. . . ." A flick of his fingers sent the pendulum in his hand spinning and flashing.

Truth looked away, lest she fall under his spell, too—or more likely, asleep. She wished there were more illumination, but every trance-worker, such as the medium, Light, was, required a different and familiar environment to enter the deep-alpha state of trance. Some worked only at night. One—Dylan used her talents frequently—only entered trance to the sound of the loudest rock music.

Julian's voice faded into a reassuring background drone, and, now that she was adjusting to the quiet, Truth could hear other sounds: a rhythmic thrumming that must be something to do with the water heater, faint scratchings of branches on distant windows.

She glanced down. Set into the black marble square beneath her feet was a multirayed sunburst the size of a half-dollar piece, as if a celestial teardrop had fallen from the sky. She looked up, but the chamber's vault was shrouded in darkness. Just barely, she could make out an area less dark, which must be where the windows reflected light from the other rooms. No wonder she'd spent the morning getting lost, if the house really was built on a hollow square. She wondered if she could get a look at a set of architectural plans. They ought to be on file in the town hall, she supposed.

Truth looked down again, to the glinting star between her shoes.

This must mark the center of the room, Truth thought with an inward chill.

She could not say why the knowledge was so instantly disturbing. She glanced at Julian, still leading Light down into trance state, the pendulum in his hand winking and spinning, winking and spinning. . . .

"Cover her bed with branches of wild herb, and lay upon her couch the fur of every beast that stalks these woods. Such is the altar of the Hierolator, the Celestial Concubine, to whose bed the Sun will be brought, and whose ecstasy will show forth the Way." Had she read that? Or imagined it?

It looked different when it was set up for rituals, Julian said. Of course it did. The altar would be set up here, in the middle, right about where she was sitting.

As it had been in 1969.

Truth felt a wave of cold nausea well up from the very marrow of her bones.

Katherine Jourdemayne had died here.

In this room, on this *spot*, her mother had died. Blood called to blood, and only the thinnest of veils separated that moment from now.

As if her horrified realization had summoned them up, Truth *saw* them here with the brilliant eye of imagination: Katherine and Irene here in the center, the others standing in a circle, the flames of their candles like diamonds on a chain. She heard the stutter and crash of thunder like distant artillery; each time the lightning flashed it bleached the lesser flames to nothingness in an instant.

And her mother was dying, dead, about to die, all innocent and helpless and unknowing; she was dying here, sucked lifeless by the powers Blackburn had called and Truth couldn't save her.

She wrenched herself out of the vision with a gasp, and Julian and Light snapped into sharp focus before her. Light, deep in trance, was gazing with trusting, unfocused eyes at Julian's face.

Just as Katherine had at Blackburn.

She'd trusted him.

He'd killed her.

He's going to kill her! Truth cried in her mind, and did not herself know which pair she meant. Blind irresistible terror crashed over her senses like a wave of the driving ocean: History would repeat itself here in Shadow's Gate, and Julian would kill Light, gentle trusting Light, as Truth stood helpless.

As Caroline had stood helpless.

As—

Truth did not hear the sharp pistol-crack her chair made as it fell over. She no longer saw the other occupants of the room. She only knew she had to get out of here *now*.

She yanked open the door and ran. The hall was twisty but there were no false turnings, she ran down it, stumbling and careening off the walls, until she reached the foyer once more. Gasping for breath but unwilling to slow down she plunged up the stairs; the last riser tripped her and she fell, scrabbling along on hands and knees for a few feet until she regained her footing. She fell rather than walked through the doorway into her room and stood there shaking, sucking air in great rasping gasps.

There was someone in the room with her.

He stood beside the window. The light from her bedside lamp cast him half in shadow.

"You're a damned fool," he said harshly. Truth struggled to husband breath for a reply and then choked, starting to cough.

She knew who he was.

"You're—" she said, gagging.

But there was no one there. Only the curtains swirling in the breeze before an open window.

*   *   *

Shocked to numbness, Truth took three wobbly steps and reached the edge of her bed. She sat down, staring distrustfully at the window, but it manifested no more apparitions.

She'd just seen Thorne Blackburn.

Impossible.

And heard him.

Ridiculous.

"Stress-triggered waking hallucination while in borderline hypnogogic state," Truth muttered shakily. "You know the drill. He wasn't there."

That he almost certainly *had* been there, sometime in that eternal 1969 that was growing to occupy more and more of her imagination, was also true, but the one thing Truth Jourdemayne knew that she was not, was psychic.

"Nuts," she said aloud.

"Would you care to explain just what *that* little display was all about?" Julian, icily angry, demanded from the doorway.

Truth turned toward him. As if her movement had given her permission, he stalked forward, moving with catlike fury.

"I thought you were a professional. Do you know what that little tantrum of yours could have *done*? But I don't suppose you—"

"Julian, my mother died on that spot when I was two years old and I don't really think I have to listen to this." Truth shot back, soaring to the attack. She heard the rage in her voice and choked it back, willing herself to coolness and calm. "I thought I could handle it. I was wrong. I'm sorry."

"Oh, my God." Instantly Julian's anger faded. "I'm such an idiot—here I was, full of myself, showing off my *théâtre sacré* and not realizing what memories it must bring back for you! I'm so sorry." He sat down beside her and put an arm around her shoulders.

His warmth and strength seemed to search out all the

frozen places within her. She wanted to take his face between her hands, take his lips with her own, feel his hard body surging against her own, blotting out the darkness. . . .

"I was stupid. I let my imagination run away with me," Truth said roughly, banishing the compelling image. "Is Light really all right?" she added in a small voice.

"Fortunately she'd already gone under. I simply brought her back up out of trance with a routine I'd already implanted in her for emergencies such as this. She's resting now. But I apologize again for subjecting you to such a nasty experience. I could have worked with her anywhere: We simply use the *théâtre sacré* in order to build up a learned response to it in the unconscious mind."

"My fault. Don't worry about it," Truth said again. *I have to get used to it sometime*, she thought bleakly, her mind roving back over Julian's last words.

Théâtre sacré. Sacred theater. Another phrase of Blackburn's: *"The first duty of the magician is to enact sacred theater."*

"Julian, do you—I mean, do you really—" she faltered.

"Believe in the Work?" Julian smiled. "Of course I do, but that doesn't mean I believe it's perfect, or should be hedged around with hoodoo. Magick is both art and science, and I've never heard that blind acceptance helps either art *or* science. While it's true that Thorne's reputation holds a lot of people at bay, and even I have to admit that he had a pretty lurid public career—"

Truth smiled weakly. Julian took his arm from around her shoulder and turned toward her, his face shining with intensity.

"—what we have to remember about Thorne Blackburn is that he was a very gifted . . . boy. He was barely thirty when he died, and he'd already been internationally known in magickal circles for over a decade. His mistakes were those of youth and overconfidence, and I've learned from them, I hope."

"So you won't make his mistakes?" Truth said, with a

crooked, wistful smile. *How can anyone ever be certain of that?*

"There's one I won't make," Julian said with assurance. "Forgive me if I speak too bluntly, Truth, but Katherine Jourdemayne—your mother—died of an entirely explicable drug overdose. There was nothing the least bit mysterious about how and why she died. If you do any studying at all of Thorne's work, you'll see that his magickal style was influenced heavily by the promiscuous illegal drug use that permeated the American counterculture in the nineteen sixties. Opium—hashish—psilocybin—even LSD, a drug that *certainly* wasn't known to the Secret Chiefs!—are part of all his rituals, and I've removed much of that from the Work. Not without being criticized for it, I assure you, but discipline, not drugs, sets the feet of the Seeker upon the Path. The drug use that killed your mother was a sign of the excess of that age; it has no place in this one."

Truth could only nod, grateful that he was speaking so plainly.

"And nothing is going to happen to Light," Julian added in a coaxing tone. "Even if you believe in coincidence—which I don't—Light is our Hierophex, not our Hierolator."

Truth stared at him blankly.

"Katherine Jourdemayne was Thorne's Hierolator, his Sacred Concubine. Light occupies the position in our ritual that Irene occupied in Thorne's—that of Hierophex, the Sacred Speaker."

"He wanted Caroline for it." What in God's name had made her say that? Truth wondered.

"Of course; it's best when the Hierophex and the Hierolator are sisters." Julian did not seem surprised by her statement, and even seemed to think it was true. "But Caroline refused, and Thorne honored her refusal."

So Aunt Caroline had been psychic—at least Julian said Blackburn had thought so.

"But you look tired, and I really should go and check on Light," Julian said. "Shall I send Irene up with a cordial? I promise, nothing harmful—or illegal."

"Oh, no, really Julian, I . . ." she faltered, her strength draining away like water from a tub. "That would be very nice, if it's not too much trouble," she finished weakly.

"I'll do it, then," Julian promised. "Sleep well, Truth." And before Truth could check him or protest, he had dropped the lightest of light kisses upon her forehead, and gone.

Too much is happening too fast, Truth thought. She couldn't focus on any of it. Her hands trembled violently as she raised them to her face, and in the sudden backwash of reaction she couldn't stop shaking. She hugged herself tightly, rocking back and forth in her own embrace as she hadn't done since she was a very small child.

I'm losing my mind. I know I am.

She'd recovered herself enough to simply be sitting quietly, staring at nothing, when Irene Avalon knocked at the door a few minutes later. The emotional storm had passed, leaving numbness in its wake.

"Oh, my dear girl—whatever's the matter? When Julian told me you'd fallen afoul of the Guardians, I never dreamed—" Irene set the tray she was carrying down on the dresser and came over to her. "And your hands are as cold as ice!" she exclaimed, enfolding them in her own.

"I saw—" Truth began, and bit the words back. Tell Irene Avalon that she'd seen her father and she'd sound like a raving lunatic—or, worse, perfectly rational by Irene's skewed standards.

"Oh, well, pet, never you mind what you saw. It's my belief that sometimes the Guardians just forget how frail we poor time-bound mortals are—a warning from the likes of them is as like to lay you out flat as tell you something you need to know. It's just that way with all the Powers," she added in a tone of faint reproach.

Truth had to smile at the image thus conjured, of Irene

fiercely scolding one of the hieratic Egyptian figures from the Temple.

"There you are!" Irene said bracingly. "I'll just run you a nice hot bath; that, and a dose of my cordial hotted up will put you right as right!" Irene bustled off to the bathroom connected to Truth's room, and in a moment Truth could hear the water running.

"I'll just pop off and get you some of my special salts for the bath and hot water for your drink," Irene said in no-nonsense tones. Truth nodded. It was easier than arguing. She was suddenly far too tired to fight.

When Irene left, Truth wandered into the bathroom—a period piece from the early fifties—and watched the steam billow up from the tub to mist the white-tile walls and the chrome fixtures. Everything was clean, white, and antiseptic, unchanging and perfect, just the way she'd always wanted her life to be, with nothing of uncertainty or doubt.

"I've brought you a—Where are you, dear? Oh, *there* you are." Irene's voice heralded her arrival long before she appeared. "I've brought you a nice warm robe to wrap up in," she announced, and then leaned past Truth to sprinkle crystals from a pottery jar into the foaming water beneath the tap. Instantly the water in the tub turned an intense blue-green, and a bracing scent of ocean and forest filled the air.

Truth inhaled, sneezed, and blinked. The scent warmed her spirit just as the steam warmed her body, and she felt better almost at once.

"What is this?" she asked Irene.

"One of my own recipes," the older woman said. "And so is this." She handed Truth a thick white mug full of a steaming scarlet liquid.

Truth took it and inhaled deeply. Strong sweet scents of oranges and flowers and honey assailed her nostrils.

"It's just my cordial mixed up with a little hot water. And as for that, there's nothing to it that can hurt you, just a bit of honey, herbs, and whiskey. You won't find a clergyman's daughter in the whole of England who won't swear by the virtue of a wee drop now and again."

Truth smiled, faintly sipping at it as the tub filled. The hot cordial went down like fiery silk, smoothing and soothing whatever it touched.

When the tub was full and the cup was empty, Irene closed off the taps and took the mug from Truth's hands.

"Now a good soak and then to bed. You'll feel altogether better in the morning."

"Thank you," Truth said. Impulsively she hugged the older woman. "You're so kind," she said.

There were tears in Irene's eyes as she answered, "Ah, child, it's no more than I owe to you—and to *him*."

A leisurely soak in the herbal bath completed the restoration of Truth's equanimity. When she got out, wrapping herself in the thick, terry-cloth-lined flannel robe Irene had left her, she was tired, but ready to take a leisurely, *rational* look at matters as they now stood.

But she did lock her door, before reaching for her notebook and settling down to gather her thoughts.

A few minutes later she'd finished her notes covering the day's events, from Ellis's cryptic warnings at breakfast to Michael's cryptic warnings before dinner. The list of people who *hadn't* warned or threatened her at Shadow's Gate was growing shorter by the day, and in the end, the only person who'd probably still be on it was Light.

Truth felt deeply guilty about her behavior before Light earlier this evening, but Julian had said the girl hadn't noticed, and from what Truth knew about trance psychism, it was very probably true. Still, tomorrow she would seek her out and apologize. Truth had a faint disturbing sense that here at Shadow's Gate she could afford no acts of pettiness or sins of discourtesy.

What a pity nobody's told Fiona the same thing, Truth thought with an inward smile.

Before getting into bed Truth checked, once more, on the security of *Venus Afflicted*, and this time drew the book forth from its hiding place. Here, in the very house where it had probably been written, its odd archaisms seemed more accessible than they had before. Perhaps, with enough study, she could extract the underlying purpose to what seemed now more akin to a cross between a recipe book and a mad playwright's prompt copy.

Truth paged through *Venus Afflicted*, picking out this bit and that as if she were plundering the blooms of a hothouse garden. Greek titles and Latin invocations, Egyptian costumes and Norse gods; Blackburn had certainly constructed his cult with a fine free syncretic hand—and then had the nerve to wrap it all up in some kind of Celtic twilight and claim he sought the return of the Old Gods from *Tir na Og*, the Land of Youth, and that he himself was a son of the *sidhe*, the Fairy Race.

"Human—or almost," Ellis had said.

Breakfast seemed a thousand years ago, but his words returned suddenly to haunt her. If Blackburn were half-elven, what did that make *her?*

Idiocy! she snorted.

But two days ago the thought would not have made her so uneasy.

CHAPTER EIGHT

REVEALED TRUTH

It takes two to speak the truth—one to speak, and another to hear.

—HENRY DAVID THOREAU

THE FOLLOWING DAY—TRUTH'S THIRD AT SHADOW'S gate, if she counted the day she'd arrived—was also clear, though less bright, but in October one accepted any good weather one got with gratitude.

As before, the house seemed almost asleep when Truth left her rooms. She would have liked to have found Light, perhaps even talked to her without one of the men around, but Light was nowhere to be seen. She'd have to make it a priority to find out where Light's room was, if she could do it without being obvious about it.

Rather than risk breakfast with Ellis or another run-in with either Fiona or Michael, Truth opted for breakfast in town, at the aluminum-sided diner on Main Street that she'd passed the day before. She took the car, both because she was not overfond of the thought of a two-mile walk before her morning coffee, and, she realized, because it would be harder for someone to stop her in the car.

But that's ridiculous! a part of her mind insisted. The

worry was perilously close to paranoia. No one was going to stop her.

Ridiculous? So is having visions of Thorne Blackburn.

Oddly enough, if Truth had been of a more mystic and dreamy-eyed temperament it would have been easier to dismiss the sight—and sound—of Thorne Blackburn as nothing more than the outliers of a stress-induced nerve storm. But Truth—at least so she had used to think—had nerves of steel, and did not begin concocting explanations for phenomena before she'd finished experiencing them. And she certainly didn't have to concede that Thorne Blackburn was a priest-king and magician to admit she'd seen him—not after yesterday's discovery that Shadow's Gate was in all probability haunted.

And she bet she knew just where the hidden spring was too.

Why else build that bizarre round room right out of a Richard Matheson story at the center of the house? The bricked-over spring must be directly beneath.

As before, her mood lightened and her thoughts cleared as soon as she left the estate, making it harder to take last night's events seriously. If that continued, Truth realized she'd have to consider very seriously whether she could, in fact, work at Shadow's Gate at all. The final decision on that could wait until she had more information, though, and the odd unsettled feelings might go away of their own accord.

She hoped. Because try as she might, she could not shake the conviction that she had unfinished business at Shadow's Gate.

Breakfast gave her the chance to make inquiries of some of the local residents, and after breakfast she drove into Hyde Park, to the offices of the Mid-Hudson Cellular Phone Company.

*   *   *

After breakfast she drove south until she found a mall, and looked around until she found a store that promised her a phone capable of immediate reliable communication, bell-like sound-quality, and the ability to also access her email from the depths of the Amazon rain-forest.

In Truth's opinion, cellphones were a waste of time, a way for people with too much free time to annoy others who were trying to get actual work done—or worse, attempting to get *away* from work. Their constant ringing on trains, in theaters, and in restaurants set her teeth on edge, and the conversations she couldn't help but overhear never seemed to be very important.

But she needed one now. And the salesman assured her that their wireless network would enable her to stay connected *anywhere*.

Take that, Shadow's Gate.

Her new purchase tucked into her purse—it was as small and light as something out of science fiction—Truth headed back toward Shadowkill. When she arrived, she could use the phone to call Aunt Caroline, just to test it out. The list of questions she had kept getting longer.

Had Blackburn knows Shadow's Gate was haunted? Who was the baby in the photograph? How many children had the feckless Blackburn fathered—and where were they now? What did Aunt Caroline know about Julian Pilgrim, the new master of Shadow's Gate?

So many questions . . .

But when she arrived, and pulled into the parking lot of the Shadow kill Public Library to make her call, she found that the time to make that call had passed.

"I'm sorry, Ms. Jourdemayne." Janine's voice was flat and robotic. "Mrs. Jourdemayne passed away early this morning."

Truth clutched the little phone tightly to keep from dropping it. A claustrophobic weight settled over her—not even guilt, but the suffocating sense of having made some fatal and irrecoverable error.

"Should I come there?" Truth asked numbly.

"There really isn't any reason for you to," Janine admitted grudgingly. "She really had everything planned. The funeral home came and took the body this morning, and Mrs. Jourdemayne left a list of people to call with a friend of hers from the library; I'm just waiting for her to get here so I can hand over the keys. She had everything all planned," Janine said, in someting like awe. "There's nothing left to do."

From a distance Truth heard herself mouth empty courtesies, and then at last the phone slipped from her nerveless fingers and clattered to the floor of her car.

She didn't remember getting out of the car. She walked aimlessly, taking no particular note of anything but the sidewalk beneath her feet. She didn't know how long she walked, but finally she stopped and, looking up, saw the graceful Gothic arch of a church door before her.

She looked at the sign out front. An Episcopal Church. She remembered Aunt Caroline taking her to Sunday School as a child, although she'd never been quite certain how much religion Aunt Caroline herself had possessed.

The door stood open. On an impulse, Truth went up the stairs and in.

The inside was quiet; dark after the sunlit street. There was a rose window behind the altar and high old-fashioned stained-glass windows on both sides of the church. It was peaceful; the polar opposite of the circular room at Shadow's Gate. As soon as her eyes adjusted, Truth found a pew and seated herself.

After a moment she began to twist uncomfortably in the seat. She'd meant to offer up some acknowledgment of

Aunt Caroline's death; some formal response to her passing, but she couldn't. The wooden bench beneath her seemed almost impossibly uncomfortable, and the uninhabited silence clamored in her ears.

What are you seeking wisdom in the temple of the dead god for, Daughter of Earth? You are none of his!

It was only hyperactive imagination that shaped the words echoing on her inner ear, but it was just the sort of mystic, grandiloquent pronouncement Thorne Blackburn would make.

Daughter of Earth. Child of the sidhe . . .

Now, when it was far too late, Truth hated herself for every opportunity she had not taken, for every question she had not asked her aunt. Now her only source for information she could trust was gone forever—the woman who might have helped her build a bridge between what she was and what she had become—or was becoming.

Oh, stop feeling sorry for yourself! Truth scolded herself fiercely. She'd known Aunt Caroline was dying—she ought to be happy that the woman who had raised her had been spared the final indignity of impersonal hospitals and clinical care. Caroline Jourdemayne had died in her own bed, that was something to be happy for. Since her twin Katherine's death, Caroline's life had been a burden and a responsibility, not a joy, and now she was free.

Truth should be happy for her.

Then why was she so afraid . . . ?

With the faint sense of another escape route closing behind her, Truth rose and left the church.

"I've found another book for you," Laurel Villanova said triumphantly.

It was just after one o'clock, and Truth had come back to the library to bury all her emotional turmoil in a search for the history of Shadow's Gate. Work had always been her escape, Truth realized, an escape so laudable that few people saw it for what it was: flight from a reality that held nothing but pain and a world in which she did not belong.

It had always worked before. It would work now. Gratefully she put away all the sadness of the day; she would solve the riddle of Shadow's Gate—and of Thorne Blackburn.

With a grateful smile, Truth took the dusty green-bound volume from Laurel and set it down on the table.

The River Where The Ghosts Walk: A Haunted History of the Hudson Valley, said the title. Truth opened it, frowning. Blackburn had also owned a copy of this book—Truth had seen it in Julian's collection.

Copyright 1938. She flipped to the table of contents.

"There's a chapter on Shadow's Gate," Laurel said helpfully. "I've marked it for you."

Truth saw the colored paper marker and turned to the indicated chapter. Facing the first page was a bound-in photo on glossy stock of a rambling Federalist house, built long and low in the style of eighteenth-century Colonial architecture and lime washed to a flat white. Beneath the picture was the legend: *"Shadow's Gate, built 1780. 1869 photo."*

She was looking at a picture of the third house.

Time fell away as Truth Jourdemayne did what she had been trained to do: search the facts and find the truth beyond. The books she had used the day before were still close to hand on the long table in the Local History Room, and Truth had the notes she had taken to help her as well.

Time passed, and slowly, cross-checked but with many question marks remaining, the story took shape.

In 1780, in the first years of the new Republic, a third building was erected—"and we shall call it Shadowsgate, after the style of Elkanah Scheidow who first settled here"—on the site of Scheidow's first trading post, which Truth now knew to have been situated beside the spring that was the source of the local *kill*, or stream. No wonder they'd called it Scheidow's *kill*, if he'd built his business right beside it.

The 1780 house, which was to vanish from the local historical records less than a century later, was built by one of the *patroons'* descendants. In the nearly century and a half since Elkanah Scheidow had first come to what was then a lush and forbidding wilderness, the family's fortunes had prospered. Each generation built upon the wealth of the last, and, through all the political shifts and upsets of fate, the Scheidow family had managed to hang on to a great deal of the land originally granted to it, and re-granted in turn by the British and the new American government. Land was wealth. The new house was to reflect this. Its windows came from Holland, its stone masons from New-York City.

It was almost enough to compensate for the other widely-known fact about the Scheidow lineage.

A century and a half previously, Elkanah Scheidow had shrewdly expropriated one of the local Indian tribes' sacred places as the site of his business. Possibly his original intention had been only to build his trading post on neutral ground in order to minimize tribal feuding, but the effect had been to make himself an envoy of the *manitou*, the guardians of the Native American spirit world. With so much invisible authority supporting him, Elkanah's business had prospered—at a cost.

The *manitou*, if gossip of the period could be believed, were quite content with the interloper's presence— providing they were served as they had always been. As early as 1780 an odd aura of misfortune already hovered over what would someday be known as Shadow's Gate.

Truth pieced together from the genealogical records a tale of nagging, recurring misfortune: this child dead in infancy, that in childhood. So many of them drowned in the spring that had been the source of stream and town alike that in 1684 Scheidow's grandson, after the drowning death of his youngest brother, had it lined and capped as if it were a well and built a well house over the site—with a door to which he held the only key. He'd died soon after, by means the sources available to Truth did not name, but it was so easy to think of him walking out from the house one night in the storm, unlocking the well house and passing within, opening the cover over the well and climbing down into it, *and pulling the cover back over the well from the inside.*

Truth gave herself a mental shake, reminding herself that she didn't know and would never know how Tobias Scheidow had died. What she did know was that at the time of the building of the third house, the well had been incorporated into the building itself, and all trace of its location destroyed forever.

With the capping of the spring in 1684, the reports of drownings disappeared from the local records, but the other afflictions seemed far from diminished. And once in each generation, a member of the family simply—vanished.

There were any number of explanations for the sudden omission: marriage, unrecorded death, family scandal. Truth fretted at her lack of ability to *prove*, but she really didn't have the resources available to determine that each disappearance really was that mysterious. But disappear the Scheidow descendants did, and not children either: once every twenty-five years or so, an adult member of the family simply . . . vanished . . . from Shadow's Gate.

The family had become important in Dutchess County, both financially and politically; in those days a Scheidow's word was law and sensational scandal something to be avoided. There was no hint in any of the local papers or family histories Truth consulted of shocking disappearances and shameful flights.

But in contrast to the newspapers and the histories, the Scheidow genealogies had been kept with a scrupulous regard for the truth, and once you began looking for the pattern you were certain of finding it. One adult, each generation, gone without an obituary to record the passing in a paper that scrupulously noted the births, deaths, and marriages of the descendants of the founder of the town.

The other things Truth uncovered, checking as far as she could the undocumented claims of *The River Where The Ghosts Walk*, seemed to fit the developing pattern—one might almost call it the Amityville Syndrome—that she had learned to look for when hauntings were inferred.

There were continuing reports of a black dog that walked through walls, of lights in odd places and times, a coldness that did not dissipate, the unexplained flight of houseguests. By the 1800s, so *The River Where The Ghosts Walk* assured her, it was commonly known as far away as New York City that the Scheidow house was haunted.

As for the crowning event the book related, it would take Truth years of research to confirm it—or deny it—in its entirety. It seemed to be the stuff of pulp fiction and supermarket press, even compiled, as it had been, some sixty years after the incident, the author claiming to have been a child living in Shadowkill at the time.

Briefly stated, the "facts," if you could claim there were any, were these: In April 1872, Elijah Cheddow, formerly a captain of Union forces in the late Insurrection of the Southern States, took an axe to his wife, twin daughters, and infant son, as well as to all servants living in the house, and then set the house on fire, burning it to the ground.

Their death dates, recorded in the genealogy, matched. There had certainly been a fire, according to the newspaper, but the story was almost maddeningly tactful, confining itself to a bare-bones report that a fire had occurred but had not spread. It did not even mention any deaths, though when Truth cross-checked the Cheddow genealogy, the death dates for Sarah, Elizabeth, Amy, and Infant Cheddow matched.

There was no recorded death date for Elijah.

As for the rest of the grisly tale, it received a resounding "Not Proven," that so-convenient verdict surviving only in Scots jurisprudence, and an entombment in local legend. A bang-up ending to what was probably a very unpleasant family, only it wasn't the end, as a distant cousin, Nathaniel Cheddow, came forward and, impelled by God alone knew what reason, built yet another house on that ill-starred site—

"Ms. Jourdemayne? It's six-thirty. We're closing."

Truth blinked up dazedly at Laurel, only now noticing the dimness of the room in which she worked. Then the librarian's words penetrated.

"Six-*thirty*!" she groaned. She was late, she knew that much, even if just now she wasn't sure for what. Truth scooped up her notes and sketches and scrambled stiffly to her feet. Slinging her purse over her shoulder, she juggled the books in her arms possessively. "Can I borrow these?"

Laurel hesitated. "Well, we don't usually like to let them circulate, but you are on the faculty at Taghkanic. . . . I guess it's okay."

Truth didn't correct Laurel's misapprehension, since she did want the books. And besides, she worked at Taghkanic, if not for it. She presented her library card, signed out the books in the local history ledger, and left the library just short of a dead run, blessing the impulse that had caused her to bring her car with her this morning. In moments she was on her way up the road to Shadow's Gate.

Which was a haunted house. A world-class, A-number-one, for-the-record-books haunted house, to rank right up there with any Irish castle you wanted to name.

And which explained everything Truth needed to know about Thorne Blackburn.

The gates up to the house were shut when she crossed the road and drove in under the gatehouse arch. She was about to get out and try to open them herself when Gareth came out of one of the gatehouse rooms, blinking in the glare of her headlights. Standing behind the bars, he looked like some kind of wild thing in a cage.

When he saw who it was he did something at the lock

plate that she couldn't see, then swung one wing of the ornate iron gate open, stepping through to talk to her.

"Good thing you showed up, Truth. I was about to bolt the gates for the night. You'd have had to phone the house then, or just leave your car here and walk up."

Gareth indicated a phone box on the wall of the drive-through, which reminded Truth of the cellphone she'd bought just that morning. She felt a hidden surge of triumph: She had resources Shadow's Gate didn't know of.

Shadow's Gate? Or Julian?

"Thanks for being here. I hope nobody was worried; I got involved in a line of research and lost track of time." She felt, obscurely, that Gareth deserved some sort of explanation. And Julian deserved an apology. She was treating Shadow's Gate as if it were an hotel!

Gareth grinned. "That's an explanation Julian can empathize with—sometimes he goes off to the library and gets lost for weeks. I'll phone him and let him know you're back so you can just go ahead and clean up. Dinner's at seven-thirty."

"Eating tonight?" Truth joked. She was instantly sorry she had at the expression that crossed Gareth's face; a slightly shuttered, slightly furtive look that did not go well with his open, generous features.

"Yeah. Um. Well—see you there." He swung the other half of the gate open and stepped back, waving her on.

She drove past him slowly. Her car's headlights cut bright arcs through the woods growing up close on each side of the drive. In mid-October almost everything still on the branches was yellow or orange or red, and the drifts underfoot made the traction slippery.

She was forcibly reminded of this when the deer suddenly appeared, standing transfixed in the headlights. It was huge; its coat was a ruddy fox color and its splendid rack of antlers gleamed like polished golden oak. It was the biggest deer she'd ever seen.

She tried to stop, but instantly realized she couldn't; the car began to skid, its back end edging forward until it seemed that rather than missing the deer, she was going to hit it broadside—killing it and probably totaling her car, if nothing worse.

Frantically Truth waged war against the laws of physics, twisting her wheel against the skid while feathering the brake. Finally the car slid to a stop.

She looked around. The deer that had caused all this fuss was nowhere to be seen.

Truth rolled her window down and scanned the horizon for it, although she knew it was probably miles away by now—*she* certainly hadn't hit it! She didn't see it, but while she was looking, a white blur off to the left caught her attention. White, and four-legged . . . She peered toward it, wondering if it were a white deer, but realized it was a white horse instead. Its eyes flashed red in the shine from her headlights as it turned and ran, becoming first a flicker in the woods, then a blur, then gone. Truth saw no rider. As she listened, the sound of its hoofbeats gradually diminished into silence, and the adrenaline rush that had sustained her passed, leaving her cold and sick.

You're lucky you weren't killed! Truth told herself unsteadily. Now that it was over she realized how lucky she'd been; she hadn't been going that fast, but running into that deer—

Truth frowned, starting the car up the drive once more. The deer that came onto the campus each Fall to steal the apples looked nothing like that. It had been about twice their size, for one thing, and its red coat a far cry from the winter-dun color of the Taghkanic deer's autumnal coats.

Not a deer at all. A stag.

What she had caught in her car's headlights had been the living image of that oft-copied Landseer painting, *Monarch of the Glen*—a great, redcoated stag; lord of Scotland and Ireland's high places.

And the white horse . . .

"The red stag and the white mare," Truth said aloud, thinking of what she'd seen and remembering Light's words again. But they hadn't been conjured up by Light's visions. Far from it—they were probably the cause of them: In this area many people kept back-bred or exotic livestock, from ostriches to aurochs, and Shadowkill was only a few miles from the famous Millbrook Hunt Country with its world-famous horse farms. Easy enough to find a red stag and a white mare in all of that—they'd probably gotten used to roving the property while it had stood unoccupied. Maybe they even belonged to Julian.

Just as long as he doesn't turn up a gray wolf, the black dog I can handle, Truth thought with a flash of saving humor.

And she was there.

The door to the house was, as it had been the night before, unlocked. Truth wondered if it was left unlocked all the time, or whether Gareth locked it each night on his way up from the gatehouse. Truth thought it was hardly fair that Gareth had such an exile forced on him, and wondered what he did there all day, but even she had to admit a gatekeeper was probably necessary. Even if Shadow's Gate were located out in the middle of the rural countryside, it was a truism of modern life that no place was safe.

When she came in Truth heard quiet conversation from the salon she'd been conducted to on her first night here. She checked her watch and frowned. Seven o'clock. It had taken her over fifteen minutes to cover the five-minute drive to the house!

Perfectly reasonable, under the circumstances. You're starting to go on like a character in one of those Whitley Streiber books—you'll be seeing short big-eyed aliens next, Truth scoffed at herself. At least she still had time to wash up before dinner.

It had been a day so full that events which would otherwise take center stage seemed to have paled into insignificance. Her "vision" of Thorne—the other children—her reconstruction of the history of Shadow's Gate, and the hints of its true nature—the red stag and the white mare—

all battled one another for pride of place, and all were insensibly diminished by the fact that Caroline Jourdemayne was dead.

But even that was wiped out by what Truth found when she opened the door to her room.

Except when sick—or exhausted, as she had been last night—Truth Jourdemayne was meticulously neat about her person and in her belongings. This morning before she'd left the house, she had carefully tidied away everything she had brought with her into its appropriate shelves and drawers until the room was once more almost uninhabitedly neat.

But when she came into her room that was not what she found there.

The drawers of the antique bird's-eye maple dresser were ajar, their disheveled contents peeked up in puffs of fabric, and the cheval-glass was knocked askew. The robe that Irene had loaned her was lying in a heap on the floor—while Truth had hung it carefully in the closet just this morning. The entire room bore the marks of a hasty—yet ruthlessly thorough—search.

The book! Her heart raced sickeningly as she fell to her knees beside the bed and scrabbled between the mattress and the box spring, searching. . . . It was gone, she knew it was, and the loss of it was more than she could bear—

A whimper of relief escaped her as her fingers closed on the spine, and her hands shook as she pulled the book out of its hiding place, undamaged. Truth closed her eyes tightly, tears of relief prickling at her eyes as she clutched *Venus Afflicted* to her chest, her body shuddering in the pure tension that seemed to be Shadow's Gate's gift to her.

This must never be allowed to happen again! Truth thought vehemently. She needed to find a safer place to store Blackburn's priceless grimoire—a place that could not be broken into at whim.

This isn't like *me*—Truth thought in a flash of despairing insight. Why did this house turn her into the next thing to an hysterical madwoman—and why did she keep coming back?

It isn't hysteria. It's reasonable, that alien inner voice assured her. *There is work here for you to do.*

She shook her head, trying to gain control of her haywire emotions. They all seemed to center on the book—maybe if she could put it somewhere safe these out-of-character panic attacks would stop. Recklessly, still clutching the book, Truth dumped the contents of her purse out on the bed. Tape recorder, extra cassettes, notebooks—the purse Truth carried was plenty big enough to hold *Venus Afflicted* and most of its original contents besides.

She slipped the book inside and folded the top flap of the purse over to conceal it. There. She'd just go down to the car and lock it in the trunk, and then come back up and find out just who the *hell* had possessed the brassbound gall to rummage through her possessions as though they were on a bargain-basement sale counter!

She swung the purse, newly heavy, up over her shoulder, and stopped. She might as well take the jewelry down too.

But when she went to look for it, it wasn't there.

Truth, anxious and angry and getting angrier by the moment, scrabbled through both of the top drawers of the dresser as roughly as any burglar. The ring and the necklace were gone.

Stolen.

Who? The question made her laugh aloud, and the sound was edgy and overwrought. Who *wasn't* a suspect? Normally she'd just suspect Fiona Cabot, who didn't seem to have any too many scruples, but considering what was missing—ritual jewelry belonging to Thorne Blackburn and nothing else—anyone could be a suspect: Ellis the cynic, Michael the mystic, Julian—who pretended to a detachment he couldn't possibly have—Irene. . . .

I hate these people! I hate this place! All I want to do is leave! a small voice inside Truth cried furiously. But it wasn't true any longer—if, indeed, it ever had been.

There was Light to think of. Light—who might even be her sister.

She hefted the bag higher on her shoulder and left her room.

Truth's only intention was to get out to the car, stash the book, and nip back in before anyone was any the wiser—unless, of course, she just got in and drove like hell. It might, in fact, be the most sensible thing to do—she could call Julian later and tell him Aunt Caroline had died; that would be reason enough for anyone . . .

Leave now and the others take what is yours.

Unfortunately for her plan she got turned around at the foot of the stairs and found herself passing the door of the room that held the Blackburn collection, a path that took her in the opposite direction from the front door which was her goal.

The door to the room was open.

Truth put her hand on the knob, intending only to close the door, and recoiled with a convulsive jerk. The handle was ice cold—as cold as if it were buried in a snowbank in deep winter. Even from so brief a contact, her fingers were tingling and numb.

Unnaturally cold . . .

Cautiously, Truth pushed the door open wider. It was dark inside, the high windows flanking the fireplace casting back the twilight afterglow. There was a fire in the fireplace too, the merest line of orange coals.

Automatically, not thinking it would really work, Truth flicked on the light switch. She felt a leap of pure scientific triumph as the fixtures overhead lit normally, then sank back to a fraction of their normal brightness, as if the power allocated for their illumination was being diverted to another purpose by some unknown agency.

Then she saw Light.

The girl was wearing the white robe Truth had seen her in the night before. She was curled in a fetal ball before the dying coals of the hearth, her hair spilling out around her like a silver spider-silk shroud. Truth couldn't tell whether or not she was breathing. If the room were as cold as the doorknob seemed to indicate, Light could not survive in there much longer.

Truth did not hesitate. Her purse over her shoulder, she took a step into the room. In the moment she crossed the threshold the bitter cold struck her to the bone. She'd been right. Getting Light out of here was vital.

She glanced up at the painting over the fireplace. Something was different about it, and after a moment she realized what it was. The painted figure of Thorne Blackburn was wearing his amber necklace and signet ring.

Oh. How very interesting, she thought with a numb detachment. She did not have time to marvel at irrelevant ghostly sendings now or to wonder what such omens meant. Only the length of the dimly-lit room separated her from Light, but to cross it was an effort equivalent to scaling the outside of a building under her own power.

As she moved forward, the wide-planked floor seemed to tilt and shift under Truth's feet, as if it were a part of some demented fun-house entertainment. Around her the room seemed to warp and shimmer as if viewed through water. She could no longer see Light, and could only pray she was going in the right direction.

Was this what Elijah Cheddow had seen, the night he tried to end the curse of Shadow's Gate by destroying his entire family?

The cold was more bitter than that of any winter she had ever known, weakening her as if she were bleeding from an open wound. As Truth forced her way farther into the room, it occurred to her for the first time that the rescue she had undertaken so rashly might not be possible, that she and Light might both die here—slain by the unreal.

It seemed horribly absurd to be fighting for her life against the nebulous paranormal here while scant rooms away there were people talking and laughing and thinking about their dinners—and living. . . .

Time lost all meaning, as in the farthest reaches of delirium. For some reason, after a while it seemed better to crawl, and so Truth was on her hands and knees when she reached Light.

The girl's body seemed cramped and lifeless, her white flesh hard and cold, but Truth, grimly determined, wound her numb and frozen hands in the girl's robe and pulled. Light's body shifted and began to slide in the direction of the pull. Truth stopped once to use the table to haul herself erect, then resumed her bleak burden.

Her blood was a sick thunder in her head, and the oxygenless air gave her no life. To stop was to die, but Truth knew she did not have the resources within her to go on. But no matter how close she was to death, she did not even consider abandoning Light.

Suddenly strong arms—arms from the First World, the world of life—circled her waist lending her strength as they dragged her backward. For one desperate eternal moment Truth thought that even this would not be enough to prevail against the force sucking her down into that room, but then the balance of power shifted, and they were free. Truth staggered backward over the threshold, Light's chill frailness a slack weight in her arms.

The cold ceased instantly.

"Julian!" Truth gasped, seeing their rescuer at last. "Oh my God—"

Julian's normal equanimity had been sorely tried. His handsome features were drawn and there was an expression almost of fear beneath a rigidly imposed calm.

"What—?" he said, looking about as if dazed. Then he knelt beside Light, taking her icy fingers in his hands, and his whole manner changed. He cradled the unconscious girl against his chest and then seemed to realize that would not help.

"Are you all right, Truth?" he asked, looking up at her. "We have to get her warm—she's freezing."

Truth nodded, shakily. She was shuddering with the cold, her teeth chattering with chill and reaction, but Light's more immediate danger outweighed her own.

Julian stood, lifting Light in his arms, and headed for the stairs. Truth staggered along behind him, glancing back as she did so.

In the Blackburn Library, the lights burned brightly and the flames of a roaring fire leapt in the fireplace. Above the mantelpiece, the painted figure in the gaudy painting wore neither necklace nor ring.

She followed Julian upstairs with Light, her muscles aching with returning warmth. The girl's room was two floors above Truth's, in what had once been servants' rooms. The only thing above this should be the front and back attics and the four tower rooms, which, although Truth had seen lights in them indicating their occupancy, she did not know how they could be reached.

The door that she opened at Julian's behest led into a small cozy room with a slanting ceiling. Curtains of crisp white lace hung at the window; as Truth drew them shut, she could see the many angles of the roof of Shadow's Gate and a bit of the central cupola below. She turned back as Julian was laying Light down upon the bed. He began to undress her with the clinical impersonality of a doctor.

"Her nightshirts are in the dresser. Get one out for me, will you?"

She found them without difficulty. Julian held out his hand for the gown as Truth returned, but Truth clutched it to her, staring at Light's frail, oddly immature body.

Thin white scars criss-crossed her back and thighs, and here and there was the deep violet crater of a cigarette burn.

Julian yanked the gown from Truth's hands. "What are you staring at? I told you she'd been in an institution," he said roughly. With deft gentleness, he worked the gown over Light's slender form. The girl's eyes remained closed, and she gave no sign of consciousness.

"She's been *tortured*!" Truth said, outraged.

"Always considered a compelling form of argument by

those who feel that others should see the world they way they do," Julian said, with tired viciousness. "Did you think *I'd* tortured her? Light the flame under the chafing dish— I want to heat her some brandy," he added matter-of-factly.

Julian covered Light tenderly as Truth found the chafing dish with its tea-light and a large box of wooden matches sitting on top of a low wooden cabinet. She scratched one alight, touching it to the charred wick of the small candle and then holding her hands out to the warmth. She was feeling better now, though she wondered if she'd ever really feel warm again, and Light had been in that room far longer than Truth had.

"Julian, don't you think we should get her a doctor? I mean—"

Julian rounded on her, gentling his expression with an effort. "Telling him what? That she nearly froze to death in front of a roaring fire in a closed room in October? Even if I could come up with a suitable lie, Light is terrified of strangers. I won't subject her to that."

He came over to the cabinet and opened its doors. Truth was surprised to see that it was filled with a variety of sweet snacks, from dried fruit and trail mix to candies made of crystallized honey and maple sugar, as if it were some naughty child's hidden store of goodies.

Some of its contents, however, were far from childish. Julian took out a bottle of brandy from the trove, and the package of crystallized honey.

"You give sugar for shock, and all forms of psychic power constitute some kind of shock to the system," he explained, "a drain on the vital energies that must be replenished." He poured a white china mug half full of brandy and set it over the flame Truth had lit, then added chunks of what Truth could only describe as dried honey until the cup was full. "Alcohol is one of the quickest ways of shutting down the *chakras*, the centers of psychic power that lie within the human body along the spinal cord. It's easy to misuse it, which is why so many of our people start out as Adepts and end up as alcoholics."

"Like Ellis?" Truth asked. She sat down on a stool beside Light's bed and reached beneath the heated down comforter to clasp one of Light's chill hands in her own warmer ones.

"If you like. The Abyss is the greatest challenge to the development of any magician. Most of them fail the test in one way or another—like Ellis. Who knows what would have happened to Thorne?" Julian said absently, stirring the gaggingly-sweet concoction with a teaspoon. "A few minutes more," he said, peering at it.

Truth gazed anxiously down at Light's still face. She was breathing normally, if shallowly, but her face was so still, so pale . . .

The memory of what they had both experienced in the library returned, and on the heels of thought came Truth's instinctive denial. Thorne's picture had not changed. *You imagined it.* Although why she should be willing to admit the cold, the disorientation, the darkness had all been objectively real and only the hallucination of the change in the painted image purely her own invention made no sense. Was she afraid that something of Thorne Blackburn survived at Shadow's Gate after all these years—survived, and moved, and acted?

"Julian, we have to talk."

"Agreed. Ah, I think it's warm enough. Lift her up, will you?"

"Shadow's Gate is haunted," Truth went on doggedly, doing as he'd requested.

She winced at the coldness of Light's skin, chill even through the flannel, and wished there was some way to warm her more quickly. But she wasn't even sure of what had happened, let alone how to treat it.

"Shadow's Gate," Julian said firmly, "is a nexus for the powers raised by the Blackburn Work, which we are engaged in performing here." He spoke in the didactic tones suitable to soothing the fears of a small child. With cup in one hand and spoon in the other, he approached the bed.

"It was a focus for paranormal activity long before

Thorne Blackburn was ever born—he bought it for its reputation as a haunted house!" Truth argued.

"Was it?" Julian asked with indifference. He carefully worked the spoon between Light's slack lips, dribbling the honey-brandy mixture over her tongue.

"You're not going to tell me that what happened tonight was a manifestation of Thorne Blackburn!" Truth said, trying unsuccessfully to suppress the memory of the transformation of the photo and the visitation of the night before.

"I bow to your superior knowledge of the Blackburn Work," Julian said coolly, conveying another spoonful of liquid into Light's mouth. Was it Truth's imagination, or was a little color returning to the girl's pale cheeks? "But if there's really something to discuss, we can do it once Light is settled."

Spoonful by spoonful Julian fed Light the mixture, until by the end of the mug there was a pale stain of color across her cheeks. Her skin seemed warmer, and her breathing had deepened into natural sleep. Gently, Truth laid her down and tucked the covers up around her again.

"All right," Julian said, laying aside the spoon and mug. "Now we'll talk. Come with me."

Julian's room was on the same floor as Truth's, on the opposite side of the hollow square forming the second story of Shadow's Gate. He had taken, as was nearly inevitable, the master suite of the house, the rooms that Thorne Blackburn would have had a quarter of a century ago.

He led Truth into a room decorated in gray and dark blue, its furniture typifying the opulent modernity that was the mark of Julian's possession of Shadow's Gate. Truth sat down gratefully on a couch of dark gray velvet that cupped her body like a sheltering hand.

"A drink—we both need one." Julian moved to the sleekly modern rosewood liquor cabinet and poured, bringing Truth two fingers of amber fire in a short heavy glass.

She sipped, and felt its revivifying heat slide down her throat and enter her blood.

"What are you going to tell the others?" Truth asked after a moment.

"The truth—as I perceive it. Thorne indicated in his magickal diary that once the Work was begun, manifestations of this sort could be expected. Of course, Light is especially vulnerable, being a medium attuned to the Work. I'll warn her, and make sure Irene stays with her—she'll know the dangers better than anyone."

Julian sipped at his drink, leaning back against the cabinet, the lean, angular, male lines of his body faintly gilded by the light from the lamp. An aura of danger hung about him, as if he were some great jungle cat—but unlike the tigers in the zoo, Julian Pilgrim was not safely caged.

"And if the cause is something other than Blackburn's . . . work?" Truth said, with what she felt was admirable restraint.

"The precautions should work just as well," Julian said briefly. "But I'm sorry; I'm tired, and so it sounds as if I'm being flip. I don't mean to minimize your own involvement—and bravery. Whatever you believe the cause to be, at least we agree that the danger tonight was mortal. You did wonderfully in the face of it."

It was a little disturbing to Truth to realize how happy his praise made her feel; how cherished—as if nothing were good or bad, worthwhile or worthless, until Julian had passed judgment on it and told her what it should be. Somewhere deep inside herself, Truth recognized the insidiousness of this new trap and began, instinctively, to fight it. She drew a deep breath before she spoke.

"I've discovered some things about Shadow's Gate that lead me to believe that it's the focus for paranormal energy—or, as laymen say, that it's haunted. I've found out enough about its history to make a pretty good argument for knowing the primary source focus of the phenomena; it could probably be fairly easily neutralized. I'd like to gather more evidence, though, so if I could just put a call in to

the Institute, they could get a team over here by the weekend; Monday at the latest. They won't be in your way—"

"No." Julian smiled to take the sting out of it, but his
refusal was absolute.

"But—Please see things from my point of view, Julian;
an opportunity of this magnitude, with such potential for
documentation—"

"With such potential for sensationalization, you mean:
'Ghosts Walk in Murder House'; 'Blackburn Haunts Shadowkill.' I'm surprised at you for falling prey to such animal superstition; the only thing Shadow's Gate is haunted
by, Truth, is memories, and I'm not going to have my house
overrun by pimply-faced grad students in *Ghostbusters*
T-shirts at such a critical time in my work."

But it was precisely during this critical time that the
haunting needed to be investigated. Manifestations could
feed off psychic talents—Dylan's team often "fed" a ghost
to make it appear. Experienced researchers could trigger
psychic phenomena at sensitive sites—and even, according
to some researchers, *create* it out of nothing more than the
human will.

Was this so very different than magick?

Whether it was or was not, the need for studying—and,
on the basis of her experience this evening, dissipating—
the psychic energy at Shadow's Gate was vital. She had to
find some way to persuade Julian that she was right, but
Truth already knew that a head-on collision was not the
way. She must divert the subject and lead it back around
at a more propitious time.

"There's something I need to know about Blackburn,"
Truth said quickly. "I think you'll know the answer. Were
there any other of Blackburn's children at Shadow's Gate
in nineteen sixty-nine?"

"Well, yes," Julian said, almost apologetically. "There
was Light."

Truth gaped at him, thinking this was almost too pat.
Julian saluted her with his glass, in token of the fact that
he was about to deliver himself of a lecture.

"Thorne, as you'll already have noticed, was not unattractive to women. We know of at least two dozen women with which he had, shall we say, relationships during his career, and that hardly begins to count the, er, one-night stands. There were about fourteen women among those people living at Shadow's Gate in nineteen sixty-nine, and it's fairly clear that Thorne had slept with all of them at one time or another. In light of all this, it's actually surprising that he didn't father more children, and not just the ones we know of."

"How many were there?" Truth asked.

"There's you, of course," Julian said, smiling faintly. "There's Light, whose mother was probably a woman named Debra Winwood—nobody's really sure, including Light, and Winwood's dead now so we can't exactly ask her."

"So Light is my sister," Truth said slowly. A sister, lost for all these years, but hers now, to care for and to cherish. "What happened to her, after . . . ?"

"Well, when the police closed the place down after the mess in 'sixty-nine, most of the children living at Shadow's Gate ended up going into the so-called child welfare system. The only reason you escaped was because you had an aunt to take you—and because she looked pretty respectable. The others were simply . . . confiscated, vanishing into foster care. It took me years, and thousands of dollars spent on private detectives, to find Light." Julian splashed his glass full again and took a long pull of the fiery spirit.

"Were there others?" Truth prompted.

There was a long hesitation before Julian spoke. "A few. I'm not really sure; no one in Blackburn's Circle seems to have thought it very important to note the parentage of the children at Shadow's Gate."

"But surely Irene . . . ?" Truth said.

"Irene does not remember . . . quite what she thinks she does. Asking questions to which she has no answers will only upset her," Julian said.

This was the second time that Julian had cautioned Truth

against questioning residents of Shadow's Gate. Why?

"What can you tell me about the children?" she said.

Julian smiled disarmingly. "You're being very patient with me. I'm afraid I don't know much. Blackburn's children haven't been lucky—yourself excepted, of course. There was one more that Blackburn acknowledged, but he's almost certainly dead by now."

There was a pause. "Who?" Truth said, when it became obvious that Julian would volunteer nothing more. But when he spoke, he was so forthcoming that Truth decided she'd imagined his reluctance.

"Your—and Light's—half-brother, born back in 'sixty, as far as I can tell, mother unknown again. Thorne seems to have taken an atypical interest in his children, keeping them with him and seeing to their care. It almost makes up for his rather original sense of naming."

"Truth and Light," Truth said, with a rueful smile. "And the boy?"

"Pilgrim," Julian admitted. "It gave me quite a turn to find my surname there in one of Thorne's magickal diaries, but it's a rather intriguing coincidence, nothing more. The boy got his name from the fact that Thorne considered himself a pilgrim in the world of men, an emissary of the *sidhe*."

"I see," Truth said. She suddenly remembered, with a palpable flash of disquiet, that her purse—with *Venus Afflicted* in it—was downstairs where she'd dropped it, probably in the Blackburn Library. She wanted to leap up and reclaim it at once, but that would be far too suspicious. The purse was shut. No one had any reason to go through it.

But thinking of it reminded her that there was a way she could get what she was after.

"I hope you'll change your mind about having the house investigated, but that decision is certainly yours to make," Truth began craftily. Julian frowned sharply, but she ignored it. "And by the way, I nearly forgot to say anything in all the fuss, but someone's been in my room. Some extremely valuable pieces of jewelry are missing."

Julian's turquoise gaze fixed on her with sharp intensity.

"Do you think I ought to go to the police?" Truth asked, striving to keep her voice innocent.

Their gazes locked, and held. Truth did not back down; she felt neither fear nor shame—only the clean bright joy of crossing swords with a worthy adversary, using weapons understood by both. Her heart beat faster, and both pain and weariness were washed away by the hot, resplendent tide of conflict. There was nothing of man and woman in it, nor of rich and poor: This was how equals strove, on equal terms, to see which brow would carry the wreath of triumph.

And so, avoiding the snare that was the dark side of trust, the abdication of all responsibility, she stepped into the opposite trap, although she did not realize that for some time to come.

At last Julian laughed and looked away. "You'll understand that I don't want any strangers here—but I don't see why you shouldn't hunt for all the ghosts you like, providing you can do it by yourself. We'll help, of course—in fact, when I consider the matter, it might be valuable practice for Donner and the others to see what approach Dame Science takes to the Hidden World. But no one else, Truth."

The terms were plain.

"Thank you," Truth said warmly. Getting Julian to do what she wanted was exciting, as if it gave them some sort of intimate connection that could be a prelude to further intimacies later. "I'll call the Institute tomorrow and see if I can get them to ship me my beads and rattles," she added lightly. She'd won, after all, and could afford to be generous.

Julian crossed to her and took the empty glass from her hands, effectively signaling the end of the interview.

"We'd probably better go on down to dinner. They'll have saved a plate for us, so we don't need to hurry on that account, but I told Irene to hold back dessert—there's an announcement I've been wanting to make. Go on ahead; I'll follow in a few minutes."

*   *   *

Truth, intent upon reclaiming her purse, was only too happy to go. In light of the earlier manifestation she entered the library warily, but everything was normal, even to the hagiographic portrait of Blackburn over the mantel. It was odd to think that an event of such magnitude could have occurred here less than an hour ago and disturbed no one, but Shadow's Gate was a big house and well made—in all probability, the others in the house had heard nothing.

And so much for a certain someone's claims of great psychic power! If Fiona were as sensitive to paranormal phenomena as she claims, she'd have been right here!

Truth tried to be sorry for her poor opinion of Fiona—after all, she barely knew the woman—but she couldn't manage it. Fiona Cabot was a type Truth had encountered often while working at the Margaret Beresford Institute: people who used the justification of great psychic ability to excuse a complete inability to adhere to even the most basic standards of common politeness. And the nastiest ones, Truth found, were the least psychic, as if possession of that gift ran by some inverse relationship to boorishness.

She found her purse sitting right where she'd dropped it on the library floor. A quick glance inside revealed that its contents were undisturbed. Truth breathed a heartfelt thanksgiving—to whom, she wasn't sure—and slung it up over her shoulder.

A flutter of movement at the front of the room caught her eye. It made her jump, but after a moment she saw what it was and relaxed. Only a curl of paper-ash blowing across the floor in the breeze from the forced-air heating.

But what papers were being burned *here?*

Reluctantly, Truth passed to the front of the room. That papers had been burned was patently obvious; the grate was choked with them, to the point that page upon page, only half-burned, filled the fireplace on each side of the grate. She wondered how she could have missed seeing them before: even from here she could see the lines of handwritten purple scrawl that covered them, turning to black against brown at the charred periphery.

She knew what they were. She'd seen them her first afternoon here.

Why—and *who*—would be burning Irene's various attempts to reconstruct the Opening of the Way ritual from *Venus Afflicted*?

Had Light done it—and if so, why? Was burning the pages the thing that had triggered the event that had nearly killed her?

More unanswered questions. Hitching her purse up higher on her shoulder, Truth headed for her car.

She returned to the house a few moments later, purse and book both safely locked in the trunk of her car. She missed the jewelry, but no matter how it had vanished, tomorrow would be soon enough to look for it. Now to see if she could find the dining room again without a Sherpa guide; Shadow's Gate had a certain fey instability when it came to the locations of its rooms.

Despite her misgivings, the house did not seem to intend to play any more tricks tonight, and through a half-open door Truth saw a familiar room. She stepped inside.

"—more time. You can't expect the results you want in the time you've allowed."

Irene.

Truth stood in the entryway of the salon where she and the others had all gathered for drinks two nights before. Through the now-closed sliding doors at the end of the room the dining room could be reached.

"I *need* the results you say I ask for. Without them I have no choice, save to act, or to countenance evil where it blooms, and so destroy myself as well. All the time in the world cannot change that, or my nature, or the nature of what I fight. And I don't think there is any more time, Irene," Michael said in his faintly foreign inflection.

The voices were coming from a small alcove—what had

been the telephone room during the house's Gilded Age. Truth took a step backward, out of possible sight. They hadn't heard her.

"There must be," Irene said, and now Truth marked the desperate note in her voice. "There must be! It isn't fair for you to judge—not yet. I've had so little time to—" Irene's voice dropped suddenly, and Truth had to hold herself back from stepping inside in order to hear better. In a moment Irene's voice grew intelligible again. "—father's seed. I think there is change already; in a few more weeks I know everything will be fine. I've worked so hard, Michael—all my life—it can't all have been for naught. If you'll just let me—"

"Do what you can." Michael's deep voice cut through Irene's words with a tone of dismissive finality. "And I will do what I must. Don't you see, child? This is no judgment—I, of all creatures, have no right to judge the shifts that others are driven to. It is a prophecy. I see no alternative before me but intervention—"

Michael's voice broke off abruptly, and when it resumed it was so soft that Truth had to strain to hear it.

"Weep not, daughter, for this ending was written in the Book of Life before the world was made, and in the end there is nothing either of us may do to erase a line of it. You have done your best, in service to your master—now you must let me serve my own."

Truth didn't stay to hear more—she wouldn't have been able to manage many more minutes of silence anyway, not with all that mystic talk of serving masters in the air. But elitism aside, there had been real sorrow both in Michael's voice and Irene's. What sort of delusion had they cooked up between them this time?

And about whom? Truth frowned. She'd assumed, after the conversation she'd had with Michael yesterday, that they'd been discussing *her*, but it could as easily have been Light—or even Julian. She tried to reconstruct the dialogue she had just heard, but the phrases kept slipping from her tired mind. Something hadn't changed, and time was running out, and now Michael and Irene were whispering in corners about it.

Julian wouldn't like that. If there was one thing Truth was sure of, it was that.

But when she finally reached the dining room—having taken the long way around—she wondered if the whole overheard conversation had merely been another haunting, because both Irene and Michael were there, seated at the table, as if they hadn't stirred from their seats at any time in this past hour.

Truth stepped into the room, blinking a little at the brighter lights. She glanced about herself for Julian, only to see him coming in behind her. The seat at his right was vacant, and a plate with a warming cover over it was placed on the table before it.

"Will somebody tell me what's going on here?" Fiona demanded shrilly.

"No," Hereward told her kindly. He smiled and his white teeth gleamed wolfishly.

The gray wolf. Realization struck Truth like a shove between the shoulder blades, idiotic and undeniable. Hereward was the gray wolf.

Exhaustion and alcohol caught up to her all at once, drugging her senses into a spurious half-dreaming state in which manifest impossibilities became plausible realities. Hereward the gray wolf was one of the four Guardians of the Gate—but where were the others?

She glanced around the table. To her dazzled perceptions, each of the diners seemed to wear another face above his own: Caradoc, the vulpine features of the Trickster; Donner, the wide, bland face of some animal she couldn't identify. Gareth's *anima* was faint, more a hint than a true seeming; Fiona's a jumbled impression of a glittering eye, and a sharp black beak—or needle fangs.

She would not look at Michael with this doubled sight. The same inner prompting responsible for these hypnogogic visions told her that she must not, and she obeyed. But she *would* find the others.

Ah. Here he is, she thought to herself with mazed satisfaction. Over Ellis Gardner's features hung, somehow, the nimbus of the black dog. But where were the white mare and the red stag?

She looked toward Julian, expecting to see the stag's golden horns—and received the greatest shock of all, for over Julian there was no halo, no nimbus, no spirit mask.

Over Julian there shone nothing at all.

CHAPTER NINE

STRANGER THAN TRUTH

What should I say,
Since faith is dead,
And Truth away
From you is fled?
—SIR THOMAS WYATT

"WELL," JULIAN SAID, AS TRUTH TOOK HER SEAT. "I SEE everyone's here now. Light won't be joining us, I'm afraid; she isn't feeling well."

Irene made an abortive move to rise; Julian smiled her down into her seat again. Truth thought he looked frazzled, somehow, although he'd seemed to be all right when she'd left him in his sitting room a few minutes before. The strange, half-fey mood that had possessed her when she'd entered the dining room had vanished with the sight of his face: People and things were now, once again, no more than they seemed, and Truth was able to dismiss the visionary insight as nothing more real than a waking dream.

Or nearly. Was this other vision the way Light saw the world all the time? Truth thought of the fearful scars she had seen on the younger woman's body and shuddered inwardly. If one did see the world in that guise, much, much better to keep it to one's self.

Truth looked down at the covered plate before her. It was still warm; the scent of meat and gravy rose up from it, making her stomach lurch profanely. The last thing she wanted in this moment was something to eat.

"I have a small announcement to make," Julian went on, "and I thought I'd take this opportunity when you are all gathered together here to make it. There is a change to our working schedule."

The announcement seemed far too innocuous to be the cause of such tense anticipation, but looking about the table, Truth could see clearly who was caught in the Blackburn mystique and who was not. Most of the men—Ellis, Donner, Caradoc—fairly vibrated with it. Gareth merely looked puzzled, as if there were something he wanted to grasp but could not; Hereward seemed aloofly intense.

But Irene looked worried rather than interested, and Fiona was clearly more interested in looking well than in anything anyone else had to say.

"As you know, we have been unable to re-create the material lost with the disappearance of *Venus Afflicted*. Despite this, we will be moving forward with the Blackburn Work. We will open the Gate on All Hallows' Eve, two weeks from tonight. This will be a full working, with all Initiates robed and sealed as to their Grades. I realize that we are under-strength, so that some of you will have doubled roles, but I think we can make it work. Now . . ."

It was bizarre, really, how Julian managed to make it all sound like an RAF briefing in an old WWII movie. Truth tried not to smile as she reached for her wineglass. All this work and all this fuss; this wasn't what magick was. . . .

"Julian, you can't be serious!"

Irene Avalon stood, facing Julian down the length of the table. The garish makeup she wore tonight made her look cruelly older, and the light from the chandeliers glittered off her earrings as she trembled with agitation.

"You know that Thorne meant that ritual to be done at Beltane—at the rising tide, not the falling one!"

"And so that was when he tried it—but did it work?" Julian asked rhetorically. "No. It did *not* work. It failed because not enough power was available in the rising tide, which is why I propose to use the falling tide instead."

"The falling tide; the *qlipothic* energies . . . It might work," Donner said slowly.

"Oh, dearie me, yes—and if a cow had an engine she'd be a Volkswagen," Ellis said waspishly. "Julian, I've been involved in the Work for more than twenty years. A little reconstruction is one thing—"

"Look—you don't know anything better!" Gareth told Ellis, rising a little out of his chair.

"I don't suppose it's worth suggesting that we try it Thorne's way first, and then yours?" Caradoc said, pitching his voice intentionally lower than Ellis or Gareth's.

Julian smiled. "A prudent suggestion, Caradoc, and worthy of your position in the Temple—only Halloween is in two weeks and Beltaine is six months after that. I don't want to wait another year to inaugurate the New Aeon, do you? We'll try my way now—and if that fails, we'll give Thorne's method a try in six months."

"You won't *live* to try Thorne's way!" Irene burst out. "Julian, Thorne knew that the powers of the falling tide were not to be lightly broached. He said it wasn't for humankind to tamper with chthonic energies, only the tellurian ones—the powers manifest in the *living* world. The chthonic powers are prehuman—*in*human—involvement with them is too dangerous; the Lodge isn't full strength— you don't even have anyone to work the higher Grades! You said—"

"Look." Julian leaned forward, palms on the table. "Unless we're going to go in for human sacrifice—and may I remind you all that even *that* didn't work in nineteen sixty-nine?—we need to find some other way of pouring more power into the Opening of the Gate that we will be able to raise and focus next Spring. We don't need a lock pick for this Gate—we need a crowbar. Now. I've recently found out some things that I'll share with you at the proper time and place, but I'll tell you now that I think that the forces we can evoke at Hallows will give us that crowbar. If we start preparations tomorrow we've got just time for the run-up to the Opening of the Gate—if you're all with me."

Silence stretched—but Julian, Truth realized, was too canny to break it. She had the frustrating sense of standing at a fulcrum point, where events could be changed as she willed, and lacking the knowledge to do it.

"What do we do about not having the ritual?" Donner asked.

"We work with what we have," Julian answered promptly, "and improvise the rest. And in opening the Gate, we complete Thorne's life's work and usher in a new golden age of gods and men."

He had them; Truth felt the weight of acceptance shift as if she stood on the tilting deck of a ship. They would do Julian's bidding at Samhain, even though they felt it was wrong. He'd dazzled them, just as Thorne Blackburn had dazzled his circle a quarter of a century ago, innocent of what the end was to be.

And despite all of Julian's promises, Truth was filled with growing dread that it would end the same way this time.

Truth didn't remember afterward what dessert had been or if she'd eaten it. She'd drunk more wine than she'd meant to, but couldn't feel any effect. Every time her mind veered away from remembering the hauntings plaguing Shadow's Gate—and *her*—the chill fact of Aunt Caroline's death would challenge her bruised psyche once more. Aunt Caroline was dead, and Truth was filled with a dangerous sense of failure.

What had she left undone that she ought to have done? What had she done that she ought not to have done—and what could she do to remedy matters? *Too late, too late, too late, too late* . . . The voice echoed in her head.

It was a relief to rise from the table when the others did. They were going about their business—Thorne Blackburn's business—and she felt an aversion growing toward Blackburn's work that was entirely different from the unreasoning hatred she'd brought with her.

She glanced toward the end of the table. Michael was standing behind his chair, gazing toward Julian with a look of anguished hunger in his eyes.

So might the damned in Hell gaze on Paradise, Truth thought, then wondered where the oddly rococo reference had come from. Her mind seemed to be sliding toward theology frequently these days, dragging up the massive questions of Good and Evil that she'd used to feel were so irrelevant to her twentieth-century life.

Michael, sensing himself watched, looked away from Julian and glanced toward Truth. She tossed off the last of her wine and turned away, unwilling to meet his midnight gaze.

'The evil that men do lives after them. The good is oft interred with their bones,' Shakespeare's words, retrieved from the lumber-room of memory, were a fitting garment for her thoughts. Evil had certainly survived its maker here at Shadow's Gate, if what she had uncovered today at Shadowkill library held any truth at all.

And where, oh where, did Michael Archangel fit in to all this? Not a follower of Thorne Blackburn, but here at Shadow's Gate for some reason he found overridingly important.

What?

She'd worry about it tomorrow, Truth decided. Whatever it was, she was too tired to think about it now. All she wanted was a bath and bed. Whatever mysteries Shadow's Gate held, surely they could wait until she was rested enough to deal with them.

But when she ascended the stairs it was not toward her own room that her steps took her, but toward Light's.

Her sister. If she could believe Julian, of course, but in her heart Truth knew that she hadn't needed Julian to tell her what the truth was. She had known Light was a part of her from the first moment she'd seen her.

A *sister*. Truth cherished the thought, and the others that came with it—that Light did not have to stay here, that Truth could take her away with her, care for her, love her as she had always longed to have someone to love.

Someone who was safe.

The stab of unwelcome self-analysis jarred her, demanding examination, but she put it aside as she put so many things aside these days. It would have to wait. As if the house approved of her goal, she reached Light's room without difficulty and pushed open the door.

A night-light burned on the table beside the bed, filling the small room with soft amber glow. Light lay sleeping just as Truth and Julian had left her. Her cheeks were faintly flushed, and her breathing was deep and regular.

Truth stepped inside and closed the door. Relief eased the tautness in her body, as if she had reached some sort of haven by reaching this room. She lifted a wooden chair and carried it over beside the bed, intending to sit for a while beside Light before seeking her own bed and whatever absolution she might gain in sleep.

She set the chair down carefully and took a moment to glance at her watch. Ten o'clock. It had certainly been a busy evening, all things considered.

"I don't know why you're carrying on so over the jewelry."

A man's voice, with the faint drawl of the stage-trained. Truth jerked as if she'd been struck and glanced wildly around, but the door was shut. There was no one in the room save for her and Light.

"If it belongs to anyone, it belongs to me. Caro didn't have any right to take it, and no right at all to give it away, even to you."

Horror crawled over Truth's skin like serpents. The mocking male voice was issuing from Light's mouth.

"Who are you?" Truth forced herself to keep her voice

low and even, lest she waken Light—and see *who* staring out from the girl's eyes?

"A prophet is without honor in his own country."

With the clinical detachment of shock, Truth saw Light's face twist in a sardonic grin, although the girl's eyes were closed and she still gave every evidence of being asleep. "You're not Saint Peter—how many times are *you* going to deny me, Truth?"

Even if Light were the greatest mimic who ever lived, Truth did not think she would be able to produce that undeniably masculine voice with such effortless exactness.

"Three times is traditional," she said evenly.

"Very well. This makes three, then—next time you should know me. And if you really want the jewelry back, it's in the top drawer of the dresser—but I warn you, it's mine. Take it, and you'll be taking more than you bargained for."

So you're claiming to be Thorne Blackburn? Truth bit down on the words before she could say them. She didn't want to hear the answer. Instead, she walked over to the dresser—two steps—and jerked open one of the top drawers.

The ring and the necklace were lying atop a neatly-folded pile of linen.

"You'd be surprised what I've bargained for," Truth said, forcing the words out past numbness.

There was no answer.

She turned back. Light was sleeping, undisturbed.

"Blackburn!" Truth's voice was a whip-crack in the stillness. Light stirred and murmured fretfully in her sleep. There was no other response.

Truth ran a hand through her hair. *I'm losing my mind. I know I am.* She turned back to the drawer and lifted out the necklace. She put it on, slipping it under her sweater. The amber beads warmed instantly, while the gold remained a chill heaviness against her bare stomach. She picked up the ring and slipped it into a pocket of her skirt.

Think. You can't afford hysterics. There's no such thing

as magick. You've dedicated your life to that. But that doesn't rule out the rest of the paranormal. Treat this just like any other haunting. I only wish I knew—

"What's going on here," Truth muttered aloud. She stroked the amulet through her sweater for reassurance. There were real-world explanations for everything that had happened here tonight. Light must have wandered into her room, found the jewelry, and taken it. Psychometry and Light's mediumistic gifts would go far to explaining the rest—she was only lucky Light hadn't found *Venus Afflicted* as well; she'd have to make a better hiding place for it than the trunk of her car.

"Truth?"

This time the voice was familiar. Light. Truth returned quickly to the side of the bed and took Light's hand.

"Did you see him?" Light said.

"See who, honey?" The unaccustomed endearment came easily to Truth's tongue. She tightened her grip on the small cold fingers placed trustingly in hers.

"Thorne," Light said. "He comes and sits with me sometimes." She yawned, as unaffectedly as a very young child. "I'm so sleepy," Light complained.

"Do you want to tell me what happened tonight?" Truth hated to press her, but this might be her only chance to ask these questions before Julian spoke to Light.

Why do I think that? Julian's been nothing but kindness itself to me since I got here—and he'd never hurt Light.

Light regarded her with sleepy trust, and Truth's guarded heart surrendered before the innocent onslaught. Light was hers, blood of her blood, hers to protect.

"Thorne and I went down to the library," Light said, unaware of the effect her words had on Truth. "He wanted me to get out some papers for him."

"Why didn't he do it himself?" Truth asked, voice carefully neutral.

Light giggled, as if Truth had said something wildly amusing. " 'Cause he's incor*po*real, that's why! And he can't touch things, mostly, because it—" another jaw-cracking yawn—"it dissipates the charge, especially if there's iron. So I did it."

"And then?" Truth asked.

"They burned," Light said, plainly uninterested in further answers. Truth remembered what Julian had said about Light and questions, and decided not to push her any further.

"They burned," Truth said. "They sure did. Why don't you get some sleep now, okay?"

In answer Light turned over, snuggling down deeper into her pillows. In moments her breath had deepened into sleep again.

Truth waited a moment longer, then tiptoed off, closing the door behind her carefully. Thorne Blackburn was dead. Like Marley's ghost, there was no doubt about it. And unless a more loquacious and well-preserved ghost than any previously documented in the annals of parapsychology was roaming Shadow's Gate, Light had not had the conversations with Thorne Blackburn that she'd said she had.

Come to that, *Truth* hadn't had the conversation with Thorne Blackburn that she seemed to have just had. Because there was, there could be, no Thorne Blackburn speaking through Light—only a fragile mind crumbling away into madness and delusion.

Even counterfeit magick could be destructive to the fragile psyche. Truth had to get her sister out of here before more damage was done. She had to stop Julian from using Light in his rituals.

But how? Truth wasn't sure just how old Light was, but if she was Blackburn's child Light had to be in her middle twenties at least—well above the age of consent. While Julian could not keep Light here against her will, neither could Truth make Light leave with her.

There seemed to be no easy answers. If Light would not cooperate, what could she do? Truth could not bear to subject either herself or her newfound sister to the glare of publicity that would result if she tried to call in the authorities to enforce her whims. Perhaps even a descent into

madness here at Shadow's Gate was better than the insti-
tutional cruelty that had left its vivid marks on Light's
body.

She reached her room without incident, and opened the
door cautiously. No one was there—though no one could
have been, of course. Not really. She entered with a sigh
of relief, and locked the door behind her. Then, catlike, she
began to tidy away all sign of the room's having been
searched, hanging up clothing and straightening dresser
drawers once more until all that remained of disorder was
the pile of books and notebooks on the bed.

Crossing to the window, Truth opened it and inhaled a
lungful of sharp October night air. Below, the grass was
green where the light of the house fell upon it, black beyond. She craned her head, but could not see the cupola of
the center room no matter what she did. When she looked
up toward the sky, she saw that the cloud cover had broken,
and the waxing moon's silvery crescent was a bright spark
through the trees. Half-full now, it would be full on Halloween, less than two weeks away.

When Julian was going to do his ritual, and trigger God
alone knew what manifestation of the uncontrolled psychic
power of that underground spring—unless she could pull
the plug on that power first.

She wished heartily that Dylan were here. Ghosthunting—and ghost-*breaking*—was his field, not hers.

'*He can't touch things. It dissipates the charge, especially if there's iron.*' The echo of Light's words came back
to her. Was this the clue to ending the hauntings at
Shadow's Gate? Psychic phenomena and magnetism
seemed to have some odd as-yet-not-understood connection
that perhaps she could use.

Truth spared a moment's pity for Thorne Blackburn. She
was fairly sure now that he'd bought Shadow's Gate after
reading about it in *The River Where The Ghosts Walk*. Had
he known how strong the psychic locus was that he trifled
with here, or did he think all the reports of hauntings were
merely trickery and illusion like his own? Perhaps what had

followed hadn't been his fault at all, but the house, using him. . . .

Truth gave herself a sharp mental shake. It was bad enough having to investigate Thorne Blackburn without making excuses for him! A "haunted" house could not have a will—hauntings were merely expressions of personalities that had attached themselves to locations in life, with no more independent will than a tape recording! Ghosts—possession—discarnate spirits—all belonged to the shadowy borderland between parapsychology and the occult, a frontier that Dylan Palmer and Colin MacLaren were satisfied to explore and Truth Jourdemayne stayed clear of. She would stick with things she could measure.

As for Thorne Blackburn, he was hardly a candidate for the role of victim. Blackburn had ruined the lives of everyone who'd gone running after his New Aeon paradise, and even after his death his reputation attracted others who were more than willing to take up his discarded mantle.

Even, Truth conceded with reluctance, Julian. Julian, who thought of himself as continuing Blackburn's work—who sought to finish it even now?

And what would Julian and his followers do when they realized that their magick had not worked this time, because magick did not work, ever—

Are you sure, Truth? an inner voice whispered, and even though she wasn't, Truth recoiled with desperate self-preservation from a world where magick was afoot, and chaos was alive in the world.

"Investigate the haunting," Truth muttered to herself, beginning to pace back and forth in front of the open window. That meant cameras, recorders—delicate expensive equipment that the Institute wouldn't just hand her for the asking. Even Dylan had trouble sometimes convincing the director to let it off the premises.

Dylan. If she called him and explained, he'd help her. He'd understand when she explained that Julian didn't want anyone else here.

He had to.

Oblivious to what she was doing, Truth wrung her hands. Dylan had to understand, had to help—without him, she couldn't do what she had to do.

But have you ever given him any reason to help you? an alien inner voice asked.

Truth slowed, stopped. Friends helped each other. Was Dylan her friend? He'd tried to be. *She* was the one who'd held back so that no friendship had grown—the way she'd held aloof from every proffered relationship for as long as she could remember. Now she wanted to use him, in the name of a friendship that did not exist—except, perhaps, in Dylan's own desires.

If that is the price, then you must pay it. Surrender yourself and make his dream real, if that is the price of his help, the inhuman inner voice said. *We pay our debts. That is the law. Who binds us in obligation has bound us for all time; this is the law of the blood.*

Truth felt the pressure of insight—or of fantasy; she could no longer tell—pushing behind her eyes, and forced it down with a fury mixed with terror, knowing it would merely come to her in dreams instead, the cold, unemotional Other that drew its strength from this house and the land it stood upon, that stood in the opposite balance from warm, human passion.

A passion Truth had always denied—until now, when she was offered the chance to root it out of her soul forever.

Truth groaned, sinking down onto the bed and doubling over until the gold medallion on the amber necklace dug into her skin. Human fallibility, or alien perfection—all her life she'd refused to make that choice, knowing that someday she must choose one or the other.

As Thorne Blackburn had chosen—and had chosen humanity, knowing it would destroy him.

"You're identifying too closely with your subject," Truth said defiantly aloud, and managed a shaky laugh. "It's called transference. And so, when any sensible person would pack her bags and go screaming into the night, you're going to start investigating bigtime."

She took a deep breath, acknowledging her fear—of change, of the unknown, of homicidal would-be magicians. First thing tomorrow she'd call Dylan—assuming she could find a phone that worked anywhere in Dutchess County—and see if there was any way she could get him to send her the ghosthunting equipment from the Bidney Institute. Then she'd see how Light was, try to have a sensible conversation with Michael, and—oh yes—try to continue the research for the biography that was the ostensible reason for her being here.

"Thorne Blackburn's message to the world: Don't buy any haunted houses," Truth said aloud. She wished there was someone here she could talk to. . . .

Irene. Truth grasped at the thought as at a straw in a malestrom. Irene had been here twenty-six years ago when it had all happened. She'd known Truth's mother—and Light's. No matter what Julian had said, Truth could ask her about the children, about Thorne Blackburn—even about the haunting. If she could get Irene to back her up about the danger of the paranormal manifestations here at Shadow's Gate, she might even be able to persuade Julian to let Dylan come to investigate.

Suddenly, desperately, Truth wanted Dylan here, if for no more reason than that haunted houses were his field, not hers . . . and perhaps because she could not go through all the rest of her life cataloging last chances and lost opportunities and not seizing any of them.

She'd talk to Irene tonight.

The decision, once made, brought comfort and new vitality—it was action of a sort. Truth smoothed down her hair and checked her face in the dresser mirror. She looked all right.

Reasonably sane, you mean.

At the last moment she took off the necklace, tucking it and the ring in her dresser drawer. Then she unlocked her door and went out into the hall.

*   *   *

Time had done another of its odd slips, or else she'd brooded and tidied longer than she'd thought; the corridors were dark when she stepped out, their only illumination dim, widely-spaced lamps on hall tables. When she glanced at her watch the hour was rising midnight. Now, where to find Irene? Her first night here Irene had told her she was just around the corner; and hadn't Julian pointed out Irene's room tonight? Yes; he'd said it was right under Light's, on the floor below, now if she could only extrapolate from that. . . .

Perhaps unfortunately, it was not too difficult. Truth rounded the corner just in time to see the door she knew was Irene's open and a man come out. Truth froze where she was, hardly daring to breathe. Staring.

His blond hair was longer than Fiona's, rippling free and spilling down his back. He wore bell-bottom jeans, their legs flared with inserts of bright tapestry fabric, and a crocheted vest of multicolored yarn over a tie-dyed T-shirt. On his left wrist, where a watch would normally be, was a wide band, black in the dim light.

She knew that figure from a hundred photographs.

He pulled the door gently shut, his every move that of a young lover concluding a visit to the bedside of his beloved, then headed down the hall away from where Truth was standing, his step springy and purposeful.

Thorne Blackburn.

A ghost out of the past. A man with the wiry whipcord body of a generation past, before megavitamins, before jogging, before personal trainers. Whether ghost or living man Truth did not know, but she did know that the retreating figure was no one she'd seen yet at Shadow's Gate.

Funny. He's shorter than I thought he would be, Truth thought, choking back the bubble of perverse laughter rising in her chest. No point in wakening Irene now—if she were asleep.

What a tangled web this was—even with nobody trying to deceive anyone. She could just imagine Julian's reaction if she reported seeing Thorne Blackburn walking the halls at Shadow's Gate. It would be about what hers would have been a week ago.

What a muddle, Truth thought again, and turned back to her room.

When she opened the door she saw, with resignation, that someone had been here while she was gone—again. The books she'd brought from the library and left in a jumbled heap on top of the bed were neatly piled on the desk, and her notebook was open on top of the pile. At least whoever'd rousted her this time had been tidy about it.

She locked the door behind her, although by now there hardly seemed any point, and walked over to the desk. Her notebook was open to a page of biographical notes about Thorne, and was written across in the raking script she remembered from the photo albums.

'Lies, all lies. But so is truth, Truth.'

It was meant for Blackburn's handwriting, and at the moment she was willing to take it as such, impossible as that was. If real, this writing was one more reason to investigate. If someone had faked it—*why?*

Her body trembled with unshed tension as Truth put on her pajamas and got into bed, but she had no intention, now, of sleeping, and risking what she would find in dreams. She wrote in her journal until her eyes burned, meticulously noting and cataloging impressions, describing the hauntings with clinical detachment: the vortex in the library, Light's apparent "channeling" of Thorne, Truth's own sighting of him in the hall. She was a scientist. She would not theorize in advance of her data.

She scrupulously indicated on each what the margin for error, misapprehension, or simple mistake was. Except in the last case—by midnight Truth hadn't felt herself to be a very reliable witness—none.

A haunting—or, in the language of her profession, a Paranormal Event: something at the reality of which the mundane world scoffed as much as Truth herself scoffed at magick. But Truth, who had proceeded not by faith, but by works until now, did "believe" in paranormal phenomena, and knew it to represent a danger that these "magicians" were not taking seriously.

Truth shook her head in weary amusement. Julian thought he could control whatever the house planned to throw at him with a few spells and incantations, just like an ancient pagan throwing virgins into the volcano in hope of a sympathetic outcome—and with about as much effect.

Assuming, of course, she was right. But there could be no other explanation—or else her entire life was built on error.

She set her notebooks aside and turned to the books she had brought back from the library. Immersed in the early history of Shadowkill, she read through the night until the sun was well risen.

In the unforgiving morning light, Truth studied her reflection in the mirror. Her face was pale with exhaustion and lack of sleep, her eyes made more brilliant by the dark purple shadows beneath them. Well, so be it. She'd had white nights before, and survived them. She'd be fine today as long as she didn't have to do anything complicated— drive, for example.

Finding that the bathroom did not, after all, include a shower, Truth took a quick sponge bath rather than running a tub, using the cold water to further wake herself up. No matter what came dragging its chains around the bedroom tonight, she was going to have to get some sleep, or else admit to defeat at the hands of a bit of boiled beef, a crumb of underdone potato—to borrow a phrase from Charles Dickens.

She dressed quickly in khakis and a warm roll-neck sweater; a little informal, but she'd packed for crawling around dusty archives, not hobnobbing with folk on Julian's level. Well, maybe she'd walk into Shadowkill this morning and pick up a few things to spruce up her wardrobe. She doubted she'd be good for much in the realms of Higher Thought. All she planned for now was to check on Light and then brave the dining room in search of morning coffee, and see how things went from there.

But when she went up to Light's third-floor room, it was empty.

"She's gone with Julian," Irene said, looking in, an armload of folded linen proclaiming her purpose on the third floor.

In the pitiless morning light Irene looked almost raddled, the purple-and-gold caftan she wore seeming like some sort of bizarre costume. All the lines of her face sloped downward with a combination of exhaustion and unhappiness. Irene Avalon looked mortally ill, but Truth was suddenly without time for compassion.

"Where?" Truth said sharply. *Where has he taken my sister?*

"They're in the Temple. But—"

Truth didn't stay to hear the rest.

Round and round, round and down—she was really getting quite good at navigating Shadow's Gate, she thought with desperate calm—Truth reached the ground floor, and then the strange narrow hallway that led at last to the great central courtyard of the house. She skidded to a halt and tried one of the brass sunburst knobs.

Locked. The door was locked.

"Julian! Open up!"

Truth hammered on the door, reckless of the consequences of disrupting a session Julian might be holding with Light—but Julian *knew* Light was fragile, knew she'd been ill, how *dare* he subject her to this now?

At last, aching and out of breath, she stopped. For all the response to her pounding Truth might have been hammering on the wall of a house six counties away. She leaned against the wall, rubbing her bruised hand and panting.

Someone somewhere in this mausoleum must have a key—and she was going to get it.

The first stop in her search was the dining room. Ellis, she was sure, would have the key, even if he'd had to steal his own copy. But when she reached there, the solitary figure taking his ease was Michael, not Ellis.

"Where's Ellis?" Truth demanded tersely. "I've got to get into the Temple."

Michael was dressed, as always, with the odd formality Truth had first noticed in him: even at breakfast in his own place he wore his dark suit and silk tie. But Michael's clothes were not an extension of his power, as Julian's were. Michael wore his garments as if they were odd native dress, and he the patrician emissary of a great empire.

Michael rose to his feet at her entrance, gravely courtly. "I think he's still asleep," he said. "Julian kept them very late last night, and Ellis has a particularly elaborate part to play in their ritual. Truth, what's wrong? You're white as a sheet." He took a step toward her.

"I have to get into the Temple," Truth repeated with dogged desperation. "Julian has Light in there, and—"

She stopped when she saw the expression on Michael's face.

"Light in the Temple? She isn't in there," Michael said, surprised. "Julian's taken her on a drive in the country. You just missed them; Julian drove off about fifteen minutes ago. They're—"

"Damn it—" Truth's voice cracked with the fury of her battered emotions. "Which one of you am I supposed to believe? Irene told me they were in the Temple—and the Temple's locked!"

Michael regarded her almost with pity. "I would not lie to you, ever, least of all about Light. Perhaps they did go there for a minute or so, but I promise you I saw them drive away just as I have told you. And Julian always keeps the Temple locked, when they are not in it." He drew out the chair beside his own at the table and resumed his seat, his dark eyes on her face, watching her.

Truth sank slowly into the offered chair, already made ashamed of her outburst of violent emotion by Michael's quiet reason. It was true she had a right to be concerned over Light's welfare, but to fly off the handle like that—

"Tell me what happened last night," Michael said. Truth stared at him blankly, and Michael pushed the thermal carafe toward her. Truth found solace in the homely routine of pouring her morning coffee and the feel of the warm china of the cup between her hands. The first sip completed the restoration of her self-command.

Self-control. That's what Shadow's Gate destroys first. And then all the rest.

Haltingly at first, then more smoothly as remembered anger warmed her, Truth told Michael about the vortex in the Blackburn Library and Light's collapse.

"—and when I told him I wanted to get it investigated, he refused. At first," she hastily amended. "But I can't do it all by myself! And Julian has to understand that phenomena like this are *serious*; he's going to have to find someone other than Light if he wants to play Sacred Theater games. He can't use her any more—not after that."

"But you're wrong, Truth," Michael told her somberly. "It is just that sort of demonstration that convinces Julian that he is on the right track and must continue with his work—with Light."

As if he had said nothing so dramatic, Michael pushed the basket of warm breads toward Truth. The jam pots glittered in the sunlight, their contents tourmaline and amber and undying gold.

"He's wrong," Truth said simply, without emotion. She reached for a roll and considered her own words. They sounded odd, somehow. "You're wrong," she amended conscientiously. "Julian's a—He wouldn't do anything like that." *Would he?*

Michael sighed as if the whole world's weight wearied him. "We are so seldom right when we are sure what another will or will not do. You are a scientist, Truth. Would you cease your investigations simply for your own convenience?"

"No—but—"

"Neither will Julian stop. It has taken him many years and unimaginable sacrifice to reach the point he has reached. He will not stop. He has so little time, after all."

Truth frowned. Both Michael and Irene had spoken about how short the time was the night before. But for a man with Julian's resources—or apparent resources—this made no sense. If Julian Pilgrim was, indeed, what he seemed . . .

"Why? Why is his time short?"

Michael smiled, making her embarrassed for her Gothic fancies. "Simply because the Opening of the Gate that he attempts is not something he can do alone. It requires a minimum of seven people, and more, so I understand, would be better. And in addition to a working trance medium, Blackburn's conception also requires an, ah, Hierolator," Michael said delicately.

Truth had only the vaguest idea, even now, of what the Hierolator's—the Sacred Concubine's—place in the Blackburn rituals might be, but she knew it was Fiona's role. She felt a distant pulse of anger, as if experiencing the emotions rightfully belonging to another.

"It requires seven people," Truth repeated dutifully. She told over the names in her mind: Gareth, Donner, Caradoc, Hereward, and the rest. "But counting himself he has nine."

"For how long?" Michael said. "Magickal alliances are by their nature ephemeral. Julian holds these people here by the force of his will."

And by paying the bills, Truth thought derisively, but she could see Michael's point. Julian had no real authority, temporal or spiritual, over his fellow acolytes of the Circle of Truth. What kept them with him was hope of magickal results—or possibly of more material gains.

"He must act soon," Michael said. "He has said he will make his attempt at Hallows; I believe him. The danger to you will end with the sunrise. . . ."

"Oh, Michael, not that again," Truth said wearily. "What

do you think Julian's going to do—sacrifice me to the Great God Pan? I think I'm a better judge of character than that."

"I have never said that Julian was your danger," Michael reminded her, and Truth blushed at her own presumption. "The danger to you will come from knowledge. If you learn what I fear you will learn if you stay here, you can never go back to your old existence, never know its peace and simple joys."

"What makes you think I have any?" Truth blurted, and the self-exposure of that naked statement made the color rise in her cheeks again. She'd as good as told him that her life was empty, that there was nothing in it she would fight for.

Because all her life, Truth now realized, had been spent fighting *against*, in a blind headlong resistance that left her no time for self-knowledge.

"I mean, if it's so dangerous, why not tell me about it, so I can decide whether or not to leave," she added in a rush, to cover her feelings. "This isn't eighteenth-century Ingolstadt, Michael—there is *nothing* 'Man was not meant to know,' and all of us live, every day, with horrors beyond imagining. Famine, war—" She stopped, gesturing with her half-full coffee cup. "What could be scarier than AIDS? Or a drive-by shooting?"

Michael smiled bitterly. "If I explain myself so well that you understand and accept the truth of my words, I have failed, for you will already have learned the truth that I wish to spare you the learning of. As long as there is hope that you may remain innocent I must remain silent—for your sake."

Look, are you really a member of the Inquisition? Or just the IRS?

The flippant words Truth wanted to utter shaped themselves in her mind and she let them die unsaid. Michael was earnest enough to be frightening—Truth believed that *he* believed what he said, and since last night she was honest enough to admit that such belief didn't automatically mean the man was crazy.

Impulsively, she reached out, placing her hand over his.

"I'm sorry, Michael. I know you mean what you say. It's probably even true. But I just can't leave. I can't."

Reaching inward, Truth was mildly surprised to find she spoke the literal truth. If she left now for whatever reason, some essential piece of the mechanism that made her Truth Jourdemayne and not some other woman would be broken forever.

Michael's hand closed over her own, offering a sanctuary that Truth knew she could not accept and remain who she was. She had a sudden vision of herself as a moth, withering in the ruthless flame of Michael's holy cleansing fire.

"I will pray for you, and hope that you find the strength to go," Michael said.

"And I guess you and I will have a long chat on November first," Truth said, striving for lightness. Every instinct screamed to her to run from Michael—not from what he would do, but simply from what he was. She forced herself to stay where she was, holding his hand.

Child of Earth, this is not your place. . . .

Michael smiled at her, with the painful gentleness of a man once more shouldering a burden too great for him, which nonetheless he must carry until the end.

"I am sorry," he said regretfully, drawing his hand away and getting to his feet, and for that moment Truth could feel his sorrow like the tolling of a great bell.

Then Michael left the room, leaving Truth alone.

The morning sun glittered off the crystal drops of the unlit chandeliers, making even their brightness dull. The friendly room with its gracious Victorian furniture, brocade wallpaper, and matching velvet curtains looked as alien as if it had been assembled by Martians for some strange extraterrestrial rite. Truth stretched out the hand that Michael had held and gazed at it as if she'd never seen it before.

Who should she be and what should she do, when all the beliefs she had always held about the nature of reality had taken such a mortal wound? What if these people weren't crazy? What if their way of seeing the world, not hers, was right?

What if the father she had hated all these years was not a monster, but a hero?

The pain of the upwelling tears was like acid, driving her to her feet. "No," she whispered. "They're wrong. It's nothing but a stupid game. I'll prove it. I *will*."

The room housing the Blackburn collection was quiet and austerely calm in the morning sun, like a temple erected to the serenity of pure thought. *Lies*, Truth reminded herself forlornly, with a distant foreknowing that the battle she was fighting she must inevitably lose.

Just as she seemed to be losing her mind. Because if she could not have seen and heard the things she *had* seen and heard, what was left for her to believe in?

The room held a faint scent of lemon polish, and she saw that the hearth had been swept clean of all the remaining ashes. She wondered who had done the cleaning—in fact, who did any of the cleaning at Shadow's Gate. Surely it wasn't Irene, despite the fact that Truth had seen her obviously on the way to make up Light's bed this morning. Irene could not do all the work around Shadow's Gate by herself, though Truth realized that she had seen no servants other than Hoskins the cook and Davies his assistant. So if not Irene, and not Hoskins, who?

But small domestic puzzles of this sort really weren't her concern, were they? She looked at the fireplace again. She must remember to ask Julian what had been burned there, although she'd already had one answer from Light—or from what spoke through her.

If she was willing to believe in it.

And if she were . . .

No. With an effort almost physical, Truth pushed unreason from her, and gathered in all the armor of logic that had protected her all her life. There was a haunting here, nothing more. She walked toward the fireplace, and as she did, Truth felt a sudden twinge of cold, as if she stood in a draft.

But there had been no draft here before. What there had been, as of last night, was a major Paranormal Event, and for such a thing to be able to occur here, there must be some sort of focus—some place in the room where the activity centered . . . and such places were almost always marked by a cold spot.

Such as this might be.

How to test it? Even the possibility of proper equipment was hours in the future—assuming she could reach Dylan and gain his aid. But she needed answers *now*!

Truth glanced around the room and saw a litter of office supplies abandoned casually atop one of the lower book-cases. Among them was a spool of thin twine and a piece of blackboard chalk.

Those would do.

A butterfly clip made a workable counterweight to a makeshift pendulum. Truth cut a length of twine the length of her body less eight inches—long enough so that when she held it straight out at arm's length, the metal clip weighting the end would hang just an inch from the floor. In less than five minutes, her preparations were complete.

She stood at the edge of the place where she'd felt the draft and held her arm straight out from the shoulder, the pendulum hanging straight down. Dylan had said that the best pendulums were copper, for some reason having to do with electricity; Truth only hoped a steel paper clip was an acceptable substitute. She'd read his paper on the mapping of cold-spot phenomena that had described what she was about to do, but she'd never actually seen the procedure demonstrated.

She'd been afraid to. It was clear now. Parapsychology was fine when it was a thing measured by computers and laboratories, but confronting the wild science on its own turf was something she'd shied away from, afraid of what she'd see.

There was so much she'd locked herself away from, afraid to look at it clearly. So much opportunity lost. And now Michael wanted her to go on hiding—didn't he see that it would be like asking her to bury herself alive?

Gritting her teeth, Truth stood fast, gazing downward and waiting for the motion of the pendulum to subside. It circled lazily, swinging back and forth, going slower and slower as it settled.

But when it stopped, it did not hang true.

Truth blinked her eyes, trying not to disturb the pendulum's stillness. It was hard to believe her eyes, even though she saw exactly what Dylan's research had prepared her to see: the pendulum cord hanging from her fingers at an angle, the pendulum at its end pulling it out of true, as though some invisible magnet called to it.

Truth marked by eye the place her pendulum strained toward. When she moved, it swung into motion again, hanging properly as though its unnatural suspension had only been a trick of the light. She made a mark on the floor with her chalk and moved a few steps to the side, holding her pendulum out once more at arm's length. She felt the cramp begin in her shoulders as she forced herself to hold the pendulum steady, waiting for it to slowly swing to a halt.

Half an hour later Truth had an aching neck and shoulders, and chalk marks edging an irregular oval about a yard in diameter on its long axis. Inside this invisible perimeter, the temperature was at least fifteen degrees colder than anywhere else in the room.

Gotcha! Truth crowed silently. Once she'd set up the polybarometer to measure fluctuations here, it would be as if she held a stethoscope to the heartbeat of the house. Peaks and valleys in event activity would be echoed in the fluctuations of temperature and pressure here.

Truth frowned. That was all very well if true. But she was nine-tenths certain that the *spring* was the center of the activity—and the spring was under Julian's Temple, not here.

Wasn't it? Truth sighed, winding the line into a little coil around the pendulum.

And stopped.

She was being watched.

The knowledge came with the suddenness of a revelation, all the more shocking for the fact that she was facing the tall oak double doors that opened into the room and knew they had not opened.

She was alone in this room.

But the sensation of being watched was so intense that it was nearly pain, and Truth surrendered to it, dropping her careful coil and sending the pendulum spinning to whip around her as she pivoted to stare at the wall behind her.

The walls in the library had the usual ornamental molding common to houses of this age, but now there was a long dark crack running down the outside edge of the molding, ruler-straight as it crossed the wainscoting to disappear into the cracks of the floorboards.

A door.

She'd taken two steps toward it before she realized that whoever had made this hidden doorway visible might even now be standing behind it—and she did not, suddenly, trust whoever that might be to harbor only benign intentions. Truth hesitated, caught between curiosity and common sense.

There was a high ringing whine, of the sort produced by rubbing a wet fingertip around the edge of a crystal goblet. Then a thump, heavy and wooden, like an axe sinking deep into a log.

Truth spun back the way she'd come, to see the immense, gilt-framed painting of Thorne Blackburn, six feet high by four feet wide, slam edge-down on the carved white marble mantelpiece, shattering the bottom edge of the ornate plaster frame. She had just time to jump back, hearing the tiny flecks of broken plaster strike the floor with a pattering sound like hail, as the enormous image tipped majestically forward, slamming face down into the place that Truth had just been standing. Its impact made a booming crash like the thunderbolt of Judgment Day.

Truth gulped. The top edge of the frame was less than a

foot from her feet. If she hadn't started over to the hidden door, she'd be under the picture now.

The door.

She turned back toward it, and saw no line in the wall. Forcing her trembling legs to obey her, Truth walked over to the wall and ran her hand down it, searching for a sign of the door that must be here.

There was no door, no join, no possibility of a door. The paint was a smooth unbroken surface, impossible to fake. There could not possibly be a door here.

It might have been an hallucination—another parapsychological event, Truth suggested hopefully, and felt a familiar anger at having to do what amounted to taking a wild guess. She simply didn't know—there was no way to tell what the rules were any more.

She turned back to the wreckage that she could so easily have been a part of. Smashed plaster from the ornate gilt frame made a white starburst pattern against the yellow pine floor. Now that it was lying face down, it was easy to see that the portrait of Blackburn had been painted not on canvas, but on a slab of wood. Painting and frame together must easily weigh two hundred pounds. Truth felt a sick chill crawl up her spine. It could have meant a concussion, broken bones, or—worse. She groped toward one of the chairs and clutched at the back for support as she lowered herself into it.

Now that the immediate threat was over, reaction began in earnest, making her muscles dance and tremble as if they answered to another's will. Fighting off the sick chill that threatened to engulf her, Truth forced herself to focus on what had just happened. The picture had fallen.

Why? She no longer believed in coincidence.

Truth heard the sound of the door opening.

"Ah, hum," Caradoc said, standing in the doorway. "I, uh—" He looked from the fallen picture to where Truth sat. "Need any help?"

CHAPTER TEN

TRUTH OR DARE

There is nothing so extravagant and irrational which some philosophers have not maintained for truth.

—JONATHAN SWIFT

TRUTH LAUGHED HELPLESSLY, LOOKING FROM THE PICture to Caradoc's face. "Despite what it looks like, iconoclasm is not among my vices. It just fell down."

Didn't it?

Caradoc came toward her. The light turned his dark brown hair red where it struck it, giving his modishly short hair a faint, fiery halo. He stood beside her, staring somberly at the floor.

"Somebody," Caradoc said after long consideration, "is going to have to pick it up and get it back on the wall. Julian's going to be pissed."

He made this pronouncement with gloomy relish.

"The panel doesn't seem to be cracked, so the painting should be okay," Truth said as consolingly as she could manage, "but I think the frame's a dead loss." Caradoc snorted eloquently.

She looked up at the wall again. High up on its pale eggshell-cream surface, there was a small shining circle flush with the wall, like a bullet hole with the bullet still in it—the back half of the bolt that had held the picture hanger. She looked down and saw the rest of it. The front half of the sheared bolt was lying in the plaster dust almost at her feet. It was as thick as her finger and looked as though something had sliced through it.

"What a mess," Caradoc said again, bringing her attention back to him. "You're just lucky you weren't under it. I was going down to breakfast and I heard it fall—at least that's what I think I heard; it sounded like the crack of doom. I thought it was thunder, at first."

Involuntarily Truth glanced toward the window. The clear blue sky showed no evidence of storms to come.

"Oh, sure," Caradoc said as if she had spoken, "but we're going to have another tree-bender by tonight—you watch."

He hesitated, like one who was willing to stay but was not sure if his presence were welcome. Truth wondered how she must have first appeared to the inhabitants of Shadow's Gate to make him behave that way. Now more than ever, she could not afford to be isolated, set apart. In the battle to come, she would need allies, and she had waited far too long to find them.

She thrust the alien intimation aside, unwilling to let it distract her.

"Caradoc," Truth said, determined to find them some mutual ground and answer her own questions as well. "Has anybody ever mentioned secret passages here at Shadow's Gate? In the walls, or something like that?"

Caradoc frowned. "There's supposed to be one under the kitchen leading out to the barn—where a barn used to be, I mean, about a hundred years ago. But I think it was closed off from this end to keep the kitchen floor from falling in— back when Blackburn had the place, Julian said. And I know there're secret staircases in the third-floor bedrooms leading up to the towers. Julian showed them to me on the plans." Caradoc regarded her quizzically.

"But not in here?" Truth said.

"None at all on the ground floor, leaving out the kitchen.

There wouldn't be room for them, would there, with the Drum Room and the hallways around it?"

"The drum room?" Truth asked.

"The Temple. Some of us call it the Drum Room. It's round, you see, and when you're in there during a storm it's like being inside a drum—everything echoes."

"Hm." Feeling her legs were steady enough now, Truth got to her feet. She stirred the scattered plaster on the floor with the toe of her shoe and bent over to pick up the bolt. She turned it in her fingers, looking at the mirror-smooth surface of the cut. The bolt holding the picture to the wall had sheared clean through, without the jagged twisted edges of normal metal fatigue.

But if it had been cut, wouldn't it have fallen the instant it had been cut, instead of waiting until she was standing beneath it? And it *could not* have been cut the instant before it fell, unless Shadow's Gate was haunted by gremlins carrying CO_2 lasers.

She tried another subject.

"Look, Caradoc, what do you think of Julian moving the Opening of the Gate like that?" *And what do you think of it, Truth Jourdemayne?* Truth wondered, hearing herself speak.

Caradoc shrugged. "Maybe it will work out the way he wants. Although, you know, with magick, we could succeed and not know it for weeks. That's how magick is."

If you succeed, you'll know it in seconds. Truth could not say where that inner certainty came from, nor the despairing conviction that Caradoc had little understanding of the real perils of the Great Work on which he was embarked. His magick was a magick of allegory and gnosis, not sheer eldritch power.

"Magick is really about personal transformation, you know, not all that David Copperfield stuff," Caradoc went on. "I believe in what Blackburn was trying to do, and I can't think of a better time for the Gate Between The Worlds to be opened than now. The human race could really use some help, you know?"

Truth glanced up from the metal in her hands to Caradoc's face. His hazel eyes were alight with conviction—as if he had seen the problem of all the world's pain and seen, too, that there was something he could do to set his weight in the balance against it, a willingness that amounted almost to reckless gallantry, holding its own comfort irrelevant so long as mercy might be served.

Truth found the thought of such a passionate idealism profoundly disturbing.

"What do you think will happen if the Gate Between The Worlds is opened?" she asked, turning from the general to the specific. And besides, Truth was honestly curious to see what he would say. She needed to know more than her own opinions of the end result of the Blackburn Work if she was to go any further with this.

"Well, according to Blackburn himself, the realms of the gods and men were separated by the will of the Gods in prehistoric times. The memory of the separation survived as the myth of the expulsion from the Garden of Eden, but in reality it's the Gods who went away, not the humans who were driven out," Caradoc began, with the air of one giving a familiar lecture.

Truth waited expectantly.

"Well," Caradoc said. "Communication was always possible between the realms—that's what magick is all about—and of course the Gods could intercede in the human world at will, but once the Gate Between The Worlds had been closed humans could no longer move freely into the world of the Gods."

"And Thorne Blackburn was going to change all that?" Truth asked. It seemed a rather ambitious undertaking for someone who hadn't even been thirty when he died.

"The *Work* would change all that," Caradoc corrected her gently. "Blackburn felt that the Ritual of the Opening of the Way—it's two weeks of rituals, really, but everyone who talks about it talks as if the last one is all there is to it—would begin the chain reaction that would merge the realm of the Gods with the realm of Men again. And we could finally ask them why they left us."

Behind his quiet words Truth heard the crying of every abandoned child: *Why did you leave me, Daddy? Mommy? Don't leave me, don't* go—

"And the Gods would permit the reopening of this Gate?" Truth asked, voice level. She had her own reservations about Caradoc's belief that the Gods—if Gods there were—would simply let human beings knock down the wall They'd raised.

"Blackburn's philosophy held that anything Man was capable of doing, Man had a right to do; that the mind of Man should not be subject to the will of either Church or State. Of course, it isn't meant to excuse things like theft and mass murder," Caradoc added, an apologia Truth had the impression he made fairly often.

"Understood," Truth said briefly, although what she understood was that Thorne Blackburn's philosophy had excused a career of irreverence and license, self-indulgence and sheer folly, all in the name of Service to Higher Truth. Even putting the most charitable interpretation possible on Thorne's aims, humankind just wasn't meant to survive adherence to such a rarefied moral code. She wanted to say something more, perhaps even to explain. But she couldn't find the words, and the moment passed.

"I guess I'll go see if Julian's up—tell him about the picture," Caradoc said reluctantly.

"He isn't here. He went driving with Light, Michael said," Truth remembered.

She was relieved to see that Caradoc seemed to take this at face value. "He does that a lot. It seems to help. Poor kid. It'll be better for her once we open the Gate."

"How?" Truth couldn't help but ask.

Caradoc stared at Truth with faint impatience. "Once the Gate is open and the Gods return, Light won't be a freak any more. She'll be *normal*," he finally said.

"Your young men will dream dreams, and your old men will see visions.' Isaiah, isn't it?" Truth said.

"Something like that," Caradoc said, suddenly subdued. "Anyway, I'll catch Julian when he comes back. Want some breakfast?"

"No," Truth said, considering. "I've got some things to do. But thanks."

Caradoc left her then, and once more Truth had the haunting sense of a challenge met—or a test passed.

"Your young men will dream dreams, and your old men will see visions," Truth quoted to herself. But when the Biblical prophet Isaiah spoke those words, he had been speaking of the Eschaton—the end of time. The last days. Ragnarok. Armageddon. He could not have known what future centuries would make of his words.

But was Thorne Blackburn's interpretation that far from the prophet's? Didn't he mean the Opening of the Way as the beginning of the end?

If that were so, then what Julian intended to do was not some joyous ritual of enlightenment, but something darker. Much darker.

True to what Julian had told her—if not to the lavish promises of the cellphone company—Truth's newly-purchased phone did *not* work the first time she tried it within the walls of Shadow's Gate. It sat in her hand, silvery and dead, and Truth found herself taking the mile walk down to Shadowkill and its theoretically functioning and available telephones. At least the errand gave her the opportunity to move the necklace and ring from their concealment in her drawer to the safer sanctuary of the trunk of her car, allowing her to retrieve her purse as she did so.

It was all like some mad treasure-hunt-in-reverse; and Truth wondered despairingly how much longer she could keep one jump ahead of the unknown scavengers determined to pillage her treasures. Certainly these frequent trips to her car—when all her luggage was already inside— would make even the most trusting soul suspicious.

Alert this time to Shadow's Gate's uncanny influence, Truth had observed herself as best she could as she walked down the road to the gate. If she could trust her senses, Shadow's Gate exerted a perceptible influence on the emotions—or the imagination. Away from the site's influence, she discovered a strong urge to dismiss everything that happened there. Passing through the wrought-iron gates at the foot of the drive was like taking two Valium and a shot of scotch. No wonder she kept going back there, like the self-destructive heroine of a Gothic novel, if everything that happened there lost its emotional resonance once she left the property.

Intrigued, she tested it, something easier to do on foot than in a car. The boundary was not sharp-cut, and Truth suspected that it moved, but it was there. She wondered why none of the others had mentioned it. Maybe they didn't leave the property often enough—but Gareth spent at least part of each day in the gatehouse. Surely they'd noticed what Shadow's Gate was doing to them.

Unless it wasn't doing it to them, but only to her— Thorne Blackburn's daughter.

Grudgingly, she admitted that it was at least possible that the Shadow's Gate event was targeting her. At the very least, there had been an upswing in the number of Paranormal Events since she had arrived.

But targeting her how? Truth wondered, once she had safely arrived in the town. At Shadow's Gate she was on an abnormal emotional rollercoaster, true—but wasn't that a reasonable reaction to the emotionally-fraught investigation of her past? And if it was, didn't that make her calmness here and now abnormal?

Once that would have been an easy judgment—surely this was her normal state, and the hysterical fantasies she experienced at Shadow's Gate the illusion.

But Light *had* been hurt. The picture *had* fallen. Let anything else you like be dream or vision, Truth told herself, those things were real—just as real as the cold spot on the library floor. Something was going on in the house that had once belonged to Thorne Blackburn. And like the heroine in the Gothic novel—but for much better reasons—Truth would go back to Shadow's Gate again, and force the house to give up its secrets.

If she could.

"Dylan? It's Truth."

"Truth! Hey, this is great! Where are you?" Dylan was unfeignedly glad to hear from her, and Truth felt a faint twinge of guilt for the fact that she was only calling to beg a favor.

"I'm in a little place called Shadowkill. It's in Dutchess, I came here to see Shadow's Gate, and—"

The practiced phrases came easily to her tongue; the history of the house as she had unearthed it; her belief that it was a center of paranormal energy, the events that had occurred in the house so far.

"—just a little PK and some channeling; a cold spot in the library but I don't think that's where the real action is. There's a trance medium living there, and—" *And she's my sister,* Truth added silently. She went on explaining what she'd learned and what she'd guessed.

"—he's not really interested in strangers showing up around the place, but he doesn't have too much objection to the monitoring equipment, so I thought—"

She'd come back to the library in Shadowkill to use its phone, and was perched on the narrow, angular bench in its old-fashioned wooden booth. Through the glass door she could see the library information desk, and the rows and rows of books in their turn-of-the-century shelving beyond.

Shadowkill was a nice town, simple and friendly. Then why did she feel so afraid—as if there were something she would soon try to protect it from, and fail?

"What? Dylan, I didn't hear you." Abruptly conscious that her mind was wandering, Truth was jolted back to the present by the interrogative note in Dylan's tone.

"I said, why not let me drive up this weekend with a

truck and a couple of my grad students and set the stuff up and run a few tests. I can take you out to dinner, and—"

"No." The refusal was so instantaneous that it was rude, and she hastened to amend it. "Julian doesn't want any strangers here."

There was a pause. "Ah," Dylan said, and now some of the warmth was gone from his voice. "Julian, is it? The reclusive new master of Shadow's Gate?"

"Honestly, Dylan, you sound like a bad Gothic novel," Truth snapped. At the moment she didn't remember her wistful fantasies of opportunities lost; she was thoroughly irritated with Dylan and it was difficult to recall that she was trying to get him to do what she wanted.

"It's just that—Look, of course the man is filthy rich and could probably afford to buy the Institute's whole array out of pocket change—"

Dylan laughed. "Not unless his pockets are two point five million dollars deep."

"Well, they may be," Truth said, thinking of what she'd seen so far. There was a silence.

"He's doing the Blackburn Work," Truth blurted out suddenly.

"Does he know who you are?" Dylan asked carefully.

"Yes." *To the devil, a daughter.* "It's just that I— I have—My sister's here, Dylan, and—"

"I'm coming down there," Dylan said, cutting her off. "You don't know what you're getting into with these people."

His matter-of-fact assumption of the right to meddle grated on her sensibilities, but a chill distant part of her was amused—that this innocent should be presuming to protect *her*, all unknowing of what she was.

The moment passed.

"If *you* know, Dylan, then I'm worried about you," Truth said, fighting for lightness. "And I, of all people, know exactly what 'these people' are like."

"A sister. You said a sister," Dylan said. He sounded flustered.

"Blackburn fathered other children," Truth said baldly. "One of them is here. That's all."

There was a fulminating silence on the other end of the line that told Truth that, in Dylan's opinion, *that* was far from *all*.

This conversation was not going well at all. Had she always been this clumsy in her handling of other people? Or was it only because Dylan Palmer took the time to try to pierce her chilly armor?

A choice, her inner intuition whispered. *You have a choice to make here, Daughter of Earth.*

"Look," Truth said, trying to bring the subject back on track. "The important thing right now is to map the extent of the Paranormal Event taking place in Shadow's Gate. Julian's willing to have you bring a team up to the house in November and do anything you want, but I really think we need to start mapping now. I need you." *It's dangerous here, Dylan, but if I tell you that you won't listen to anything else I say.*

Truth broke off, sighing, and rubbed her forehead with her free hand. Her sleepless night made her bones ache with exhaustion, but it wasn't only that. Everything seemed to be tiring these days, as if her weariness formed the invisible walls that constrained her to follow the path appointed for her.

"I need you," she repeated, "to get me the equipment. The cameras. Some of the monitors. I know what I'm asking, Dylan—"

"No, I don't think you do," he said quietly, and the conversation died again.

"What do I have to say to make you do what I want?" Truth blurted out in frustration. If this was a sample of the sort of so-called normal life people were always urging on her, she'd stay the way she was, thank you. "I need those monitors. I need to *know*. Before someone gets hurt," she added in an undertone.

Over the long-distance line she heard Dylan sigh.

"Truth, it's not that—These monitors aren't cheap. Even

if I only bring up one of the barometric arrays and a camera . . . Do you know that film costs one hundred twenty dollars a roll? Which budget line am I supposed to hide those costs in?"

"I'll pay for it myself," Truth muttered.

"It doesn't work that way. Truth—" She heard him sigh again, and imagined she could feel his breath stir the tendrils of hair coiling against her cheek—and did that image repel or attract her? "What are you *doing* up there?" Dylan asked helplessly.

This time her emotions went spinning out of control, and her self-command shattered like a thrown plate. "What am I *doing*, Dylan? I'm doing what you and everyone else has always badgered me to do. I'm getting involved. I'm being reckless. I'm getting in touch with my feelings. Hell, I'm even getting in touch with my father." The laugh that followed was mocking and barely controlled. "I'm getting to know my father better, Dylan—isn't that something you'd think was appropriate?"

She felt the song of power rise up in her; the headiness of knowing that if she only chose to use it she had the ability to wound with a word, to change the course of others' lives, to force them to obey because she had the power to command—

"I'm coming up there and I'm bringing you back with me. And if this Julian of yours tries to stop me—" Dylan's voice was edgy, harsh. Truth could feel the tension thrill between them like a tight-drawn whiplash, shocking her back to the world.

" 'This Julian of mine' will rightly point out to you, Dylan Palmer, that you've got no grounds for treating me like a teenaged runaway," Truth said. She held her trembling voice even and low with an effort; every instinct urged her to shrill at him; if he were here she would *claw.* . . . "I'm a grown woman. I need that equipment. I thought you'd help me. You won't. That's all." Her hands were shaking. She took a deep breath.

"I'll help you." Dylan's voice was so low she had to

strain to hear it. "I'll see what I can sign out. Is there a number where you can be reached?"

She'd won, but the victory didn't make her happy. "I'm staying at Shadow's Gate, but the phone service isn't very reliable. I've bought a cell, only it isn't working either, most of the time. You can try them both, though." She gave him both numbers; he read them back to her.

Truth hesitated; Dylan did not deserve this treatment from her. "I'm sorry I snapped at you, Dyl. I—"

She wavered over telling him about Aunt Caroline's death, then recoiled from the thought of using her aunt's death to buy cheap sympathy. No matter what, she would not do that.

"I've been having some personal problems lately," she finally said. "And I'm worried about these people. They're playing occultist in a haunted house and I think they're playing with fire."

"And with the money you say this Julian's got, they can afford a really expensive box of matches," Dylan said, finishing her unvoiced thought. "If there's—If there's anything else I can do, Truth, just tell me. Maybe Colin—"

"No outsiders," Truth said quickly. "Julian . . ." What could she say that wouldn't rouse Dylan's misgivings again? "Just wait a few weeks, Dylan, okay? After Halloween everything will be all right." Even to Truth, the sound of her words had a forlorn echo: whistling past the graveyard.

"If you say so," Dylan said doubtfully. "I'll do what I can."

"Thank you," Truth said honestly. She wanted to say something more, but hated the thought of saying something that wasn't true. "When I needed help, I thought of you," she finally said. The words came with reluctant honesty.

She could hear Dylan's pleasure in his indrawn breath, and had a sudden disturbing insight into the strength of his feelings for her. She'd done nothing to deserve them; that Dylan felt so strongly about her made her feel trapped, almost unworthy.

No, not unworthy. Almost sorrowful, as if to love her was to court destruction.

"Well, just keep thinking of me, okay? And I'll give you a call tomorrow, assuming I can get through," Dylan answered.

"Sure." A few minutes later Truth hung up the phone, most of the conversation already fading from her mind, leaving the memory of Dylan's hurt feelings and willingness to help behind them like a psychic sore tooth. Dylan deserved better than to wait for a kind word from *her*.

For a moment she let her mind run free to speculate about what it would be like simply to talk with Dylan about inconsequential things, to wander across the Taghkanic campus with no ulterior motive or end in mind. To find out what Dylan Palmer was like—and what she would be like with him.

Then reality intervened like the closing of an iron-bound door. Even assuming Dylan was interested in such a colossal waste of time, why should he be interested in wasting it with her? If he knew what she was—

And what is that, precisely?

But he did know—didn't he? And he hadn't run screaming into the night yet.

Ready to run screaming into the night yet, Truth? Hereward's voice from the first night she'd come to Shadow's Gate echoed in her memory.

But this time the words weren't funny.

Truth dawdled in Shadowkill as long as she could, buying lunch at the Chinese restaurant on Main Street, browsing through all the pricey little boutiques for some accessories to freshen up her wardrobe. If she was going to be staying at Shadow's Gate for an extended period she was damned if she'd do it looking like a poor relation.

At one of her stops Truth found an exquisite chenille shawl in dark blue yarn; silver threads of Lurex woven through it gave it the look of the sky on a starry night, and though she had no idea what she might possibly wear it with she bought it on the spot. A long vest in bright patchwork velvets from the same store joined her purchases, and a pair of green onyx and marcasite-set silver earrings. She was on the street again, having regretfully decided she'd already spent far too much, when she saw the dress.

The store's name was *"innovations,"* and Truth had decided, looking at the chaste gold-lettered sign in the display window's bottom corner, that she'd better not even look inside. That was before she looked at the dress in the window.

It was on a dressmaker's form of woven wicker, and the sand-washed silk clung to the wicker's weave like poured cream. It was all the possible shades of green, from the blued fire of an emerald's heart to the peridot-yellow of a tiger's eyes. The silk had been marbled; the dye colors laid on with a wavy flame pattern of a book's endpapers.

The cut was simple—a princess line, with a sweetheart neckline piped in green velvet cord—but it was the skirt that truly made the dress special. Even seeing it hanging on the dressform in the window, Truth could see that the handkerchief hem of the skirt had been inset with a dozen gores of opalescent silk-illusion netting, giving the long skirt a fairytale fullness, as if one of Cinderella's ballgowns had wound up in the village of Shadowkill by mistake.

The dress sparkled.

"How much is it—the one in the window?" Truth found herself asking a few moments later. The saleswoman she spoke to was far too wise to answer straight away; she took the dress off the dummy in the window and handed it to Truth first. The fabric slid over Truth's hands like wintery cream, supple and heavy and gleaming in the light.

"It doesn't really need any jewelry," the saleswoman said cannily. "You could just tie a green velvet ribbon around your throat. I think I've got some back here if you'd like to see how it looks."

Truth held the dress up to the light. It looked as if it might fit her.

"How much is it?" she said firmly, refusing to be seduced by patterns like kingfisher wings against the sky, or a gleaming surface like mist on morning grass.

The saleswoman, defeated, named a figure approximately the size of one of Truth's weekly paychecks.

That isn't too bad, Truth found herself thinking. *I'd pay twice that in the city.* And she deserved something, some reward, some comfort, a dress to wear to the ball. . . .

"And that shawl you've bought will go wonderfully with it," the clerk said hopefully. Truth looked down at the tell-tale corner of Prussian blue chenille peeking out of one of her bags. She doubted the saleswoman could be right, but when she held them up together in the light from the window she saw it was true. Midnight and meadowsweet, and the wild freedom she had denied herself all her life, here for the taking.

"It probably won't fit," Truth said, grasping at straws.

"Oh, it probably will. Why don't you try it on?"

It fit, of course. Standing in the tiny dressing room, Truth gazed into the mirror and exchanged the sensible gold knots in her ears for the dangling silver earrings. The green in the long, lozenge-shaped stones echoed the greens in the shifting painted surface of the dress, and around her legs the skirt clung and swung, sparkling and flashing, showing bare limb here, patterned silk there, and at the next moment a froth of incandescent gauze.

When she swung the shawl over her shoulders a gypsy princess stared back out of the mirror, powerful and self-possessed.

Clothing is power. That's one secret the mages always knew. How you dress becomes who you are; you can put on power like a robe and become anyone you choose. . . .

She shook her head and the earrings flashed, and now the only thing out of place were the good brown sensible walking shoes Truth wore on her feet.

She left *"innovations"* fifteen minutes later with the

dress wrapped in tissue and boxed, a viridian ribbon still tied around her throat, and the address of the village shoe store in her hand. Who cared if there was nowhere to wear such a fabulous costume—she could make a place and a time to wear it, or wear it anywhere she chose.

When she reached the shoe store the woman sitting behind the cash register looked vaguely familiar. Truth stared at her, trying to place her.

"I'm Mary Lindholm, remember? The Bed-and-Breakfast?"

"Oh, of course. I just didn't expect to see you here," Truth said. "How are you doing?"

Mrs. Lindholm made a face. "The adjuster said he'd never seen anything like it—as if somebody'd taken the roof off and soaked the place down with one of those thirty-thousand-gallon-a-minute firehoses. The whole business is going to have to be rewired just to start; I just don't know how it could have happened. . . ." With an effort she roused herself. "So I'm helping my cousin out here just to get away from the mildew. And what can I do for you today?"

Truth explained what she needed. "I'm hoping to match this color," she added, pulling out the dress so that the green velvet trim showed.

Mrs. Lindholm smiled. "I think I have just the thing. What size do you take?"

She came back from the back room a few minutes later with a box in her hands. "I thought these were still back there; Roxy was supposed to send them back at the end of the season but she forgot all about it and the jobbers won't take returns after the cut-off date. Try these and see if you like them—I can make you a good price."

Truth took the box and looked inside. The pumps were green velvet with a gold Cuban heel studded in *faux* emeralds. The vamp of the shoe was garnished in gold lace and studded with more glass emeralds—shoes worthy of the Queen of Elfland. She glanced at the designer's name, gold-stamped on the insole, and gulped. No way could she afford these—especially after buying that dress.

But wouldn't it be fun to try them on, to pretend. . . .

Truth sat down and unlaced her sensible brown walking shoes. She put on the anklets Mrs. Lindholm offered her—she hadn't meant to be trying on dress shoes today and hadn't come prepared for it—and then slipped the shoes on.

She walked over to the mirror, conscious of the twinkling flash of the shoes at every step. She felt like Dorothy in *The Wizard of Oz*, only her shoes were emerald, not ruby.

"They're perfect," Mary said, and named a price that was only slightly more than the dress had cost—and a third of what the shoes ought to cost by right.

"But these are Stuart Weitzmans!" Truth said. The glamorous designer's shoes were the last word in elegance—and more than a thousand dollars the pair.

"We all have our moments of reckless indulgence," Mary Lindholm said. "Why shouldn't this be yours? Roxy saw them at a trade show and couldn't resist them either, but you'll notice they're still here. I told her they wouldn't sell in Shadowkill."

"You were wrong," Truth said firmly, handing over her charge card without a fight. Mary Lindholm was right. Let there be one reckless indulgence, one memorial to the woman Truth Jourdemayne might have been.

Truth stepped out of the shoe store with yet one more shopping bag, as breathless as if she'd outfaced demons, and knew it was time to go home.

On the walk back to Shadow's Gate Truth let her mind ramble, hoping her unconscious would come up with some answer to all of the problems and puzzles surrounding her. Her mind, unreasonably, refused to settle any of them, fastening instead upon the most nebulous and least urgent of her present concerns—her future.

What was she to do with the rest of her life? She had as much job security as anyone did, until recently she'd found the field of statistical parapsychology to be exciting and challenging, and her personal life was—

Was nonexistent. She had colleagues and acquaintances, but no close friends. Dylan was the closest thing to a friend she had, and she knew she'd taken unfair advantage of that this morning, trading on his kindness to get what she wanted.

Oh, but he doesn't want me! Truth protested inwardly.

Why not let him decide for himself? a Blackburnish inner voice responded. *Stop biting his head off every time the conversation veers beyond 'Good morning, Ms. Jourdemayne.'*

Okay. She might. But what was she doing with the rest of her life? Was she going to spend it sitting behind a desk at the Bidney Institute? If she wrote the book she planned to write about Thorne Blackburn and saw it published, things would inevitably change for her. Lectures, tours, fieldwork . . .

If she stayed in the field at all.

But at that point even imagination faltered, since if Truth were not working at the Bidney Institute or one of its sister organizations she could not imagine what she would be doing. For all the years of her life her tastes, education, interests, and training had led her to the field of parapsychology, just as if she were an arrow streaking unerringly for its target—or a religious with a calling.

But now for the first time she was taking a good look at herself, and, examining her past with brutal honesty, Truth wondered if her serene satisfaction with her career path weren't just one more link in what she now saw as a long chain of errors of judgment. What if her life had been aimed, not at parapsychology, but at its darker sibling?

Was Science her calling—or Magick?

When Truth came up the drive toward the house she could see one of the men—Donner, at a guess—riding a lawn tractor around in circles across the wide side lawn, its vacuum attachment sucking up the fallen leaves and leaving velvet greensward behind. He waved as he saw her and Truth waved back. Behind him, atop the rolling hills that were all New York State could claim in the way of mountains, thunderheads piled up, a more concrete promise of the coming storm than Caradoc's prediction from this morning.

Considering what had happened during the last storm she'd been here for, Truth thought it was a good thing that she'd be retiring early and sleeping hard.

Julian's sleek black BMW was back, parked under the portico next to Truth's Saturn and the white Volvo. Its presence reminded her that she needed to talk to him—and see Light. She shifted her bags to a more comfortable distribution in her arms and started up the steps to the front door of the house. As she gained the topmost step, Gareth came around the side of the house, dragging two enormous bags of lawn waste. He brightened when he saw her.

"Hi," Gareth said, abandoning the bags for the moment. "Been down to town? Say, did you hear what happened last night?" he went on before she could answer, his enthusiasm obvious. "And this morning? The Powers are gathering— Julian says we're already having manifestations of the Elemental Kings, and soon we should be seeing the astral vessels of the Guardians of the Gate as well."

It was peculiar, Truth reflected, and not for the first time, to see someone like Gareth, wholesome and normal looking in his worn denims and grass-stained T-shirt, spouting cant that belonged at some decadent Bloomsbury opium-and-absinthe gathering. To hear it in the cool Fall sunshine of the Hudson Valley was even more of a shock.

"Well, that's nice," Truth said inadequately.

Gareth grinned at her, the expression so endearing and normal that for just an instant Truth felt that *she* was the lunatic.

"But you were there—I forgot—you've *seen* it happen. Isn't it terrific?"

This time he stopped and waited, obviously expecting

her to agree—that psychic vortexes and falling pictures and ghostly stags were, indeed, terrific.

Only Gareth didn't know about the stag, because she'd told nobody about the animals she'd seen on her drive back to the house yesterday. Julian had prophesied that one on his own.

But if ghostly stags—and, she supposed, horses, wolves, and dogs—were a manifestation of the Blackburn Work and not a symptom of the Paranormal Event native to Shadow's Gate, what did that do to her theory that all of Blackburn's problems had been caused by his haunted house—not by his magick?

Which came first—the magick or the magician?

"Truth?"

"Oh. I'm sorry, Gareth. I was just—thinking."

"It's pretty awesome, being on the spot when the New Aeon starts, isn't it?" Gareth said cheerfully. "Say, are you sure you don't want to join us? You could probably go right through Neophyte and become a Zelator almost overnight, and then you could have the Freedom of the Temple and come to all the rituals and everything."

For a moment Truth hesitated. She didn't have the faintest idea of what a Zelator actually was, although it seemed to be the Blackburnian equivalent of a Brownie Scout, but the idea of being able to decide on the evidence of her own senses what was really going on in whatever rituals the Circle of Truth was holding now seemed more attractive than repugnant.

"Well, I'll think about it; good enough?" she said.

"Sure!" Gareth's delighted grin widened, and Truth had a sudden cruel insight that part of Gareth's pleasure stemmed from the status that being able to report he had gained even this tentative assent from her would bring him. With her growing intuition, she sensed that Gareth Crowther was very much an outsider here—in one sense, even more so than Michael was.

Because Gareth wanted very much to be a part of things here—and Michael did not.

Gareth's attention returned to the leaves. "Well, I'd better get a move on with these. We've got an incinerator on the grounds to burn trash like this, and there used to be a zoning variance for it, but the village says it's lapsed and they'll only issue us a two-week permit now, so we've got to store all of it until November. What a pain."

Truth smiled in sympathy. It was easy enough to imagine that the village's objections stemmed less from any real-world cause than from its profound unease with Shadow's Gate and its tenants. *All* its tenants, stretching back to old Elkanah Scheidow himself—

Who had bound what must be free, who had tampered with that which was inviolate, with that which would rage against its shackles until it was loosed to take its rightful place among Those Who Ride ...

Truth blinked, and found that Gareth was halfway down the upper loop of the drive, dragging the bags behind him.

"Gareth!" Truth called. He stopped. "I need to talk to Light—do you know where she is?"

"Out by the maze, I think. You can go around the house to get there—leave your stuff there if you want; I'll take it up."

"Oh, don't bother," Truth said. "I'll come back for it." She piled her bags on the settle bench to the right of the door. She only intended to be gone a few minutes, and after all, who was going to steal her things here?

She walked around the side of the house, through the portico where coaches once had drawn up to take on and discharge passengers in inclement weather. By rights there should be a carriage house somewhere in sight, but all Truth saw was the back terrace, the garden, and the boxwood maze off to the left. Maybe the carriage house had burned down.

"Light?" Truth called softly. She'd passed the house and drawn even with the entrance to the maze but she still didn't see Light anywhere. Hadn't Julian said that Light went wandering in the woods sometimes? If she'd gone there now, Truth could hunt until Blackburn's New Aeon showed up and probably still not find her.

Truth peered into the maze, wondering if Light were anywhere to be found down its white-pebbled pathways. The key to this maze was easy; like many of them, you simply alternated left and right turns in order to come to the center, and used the same method to leave.

Truth took a step down the path, and stopped when she heard voices. A moment later Light and Michael came into view. He had an arm around her shoulders, and Light was laughing up at him, her silver hair spread over his arm and lifting on the breeze like scrolls of cloud. Michael tapped her on the end of her nose with a finger, smiling, and she shoved playfully at his chest. Then they saw Truth.

Light flinched, like a child with a guilty secret. Michael watched Truth to see what she would do, but duplicity was not in his nature. He did not try to hide what Truth had just seen, or make her think that she had not seen it.

"Hi," Truth said, in what she hoped were neutrally friendly tones. "I was just looking for Light, and Gareth said she was up this way. I wanted to make sure you were all right after last night," she said, addressing this last directly to Light.

"Oh." Light looked uncertain. "I'm all right," she said hopefully, and it came to Truth that Light probably had no memory of the events of the previous night, only memories of all the other times that people had badgered her for information that she didn't have, about events she couldn't remember.

"Well, that's all right then," Truth said, smiling encouragingly. She wondered if Julian had told Light who Light's father was, and, if he had, if Light had made enough of a connection to realize that she and Truth were sisters. "I just wanted to see you again. That's all."

"You don't want to talk about Thorne?" Light said doubtfully.

Out of the corner of her eye Truth caught sight of Michael's faint warning frown.

"I don't want to talk about anything you don't want to talk about," Truth said honestly. "What would you like to talk about?" She spoke slowly and plainly, as if to a backward child, though there was nothing about Light that suggested impairment, only a *difference* so profound that the vocabulary to describe it simply did not exist.

Light giggled and hung her head, peeping slyly up at Truth through her lashes. "You know a secret," she said.

It took Truth a moment to realize that the pronoun she'd heard was not the expected one. "*I* know a secret?" she said.

Light nodded, still smiling. Truth looked at Michael, hoping for guidance.

"Do you think Truth wants it to be a secret, or will she tell it to us?" Michael said.

In answer, Light slipped out from under his arm and stepped toward Truth, holding out her hand. Truth reached out in return, and Light's fingers closed around her, in a surprisingly strong and assured grip.

"She's . . . worried," Light said, as if she were reading sentences in an unfamiliar language. "About me knowing? No, about what others will do when they know. But she still thinks it will be better if everyone does. Truth doesn't like secrets," Light announced, staring into Truth's eyes with a silver-eyed gaze.

Truth refused to be spooked by this demonstration, which might be anything from genuine telepathy to guesses so accurate they might simply seem supernatural.

"Light's my sister," Truth said to Michael, glancing up at him. Light's fingers tightened around hers. It had been the right thing to say, then.

Perhaps it was the proximity of the strongly psychic Light, but when their gazes met suddenly Truth imagined she could hear Michael's unspoken thoughts:

If you will not leave for yourself, won't you leave for her? Take her far away, keep her safe?

Truth shook her head reluctantly. *And what would you do with my sister, if you had the right?* she thought back.

"I've been talking with Light about her gifts," Michael said aloud, as if her were answering her unspoken question.

"Michael says I shouldn't see things," Light said, but not as if this disturbed her.

Michael says," corrected Michael, coming closer to the two women, "that all the human senses are a gift from God, and Man's gift *to* God is his discipline of those same senses."

"Meaning that Light shouldn't use her powers?" Truth interjected sharply.

"Meaning that we are sent to live in this world, and while we are here, our task is to fit ourselves for those things we will be called upon to do in this world, not to try and live in another. Light has great abilities, but it may be that her task in this world is to set them aside."

"Of all the—" Truth began, but Light's pressure on her hand stopped her. To be normal—was that so bad, when being different had brought Light such pain?

"You would not say that your sister should speak to every person she meets, much less invite them into her home. How much less ought she to do that when the visitor is unseen, and she has no one's judgment or help to rely upon but her own?"

"So you just want her to . . ." Truth couldn't think of a tactful description for what she thought Michael wanted.

"To accept the protection of One who will bar the door of her soul to any malignant forces," Michael said firmly. "To deny what she is when that is the handiwork of God would be impertinent, to say the least, but to deny her protection in her vulnerability would be folly." Michael smiled gently, to take the sting of fanaticism out of his words.

"I see *your* soul," Light said softly to Michael. She was about to say more, but Michael gently laid a finger on her lips.

"You must hush, or your sister will say I am a bad influence on you, a religious fanatic who believes that everyone must seek the Divine as he does."

"And are you?" Truth said boldly, carrying the war to the enemy.

"There are many ways to approach the Divine," Michael told her. "But only one of them, so I believe, is safe, and that safety was purchased at a cost of pain, sorrow, and tears that is being paid to this very day. But I perceive that I am annoying you, Truth, and you already think me quite tiresome. Shall I leave you with Light?"

"Oh—no," Truth said, thinking both of her purchases waiting for her on the front steps and how happy Light seemed with Michael—at least when Julian was not around to disapprove. "I have some things to do—I really did only want to see if Light was okay."

"Yes," Michael said. *For now*, his eyes told Truth. *But what of the future?*

When she got back to the front steps, her bags were gone. It did not occur to Truth that they had been stolen; she was baffled more than worried, until she remembered Gareth's offer to take them inside.

Must have done it anyway, she thought to herself. Gareth tried too hard to please, trying to buy himself a place in the Circle as if they would not grant it to him by right. Certainly checking her room would be the first thing to do.

When she stepped into the foyer, the faint salt-sea-sugar-pine scent of incense thrust her suddenly back to her first night at Shadow's Gate. She shook it off. Smell was the most primal of the five senses, the one most likely to trigger illogical associative memories. It meant nothing—other than, possibly, that the door of the Drum Room/Temple was open. She tried to remember if she'd smelled incense the one time she'd been in there and couldn't. She went on up the stairs, to find that the Temple's door was not the only door that was open.

The door to her room stood open, and Truth could hear rustling sounds within. Was Gareth unpacking her things as well? That was going a little too far.

Truth hurried through the doorway and stopped dead.

Fiona Cabot was in Truth's room, wearing one of her usual exiguous outfits—a bodysuit in burgundy crushed velvet with a translucent chiffon skirt—though why someone who desired respect so desperately should dress as if she shopped out of the *Frederick's of Hollywood* catalog was a riddle that Truth had not yet solved.

Tissue from the shopping bags was strewn all around the room, and the bags themselves had been thoroughly ransacked. As Truth watched, Fiona tried on the velvet vest— *Truth's* velvet vest—and turned toward the mirror on the dresser, admiring her reflection. As she turned back she saw Truth.

"Oh, there you are. I saw that blond idiot bring this stuff up here, so I decided to see if there was anything here I liked."

Her face was serene and untroubled. Truth had a moment to wonder why Fiona had been hanging around her room before being consumed with an anger so great it was literally paralyzing. "Get out of here," Truth said. "And take that off while you're at it—it isn't yours."

"Make me." Fiona's smile was an ugly thing. "It's like your dear old dad said—I've got the right to do whatever I want and you've got the right to cry about it. You're not going to yell to Julian because that'd make you look like a wimp and maybe he wouldn't let you hang around here any more, so I guess you're just going to put up with me."

Fiona stripped off the vest and threw it into a corner, then turned back to the shopping bags, humming under her breath.

"You . . . bitch," Truth said.

The hot anger was gone, replaced by a cold contempt and the wonder suitable to the discovery of a new species. She'd seen them in books and on television, but she'd never expected to meet with one in real life; a bitch; a woman who put as much thought and effort into making other people unhappy as most people did into making themselves happy.

Fiona turned back to her, smiling sweetly, and responded with a word so foul it actually made Truth's ears ring with shock to hear it. She picked up Truth's nail scissors from the dresser top, then reached into one of the bags at her feet and pulled out a fistful of marbled green silk—Truth's dress.

Truth took a step into the room, wondering if she could grab the scissors out of her hand before Fiona carried out her obvious intentions.

"I wouldn't," Julian observed mildly. Each woman froze, as if the remark had been addressed to her alone. "Fiona, my angel, have you been being naughty?" Julian said.

"Truth was showing me the new dress she'd gotten in town," Fiona lied silkily, "and I was going to trim a loose thread. Only I don't see it now."

She dropped the dress and scissors to the floor together and kicked them to one side, smiling at Julian with the perfect confidence of the woman who knows she will be believed not because she is truthful, but because she is beautiful.

"Fiona, darling." Julian's voice was warm and sympathetic, and Fiona flowered beneath it like a rose in the sun. Truth wondered that she couldn't hear the fury underneath; it spilled off him like smoke from a cake of dry ice, arctic and burning.

"If you ever bother Miss Jourdemayne again—in *any* way—I'm going to have Hereward drive you to the nearest bus station and you'd better pray you have enough money in your pocket for a ticket to somewhere because I guarantee the gravy train will have been derailed. I don't need attitude cases here at Shadow's Gate—which means I don't need you. I hope I'm being very clear?" he asked graciously.

Whatever Fiona had been expecting, it was not this dispassionately savage shaming. As Truth watched, the girl went so pale that her sluttish makeup seemed to lie on the surface of her skin, chalky and inert. Her eyes seemed to grow larger, brilliant through the lens of welling tears.

"Fiona?" Julian said, in that same mild voice.

Fiona gulped, her lips stretching in a sickly rictus of appeasement. She shook her head, unable to speak, the velvet costume suddenly lurid against the ashen pallor of her skin. Julian took a step to the side, and Fiona took the escape offered, running from the room.

Julian looked at Truth.

"I'm sorry," he said. "Are your things all right? I suppose it's no secret to you that magick—like parapsychology— attracts some inherently unstable personalities." He smiled ruefully.

The fury that Truth had felt Julian wield like a lash was gone, carrying all Truth's anger at Fiona with it. She felt drained but calm, her only emotion a faint pity for Fiona, who had been so brutally put in her place. Now, only a few minutes later, it was hard to believe the words spoken here—Fiona's and Julian's—had ever been said.

She walked over and picked up the dress, lifting the scissors carefully clear first. She inspected it closely, but Fiona's handling had left no marks on its shimmering surface. She draped it over one arm and went on to retrieve the vest. She wondered if she'd ever be able to wear it without remembering this scene. She laid both garments out on the bed.

"Pretty." Julian's verdict was frankly appreciative and frankly male. Truth found herself coloring slightly at a remark that was far more than casual—and at her reaction to it.

"It's like the old joke—'I saw it in the window and I just had to have it,' " Truth said, trying to deflect the compliment.

"You have good judgment," Julian said, couching his next tribute in more carefully neutral terms, though his smile was warm and intimate. "Any act of judgment is a risk. Most people are afraid to take risks."

"I'm not afraid," Truth said, meeting his eyes.

"No," Julian said with an inward smile. "I don't imagine that you are."

*   *   *

Dinner was a quietly hurried affair, from which Fiona was absent without explanation. The others, having by now accepted Truth's presence entirely, spoke freely in front of her—but in the technical vocabulary of high magick, which employed a terminology as alien to Truth as that of any physicist.

What, for example, was a Lesser Banishing Ritual? It seemed to be similar to a Middle Pillar Exercise, for all the good that information did her. Talk of paths, pillars, gates, and houses—and left- and right-hand trees—gave Truth the Mad Tea Party feeling she'd been dropped down into a gardeners' convention—at least until they started talking about operations and workings. She didn't know what any of this meant, but she was beginning to grant it a grudging respect.

Light was radiant, as caught up in this as any of them and in impish high spirits. All of the others, even Ellis, treated her as an adored baby sister, but Truth had seen what the others seemed to ignore—what the exercise of Light's powers cost her—and knew that even loving ignorance could kill.

She had to get Light out of here, and it seemed that in this Michael was her only ally.

It was odd, Truth reflected, that what she would not do for herself—leave Shadow's Gate—she would do on the instant for a woman she had known for barely a week. But Light was her sister, her blood, and blood called to blood.

"I'm afraid we have to leave you now," Julian said, interrupting the train of Truth's musings. He leaned proprietorially over her chair, his hand on her shoulder. "But as Gareth says, you are always welcome to become one of us."

Truth forced herself not to look at Michael, sensing it would be a tactical mistake. It was a bad thing when you knew you really couldn't trust your only possible ally.

"Give me more time," Truth said, and the coaxing pressure was withdrawn.

"All the time you need," Julian said, smiling, and followed the others from the dining room, leaving Truth and Michael there alone.

"Michael?" Truth's question stopped him as he was rising from the table. He stood and waited, head inclined at a courteous angle of attention.

"If I asked you your opinion of my joining the Circle of Truth, you'd say I shouldn't, wouldn't you?"

Michael pondered the question for a moment—choosing his words with the care of a lawyer or a judge, Truth realized.

"If you were to join Julian's Circle, you would find neither happiness or rest in doing so, and would probably destroy any hope you had of finding either in your lifetime," he said at last.

As nice an equivocation as she was likely to find outside a Jesuit rectory, Truth thought sourly.

"Michael—you don't believe in magick, in the Work, do you? You think my father was crazy, right?" *And that being the case, why are you here, Michael Archangel?*

"No. I think he was right," Michael said simply. "That's the problem. Everything he said was true. Good night, Truth. Sleep well."

And with that Michael left her, and Truth was alone in the dining room of Shadow's Gate.

After the affair with Fiona and the conversation with Michael, sleep should have been elusive, but Truth had taken a long walk in the fresh air that day and had endured a sleepless night before it. She barely kept her eyes open during a quick bath in the new bath salts that had been another purchase today in Shadowkill, and was asleep almost before she turned off the light.

She was awakened—she thought—by a crash of thunder, and opened her eyes to the strobe-white flicker of lightning bleaching her bedroom to a grayed monochrome image of itself.

There was a man sitting in the chair beside her bed. She drew a deep breath. To scream? She wasn't sure herself.

"Shut up," he said sympathetically. "I hate screaming women."

The lightning flickered again—more distant this time—and died, leaving the room dark, filled with the sound of the hammering rain. But Truth had already recognized her midnight caller. Forcing herself to move through the terror that gripped her, she stretched out a hand toward the lamp beside her bed.

"Don't," Thorne Blackburn said.

Truth stopped. If this were a dream—it could be, it *could* be, she told herself desperately—it could end, and she struggled to awaken. But every sense was already at shrieking attention, and the man in the chair—only an indistinct shape, without the lightning to illuminate him—was still there.

"What do you want?" Truth said. Wasn't that what you were supposed to ask ghosts? Lightning flickered again, quick as a snake tongue, showing her the Thorne from the pictures—long blond hair, headband, denim vest, and tie-dyed T-shirt.

"My necklace and ring, for a start. Where are they?"

For a paralyzing moment she couldn't remember. She was too frightened at this moment to be self-conscious; she believed, sincerely and with primitive terror, that this was her father, Thorne Blackburn, returned from the dead.

"In my car," she finally managed.

"Well, hell; I can't send you out in this to get them," Thorne Blackburn said. The thunder followed his words with a sharp crack and a dying rumble. "Leave them somewhere around the house, will you? They're mine. I need them. More than you do, anyway."

Raindrops drove at the bedroom window with the force of thrown gravel. Lightning again: and in the flash Truth saw Thorne's shadow printed on the wall, real and substantial as the ageless apparition before her. She closed her eyes tightly, nauseated with primeval dread.

"You're dead," she said through clenched teeth. "You can't need anything." The thunder following the lightning was several seconds later; the storm was moving away.

"And you're just as stubborn as your mother," Thorne said fondly, "but it's hard enough to pull this hat trick off without wasting my time arguing. I came to tell you: Get the hell out of my house before you get your rationalist ass singed. Who the hell do you think you are, Hans Holzer? You're not like other people baby, you're my daughter—"

It was difficult to remain terrified while being affectionately scolded by a dead parent in a voice with faintly working-class undertones. Truth lunged for the light switch and pressed it frantically.

The lamp at her bedside came on. There was no one in the chair.

And who in God's name was Hans Holzer?

The room was dark, lit only by the sickly pale glow that emanated from television and VCR.

"—thank you, future Epopts of the New Aeon, it's really groovy being here with Ed tonight and we've got a really far-out cosmic trip planned for all of you—"

Truth red-eyed and sleepless, sat in the room containing the Blackburn collection, running tapes through the VCR. Looking at her father.

"I came to tell you: Get the hell out of my house before you get your rationalist ass singed."

She'd run this tape five times already: Here, transferred to videocassette, were copies of every one of Thorne's appearances caught on film: Carson, Sullivan, *The Dating Game*, the Hollywood Bowl—even a few minutes at Woodstock. Before, she hadn't been able to bear the thought of seeing Thorne, even in the electronic flesh. Now she couldn't look away.

He was so young. In his twenties in these clips, a leading

light of what had been called the Youthquake, that dazzling demographic surge in which kids in their teens and twenties took over the popular culture of the nation, from music to fashion. The Youthquake, the British Invasion: the faint Liverpudlian accent she'd heard—

—in her dreams? Oh, please let it have been a dream—

—was still discernible here in these taped performances, if you listened carefully and knew what you were looking for, although Thorne Blackburn had worked hard at some point to attain the bland measured diction of a radio announcer. Or was the Liverpool accent an add-on, an afterthought, to capitalize on the 1960s American fascination with things British? None of the biographical information on Thorne Blackburn had been really certain about his nationality; Truth had just assumed he was American.

She'd made, she knew now, far too many assumptions.

After Thorne's appearance in her room, sleep, no matter how her body begged for it, was out of the question. After an hour spent flinching at every retreating thunderclap, fighting the impulse to simply grab her car keys and flee—

Without Light? And where would you go? You've never run away from anything in your life. Except from being Thorne Blackburn's daughter.

—she'd given up and gotten dressed. And come down here, looking for proof of a sort. The tapes that Julian had gathered. All the footage there was of Thorne.

"Who the hell do you think you are, Hans Holzer?"

No. Hans Holzer was a lecturer and author of numerous popular books on ghosts, hauntings, and the occult whom Thorne had affected to despise for his bland middle-of-the-road approach to the world of the supernatural. For that reason if no other, his books were represented in the Blackburn collection. She must have heard of him from Dylan or someone, little though she remembered it. It was not possible that her information came from Thorne Blackburn.

Seeing the tiny, moving figure, preserved forever on tape, Truth was able to wonder about what she had seen—or dreamed. If it had been a dream, then certainly the man in her room had been Thorne Blackburn.

"You're not like other people, baby, you're my daughter—".

The voice, the face, everything was the same. Even though her unconscious mind had not had these tapes to draw upon, she'd certainly had access to enough material to create a dream image so close to the reality that her waking mind could merge the two.

Then what about the handwriting in your book? Or what spoke through Light? Or the man you saw in the hall outside Irene's room? What about them?

Truth put her face in her hands. Helplessly, hating it, she believed.

"Oh God damn you, Daddy. God damn you to Hell."

CHAPTER ELEVEN

TRUTH OR CONSEQUENCES

This truth within thy mind rehearse,
That in a boundless universe
Is boundless better, boundless worse.
—ALFRED, LORD TENNYSON

BUT HAVING TAKEN THAT FIRST STEP INTO THE ABYSS OF
unreason, Truth didn't know what to do now. A True Believer, she supposed, stepping off the curb of Reality,
would be looking for signs and portents to point him in the
direction of his new delusion, but she didn't even want the
proof she had, much less to get any more of it.

At least she didn't have to believe in magick, Truth told
herself desperately. She only had to admit to seeing—and
listening to, and talking to—ghosts. *A* ghost, anyway.

But ghosts were worlds away from the safe sane sterile
world of clinical parapsychology, of PK and ESP, of test
series run in modern, brightly-lit buildings.

And she was afraid that ghosts were just the beginning,
as if she'd fallen into some weird shadowland between
Magick and Science; a place controlled by the rules of neither one. And now Thorne, too, was demanding she leave
Shadow's Gate.

Before I get my rationalist ass singed. But I'm not a

*rationalist any more, am I, Daddy? No, I'm afraid Daddy's
little girl has gone right off the deep end.*

She wanted to cry, but her eyes were aching and tearless,
as if she had already cried all the tears she had to weep.
Truth shook her head, wearily.

A hiss of static startled her. The tape in the VCR had
come to the end again. She muted the sound and hit the
"Rewind" button and got up, stretching stiffly, to turn on
the lights. Sitting in the dark hadn't gotten her anywhere.
She looked at her watch. Almost five o'clock in the morning. So much for the peace of a night's sleep.

*Everybody—well, counting Thorne and Michael as
everybody, anyway—wants me to leave Shadow's Gate. But
it isn't because I'm in danger, not really. Neither of them
has said that.*

She tried to concentrate on what Michael had said to her
in their maddeningly inconclusive conversations.

*Not because I'm in danger. That's not why. It's because
I'll* learn *something.*

What? Truth's lifelong mistrust of Thorne Blackburn returned full force—if there was something he didn't want
her to know, she was determined to find out what it was.

Her hand was still on the old-fashioned push-button light
switch when the library door opened.

"Oh—it's you," Irene and Truth said in chorus.

Irene Avalon was obviously either just on her way to bed
or had just gotten up. Her white hair was pulled back neatly
under a silver hairnet and her face was bare of makeup.
She wore fluffy purple scuffs on her feet, and her stout
person was swathed in a heavy flannel robe the twin of the
one she'd loaned Truth. Truth contrasted the woman before
her with the slim laughing redhead in the pictures—who
could not have been young even then, if twenty-five years
had aged her so—and thought that Time's magic was the
cruelest sorcery of all.

"I saw the lights were on in here," Irene said. "I was
meditating in the Temple after the Work tonight and I was
on my way up, but I just wanted to make sure none of

those rascal boys had left the lights on again. Good boys, all of them, but not one of them has ever had to worry about where the next penny is coming from, if you ask me."

"The storm woke me up," Truth said. A half-truth, after all, was better than none. "I thought I'd come down and do some work while it was quiet."

"Not sleeping well?" Irene studied Truth's face closely. "No," she answered herself. "Child, you look positively haggard. What you want is a good cup of cocoa and a nice lie-in; it's my belief you're half-attuned to the Work already; no wonder you can't sleep when the Circle is working."

Irene's explanation, smacking strongly of mumbo-jumbo as it did, was still preferable to having to admit the reality, at least in Truth's opinion. She let Irene lead her off to the kitchen, where the older woman took down a small saucepan and set it on the stove.

"Real cocoa, and none of those nasty modern mixes full of chemicals and hydrogenated vegetable fats—pah! Just a pinch of saffron in it, to help you sleep. They used to use it in possets all the way back to the Middle Ages; there's no harm in it," Irene said soothingly.

"Just as long as I don't have to go back to the Middle Ages to drink it," Truth joked feebly.

Irene laughed, pottering around the kitchen, taking the milk from the refrigerator, adding saffron and vanilla and brown sugar and cocoa, and finally whisking the steaming brew into a froth and pouring it out into two large mugs.

Truth held the cup under her nose and inhaled deeply. The honey-sweetness of it was like a field of edible flowers in the sun; the strong scent of vanilla and the luscious tropical chocolate smell were underlain by the faintly winy tang of molasses and the delectable, earthy savor of saffron. She sipped at it. It tasted even better than it smelled.

"Delicious," Truth pronounced, but even if she drank a swimmingpool full she didn't think she'd be able to get back to sleep.

They talked inconsequentials—the weather, the shops in

town. Truth had a sense that there was something Irene wanted to say to her, and for her own part, Truth's tongue was tangled with unasked questions.

Irene was just topping off their cups with the last of the pot when there was the sound of a key in the door that once had been the tradesman's entrance, and a moment later a man came in, shrugging off a heavy corduroy barn coat. There was a woman, similarly dressed, behind him.

"Oh, Mr. Walker," Irene said. "This is Mr. and Mrs. Walker, Truth—they do the housekeeping here—in the morning, while there's no one to get in their way."

"Good morning, ladies," Mr. Walker said—civilly enough, but his desire to have his domain to himself was plain.

So that was why Truth never saw the people who cared for Julian's house—they were probably gone before nine o'clock, and Mr. Hoskins left by eight P.M., leaving the house—and the night—to Julian and his apostles.

"Oh, and here I've gone and dirtied up your kitchen, and I dare swear you won't let me hear the end of it, Mr. Walker," Irene said ruefully. She made as if to take the offending pot and wash it, but Mr. Walker waved her away—curtly, Truth thought.

"Come on, Irene, let's go somewhere else and leave the poor man to do his work in peace." Truth took the older woman's arm and, carrying their unfinished cups of cocoa with them, they left the kitchen.

Truth would have chosen any other room in the house for a cozy chat, but Irene's destination turned out to be the Temple. It had not been completely tidied away from the events of earlier in the evening; when Irene and Truth came in there was still a ring of stools in the middle of the floor, giving the space an eerie resemblance to a deserted classroom.

Irene pressed the button that turned on the lights, then sat down on a stool and patted the one next to hers invitingly.

Truth sat as she'd been bidden and stared into her cup.

The fact that Irene had brought her here showed plainly enough that for Irene, this room held no terrors—and she had actually been here the night Katherine died.

"Tell me about my mother," Truth said. "Did my—did Thorne love her, do you think?" she blurted out, flushing.

It was a childish question and an awkward one, but Irene gave it serious thought. Truth saw a faint smile tug at the corners of her mouth and light her eyes, as though whatever memories Irene had of those times were happy enough to blunt the horror of its end.

"She was his soul mate; there's no doubt of that in my mind. There were two women he loved that way—oh, not the way he loved me, but I don't grudge it them; better to have one-tenth of a man like Thorne and the memories afterward than all of something you'll only regret. But for Thorne—

"There were the two of them, Katherine and, well, let's just call her the other one. He couldn't have them both, and when he had to choose, he chose Katherine, even though it meant losing the other. Oh, it wasn't about jealousy—we were none of us jealous that way in those days, we were building a new world and all the rules were going to change. I think it was you as made the difference to Thorne when it came to Katherine, but there I'm telling tales out of school, and I haven't a right to. But he loved them both, and gave up one of his loves for the other, so never doubt Thorne loved your mother."

Irene sipped at her cocoa, her mind obviously caught up in memories of those days.

"In a way it's as if Thorne Blackburn—of all people— was put on this earth to curb Katherine's wildness. You've got the look of your mother but there's more of Caro in you, to my mind. Stubborn, that one—Thorne always said that nothing could shift Caro but Caro, and once she'd made up her mind you could save your breath to cool your porridge. Oh, but Katherine, she was a one for desperate chances; reckless as Lucifer and just as proud. That night . . .

she just went too far, that was all. She went too far." Irene shook her head, the memory of the pain dimming the joy.

"Aunt Irene, what happened to Thorne that night?" The honorific slipped out before Truth realized it; she felt a sudden fierce love for the old woman, and for a moment she could almost imagine she remembered Irene from before.

"He . . . saw that she was dead. There's more to it than that, but I'm afraid I can't tell you; I'm sealed to the Circle." Irene took up the tale easily. It was not necessary to specify which night—in the tale of Thorne Blackburn there was only one. "But he knew she was dead. He stripped off his jewels—they're like badges of rank, lovey, you can see him wearing them in those old photos—and threw them away; a ring, a necklace, and a bracelet—and cradled her in his arms, crying like a baby. But the police never found him, though they looked all around here for two days and put roadblocks as far south as Fishkill."

She sighed and shook her head. "I tell you, it gave me quite a turn, seeing Julian wearing Thorne's bracelet. But it isn't the original, he told me, just a copy made to the specifications in the workbook. You take nine iron bands, you see—"

Irene rambled on, like a partridge fluttering in front of the hunters to draw attention away from her nest, but Truth refused to be diverted.

If this were true, then she'd been wrong. All these years, when she'd blamed Thorne Blackburn for her mother's death, she'd been wrong.

"You said Thorne saw Katherine dead? How did she die? Julian said it was a drug overdose—was it? What happened? What happened to Thorne?" Truth demanded.

"I can't tell you," Irene said simply. "You aren't sealed to the Circle. I swore, you see: to protect, conceal, and never reveal any art or arts, part or parts—"

"Yes, all right. Does Julian know?" Truth said impatiently.

"Oh yes. He asked me, and as soon as I was satisfied

that he could work the proper Grade I told him."

And that was something Truth couldn't do if she sat here till doomsday. "But the police—" she said in frustration. Surely *they* hadn't accepted an explanation like that? People who pleaded the Fifth Amendment these days went to jail, and that was reporters, never mind what would have happened to nut cultists in the sixties who tried it.

Irene shook her head sadly. "I'm sorry, pet; I'd tell you if I could, but it's like asking a priest what goes on in the confessional, don't you see? Oaths are real things and you can't break them. I can tell you what I told the police, though, and it's every bit of it true."

She patted Truth's hand, and Truth forced herself to smile. It wasn't Irene's fault. . . .

That she was crazy? Or conscientious? Or simply loyal? Truth didn't know. It seemed that suddenly there were no villains any more, and that frightened her as much as evil might have.

"What I told them was this, and it's true enough, being all that outer eyes could see. A sudden storm blew up while we—the Inner Circle, all thirteen of us—were in the Temple, and it blew open the doors. The front doors, and the ones in here. Katherine—your poor mother—went into convulsions. They did decide later it was a drug overdose, which Thorne would never have permitted if he'd known, you must believe that—but at least they called it an accident, or we'd all have been facing murder charges. But Johnny's father—that's our Johnny; one of us—the Circle as we were then—poor lad, he's been in the ground these fifteen years—had the money for some fancy lawyers, and if they didn't charge him, the rest of us had to get off too. I don't think they cared much, the police didn't, although if they could have got their hands on Thorne it would have been a different matter. . . ."

"Yes, Aunt Irene. But about that night. You said there was a storm?"

"Yes. Thorne liked to work during storms; he said the power was easier to manipulate then. But the storm that night . . . Well, the doors blew open and of course the candles we were using went out—it was the wind, you see. We tried to turn on the lights, but there was a power failure because of the storm, and by the time we got the flashlights and sorted everything out, Thorne was gone and Katherine was dead."

"So he could just have run off?" Truth said uncertainly. But even if the police weren't still looking for Thorne after a quarter of a century, Julian would have been—and Julian, Truth was willing to bet, would have found him.

"That's what the police said, and I'll grant them, they did give the old place a good turning out, and of course we did nothing to stop them. We couldn't," Irene added with an apologetic laugh. "It was Thorne as owned the place, you see—they called the rest of us squatters and said we had no right to be here. Arrested us too, they did, all but Caroline, though in the end they had to let most of us go, after Johnny's da had got through with them. But took Debbie's baby away from her, poor girl, and when they told her she was an unfit mother she hanged herself in her cell. All so long ago," Irene said mournfully.

The 'Debbie' that Irene spoke of must be Debra Winwood, Light's mother, and Johnny would be Jonathan Ashwell, whose father had been quite as rich and well connected as Irene's scattered narrative reported. But what a horrible thing to do! Truth felt her anger rise in defense of that long-ago helpless girl, even though common sense said there might be another side to things than the one that Irene knew.

"What about the other children?" Truth asked.

"Pilgrim ran away the night of the storm. He was a wild boy; nobody but Thorne could ever make him mind; he must have been uncontrollable after Thorne . . . was gone. They caught up with him while the rest of us were still being held; we heard that much. The poor wee thing was only eight; I don't know whatever happened to him. Caro tried to make them give him to her but they wouldn't, and she tried at least to keep both you and Light, but—oh!—

the pigs—as we called them then—were out in force, determined to stamp out the massed forces of the ungodly: thirty hippies working magick in a big old house."

Irene paused, looking off into the distance. When she spoke again, her voice was taut with remembered anger.

"All the children were taken away—there were more than just Thorne's, and some of their parents were legally married and all. It didn't matter. It was six months before Caro got you back, and that was only through friends in high places, so I imagine. It was in the American papers, so I got to see the clippings even after I was sent home, but she came to me while I was still in jail and asked me to stay away and keep the others away—from you and from her. I think she already knew she had a fight on her hands.

"The other children, I don't know what happened to them. I'm not really sure about most of what came after they gave up on the murder charges; I was deported back to England. Silly buggers labeled me an 'undesirable alien,' and you know *that* doesn't come out of your file easily. Why, from that day to this I haven't been back to America."

Irene sighed again and shook her head. "Oh, it's caused me more than a bit of trouble down the years, but Thorne was worth it, all of it." She smiled reminiscently, in a fashion that once would have angered Truth but now only made her sad.

"I don't know how Julian ever got the Minister to issue me a new passport and American visa and all," Irene went on in a faintly troubled tone, "but he managed something, the dear boy. I was down in Brighton—the seaside crystal-ball-and-teacup trade, you know, and even if my powers aren't what they once were I can still read a heart-line to some purpose. I'd even kept in touch with the Circles still doing the Blackburn Work—oh, we were snubbed royally in our day, by the O.T.O. and the Golden Dawn both; they thought Thorne wasn't serious enough, but after he'd gone there were enough people Thorne had touched with his work to carry on, after a fashion—Smoothing the Path, at least, even if without *Venus Afflicted* no one could Open the Way. Until Julian, of course—"

Truth let Irene ramble gently on, all the while thinking furiously. One thing stood out clearly through Irene's reminiscences—that Thorne Blackburn's body had never been found. Irene had said that he'd disappeared, not died.

"So Thorne could still be alive?" she finally asked.

Irene stopped, interrupted, and stared at her. Finally she gave a little startled laugh. "No! Thorne still in the world? Oh, Truth, I can't tell you anything, truly, but I tell you: no. If you're thinking he'd run off that night, it isn't true."

Irene hesitated, as if debating whether her conscience would withstand the bending of a confidence. Finally she drew a deep breath. "He never left that room, not by door nor window. I was there and I'm telling you. And that's *all* I'm telling you."

At Irene's insistence, Truth went back to her room, promising to lie down at least for a few hours. Already the midnight conversation with Thorne Blackburn was receding into unreality; it was hard to believe it had ever happened.

But she did believe that Thorne was here. Somewhere. Somehow. And because she was a scientist by inclination and training, the fact that he was here was not enough. She wanted to know why.

Why here? Why now? Why *her*?

Despite herself Truth fell asleep, and when she awoke it was early afternoon, She felt rumpled and grubby from sleeping in her clothes, but a vigorous application of cold water to her face brushed away some of the cobwebs, and she thought she might as well continue with what she'd come here for, difficult though it was to keep her mind on her original goal now—reviewing Julian's collection of Blackburniana and making notes for her biography.

If Blackburn truly was English, maybe she could prevail on Dylan to see if any of Dylan's friends in England could turn up anything on Thorne's early life. Or maybe even trace him through the passport office.

Passport. If the British government had indeed revoked Irene's—and the American government her visa—how *had* Julian gotten both of them back for her?

Maybe Irene had just been misinformed, Truth decided dubiously.

As her mind turned over approaches to her subject, Truth changed clothes, defiantly layering the velvet vest over a white cotton blouse and dark slacks. If she wasn't going to run from a ghost, she was damned if she'd back down for Fiona's tantrums. And Julian had pretty well put an end to those, if Fiona had any sense at all.

But does she? Ah, there's *the question . . .* Truth thought wryly.

A rebellion from her stomach reminded Truth that she'd missed breakfast, and that if she was going to run short on sleep she at least needed food. She remembered from her undergraduate days that sleepless nights of study had been fueled largely by take-out pizza and fistfuls of candy bars, and although she wasn't willing to go quite that far, a hearty lunch wouldn't come amiss. When she left her room, she headed for the dining room.

Lunch at Shadow's Gate seemed to be served buffet style, with the two sideboards cleared and set with a soup tureen and a variety of salads and cold meats. Apparently lunch, like breakfast, was a very casual affair, with people coming and going as they pleased.

When Truth came in, Ellis, Hereward, and Light were already seated at the table. Light had a plate filled with desserts at her elbow, and was poking desultorily at a bowl of soup. Her face lit up when she saw Truth.

"Oh, good! You're feeling"—she cocked her head as if she were listening, still staring at Truth, although Truth could see that her eyes had lost focus—"better," she concluded a moment later.

"You're going to make yourself sick if you eat all that sugar on an empty stomach," Truth found herself saying.

Ellis snorted, in a fashion that suggested he'd said the same thing. The water glass at his plate was half-full of an amber liquid that Truth was willing to bet wasn't iced tea. Light hunched her shoulders defensively and dropped the spoon back in the bowl with a splash.

"Oh, well," Truth said hastily, "I don't suppose it matters what order you eat lunch and dessert in, as long as you do eat both of them."

"Kids," Hereward said to no one in particular. "Can't live with 'em, can't live without 'em." Light stuck her tongue out at him and he grinned at her. She pushed the soup away and reached for a brownie, biting into it with triumphant satisfaction.

"There's sandwich makings over there, and soups and salad under the window. Coffee and dessert are set up in the kitchen—we're allowed the freedom of the sanctum at lunchtime because that's when Hoskins does the shopping," Hereward told Truth.

She filled a plate at the sideboard and set it down in the place next to Light, then went into the kitchen in search of coffee. When she came back, a cup in one hand and a napkin full of still-warm cookies in the other, it was to see half her egg-salad sandwich gone and Light wearing a mischievously innocent expression.

"Hmp. I know a trick worth two of that," Truth said, and paused to add a couple of slices of roast beef to her plunder. Light wrinkled her nose and turned back to her dessert.

Truth bit into the roast beef. It was delicious as all the food at Shadow's Gate had been, and just what her ravening stomach required. She sat down, and used her napkin to remove a smear of mayonnaise from Light's cheek. The protectiveness she felt toward her newfound sister was almost frightening in its fierceness.

"So. What are all of you doing this afternoon?" Truth asked cheerfully. She thought glancingly of the conversation she'd had with Caradoc—could it have been only yesterday?—about Magick being the art of personal transformation, a tool for the mind of Man that should not be circumscribed by the will of Church or State. Noble sentiments—but what was the reality?

"Temple's dark tonight, so we won't be working," Hereward said, answering her question. "But most of us have lines to learn for the ritual tomorrow. Not the first time any of us has done it, but I'd hate to go dry in *théâtre sacré*," he added.

The way Hereward spoke triggered a memory in Truth. "You're an actor, aren't you? When you're not—here?"

Hereward laughed. "Oh, I'm always 'Here,' but you're right. I won't ask if you've seen me in anything, because you haven't, but—how did you know?"

"I dated a Broadway gypsy while I was in college. I remember he used to talk about the theater having dark nights—I thought it had something to do with the light bill."

Hereward laughed. "No; just that it isn't in use. But I'll have to watch myself. I wouldn't want to give anything away." His gray wolf-eyes watched her steadily, giving another layer of meaning to his words.

"Well at least, my dear fellow Guardian, you don't have to haul a bloody great sword around while you're rattling off *your* bit," Ellis said. "I thought our Julian was going to put the thing through me last night." He took a long drink of what was in his glass—sherry, Truth thought—and set it down again.

"Well, you *did* drop it," Hereward said, his eyes still on Truth. "But that's what dress rehearsals are for, my dear Gatekeeper. And speaking of dresses, Truth, what *did* you do to little Fee, our Titian-tressed angel of compassion? I haven't seen her blow her cues as badly as she did last night since I've met her."

Since he'd mentioned dresses, Hereward must know perfectly well what had happened, and Truth was damned if she'd provide him any more details.

"How long have you known her?" Truth asked instead.

It was only after the question had been asked that she realized how interested she really was in the answer.

"The Circle's been working together for about a year. Both of us—Ellis and I—had experience with the Blackburn Work before, and of course Irene and Doc—that's Caradoc—did too, but I'm willing to swear that Fiona didn't know an Airt from an Epopt before she met Julian." Hereward shrugged.

Airt was Gaelic for "direction," but in Fiona's defense, Truth didn't have the faintest idea what an "Epopt" was either—only hadn't Thorne used the word? She looked inquiringly toward Ellis, but enlightenment was not forthcoming from that quarter.

"True—for what it's worth. There are times I think Thorne would have done us all a great service if he'd designed a magickal system that didn't rely so heavily on . . . female participation." Ellis said.

"Why, Ellis. You talk as if you didn't *like* women," Hereward said archly.

Ellis grimaced sourly. "All I'm saying is that the Blackburn Work is built around the Hierolator and the Hierophex, and they're both women."

"There's always the Ritual of Anubis," Hereward said provocatively.

"Yes," Ellis said without comment. He saw Truth's look of incomprehension and relented, taking another sip from his glass. "Since you'll probably run into it in your research I'll tell you: The Ritual of Anubis is Blackburn's Smoothing of the Path with men substituting for the women's roles. It was published by the Circle of Fire—that's the Blackburn Lodge in San Francisco—"

"Naturally," put in Hereward.

"But I don't know if it's ever actually been performed. If it had been, there'd be no trouble finding out where Thorne's grave was—all you'd have to do would be listen for the noise of him spinning in it."

No matter how much Ellis had drunk—and Truth was beginning to suspect it was rather a lot—his sarcastically overprecise speech remained clear. And it was beginning to seem to Truth that the occult and the academic world had more in common than she'd originally thought—faction fights and disputes about material, a small, closed community where every one knew—and dished—every one else.

"Not to mention the trouble of finding a male trance psychic over the age of consent for your Anubian Hierophex. Isn't it true that most mediums are women?" Hereward asked Truth.

She felt a gratitude at being asked a question to which she actually had the answer, and wondered if that had been Hereward's actual point.

"It does seem that way, but one of the most famous mediums on record—R. L. Lees—was male. He lived in nineteenth-century London and was even consulted about the Ripper murders. Another famous male medium from the period was Daniel D. Home; Houdini tried to debunk him and failed. But it's true that women outnumber men in the field by at least three to one. Maybe women are more comfortable with admitting that the world isn't, well, entirely susceptible to logical analysis," Truth finished weakly.

"Isn't that the truth," Ellis said bitterly.

"If the world were a logical place we'd all be Unitarians," Hereward said, "and nobody'd fight over anything. But I've got to run—Julian gave me a shopping list, and I've got to go all the way to New York to get some of the items."

Hereward stood up.

"If you're going to New York I'll go with you. I want to stop by my apartment and pick up some things," Ellis said, finishing his drink and standing as well. He swayed a little and steadied himself with a hand on the table.

Hereward stopped in the act of pushing his chair in and looked sharply at Ellis.

"Yes, I know what he said," Ellis said, as if Hereward had spoken, "but it isn't as if I contemplate appearing on

The Tonight Show—which Our Founder did, in his day, may I remind you?—I just want to see if Dorian's watering the plants, pick up some winter clothes. It's freezing up here."

Hereward raised his eyes ceilingward, as though soliciting heavenly help, and exhaled slowly. "On your own head be it, my dear Gatekeeper," he said at last. "But I'm not going to lie to Julian for you." He picked up his—and Ellis's, Truth was relieved to see—dishes and headed for the kitchen.

So there was a rift in Julian's lute of New Age harmony, Truth thought, after the two men had left. The patter was glib and the anecdotes amusing, but underneath it all there was something they weren't saying, and she would dearly love to know what it was.

Light, dessert finished and soup abandoned, gathered up her things and stood to go.

"What about you?" Truth asked.

"I'll stay with you," Light said.

Though welcome, Light was an unnerving companion to have. She followed Truth into the library and curled up in a sunny spot like a little cat, staring unblinkingly off into space. A few minutes later, Truth's speaking her name failed to rouse her.

Where had she gone? Truth looked into the wide-staring silver eyes and wondered. She did not try to rouse Light again; let the child alone, after all that people had done to her trying to change her.

Child? Truth questioned her own thoughts. If Light was indeed Thorne's daughter—and there didn't really seem to be much doubt of that—then she was twenty-seven at least, having been born—if she were indeed Debra Winwood's daughter—sometime before April 30, 1969. Truth thought again about Light's mother's suicide and flinched. What a dreadful beginning to a life that had held nothing but shadows.

Until Julian came along. Every time she started to cast Julian in the role of the Napoleon of modern crime, Truth told herself, she ought to remember how much he'd done for Light and knock it off at once. Julian, like everyone, surely had his dark places, but the good he had done was a matter of public record.

With a sigh, Truth turned to the file drawers, and Thorne Blackburn. He was still the one certain thing in her life— but it was hard, now, to remember that he wasn't a devil— only a charlatan of the occult: a showman, a fraud, a hypocrite.

And coming back from the dead, Truth told herself absurdly, didn't change what he'd done in life.

She began to read the letters that Julian had carefully collected and placed in chronological order. Thorne had kept up an extensive correspondence entirely in pen, and his letters often slid into illegibility, as well as gibberish— but the earliest one was dated 1959. Thorne was in New Orleans, and had a number of scathing things to say about the "tourist trade" Voudoun, ending with:

> —*I should throw open the Gates of Death and bring back Marie LaVeau to walk among die mundus, if only I weren't uncertain which of them would recoil in more horror—those corn-fed rubes, or the Witch Queen herself. Things have changed since the last time I was here—*

At that point Thorne went on to blithely assert that the last time he'd been here, New Orleans had still been in French hands and that he found the city, especially Natchez Under Hill, much changed. The letter ended with a gracefully-disguised plea for money, and several lines of what looked like Greek. Truth mistranslated it whimsically: "*That is not dead which can eternal lie/And with—something, something—even Death may die.*" In 1959 Thorne's apparent magickal mentor was H. P. Lovecraft, or at least

Giuseppe Balsamo, Count Cagliostro—at least if he was claiming he was over a hundred years old.

"My father, the Vampire Lestat," Truth groaned.

The letters got longer and longer, pages of minute script filled with elaborate explanations or refutations of occult theories, but no matter what else he said, Thorne had been explicit from the first references that Truth had found that there was a gate between the world of the gods and the world of men that could be opened through magick.

In later letters he added the claim that he was of the "Old Blood"—the *sidhe*—and had been chosen by the gods to open the gate between the two worlds once more. Thorne referred to "the war" in several of the letters, and at first Truth thought he meant Vietnam, before realizing he meant World War II.

If Thorne had been thirty when he died or anything approaching it, he would have been born somewhere around 1939, and spent his earliest childhood with the war as backdrop. But references to his past were extremely slight, nearly inadvertent:

>   —*since the war it has been clear to all individuals attuned to the higher vibrations that we are approaching the end of an era. Crowley thought the New Aeon had been declared in 1904, but he did not understand Aiwass; he was only a voice crying: "In the Wilderness, make straight the path!"*—

It was fortunate, thought Truth, looking at the date on the letter, that the Great Beast had not lived to see himself demoted from Lucifer to John the Baptist. But Crowley had died in 1947; if his signature in the book from Thorne's library was not a forgery, it meant Thorne had known Crowley while Thorne was still a child.

Truth made a note to see if she could check out the Blackburn/Crowley connection, but Crowley's modern followers were a secretive lot, reasonable when you considered how much nonsense had been written about them.

So much to do . . .

Thorne's correspondence decreased—at least Julian's files held fewer letters—when Thorne started his underground newspaper in San Francisco. That purchase had been bankrolled by one of his followers—as was the acquisition of the Haight-Ashbury house, the purchase of the Mystery Schoolbus, and, in the end, the acquisition of Shadow's Gate—all of which ended up in Thorne's name because, as he airily told his backers: "I cannot bear to live on charity, subject to another's whim."

He'd been willing enough to accept large cash donations, though, and Truth, finally looking at the matter with something approaching dispassion, wondered how he'd gotten all of them; people with a lot of money were usually more careful about whom they gave it to.

But Thorne had seemed to possess an unerring radar for those who had money, and a totally unself-conscious charm that got it for him. The people living at Shadow's Gate in 1969 hadn't been ultimately released and cleared from any shadow of complicity in the death and disappearance out of a liberal spirit on the part of the local police, and certainly not because they were hippies. But they'd been *rich* hippies, if what Truth was turning up here was any indication.

"Not one of them below the rank of a stockbroker," Truth murmured aloud. "Well, you know what they say; it's as easy to love a rich man as a poor one." And Thorne had apparently found it easier.

But Truth found no indication, either in the letters he wrote or in the ones written to him, that Thorne Blackburn was fleecing his followers and funneling the money into his own pocket—at least not in the way she'd once thought. In the strictest sense, then, Thorne Blackburn was *not* a cheat, fraud, scoundrel, and con man.

It was true that Thorne had run through several fortunes that hadn't, originally, belonged to him, but he'd spent it all on what he called *the Work*—on extravagant follies like inlaying the floor of the Temple at Shadow's Gate with sterling silver. He'd certainly been manipulative and probably unscrupulous. . . .

"But his intentions were pure," Truth said with a sigh. *Oh, Daddy, what am I going to do with you?* In the money-conscious, anti-greed nineties, she could ruin his reputation just by reporting his finances.

But did she want to do that? Really? Still?

"Julian's coming," Light announced. Truth jumped at the unexpected sound of her sister's voice, and a moment later heard a gentle rapping on the door.

Julian was wearing a raw silk sweater with tweed slacks, and the combination gave him the air of a raffish jewel thief on vacation. He crossed the room to where Truth was standing and looked down at the papers.

"The story of a life interrupted?" he asked, picking up one of the letters and looking at it.

Looking at it in his hand, it was impossible not to calculate the capital outlay on Julian's part that the entire folder represented, these priceless, irreplaceable documents . . .

"Julian, how did you—I mean, it must have been difficult to . . ." Truth floundered.

"How many houses did I burgle?" Julian finished playfully.

His high spirits bordered on euphoria; Julian was more lighthearted than Truth had yet seen him. "There's no need to frown; the reality is far more mundane: I ran advertisements in the leading magickal journals and *bought* them, one way or another. Unfortunately, Thorne rarely kept the letters sent to him, so I'm afraid it's a rather one-sided correspondence, except in a few cases."

She'd already noted that the files contained very few letters *to* Thorne, and if Julian's means hadn't turned up any other letters than these, it was hard for her to believe she could do any better with her own resources.

"Is this my cue to say there are some things money can't buy?" Truth asked lightly.

"True, oh, true—but very few," Julian said, almost sing-songing. He seemed to collect himself, as if reigning in his febrile high spirits with an effort. "But those are the most important things—the ones money can't buy—so I've found. And what have you found out about Thorne?"

"Not much—unless you count the fifty-cent tour of his magickal beliefs—and financial conquests," Truth couldn't help but add. "Julian, you'll know if anyone will; where was he born? How did he get, um, involved in the occult?"

"How tactful," Julian said, smiling at her, "when I'm sure that what you nearly said was 'How did he get mixed up in this idiocy?' " He pulled out a chair beside her and sat down. "But that hardly answers your question."

He held his hands out before him on the table, staring at his fingertips as if perhaps words might be written on them.

"As for what I know . . . Thorne was probably English, or at the very least, spent a great deal of time in England. His past is rather like an unfinished murder mystery, with a handful of clues and no explanation, and I'm afraid that all I have to offer you is a quarter century of accumulated legend and no more concrete facts." Julian continued to study his fingertips, and inevitably Truth's gaze followed his, until they were both staring at those perfectly mani-cured ovals.

"One possibility is that Thorne's mother was an English-woman who married an American, as so many did in the forties. She would have returned to the United States with her husband, of course, and Thorne would have been born here," Julian said. "Then, assuming his parents were dead, he might have returned to England to be brought up by his grandparents. The FBI had a file on him, and I've been able to get to see parts of it through a major magickal operation: the invoking of the Freedom of Information Act. Thorne was certainly an American citizen at the time the Bureau started watching him." Julian glanced up at her, and Truth was instantly ensnared in his brilliant turquoise gaze; dazzling and soothing all at once, like Caribbean seas.

"But don't *they* know any more about him?" Truth asked after a long moment. She felt some invisible net release her as she spoke, and Julian smiled.

"They were more interested in who he met in the Weather Underground than who he'd gone to school with," he said ruefully. "Careless of them, when you consider how secretive Thorne was going to turn out to have been. Since backtrailing him hasn't been my highest priority I haven't pursued the matter, but I rather suspect that Thorne was given his mother's maiden name as one of his *soi-disant* Christian names, so anyone backtrailing him might begin by tracing the Thornes. That was Thorne's middle name, incidently; his given name was Douglas."

"Somehow I can't see Blackburn as a Doug," Truth admitted. "It won't be easy to trace, but I suppose there'd be records kept of military marriages, and I already know I need to be looking around a base in the north of England."

"Why do you say that?" Julian asked, and Truth answered before she realized what she was saying.

"You can hear it in his voice; it sounds like Liverpool or Birmingham; it's a different inflection than the south. If he went to live with grandparents, he'd pick up their ways of talking. . . ." she trailed off, hearing her own words.

"In his voice?" Julian prompted. *When did you ever hear Thorne talking?* hung unspoken in the air between them.

Oh, yes, you could hear Liverpool in his voice—but only when he was speaking casually, telling his daughter to leave Shadow's Gate—not on the tapes that Julian had carefully collected. Truth's cheeks crimsoned as she realized the magnitude of her slip.

"I've been listening to the tapes," she said. "You can hear it there if you listen." Her voice sounded flat, unconvincing, but would the truth be any more believable?

Julian gazed at her, luminous eyes glowing with an inner light. "If he would come back for anyone, it would be for you," he said, almost to himself.

What could she say? That she didn't believe in ghosts?

When she'd all but blackmailed Julian into letting her bring in the recording equipment because she was so sure Shadow's Gate was haunted? She looked away, only then noticing that Light was nowhere to be seen.

"Light," Truth said, getting to her feet. She looked around.

"She was here when I came in," Julian said, unconcerned. "She must have gotten bored and gone out. Don't worry, Truth, you'll find that Light slips in and out on little cat feet. She's old enough to get out of most trouble on her own; just as long as she's in the house by dinnertime, I don't worry too much."

"But—" Truth began.

"Don't *worry*," Julian said firmly, placing his hand over hers, and Truth sank back down reluctantly, a little thrill running through her at the warm pressure of his hand. Whether she liked it or not, there was some truth in what Julian said—and either she believed Light could be self-responsible, or else she believed that she belonged back in an institution like the one Julian had rescued her from.

"You're right," she admitted, though everything in her rebelled against saying the words—but wasn't that just false pride? The self-sufficiency she'd cherished all these years was just another form of trap, wasn't it?

She had never felt so uncertain. She knew she had to protect Light—she just didn't know *how*.

"Don't look so worried," Julian said, a note of teasing intimacy in his voice. "My work is proceeding splendidly, and from the sound of things, yours has made a promising beginning. If you think a trip to England will help your research, I'd be honored to underwrite the expenses. And I'm—not without resources in a certain segment of society. I'll be happy to provide you with all the introductions you'll need."

"That's very generous, Julian," Truth said slowly.

"It's very selfish," Julian corrected her affectionately. "I'm as eager to unfold the secrets of Thorne's past as you are. Is it true he was Aleister Crowley's godchild? Was

Thorne's grandfather a member of the Golden Dawn?" His smile invited her to share his curiosity—and more.

"Does our theory even hold water if Thorne was born in nineteen thirty-nine?" Truth shot back. "The war ran from 'forty-one to 'forty-five, at least for the Americans. If your theory's right, that would put Thorne's birth in nineteen forty-two at the earliest."

"It's not impossible," Julian said. "That would make him twenty-seven in nineteen sixty-nine."

"When he died?" Truth asked sharply. Whatever Irene Avalon knew or thought she knew about that fatal night, she'd told it to Julian Pilgrim.

"When he vanished, at any rate," Julian said, turning the question smoothly. "Never to be found again on Earth by the best efforts of the Dutchess County Sheriff's Department, the New York State Police, and the FBI."

Truth shook her head in frustration. The simplest questions about Blackburn seemed to be hedged about by a thicket of ego and mystification.

"Go to England for me?" Julian asked coaxingly. "Or we could go together, in a few weeks. Christmas in Paris, perhaps?"

"You sound like you're trying to seduce me." Truth spoke before she thought. "Oh my God, Julian—I didn't mean—" she gasped, cheeks flaming.

"Oh, it's quite all right: I did. In the politest possible way, of course." Julian lifted Truth's hand from the table and turned it over between his. He ran his thumb up the hollow of her palm. "Truth, you're very perceptive, and far from naive. I'm sure you know that there're very few things that someone with as much in the way of resources as I have has to ask for. But I would very much like to see you—socially. Would you have dinner with me tonight— somewhere other than Shadow's Gate?"

He smiled into her eyes. Truth was so flustered that it took her a moment to realize what he was asking, and when it sank in she could only nod, as if responding to the promptings of another.

*　　*　　*

The River View Inn was an hour north of Shadowkill, in Columbia County. It had a magnificent view of the Hudson, a Culinary Institute–trained chef, and a glassed-in terrace from which both could be experienced in opulent comfort. The moment Julian's BMW had turned up the long curving drive of what Julian had described as "the usual sort of country roadhouse" Truth had been devoutly grateful not only that she'd bought the green silk dress in town but that she'd put aside false modesty to wear it—it was the perfect dress for this setting.

"Ah, fair beauty, at last I have you to myself," Julian teased, as he slid the storm blue wrap from Truth's shoulders. She smiled at him as he handed his coat and her wrap in at the coat check.

"Just have me back by midnight—or I turn into a pumpkin," Truth rallied, trying to match his tone. Julian smiled, and offered his arm, and they proceeded into the restaurant.

The River View Inn had once been a Hudson River mansion from about a generation later than Shadow's Gate; an opulent Jazz Age playpen whose private dock had seen the off-loading of many a case of illegal Canadian whiskey in the days of Prohibition. It had suffered various reversals of fortune, Julian had told Truth on the drive here, until it was bought in 1979 by Jillian and Peter Randollph, both graduates of the CIA—which in this part of New York State meant Culinary Institute of America, not the Central Intelligence Agency. After almost twenty years of hard work by the Randollphs and a write-up in *New York Magazine*, the inn was an overnight success; a preferred spot for area weddings, its few overnight accommodations booked months in advance.

"Did you know it even has a ghost?" Julian asked as the maître d'led them to a table on the terrace.

"You're kidding!" Truth said.

They were seated, and Truth took a moment to admire the view. Though the sun had long since set and it was too dark to see much, the bushes lining the path down to the water were strung with fairy lights, and on the river itself, a determined tanker could be seen plugging its way down-river.

"No, truly," Julian protested. A waiter appeared, with the attentiveness of very expensive service, to take their drink orders.

"Shall we be trite and have champagne?" Julian asked. "Unless you'd prefer a cocktail, of course."

"Oh, no, champagne would be fine." The fizzy white wine Truth associated with the name wasn't something she'd be tempted to overindulge in, and she felt a need to keep her wits about her, even as another part of her wanted to give Julian his head and see if the old adage about "enough rope" was true.

Now why would I want to do that? If there's anyone at Shadow's Gate without extra added dark secrets, it's Julian.

"About the ghost?" Truth prompted.

"Cristal if you have it on ice, otherwise Perrier-Jouët will do," Julian told the waiter. "And ice the P-J nineteen eighty-two *grande cuvée* for dessert, will you?" The man bowed and left.

"Ah, yes, the ghost. Well, old Joseph Peladan who built this place was your usual sort of turn-of-the-century robber baron in the William Randolph Hearst mold. You can't tell so much here on the first floor since it's been redone as a restaurant, but to finish and furnish the place Peladan denuded a large number of stately English homes of plaster and paneling and *objets d'art*—as well as of a great deal of the furniture. This place must have looked like a museum in its heyday. Well, anyway, among the items Peladan ordered—and was duly shipped—was a ghost."

The champagne arrived, and was opened and approved. Truth took a small sip, and then a larger one. This was light-years beyond the so-called champagne served at the faculty mixers at Taghkanic College.

Just be careful, Dorothy—you're not in Kansas any more.

She sipped her drink as Julian rambled on charmingly with what Truth came to suspect was a shaggy ghost story—if not an outright piece of local folklore about the millionaire and his haunted library.

"—so if you see a lady in old-fashioned evening dress about the place," Julian finished, "whatever you do, don't ask her the time."

Truth laughed as she was meant to, and a hovering waiter, sensing his moment, approached with large leather menus.

"If you don't mind, I'll just ask Peter to decide what he'd like to feed us; it can be more amusing that way," Julian said.

He looked an inquiry at her; Truth nodded. Julian gestured; the waiter took his menus and retreated.

Truth meditated upon her unaccustomed passivity. It was as though she were on some sort of magickal quest, where to find the answer to the riddle at the end of it she had to answer yes to every question along the way.

He's up to something and I wonder what. I can't think of any reason I deserve a snow job. How could I have anything he wants—or couldn't buy cheaper elsewhere?

But it was difficult to retain such cynicism in the face of Julian's charm—charm which, manifestly, he was exerting tonight, making all the normal inconveniences of everyday life melt away, leaving behind a sort of Hollywood version of reality.

"I assure you, I have an ulterior reason for bringing you here," Julian said, as an appetizer described by the waiter as gravlax in puff pastry with wild asparagus was placed before them. "I'm very . . . attracted to you," he said, almost shyly, "and I behaved like such an idiot the other day that I'm here hoping to recover lost ground."

"Oh yes," Truth agreed gravely. "You behaved so badly that I can't quite remember the occasion, myself." She speared a forkful of the delicate appetizer. It seemed to melt upon the tongue without any need for chewing. She shuddered to think what the tab for this dinner *à deux* would be; if this was the sort of life the wealthy led, she could easily get used to it.

And wasn't that what she was being offered?

The chill that struck through her then nearly made her choke. Julian had led her up to a high place and was offering her . . . what?

He'd been speaking. "I'm sorry, Julian: What were you saying?"

"Oh, nothing that matters. Merely that I didn't want you to think I objected to Shadow's Gate being investigated. In fact, I hadn't quite made my mind up when I spoke to you before, but I've decided to close up the house in November. If your friends would like to come up with their strange devices, I could just as easily leave it open and keep Hoskins on, if you think that would suit."

"That would be great," Truth said. *And too late; whatever's coming will be here next week, on Halloween.* "I've spoken to Dylan—Dr. Palmer is the Institute's resident ghost-hunter—and he's very interested"—if calling her an idiot was an expression of interest, anyway—"and he'll be sending some of his equipment on ahead. It should be here soon. You don't mind, do you?"

It was odd, Truth noted with detachment, how all the manipulative wiles she'd scorned in others came so naturally to her the moment she felt a need for them. How could Julian say he minded without looking like an idiot?

"How could I mind, when it keeps you interested in us?" Julian answered. "What's rather a sore point with me—and I know you understand—is word of this getting out, and Thorne's name being linked with some sort of Amityville idiocy. By now you know us well enough to know that the last thing we're looking for is publicity."

Know you? But I don't know you, Julian . . .

"Thorne seemed to court publicity," Truth pointed out, discovering the appetizer appeared to have vanished. The hovering waiter swooped in to remove the plates.

"That was long ago and in a far country," Julian said with a crooked smile, "and that sort of innocence is long dead. I think of Thorne as a profoundly innocent man in some ways, don't you?"

The waiter returned with the immense serving plates upon which the dinner plates would be set. Julian refilled their champagne glasses.

"Innocent?" Truth pondered. "I don't know if I'd call him innocent. Sincere, certainly, but . . ." Passionately sincere, in fact, and infused with the idealism of his time, only in Thorne it had taken that bizarre turn into the occult sciences. Like all his generation, Thorne Blackburn had wanted to fill the world with peace and love—though in his case, he intended to do it by making the Golden Age come again, when gods and heroes had lived among men.

He'd never stopped to ask whether this would be a good idea.

"Anyway," Truth said, shrugging, "that's a judgment for the biographer to render—or not—when all her material is in hand, don't you think?"

"Touché," Julian said, raising his glass in salute. "And I can only hope that she is as insightful as she is beautiful."

Thorne Blackburn, it seemed, was to be the invisible guest at the feast. Ignoring—or merely overlooking—her attempts to draw him out about himself, Julian spoke of Thorne throughout the meal: the San Francisco period, the Universal Mystery Tour, the cross-country odyssey in the Mystery Schoolbus, the eight months spent in Mexico, during which Thorne's determination to perform the rituals that made up *Venus Afflicted* had crystallized.

Abandoning her attempts to question him, Truth felt the growing temptation to tell Julian about Thorne's appearances at Shadow's Gate instead—but surely Thorne had appeared to Julian as well?

If she weren't simply going mad.

It was a possibility, after all.

"I would give up ten years of my life just to know where the book is now," Julian said, as their plates were cleared away. *"Venus Afflicted* was there at Shadow's Gate; we know that much. Thorne was adding to it and correcting it all the way up to the end. The police looked for it and didn't find it, and of course when I took over Shadow's Gate I turned the place inside out. Nothing."

"Why would the police want a grimoire?" Truth asked. The turn the conversation had taken made her uncomfortably guilty. The book that Julian sought so fervently was within his reach : *Venus Afflicted* was currently in the trunk of her car.

Truth had never liked keeping secrets, and Julian seemed—oh, not to *suspect* her, but in some strange way to *hope*—

And meanwhile some still, small inner voice—of self-preservation?—told her that she must keep the book a secret—just as Aunt Caroline had.

For if Julian had sought Thorne Blackburn's artifacts everywhere, it was not possible that he would have overlooked Caroline Jourdemayne.

Truth had the teasing sense that she was on the verge of making an important discovery, but whatever she was about to uncover vanished as Julian spoke again.

"They were still trying to make a case against Thorne and thought Thorne's grimoire would be evidence of God knows what. The book was fairly famous in the magickal community; Thorne referred to it often in his diaries and essays," Julian said with a certain air of wistfulness.

All of which she was going to have to read, as well as reading his letters, Truth realized with a sinking heart. Maybe she could ask Thorne to come back from the dead to explain them to her, she thought flippantly.

"But you don't really need Thorne's spellbook, do you? You're doing the—" Truth was reduced to waving her hands, uncertain of the proper terminology to describe what she meant.

"Our Circle is indeed doing the Ritual of the Opening of

the Way, sometimes called the Opening of the Gate," Julian supplied with a teasing pomposity. "Without the book.

"Since you've given me the opening, I'll go on to explain that the Opening is the last part of a series of rituals that take about ten days to perform; they're keyed to the Tree of Life—which is, oh never mind; the Kaballah would take me years to explain. To make a long story positively cryptic in its brevity, the first part of the Opening has been published—in a number of variorum forms, I might add— and forms the principal part of the Blackburn Work as it is done today. These nine rituals are collectively called the Smoothing of the Path, and form a complete Working by themselves. Thorne prescribed that the Smoothing be done several times as an end in itself to get a Circle working fluidly, but when it *must* be done is as a prelude to the Opening of the Way."

It was amazing how plausible all this was, even logical. In her own mind Truth hesitated; if magick as Julian described it was more than the mere elaboration of a delusion, how *much* more was it?

"Which you don't have," she said again, bringing the discussion back to ground she was sure of.

"Neither did Thorne—once," Julian said, almost snappishly. "I'm sorry, it's just that I've been hearing the same thing from Irene and Ellis for weeks, and it's true: I *don't* have the Opening as it is written in *Venus Afflicted*. But I have Irene, who rehearsed it with Thorne's original Circle several times, and I have . . . well, I won't tax your magnanimity with a blow-by-blow account of more forays into the home life of Science's Dark Twin."

That was a phrase of Colin MacLaren's that Dylan was especially fond of quoting—and Thorne had known Professor MacLaren years ago. She looked at Julian. Charming, sane, and nearly normal—and handsome and rich besides! It would be so easy to ask Julian about Thorne and MacLaren—and to tell him. . . .

To tell him . . .

About Thorne. About the book. That she had it, it was

here, he didn't have to try to re-create the ritual, that—

"What do you suppose the chef has planned for dessert, Julian? Do you know?" Truth said brightly, shattering the spell.

Dessert, when it came, was breathtaking; individual compotes of fresh fruit lightly poached in liqueur and sugar and piled into a dish made of colored spun-sugar.

"It's too pretty to eat!" Truth protested.

"It will only melt if you don't," Julian responded with cheerful ruthlessness. To Truth's relief, Julian seemed to be willing to abandon the subject of Thorne Blackburn and *Venus Afflicted*, and become once more what he appeared to be—a man of wealth and sophistication.

As the waiter who had placed the dishes retreated, the wine steward approached with a sweating, white-swathed bottle. Another uniformed attendant carried away the standing ice bucket that held the melted ice and empty champagne bottle.

"Your champagne, sir. The cellarer couldn't supply a nineteen eighty-two *grande cuvée blanc,* but we did have an 'eighty-five double *cuvée* pink, which I hope you will find acceptable." He paused, waiting for Julian's decision.

It was very odd, Truth decided, to look into a world not only where sentences like this made sense, but where the questions those sentences framed actually mattered, and mattered desperately: the world of great wealth, a world polished so smooth by the application of privilege that any flaw in the seamless perfection was seen as an enormous defect.

Julian frowned, and for a moment Truth even thought he might make a scene, but then he smiled and the anxious steward relaxed.

"Of course. Pink champagne, Truth?"

Cuvée, Julian explained, was a sweet dessert champagne. The wine in their glasses was a delicate shell pink, and its sweetness made it slide down her throat as if it were the scent of roses made liquid. It would be easy to become reckless, irresponsible, drinking this, and part of Truth welcomed the thought.

But if I'm going to do anything rash, I'm going to do it because I want to, and not because I'm hopped up on expensive booze. She put the half-empty glass down.

"Don't you like it?"

"It's lovely. But I'm afraid academics don't see much of the high life. I'm not used to it."

"We'll just have to accustom you, then. Do you dance?"

Truth would have bet hard cash that there wasn't any place in the Hudson Valley where you could still find ballroom dancing; and if she could have found anyone to take her bet she would have lost her money. Julian found such a place—in fact, he found three of them, beginning with the River View Inn itself, which had a small dance floor tucked off in what had once been the conservatory wing, and a live band to provide the music.

So it was very late indeed when Julian's BMW drew up at the front door of Shadow's Gate.

"I'll let you off here and go put the car away around back. Oh, and if you're looking for yours, I had Gareth move it today. With the bad weather setting in, it's just as well to have everything under cover."

"How did he move it?" Truth asked. "I didn't give him the keys." Nor would she, when the ignition key opened the trunk as well, and the trunk contained *Venus Afflicted.* She'd even made sure to take them with her this evening.

"No? He might have left it then; he'll probably ask you for the keys tomorrow. But sleep well, darling."

So there wasn't to be a proffered nightcap and a skillful pass, subtle or un-. Truth felt a sense of relief; she couldn't handle one more complication in her life just now and Julian seemed astute enough to know it. She got out of the car.

"And you," she said, turning back to close the door. Julian reached out and took her hand, raising her fingers to his lips for a quick Continental salute; the gesture had enough of conscious self-mockery in it that she didn't find it embarrassing. Truth turned away and heard the car move off behind her.

Though her head was mazed with wine and music, the sense of responsibility that was so much a part of her nature made her follow the drive around to the pass-through where she'd left her car the last time she'd driven back from Shadowkill.

It was still there, untouched. Relief combined with the champagne made her suddenly giddy, and the distant sound of a car door closing, carried on the still night air, warned her that if she didn't want this evening to continue in a direction she wasn't ready for, she'd better get inside before Julian returned.

Despite her distraction, the sense of sanctuary that she'd thought dispelled forever filled her senses as soon as Truth stepped into her room.

She knew what to call it now. It was Thorne's presence she sensed. He would never hurt her. She knew that with the unquestioning intuition of a child; felt the burden of hatred for him she had carried in her heart all these years simply . . . vanish.

Know the truth, and the truth will set you free. Thorne Blackburn might be dead, he might have returned from the dead, the things he'd done in life might still be weird, hateful, or simply puzzling to her, but he would never knowingly or intentionally hurt his daughter.

He'd loved her.

He loved her now, and with that certainty some needy, stunted part of Truth Jourdemayne began to flex and spread its wings.

"Champagne talking," Truth muttered aloud, embarrassed at the tenor of her own thoughts. She flopped down on the bed and groaned, kicking her shoes off. Her *new* shoes, in which she'd gone dancing the first time she'd worn them. So much for common sense.

She lay back on the bed and stared at the ceiling, frowning.

Love was all very well, but it certainly wasn't enough to bring somebody back from the dead; if it was love alone that mattered, surely there would be thousands—millions— of the dead come back to comfort grieving loved ones. Love alone could not explain Thorne's presence.

If he really were here. If this wasn't the self-delusion of a woman heading full-speed for a world-class nervous breakdown. Her very conviction could be a symptom of her sickness.

What proof did she have? What proof could she get? Something tangible—or, failing that, some information only Thorne could have, something that she could check. What had he been doing in her room anyway?

Oh, of course—he wants his jewelry back. It's still in the car with Venus Afflicted. *I'll have to get it for him* . . . she found herself thinking.

And maybe her unquestioning acceptance of Thorne's reality ought to be the most frightening thing of all.

CHAPTER TWELVE

TRUE LIES

When my love swears that she is made of truth,
I do believe her, though I know she lies.
——WILLIAM SHAKESPEARE

"AUNT CAROLINE TOOK VENUS AFFLICTED AWAY WITH her that *night*. She's the only one who could have. But why? Tell me why!"

A drumming in the distance, like the clamor of approaching hooves.

"You're a bright girl, Truth. You've got all the facts. You've even got the book. You figure it out."

Not horses—

"But—" Truth protested, even she felt herself—

—jerked out of sleep to find herself lying abed, dizzy and dazed, and the hammering having followed her into the world.

"The door," she said at last, pleased to have figured this out with a brain that seemed to be full of butterflies.

"I'm coming," she said. She glanced at the clock. Nine o'clock. *Nine o'clock* A.M. *in the morning?* an outraged part of her mind protested. She'd had less than four hours' sleep—no wonder she was so disoriented.

"Truth?" Gareth called through the door. "There's a big truck here with six crates—they say they're for you."

Ten minutes later Truth, hastily dressed and far from awake, was standing in the foyer looking out the drive at a white truck standing in the drive. Three four-foot-high crates stood on the gravel, and a fourth was being gingerly downloaded from the truck's ramp. All four of them were stenciled FRAGILE and THIS SIDE UP and MARGARET BERESFORD BIDNEY INSTITUTE—DO NOT DROP.

Dylan had come through for her. This was the equipment she'd requested.

"Somebody's got to sign for this. Are *you* Ruth Jourdemayne?" the driver demanded, as if it were a question he was tired of asking.

Truth recognized him vaguely—this was the usual freight service the Institute used; she'd seen the driver before. She felt a pang of relief that Dylan hadn't come himself. What could she say to him; *'Hi, Dylan, I've had a long talk with my dead father and you were right all along'*?

"*Truth* Jourdemayne," Truth corrected. She reached for the clipboard.

"Good morning," Julian said.

Unlike Truth, Julian had made no effort to get dressed; he wore a paisley silk dressing gown over black silk pajamas, and his black hair fell across his forehead in an unruly comma. He narrowed his eyes in the bright morning light and looked at Truth, raising an eyebrow quizzically.

"The Institute seems to have sent the equipment I asked for," she said superfluously. A fifth crate joined the other four on the gravel. Truth looked down at the clipboard in her hands.

"They have a wonderful sense of timing." He raised his voice slightly. "You can bring them inside. We can open them at a more civilized hour," Julian added to Truth.

"Hey, fella, all they told me to do was bring 'em here—

they didn't say nothing about anything else," the driver said argumentatively.

Julian went completely still.

"*Oh* boy," Gareth said, very softly. Truth glanced back at Julian. She didn't need any psychic powers to know that the level of tension in the foyer had soared—all she had to do was look at Gareth's face.

Julian took a few steps forward, until he was standing at the edge of the steps. As he passed Truth he plucked the clipboard from her hands. The morning sun turned his hair to a black halo, blinding as a raven's wing.

"But I'm sure you won't mind bringing them inside?" Julian said pleasantly. "You certainly can't expect the lady to carry them inside by herself, can you?" There was nothing in the words, in the even, measured voice, to make what Julian had said so frightening. But Truth *was* frightened. And so was Gareth.

"Hey, mister, I didn't mean to—It's just extra, that's all."

"The Institute—" Truth began.

"Naturally I'll take care of any additional charges," Julian said, smiling. But Truth wasn't comforted, and when she glanced around, she saw that Gareth had fled.

"There now," Julian said turning back, all mildness once more. "An improvement, anyway." He stifled a yawn. "Gareth, is there room . . ."

Julian only just then seemed to notice that Gareth wasn't there, and once more Truth felt that sharp bolt of tension.

"*Gareth* . . ." Julian said, very softly.

"Why don't we put it in the library?" Truth said quickly. "Some of it's going to be used there anyway."

"Fine. They can put them all there."

Truth watched as the first of the six crates was brought up the steps with planks and dollies. She went ahead, into the library, leaving Julian in the front hall.

The room looked odd and unfinished without the portrait of Thorne Blackburn looming over it. She wondered what

Julian had done with the damaged painting—she hadn't thought to ask him about it last night.

The crate was wheeled in, and Truth gave instructions that they should place it in the middle of the floor and move the tables back if they had to. While the workmen were doing that, she stepped back to the doorway.

And saw Gareth come toward Julian, unwillingly, like a small boy being dragged. Saw Julian's smile widen—and his hand flash up in a vicious backhand slap that left Gareth staggered. The sound was loud, flat, and final.

Truth flinched back inside the doorway, putting her hand to her own jaw in sympathetic reaction. Why had Julian done something like that?—Gareth was the most harmless creature she knew!

The workmen trundled out of the library, going for another crate. After a moment, Truth steeled herself and peered out the door again.

Julian stood there alone. He looked toward her inquiringly, and for the first time Truth really felt the tug and flow of the sleeping mind of Shadow's Gate as it eddied around her, bent on its own fulfillment. Using them all as tools.

After all, what she'd seen had probably been some part of the Blackburn Work. And if Gareth didn't like the way he was treated, as far as Truth could tell he was perfectly free to leave.

And maybe what she'd seen hadn't happened at all.

Julian walked over to her.

"You're looking peaked this morning," he said, putting an arm around her. The warmth of his body was palpable through the thin layers of silk he wore, the heat passing from his body into hers, and she was close enough to smell the faint skin-warmed scent of his cologne.

"I'm just . . . not a morning person," Truth floundered. The awareness of the thin layers of silk as they shifted over Julian's bare skin was maddening; a painful eroticism that replaced the confusion of her rough awakening and her earlier fear. It would be so easy to respond to his subtle invitation; to raise her hand to stroke his cheek; to follow where he led.

When the workmen came back with the second crate it was almost a relief.

By the time they were done, most of the rest of the household was roused and Truth could see why the carriers had been so reluctant to do the work of bringing their load inside. By the time the last crate had been set to rest, all three men were sweaty and red-faced.

"Would you like some coffee before you go?" Truth said, feeling guiltily responsible.

"All I want is to get out of here, lady, so if you'll just sign this—" The driver held out the clipboard one more time. Truth took it.

"Maybe you ought to have them unpacked first and check for damages?" Julian suggested with malicious sweetness. Beside him, Caradoc snorted.

Julian leaned against the doorway, holding a steaming mug of coffee. He'd taken the time to dress while the crates were being moved, and now looked formidably casual in a collarless linen shirt and a dark Armani suit.

The driver looked at Julian; a hopeless hostility in his eyes, like a dog cornered by a leopard.

"I'm sure they're fine," Truth said quickly. "And if they aren't, I have no way of knowing just by looking." She scribbled her signature on the top sheet and handed the clipboard back. The driver took it and hurried out.

"Drive safely," Julian called after him cheerfully.

"Julian, that was mean," Truth said, torn between reproof and a sneaking admiration for the deftness with which Julian had gotten his own way—and a little of his own back.

"A confession," Julian said, sipping from his mug. "I hate thieves, particularly stupid ones."

"Thieves?" Truth said, surprised. She'd expected Julian to say "bullies."

"He was stealing services you had a right to expect and

keeping the potential labor for himself. He wished to charge an additional fee for bringing the crates into the house, but I somehow suspect that of hardly being the terms of the original delivery agreement. Extortion, plain and simple."

When Julian explained it that way it seemed flawlessly logical.

"I guess you're right," she said reluctantly.

"What Man is capable of, Man has a right to do," Caradoc said. "The Blackburn Work."

"But," said Truth, confused to be arguing philosophy at this early hour, "that means the driver had the *right* to cheat me."

"If he could," Julian agreed meditatively. "But he couldn't."

"Breakfast," Caradoc announced, making it a general invitation. He ambled off, leaving Truth and Julian alone.

Julian smiled at her.

"But enough Jesuit logic. Come; we're here, we're—God help us—awake, it's a beautiful morning, and my time is my own until this afternoon. What would you like to do?" Julian asked invitingly.

Truth looked through the open doorway at the crates. "I suppose that duty calls," she said reluctantly.

"You'll at least join me for breakfast, stunning Monsieur Hoskins inexpressibly," Julian said. "Oh, and give Gareth your keys, will you? The car's still there, I noticed."

"I can move it myself after breakfast," Truth said. "I have to get some things out of it anyway." *And that way I'll know where it is—if I need it in a hurry.*

"Fine." Julian's smile did not indicate that his will was being crossed in any way. "After breakfast, then. Gareth will show you where to put it."

Four hours' sleep was enough to give her at least the illusion of restedness for a few hours, and good food could offset some of the fatigue. Julian seemed to be a believer in hearty breakfasts in any case; he seated Truth at the dining room table with a cup of coffee and returned from the kitchen a few minutes later balancing two high-piled plates.

Though Caradoc had mentioned breakfast, he was nowhere to be seen, and Truth wondered where he'd gone.

And she wondered, in some small ungracious part of her mind, if Gareth would have a bruised cheek the next time she saw him.

"Here we are," Julian said, setting one of the plates in front of her. "Not everyone eats breakfast at Shadow's Gate, but Mr. Hoskins stands ready to abet those who do."

"Oh, Julian—I can't eat all this!" Truth protested, looking at ham, omelette, fresh fruit, and muffin. It appeared that in addition to supplying breads and coffee, Mr. Hoskins cooked breakfasts to order.

"Certainly you can," Julian said, forking up a bite from his own plate. "You're body's a machine; do you expect it to run without fuel?"

"You make it all sound so simple," Truth said protestingly.

"Just as I expect you'd make—what was it? Statistical parapsychology?—sound simple. It all depends on what you know."

What I know is that I don't know very much, Truth said to herself.

Caradoc and Gareth came in together. Gareth headed for the kitchen, returning a moment later with a plate piled high with ham and biscuit sandwiches dripping with butter and maple syrup. He proceeded to demolish the food with an easy efficiency that Truth admired.

There was no bruise.

"When everyone else gets up I can have them help you with getting the stuff set up—if that's what you call it," Gareth said between bites.

"Everyone being Hereward and Donner," Caradoc said, "as Ellis isn't likely to be any help. To put it mildly."

"Ellis is all right," Gareth said, in good-natured defense of his absent comrade. "And if you want to move your car into the back . . ." he added to Truth, letting the sentence hang.

"I'm sure Truth will enjoy the chance to present parapsychology's case against the occult," Julian said, drawing Gareth into the conversation, "as well as explaining what all of those formidable engines actually do."

"I'm not the expert," Truth reminded them. "Where I come in is usually after the raw data has been generated— probabilities versus possibilities, that kind of thing. We've even gathered statistics on the spontaneous failure of random lots of infrared film, so we have a basis for positing that the pictures we have are a ghost, rather than a flaw on the film."

"Other than the testimony of the observers on the site," Julian said.

"But that just isn't reliable," Truth said, warming to the subject and the education of her small audience. "There are too many ways to fool the human mind and eye. Only the machine is objective."

"There is, of course, no way to fool a machine," Julian murmured, and Truth felt a flare of indignation.

"They're poor tools, but they're all we have. If you insist on waiting for perfection, you aren't going to get very far," she said sharply.

"True," Julian conceded, "and so perhaps you'd agree that some balance of trust between human and machine should be observed? I do wonder why no skeptic, noting what he would term the widespread delusional perception of ghosts and space visitors, has ever asked *why* people see what they see." He buttered his muffin and bit into it with relish.

It was a good point, and Truth acknowledged it as such.

"That's a question I'm not equipped to answer," Truth admitted. Under Julian's minatory gaze she took a bite of omelette, then another.

"Well, then, if we agree with Sir Isaac Newton that we are all standing at the edge of a vast ocean picking up bits of colored shell while the sea of absolute knowledge foams about our feet, that's enough," he said.

Maybe it is, Truth admitted. *But I don't think we agree on—on why the sea is boiling hot, and whether pigs have wings,* Truth protested silently.

"Since you'll deny me the chance to run and play hooky," Julian said when breakfast was over, "I'll be in my study, catching up on some correspondence. Don't hesitate to interrupt me," he told her with a grin.

"I promise," Truth said. She abandoned her breakfast mostly unfinished and went upstairs to get her keys.

Coming down the steps, her car keys in her hand, Truth wondered where she could hide *Venus Afflicted* once she had it back in her possession. Fiona's unwelcome visit had shown her that her room was far from sacrosanct, and even though she didn't think Fiona would bother her again that left half-a-dozen other candidates.

Light.

The idea appealed through its very perversity. Why would anyone search Light's room when they were sure that the unworldly psychic had nothing to hide? And Truth had seen a number of nooks and crannies in that attic room into which she could insert the book. So long as Light didn't suspect it was there, it would be safe—there was no reason for Truth to believe that Light would not instantly hand *Venus Afflicted* over to Julian if she once suspected its existence. But if Thorne were real—and not merely her compelling delusion—surely his protective interest would extend to his other daughter as well?

She went outside, shivering in the morning chill.

Her car was just where she'd left it; she glanced around furtively to see if anyone was in sight, feeling ridiculous as she did so, before she opened the trunk. The necklace and ring were there, and so was *Venus Afflicted*. With another covert look around herself, Truth shoved the book and jewelry into her purse and closed it tight. Then she shut the trunk.

But where was she supposed to put the car? There was

nothing beyond the pass-through and side entrance besides the back lawn and the boxwood maze. It appeared she needed Gareth's help after all.

Just like some fainting Gothic heroine? Forget it!

A little detective work solved the mystery; remembering where Julian had gone last night with his car, she simply followed the drive along its curve past the front of the house until she came to what looked like an old carriage house behind a stand of trees. The doors were open, and she saw Julian's immaculate BMW, parked next to the white Volvo station wagon that showed signs of hard use. A gleaming black motorcycle, its gas tank painted with silver stars, stood in a corner. She imagined it must be Hereward's—he looked the sort to have a dashing bike like that.

And when did you start to think that bikers were dashing? Truth asked herself. It was beginning to seem to her that she had sleepwalked through her entire life—suddenly, upon awakening, to be presented with an unknown self that had a great many positive likes and dislikes, none of which she recognized as her own.

Who was she turning into? *What* was she turning into?

She sighed. All she had to do was make it through to next Tuesday alive. Julian would do his ritual on Monday—Halloween—have no result, of course. . . .

Of course? It killed your mother.

Drugs *killed my mother—not magick. And Thorne was innocent!*

Are you sure? Really sure?

Thorne wouldn't have killed Katherine Jourdemayne. He loved her.

You're sure of that too, the snide inner voice commented. *Has it ever occurred to you that the great Thorne Blackburn was just as surprised by what happened as everyone else was?*

I'll have to ask him when I see him, Truth told herself grimly.

When I see him.

*   *   *

Now that she knew where to go, it was a matter of minutes to slide her Saturn into the empty space provided. The weighted-down Coach bag slung over one shoulder in what she hoped was a casual attitude, Truth walked back up to the house.

It was hard to believe, looking at Shadow's Gate, that it could really be the sinkhole of madness and doom that basic research and lurid imagination insisted. The Elijah Cheddow murders of 1872 were over a century ago; Katherine's death and Thorne's disappearance twenty-six years in the past. Standing here, it was hard to remember that she'd nearly frozen to death in the library just a few nights ago—or heard Light speaking in her father's voice.

As Truth came up the drive, she saw the front door open. Without conscious volition she stepped back off the gravel path into what shelter the bare trees provided.

Michael came out the door. His hair shone blue-black in the sunlight, and he was dressed as usual, in a dark three-piece suit with tie that echoed the formality of the canonical garb that he might or might not be entitled to.

He turned back, holding out his hand, and Light came through the door.

She was wearing clothes Truth didn't know she owned—a skirted suit with a dark blouse. Her hair was pinned up; the effect was severe and jarringly adult, as if the fey woman-child Truth knew was only a mask to be put off at will. But Truth had been willing to bet that the Light she had seen was genuine.

This must be the mask, then.

Why?

Michael put his arm around Light, leading her down the steps. In the white morning radiance, both of them seemed to glow. He smiled down at her; Light reached up to touch his face. Then, as Truth watched, the two of them began to walk toward town.

Oh, please, let him be taking her away. . . .

Truth rubbed her forehead in confusion and the beginning of a headache: it wasn't noon yet, but the morning
had been incredibly tense. But she didn't want Michael to
take Light away from her—only away from *here*, and he
wasn't going to do that, was he?

Then what *was* he doing?

"It doesn't matter so long as it means there's nobody in
her room," Truth muttered with brutal practicality. She
waited until the pair had vanished around the curve of the
drive, heading for town, before she moved.

The house let Truth find Light's room easily. She listened
to herself think that, and winced. It was all too easy to slide
into anthropomorphism, imputing human reason to inani-
mate objects. Houses were not alive. They could not need
or desire—or act.

But their inhabitants could. And what did the inhabitants
of Shadow's Gate want?

Truth opened the door to Light's room and 'stepped inside, half her mind still on that problem. What *did* all of
them want . . . and how far would they go to get it?

The window seat had a lid that opened; the storage was
filled with sheets and blankets. They smelled musty, as if
this storage space weren't one in common use. Truth
slipped *Venus Afflicted* into a pillowcase and buried it at
the very bottom of the chest. The hiding place was neither
perfect nor foolproof, but it was better than nothing.

She weighed the amber necklace with its heavy pendant
in her hand, measuring. It would be a good idea to hide the
ring and the necklace somewhere outside her room too—
and if she hid them here, anyone who stumbled across them
might not look further.

Or finding them might motivate them to look hard
enough to find the book.

" 'You pays your money and you takes your choice,' "
Truth said aloud, quoting. After another moment, she

slipped the necklace back into the drawer she had taken it from, a day or two ago.

"Do you want it back, Father? Come and get it."

She took the ring with her when she went.

Where to hide the ring—so she (and perhaps Thorne) could find it? Thus armed and motivated, the whole of Shadow's Gate took on something of the out-of-season air of a site for an Easter egg hunt. Most of the possibilities that presented themselves were too obvious—or too hard for her to get to in a hurry. At last she gave up and brought it back to her room with her—and with sudden inspiration concealed it at the bottom of the jar of bath salts she'd bought.

There. That was taken care of.

Now there was only the matter of six crates of delicate machinery to consider.

By four o'clock that afternoon Truth was seriously considering a career in some other profession. While she had been given the free use of four strong males—Caradoc, Hereward, Donner, and Gareth—to do most of the heavy lifting and uncrating of the apparatus, getting the equipment out of its crates was just the beginning.

At lunchtime, when her assistants were finished and the crates and padding stored away for later, Truth found that she had three cameras, which could be set to take pictures automatically at anything up to one-hour intervals. Two of them were loaded with superfast high-resolution film that should allow her to take recognizable photographs even in near total darkness. The third was loaded with infrared film, which was sensitive not to light, but temperature. Dylan hadn't sent any spare film, and Truth wondered why.

She had an industrial-model tape recorder, six reels of recording tape, and a number of mikes sensitive enough to pick up the sound of water in the plumbing from a floor away.

She had not one, but two polybarometers, specially built for the Institute, which would do their best to chart and record all fluctuations of temperature and air pressure, along with noting any stray earthquakes that happened to come their way.

She had battery packs for all six machines.

All she was lacking was a strategy.

Nearly everything was on casters, so Truth didn't think she'd have too much trouble moving it herself to where she wanted it—although carrying any of the objects except the tape recorder up a flight of stairs would have been impossible for her—so she released her willing servants and was left to wrestle with thirty pages of handwritten instructions from Dylan, plus the manuals that came with each machine.

Gareth brought her a sandwich, and only after he left did Truth realize that she'd missed a golden opportunity to question him about what had—or possibly hadn't—happened this morning. She sighed—so much bad luck was really bad planning, giving her a choice of thinking of herself as stupid or merely inept—and turned back to Dylan's notes.

The more she read, the more she was convinced that fieldwork was not for her.

By two in the afternoon she was even desperate enough to call Dylan. Today her cellphone phone worked just as it ought to.

"Truth! How are you?" Meg's voice came cheerfully through the handset.

"I'm fine, Meg." What else, after all, could she say? "Is Dylan around?"

But Dylan was not around, so all Truth could do was leave him, once again, the number of her new phone—though if she were not within earshot of it when it rang there would be little way for her to know if he had called—and returned to the equipment and instructions.

She had never felt so inadequate.

Now that she had the equipment she'd asked for, where

was she going to put all of it? She should have thought of that long before.

The library was an obvious place, and one that had been the center of a previous event: It was reasonable for her to put one of the cameras and one of the polybarometers here to see what she caught.

But the obvious place for the other one, plus both cameras and the tape recorder, was her bedroom. Thorne had come there before—he would probably return there again. And when he did, she could nail him.

But if she did that, she'd have to admit she was being haunted—and by whom. Sanctity of the scientific method or no, Truth was unwilling to expose herself to the attention she would receive from Julian's Circle of Truth if that particular truth came out. There must be some other way.

So she decided to put the other polybarometer in the Temple.

Julian poked his head in to see how she was doing around three. He had no objection to the polybarometer going into the Temple, although he would not permit either the camera or the tape recorder there.

"Our rituals are secret, Truth. And even though one day I hope you will be inside the Veil rather than outside, photographing or taping what we do—no," he said.

In the end—running out of both ideas and patience— Truth decided to set up the other two cameras to provide a parallax image in the library, and that gave her the perfect excuse to take the tape recorder upstairs with her. Let them think she only wanted to keep it out of the way. Maybe she could get proof without anyone knowing.

But what would she do with it when she had it?

By the time she'd wrestled the tape recorder upstairs it was after six, and while Truth had no idea by this time if any of the Institute's equipment would even work, she was pretty sure she hadn't broken any of it.

She glanced out through the windows. The sun had already set, leaving only a faint indigo line of light upon the horizon, but ornamental floodlights shone out over the garden and maze. After a day spent indoors, a walk in the fresh air seemed especially inviting.

Saint Martin's summer—that brief warm period after the first frost—was still ahead, and the evening air was cool and inviting on Truth's face as she walked out down the white pebble pathway. Glancing back over her shoulder, she could see that most of the rooms of the big old house were lit, including one high in the corner. Light's.

I wonder where she and Michael went today? For a moment Truth let her mind run free to speculate upon the future. After everything here was over, she would take Light away with her. She had a two-bedroom apartment; it would be only a small inconvenience to move her office into her bedroom and give Light a room of her own. Light could wander the Taghkanic campus as easily as this, and Truth—

But there imagination foundered, because Truth could not see herself slipping comfortably back into her old life. And what if she took Julian up on last night's offer and went to Europe with him? What would happen to Light then?

We could take her with us, Truth thought, even as she realized that Light was utterly unequipped to deal with the crowded chaos of European travel.

But it isn't going to matter, Truth thought with a strange detachment. *That won't be my decision to make.*

The fey impulse faded, and Truth saw that her footsteps had brought her to the maze. She hesitated at the entrance. Going in was tempting, and if they hadn't changed it from the map she'd seen in one of the books, she'd be fine.

And even if they had, how lost could she get in something this small? It wasn't as if she were daring Hampton Court Maze. Truth started down the path.

She'd just had time to get inside, for the high boxwood hedges to cut off the light and for her to realize how really foolhardy an idea it was to come in here after dark when . . . something . . . *changed.*

If this had been California and not New York, Truth would not have hesitated to name it an earthquake; it had the same rolling disorienting quality that made its victim need to stop and remember his own name. She felt as though she'd tripped over a step that wasn't there, although the path was perfectly smooth.

Then she realized that something was burning—she smelled the smoke and heard the crackle of flames like far-off gunfire. She turned.

There was no hedge between her and the burning house. She started forward, and stopped as the realization came to her that something was wrong, that a fire like this could not have spread in the few minutes she'd been out of the house. Then she realized that the house that was burning was not the one she had left.

The burning house was a long low rambling white clap-board structure, its small windows set high under the eaves. It was filled with fire, and every window showed the hot gold of a jack'o'lantern's eyes. Shadow's Gate—just as it had been the night it burned, as it had been in 1872, one hundred twenty-three years before.

As if she possessed the clairvoyance she tested in others, Truth stared into the fire and seemed to see *through* it—to see with snapshot clarity a whitewashed bedroom with a high-canopied tester nestled beneath its slanting ceiling. The fire was all around, but even the fire had not eradicated the lacy sprays of blood that patterned the walls of the room.

In the middle of the room stood a man, his skin baked glistening red by the flames and his shirt soaked with blood and sweat, holding an axe and sobbing as he plied it past all necessity. Bringing it down again and again, though its targets had long since ceased to struggle and, even, to breathe.

Elijah Cheddow. Who, on this site, had killed his family and vanished—burned to death in a fire he himself had set.

And no one had ever known why, though Truth was beginning to suspect.

The flame-fed vision faded as a section of roof caved in, sending a pillar of sparks skyward. In the distance she could hear a bell tolling to waken the villagers of Shadowkill to the disaster in their midst.

But somehow, for all its horror, the scene Truth watched held no power to frighten—its emotional impact was as diminished as if it existed in the shadow of even greater terror, of power which—once bound—must be fed.

"I know a bank where the wild time grows," a familiar voice said behind her. "No, don't turn around."

She glanced sideways as Thorne spoke, and as she looked away from the fire felt it suddenly cease, tucked back into the past once more. The evening breeze rustled in the leaves of the boxwood hedge.

"Hello," Truth said, and then, reluctantly: "Hello, Father."

The fear she had not felt watching the fire came now—not of Thorne Blackburn, but for herself, her sanity. She understood now what Michael had been trying to tell her about leaving while there were things she didn't know—about leaving while she still had the serene certainty that there was only one way to see the world.

"Wouldn't you like to walk down the drive and get in your car and leave? You could send for your things—and if you don't get them, so what? You dress like a straight anyway," Thorne added with faint scorn.

"Why should I leave?" Truth forced herself to ask. *Now that I'm finally beginning to find out who I really am.* She stared straight ahead at the hedge-wall of the maze. She could still see the entrance off to her right. There was no house burning there now.

Or should that be . . . yet?"

"So you could always be certain about everything—including your sanity," Thorne said in response. "You're not like the others—you're *my* daughter. And you don't even understand what that means," he added.

Don't I? When blood calls to blood?

Truth turned around abruptly. There was no one there. She glanced up the path, although she knew that if someone had been standing there they had not had time to get out of sight.

She reached out her hand and brushed the leaves. There was no path through them.

"I'm already crazy," Truth said aloud. "I've read about hallucinations—they aren't like this. Normal people don't see things that aren't there and have conversations with people that don't exist. And what about Light?"

There was no answer.

"Thorne!" Truth's voice was preemptory, demanding, the question of reality set aside. "What about Light? What will happen to her if I go? She won't go with me. She's your daughter too—our blood—what will happen to her?"

I'm standing out here in the dark yelling at the bushes, Truth realized suddenly.

"Thorne? Father?" *Oh please answer me.*

"The Light and the Truth are the Way," Thorne Blackburn said. Truth couldn't tell what direction the voice was coming from, though she could hear the smile in his voice that told her he was pleased with his own cleverness. "And the Way is the Way of the Pilgrim. Your blood has chosen for you, daughter. Beware." The voice faded like a theatrical special effect.

"Oh Jesus Christ!" Truth snapped in nervous exasperation. Not another florid melodramatic cryptic warning! She thought of all the things she wanted to say to Thorne Blackburn at that moment and decided that none of them was suitable for addressing one's father, living or dead.

I'm going crazy. I'm having all the arguments with my father I would have had when I was a teenager, only I'm not a teenager and he's dead.

But it doesn't seem to change anything. . . .

Truth retraced her steps quickly and went back into the house.

*   *   *

Wherever Michael had gone with Light that afternoon, they were both back at the house in the time for dinner. Fiona was also at the table, carefully not looking at Truth.

Julian presided over them like an antique god over his unruly children, coaxing, chiding, and proclaiming by turns. He reserved a special smile for Truth, and it warmed her as if she still stood before the fire that had burned tonight in the parlor fireplace. Only later did she realize it should have triggered an associative memory of her vision of the burning of the previous Shadow's Gate, but it was as if those memories were in a class by themselves, untouched by mundane reality.

Conversation eddied around her, excited and anticipatory. The Circle would be working tonight, beginning the rituals that would culminate in the Opening of the Way. The Circle would meet every night from midnight until dawn right through a week from Monday—Halloween— for six hours of Blackburn's elaborate *théâtre sacré*. On Halloween night they would start at dusk, and work the final ritual of Thorne's liturgy—the one that would reconnect the worlds of Gods and Men.

And then what?

Though she'd been here only a few days, Truth had become fond of most of Julian's Circle: the aloof Donner; Hereward with his backhand mockery; Ellis, who seemed always to be consciously satirizing himself; Caradoc, whose involvement in something this outré appeared so out of character; Gareth who wanted so passionately to belong— and who was so unsuitably in love. They weren't just dry case histories in a monograph on cults—they were people heading for disaster as surely as if they'd been let loose in an armory to play with the guns.

Why was she so sure of that?

The question took on fresh urgency the longer she considered it. She was—she was having some sort of breakdown, because if she was not, what *was* happening to her?

And Thorne kept harping upon the fact that she was *his* daughter, as if that fact put her in a special class of danger—but what?

The longer Truth stayed at Shadow's Gate, the more questions—and fewer answers—she had.

The members of the Circle excused themselves directly after dinner; Truth gathered that there were a number of preparations that preceded the ritual. Julian hung back, and, when she got to her feet, walked with Truth back into the parlor.

The lights were turned low, and the fire in the fireplace was burnt down to coals. The litter of glasses, abandoned from the predinner cocktails, was still present. Truth walked over to the fireplace, staring down into the dying fire. Who was Thorne Blackburn—and *what* was his daughter?

Julian came up and put his arm around her; his hand was warm where it cupped her shoulder. She could feel the thrum of power running through him, like the low purr of an idling engine.

"Your equipment should have recorded some interesting data by tomorrow," Julian said.

"I hope so," Truth said, but even the possibility of graphing the fluctuations in energy produced by the workings of an occult Lodge could not distract her from the feeling of doom that hung over her.

"Tell me that you'll join us," Julian urged. "For Thorne's own blood to be absent from the scene of his greatest triumph would be a crime, don't you agree?"

"Light will be there," Truth said without thinking.

"True," Julian agreed. "But all Thorne's children should be."

"I . . . I'll think about it," Truth said as she had before.

"I'll even admit that part of my desire is purely selfish: If you aren't working with us, I'll hardly see you at all in the next week," Julian added.

"Are magicians supposed to be selfish?" Truth asked, striving for a light tone.

"Join us, and I'll show you just what magicians are," Julian said, his voice a velvet promise. But he took her continued refusal in good humor and, kissing her lightly upon the forehead, departed to his magick.

After he was gone she almost wished she had gone with him. She'd never before noticed how flat and empty Shadow's Gate seemed at night—as if, in Julian's absence, it was a theater without a play.

She glanced at the mantel clock. Nine twenty-three. So much for the frantic night-life of the super rich. Truth yawned, remembering how short on sleep she'd been these past few days. An early night would do her no harm, either.

She went upstairs to her room. The bed was turned back—it must be Irene who did these things, as Truth could not imagine this much domesticity from Fiona, nor that Fiona would do these things for her even if she did them for everyone else—and her nightclothes were laid out. She'd just write up the day's events in her diary before turning in.

She undressed and got ready for bed, switching on the enormous tape recorder as she did so. Most of the failures to record psychic phenomena, Dylan had always said, stemmed from failure to turn on the recorders. Truth wouldn't make that mistake—especially as events at Shadow's Gate seemed to wait on no particular calendar.

The massive reels began slowly to turn, and the needles flickered alertly across the dials. The machine made a muted "open mike" sound, faint enough that it could not be heard even from a few feet away. Each reel held twelve hours of tape—the machine should be set up to record through nine-thirty tomorrow morning. Truth checked that all the wires were tucked carefully out of the way—to minimize disruption, none of the Institute's ghosthunting equipment ran off house current; each had it own massive rechargeable battery pack, which should power it for at least a week. And a week's time was all she needed.

She pressed the "test" button. The battery's LED display lit redly: 87 percent power. More than enough.

Testing the recorder's battery reminded her once again of Julian's warning about battery life at Shadow's Gate, and she tested her cellphone, dialing her home number and being miraculously rewarded with the sound of her answering machine. The phone was working, at least. Why some times and not others? It made no sense.

Nothing here made any sense.

She hesitated over trying Dylan again and finally dismissed the idea. It was late, she was tired—and the equipment was working as well as it was going to, anyway. Truth got into bed with her journal and began to record the day's events.

She was feeling pleasantly sleepy by the time she was done, and got up to take one last look at the recorder.

It wasn't working.

It took her a few moments to register the fact. How could it not be running? Nevertheless, the needles all lay flat at the end of their dials, and all the status lights were out.

Had the plug worked loose? But this equipment was designed to foil poltergeists—the plug was locked into the battery with two metal flanges. Truth flipped up the guard on the battery's "test" button and pressed it, but the LED display stayed dark.

But it had been working earlier. It had been at nearly full charge earlier.

She glanced at the wall socket. She could plug the recorder directly into the house current. It was tempting, but she already knew how untrustworthy the power was here— if she plugged the recorder into the house she risked a power surge that would scramble its delicate little innards for good. Sighing, all thought of sleep banished by exasperation, Truth switched off the reel-to-reel and unhooked it from the battery pack. She plugged the battery into the wall, where a green "charging" light and a weak flutter of needles reassured her that the laws of physics still worked.

What about the others? Truth groaned, belted on her bathrobe, shrugged her feet into slippers, and went downstairs.

There were three cameras and a polybarometer in the library. The battery pack on one of the cameras was dead; the other three batteries showed 33, 17, and 40 percent power, respectively, although they'd all been between 80 and 90 percent when she'd hooked up the equipment and tested it. The timers on all three cameras were scrambled as well; not knowing the cycle for the manifestations centering on the library, Truth had set them each to take a picture once an hour. One of the cameras had run through its entire roll of film already—Truth winced; as Dylan had said, the fast film was expensive—and one had been reset to take a photograph every six hours. The third had been changed to manual operation.

It would be so comforting to think this was sabotage, Truth reflected. Comforting, but unlikely—Julian had shown very little interest in interfering with her investigations, and she doubted that was an act.

She switched the polybarometer to the battery with the 40 percent charge—though at the rate the batteries were draining it probably wouldn't last out the night—and looked around for outlets to plug the other three batteries into for charging. She found outlets for two in the library— the batteries seemed to charge normally once they were plugged in, at any rate—and decided to forget about the other one for the time being. At least she now had some proof of Julian's claims about failing batteries.

When she was done with the equipment in the library, sleep seemed the farthest possible thing from her mind, and a rumbling in her stomach reminded her that she'd been too keyed up to eat much at dinner.

A nice cup of cocoa, as Irene would say, heals all wounds. That's what I need.

The thin line of light beneath the door warned her that the kitchen was already occupied, but although he was the only possible person who could be there tonight, Truth wasn't really prepared to see Michael standing in front of the stove, intent upon a saucepan.

His jacket and vest were thrown over a chair and the

sleeves of his white shirt were rolled up to just below the elbow. His shirt collar was unbuttoned as well—without the armor of his formal dress Michael seemed absurdly young. The strong odor of chocolate wafted up from the saucepan as Michael gave its contents another stir.

"I guess we both had the same idea?" Truth said. She supposed she ought to be embarrassed showing up in front of Michael in a robe and pajamas, but it was a good heavy robe and the pajamas were far more concealing than many street clothes. And Michael was not her idea of a romantic object, anyway. There was something too ... alien ... about him.

What a peculiar thing to think. Light likes him.

"Cocoa?" Michael said. He smiled at her. "There's enough for two."

Truth nodded, and took one of the brownies left over from the evening's dessert and sat down at the kitchen table. Michael brought over the saucepan and two white china mugs. Deftly, he poured each of them full and sat down.

"Julian plans to close the house in November," Truth said, approaching her subject obliquely.

"I believe he would," Michael said.

"Would," not "will." "Don't you believe him?" Truth challenged.

Michael met her eyes directly, and once more Truth had that unsettled feeling of peril.

"I believe that Julian believes ... that there is no reason to plan beyond October thirty-first," Michael said carefully.

"The day of his final ritual," Truth amplified. Michael nodded.

Was Michael implying that Julian was crazy? And how reliable a source was *Michael* anyway, if it was sanity that was in question?

"What do you suppose will happen, when ..." *When he finds out it hasn't worked,* Truth couldn't quite bring herself to say.

"Let me ask you a question in turn: What do you think

Julian will do with the power he gains from opening the way for pagan gods to walk the Earth once more?"

"Thorne Blackburn always said that Opening the Way would inaugurate a new golden age," Truth said slowly.

"Admirably vague," Michael said with an angry smile.

"So you think Julian doesn't have the human race's best interests at heart?" *Just what I need; another inconclusive conversation with a nutcase. Well, at least this one's alive.*

"Do you?" Michael shot back. "Think carefully: Pure altruism is nearly as rare as disinterested kindness in this world."

"I thought you were supposed to be his friend," Truth said, starting to get annoyed. Her feelings for Julian were too confused to withstand much examination, but she did know that she didn't like hearing this tissue of innuendo from Michael.

"I am his friend," Michael said. "Perhaps the only one he has left—and certainly the one he needs most."

"Well isn't that just peachy for both of you," Truth snapped. She drained her cup and stood up. "Just tell me one thing, Michael: You hate magick, don't believe in studying the unknown, and you think Julian's crazy. Just what are you doing here?"

Michael looked up at her, and in his eyes Truth saw a fury and pain that made her irritated frustration seem in the worst of taste, as if she mocked a man who had already received his death wound.

"I am here because here is where I must be," Michael said, "because Good cannot act in the absence of Evil. I have fewer choices than he has."

"Michael, I need you to talk rationally to me," Truth said desperately. "I need you to tell me the truth."

" 'What is truth? said jesting Pilate,' " Michael quoted bitterly. "Very well: the truth. If you remain here, you imperil your immortal soul. It is possible that you will be offered the chance to renounce your certainty of heaven. It is possible that you will take it. That renunciation will cost you the light, Truth—you will walk in shadows all the rest of your days."

"That's . . . gibberish," Truth said forlornly.

"It is the truth," Michael said sadly, "but you do not understand it. And once you do—I think you will have passed beyond the time when you are still free to choose."

"I've told you I don't believe in . . . your religion," Truth said diffidently.

"Your belief is not necessary for its existence—or its truth," Michael said. "It *is*."

She could talk to Michael no more than she could to the others, Truth realized sadly. Michael held to a faith that shaped his world—and without accepting its reality, how could the two of them talk together?

"Good night, Michael," Truth finally said, going to the sink to rinse her cup.

"Sleep well," Michael Archangel said.

On her way up to bed she detoured past Light's room. Light was already down in the temple with the others, and her room was empty. *Venus Afflicted* was still where Truth had left it.

It remained there for the next nine days.

CHAPTER THIRTEEN

THE HOUR OF TRUTH

Time's glory is to calm contending kings,
To unmask falsehood, and bring truth to light.
—WILLIAM SHAKESPEARE

OCTOBER 30TH WAS A SUNDAY, AND TRUTH SPENT IT AS she had spent every day of the past week or more—in the Blackburn collection at Shadow's Gate. By now she had a pile of notes that rivaled her source material for sheer word count, and even a rough outline of her book. There would be chapters covering Thorne's early life and the evolution of his "followers" after his death, but the meat of the book would still be Thorne's public career in all its scandalous excess, just as she had originally planned.

Only the excesses didn't seem quite so scandalous any more.

She tried to ignore the inner voice that told her Thorne was no more excessive than his contemporaries, that his own sincere belief blurred if not eradicated the line, if not between con man and visionary, then at least between con man and crackpot. Thorne had *believed*—he hadn't been trying to steal money to enrich himself.

And in one sense he had not stolen at all—the wealth

which his devotees had heaped upon him had all gone into achieving his vision, leaving nothing behind.

Even his lies had been an exercise in honesty—if he told his followers unbelievable stories about his past and his exploits, it was precisely so they wouldn't believe him— or anyone else who tried to fool them. Thorne had been raised in a world where the example of Hitler's madness was still fresh—what he had wanted most was to create a world of demigods, not followers.

How could it all have gone so wrong, Father—how?

But chasing Thorne had not been all that Truth had to occupy her during that time. There was also the matter of the batteries.

When she'd finally gone back upstairs that night, the cellphone had been dead as well, and Truth had repressed the momentary impulse to fling the useless thing out of her bedroom window. She'd told herself she'd see tomorrow if she could get it working again, and thus had begun a frustrating and intermittent week-long struggle with batteries and chargers that had finally caused her to give up in disgust. But that wasn't the worst of it.

To Julian's affectionate, ill-concealed amusement, none of the battery packs for Dylan's ghosthunting equipment would hold a charge for more than a few hours, no matter what she did. It hardly mattered that Dylan hadn't sent more film for the cameras—she hadn't managed to use up what she had.

Not that she'd missed much by having no equipment available. Except for its pernicious effect on her batteries, Shadow's Gate had been meek as a little lamb. Rooms stayed where they belonged and so did pictures. She didn't even see Thorne Blackburn, and Truth was surprised to find how much she missed that. She'd been becoming fond of the old rogue; as if he were a wicked uncle with deplorable habits who was, nonetheless, part of the family. She would miss him when she left Shadow's Gate.

She looked around the library room, chewing on her pen.

The curtainless windows admitted cascades of white October light. Caradoc was sitting at the other table surrounded by several books on magick. Truth had looked into them and found them incomprehensibly technical, but Caradoc did not seem to be having any trouble—he worked steadily, checking one against the other, and making notes in a large, black-bound sketchbook. He was wholly engrossed in his work—these days, all the Circle of Truth was occupied by the Work, focusing all their attention on perfecting their performance of Thorne's elaborate rituals. She hardly saw any of them these days, except at dinner.

A theater built for one . . . and one they aren't even sure is coming, Truth thought to herself whimsically. To her uninitiated perceptions, it was very much as if Julian's Circle were putting on a long elaborate full-dress play every night—and spending all their other waking hours rehearsing for it, as well as building the sets and compounding the makeup. Well, better them than her, although she'd been laboring hard herself, and her work with the Blackburn Library was nearly done.

She'd be leaving soon, Truth thought idly. She'd copied out by hand most of the documents she'd need to refer to later. And besides, Julian would be turning his attention to other matters once the Opening of the Way was done; there'd be no place for her here.

The final ritual was tomorrow night.

Truth blinked and looked around, as mazed as if she were awakening from some long dream. Tomorrow night was Halloween, and Julian's final ritual.

Where had the time gone? Over a week, and she'd drifted right through it as if she had all the time in the world. And now there was no more time.

That knowledge was as alarming as anything else that had happened to her here, and the sudden sense of urgency that replaced it was smothering—as if the house itself had abruptly awakened.

Where in God's name had her mind been—she hadn't

even driven home to Stormlakken for Aunt Caroline's memorial service!

Truth got slowly to her feet, feeling slightly dizzy. On the floor beside the fireplace, Light looked up when Truth looked at her, and smiled, then went back to playing cat's cradle with a length of white string onto which one silver bead had been threaded.

Truth groaned inwardly. She'd felt so smugly industrious, and now she realized that she'd been concentrating on busywork to shield her from her real work. She should have tried harder to get Light away from here; found out more about the backgrounds of the others and their reasons for being here—found out more about Julian, for God's sake; money like that didn't just sprout out of the ground like dragon's teeth . . .

She hadn't even tried to call Dylan back once she'd given up on the cellphone. Meg would have given him her message, but after that—nothing.

Well, that much she could remedy right now.

She felt no qualms about going into Julian's office—if he had the only phone at Shadow's Gate he must be used to all sorts of interruptions by now—but in fact she was not interrupting him; Julian wasn't there.

Truth went to the desk and raised the phone from the cradle. She held it to her ear. Nothing.

She joggled the button a few times—a useless habit picked up from old movies—and as she did Truth became aware of a strange smell in the room, a bitter, musty scent, pervasive but oddly pleasant.

The phone was obviously useless, though the weather had been reasonably clear, so its present failure could not be blamed on power outages. Truth returned the receiver to the cradle, and as she did her eye fell upon Julian's Day-Timer, open on the blotter.

I shouldn't look, Truth told herself, and did. Not that her snooping gained her anything. Most of the entries were in strings of gobbledygook symbols, except for one today that was written in plain English: *See Ellis.*

About what, I wonder? Truth mused, but this really was none of her business, so she forced herself to leave the desk diary alone and leave before anything embarrassing happened.

She went back to the library, but she now felt as restless as she'd been placid. Light stared at her for a long moment before returning to her elaborate game of making the silver bead slide back and forth among the cords. Watching her, Truth made up her mind to go down to Shadowkill and try to phone Dylan from there when an even more useful idea occurred to her.

She would do what she ought to have done much earlier. She would send all her log notes to Dylan and ask him to review them. He wouldn't see her visions of Thorne as evidence of a moral failing—anything from self-delusion to true psychism, yes, but not as some nebulous indicator of Truth's personal immorality.

She could trust Dylan.

And she'd send *Venus Afflicted* away from here too—to herself at the college. Maybe she could get it copied in town and send a copy to Dylan—she suspected that Dylan was more of a Blackburn scholar than he'd ever wanted her to know, though without crossing the line into occultism. Perhaps he could help her think of a way to defuse that dangerous book.

She hadn't wanted to do these things before—but that was, Truth knew now, because she hadn't felt *strong* enough before to survive their inevitable aftermath. But as she'd all but slumbered here at Shadow's Gate something deep within her had changed, something about the way she defined herself; and admitting to Dylan that she needed help no longer frightened her. Needing help did not diminish her. Everyone needed help sometimes; that was the way of the world.

She gathered up her notes and left the library. Today was

Sunday—she would put her package in the mail the moment the post office opened tomorrow.

The first thing to do—while she knew where Light was—was to retrieve *Venus Afflicted*.

Truth ascended the stairs to Light's third-floor aerie. The book was right where she had left it—so, for that matter, was the necklace, despite Thorne's demands—and she retrieved both and brought them back to her room. She tucked the necklace into a drawer and began making up a parcel of the items she meant to send to Dylan—her voice tapes, her notebook and log, the material she'd gathered on the haunted history of Shadow's Gate. The finished stack was large enough that she'd need a sturdy box for it.

Perhaps there was one downstairs. Probably Hoskins would know—or she might be able to find Irene.

She took one last glance at the pile from the doorway. The book was thoroughly buried in other papers, unnoticeable. She went out, closing the door behind her.

It took her about half an hour to track down box, tape, and wrapping paper, but Hoskins was helpful and she didn't have to bother Irene—not that finding Irene would have been easy. These days the entire house was like an enormous engine, dedicated to the Work, and everyone's waking moments seemed to be focused on it, either in meditation, rehearsal, or private ritual, or in fashioning the various paints, oils, teas, and incenses that seemed to be so necessary—freshly-made—to each night's performance. It made Truth a little uneasy, although she was well used to such discipline when she encountered it in academic circles.

She got back to her room, thought of composing a cover letter for the material, then decided she could just as well tell Dylan it was coming when she called him. She'd pack the box, leave it in the trunk of her car overnight to be doubly sure it was safe, and walk on down to the village today and give Dylan that call she owed him. The walk would be good exercise: She couldn't remember the last time she'd left Shadow's Gate, once the house had stopped trying to push her away.

And if it had, why?

It was as if, in some bizarre fashion, Shadow's Gate had finally welcomed her in.

She opened the box and started filling it.

Venus Afflicted wasn't here.

At first she thought she had to be mistaken. She searched the pile paper by paper, then all the other piles of paper, then every inch of the room.

It wasn't here.

They'd gotten it. After all her care, after all her *planning*, just when she'd been about to put it beyond their reach forever, they'd gotten it.

She felt an anger all out of proportion to the offense, as if the house, awakening, was feeding all its surging madness through her. Pure unreasonable fury surged through her veins, as if her blood had been turned to fire. She was tired of making nice, of letting them lull her with how reasonable they were. She was tired of going along, of being sensible. This was too much.

She was going to Julian. She was going to demand her book back—it was *hers*; Thorne was dead and it was *hers*—it was her heritage!

She didn't think past that moment of confrontation; she couldn't. When she threw open the door to her room it hit the wall with a popping sound like a rifle shot.

She felt the house try to pull her away, to confuse her, and used her anger like a sword to cut through its coils of influence. For the first time she tasted the power that went with her birthright, and embraced it gleefully even as some part of herself recoiled. She felt the house's power rebound upon itself, impotent, as she ran down the stairs.

"Julian?" Truth called, halfway down. Her voice had a dangerous edge.

Hereward crossed the black-and-white marble of the entryway, heading for the door. He glanced up as he saw her, but then the door was open, Hereward was holding the door as the men in white came in, carrying a gurney.

The sight jolted her back to some semblance of reason.

"Hereward?" she said, but he didn't stop, leading the EMTs down the hall.

Slowly, baffled, Truth came the rest of the way down the stairs. The front door was open. She could see an orange-and-white ambulance, its blue lights still flashing, parked in front of the steps.

What's going on?

"Isn't it *horrible?*" Irene said. She came through the parlor into the foyer. "It was—Oh, how *could* Ellis have done it—he'd been up and down those stairs a hundred times!"

"What did—" Truth began, but then the EMTs came back, wheeling the gurney slowly and carefully. Gareth and Hereward followed, faces grim.

Ellis was on the gurney, strapped to a fracture board that spoke volumes for the seriousness of his condition. His face was gray with pain and his eyes glittered. When he saw Truth he moved weakly against the straps, his mouth opening and closing.

Truth ran over to him. "Ellis?"

"He fell down the stairs. The servants' stairs—we don't use them, they're so steep, and—" Gareth said.

"He fell on his head," Hereward said harshly.

Ellis was plucking at Truth's hand with ice-cold fingers. She stared into his eyes; they were fixed on hers, and welled with tears of pain. His mouth worked desperately, but the words he was trying to say wouldn't come.

"It's all right," Truth found herself saying. Ellis's pain had defused the last of her rage, and all she felt now was a vast, aching pity. Ellis closed his eyes—in frustration? Resignation?

"Miss?" one of the EMTs said, and Truth let herself be moved back out of the way. The two technicians maneuvered the gurney carefully down the steps.

Truth glanced back the way it had come and saw Julian, all in shark-gray Armani silk. He was staring after Ellis with an unreadable expression on his face.

What would Julian do now? She didn't know much about the workings of his Circle, but she did know that Ellis had occupied an important position in the ritual. Ellis was the Black Dog—one of the four Guardians. Could Julian find someone to replace him?

"Truth?" said a voice from the open doorway.

She turned around.

It was Dylan.

Dylan Palmer stepped into the foyer. He glanced backward, to where the driver of the ambulance was closing the doors on its injured cargo.

"When I drove up here and saw that thing, I thought . . . Well, I'm just glad it wasn't you." His voice was ragged with relief.

Dylan was wearing a gray corduroy work shirt with the sleeves rolled up a few turns, faded jeans, and work boots. His sandy hair was in unruly disarray, and he looked as if he stood in a different light than the others.

"And you are?" Julian said before Truth could sort out the conflicting emotions surging through her and speak. Julian stepped forward, and the difference between him and Dylan was as jarring as that between Julian and Gareth—yet somehow Dylan did not come off the worse in the comparison.

"Dr. Dylan Palmer," Dylan said, stressing his title slightly. "Of the Margaret Beresford Bidney Memorial Psychic Science Research Laboratory at Taghkanic College. You must be Julian Pilgrim." He held out his hand, smiling.

"And what brings you here?" Julian said, his voice neutral. He did not offer his hand. Though Julian didn't look in his direction, Truth saw Gareth start uneasily, and she remembered the morning the crates had been delivered.

Julian didn't like surprises.

"I'd better go back down and close up the gate," Gareth said.

"Don't bother. I don't imagine Dr. Palmer will be staying long," Julian said.

Dylan lowered his hand but did not stop smiling. "Well,

actually," he said. "I came here to see Truth."

"There she is," Hereward said.

"Hello, Dylan." Truth said uncomfortably. *What the hell are you doing here?* Finally—as though something inside her had decided what defense to offer—anger began to well up, threading itself through all her perceptions. How dare Dylan come here?

As if summoned by some inaudible alarm, Caradoc came out of the library and Donner appeared from the back of the house, and suddenly the grouping in the foyer had all the earmarks of a confrontation spoiling to happen. But this wasn't right. Dylan was hers, to punish as *she* chose—it was not for these others to judge him.

"Julian, could we use the parlor for a while?" Truth asked. Julian nodded, smiling faintly. Truth crossed to Dylan and took his arm, leading him away from the others.

"What's with the Mad Scientist and his crew of muscle boys?" Dylan said, nodding toward the closed door into the foyer.

"What are you doing here?" Truth demanded. The anger rose up in her in sweet seduction—the fury that she'd felt earlier came surging up, rinsing away confusion and doubt now that it had found a new target, and that target was Dylan.

"I could ask you the same question," Dylan said, his voice rough with confusion and concern. "Two weeks ago you up and vanish, telling me you're going to write a bio of Thorne Blackburn and start here. Ten days ago you call and tell me you need monitoring equipment for Shadow's Gate—which I got for you—and then . . . nothing. I tried the cellular number, I tried the house number—nothing."

"So you came up here to check on me," Truth said accusingly.

"So I came up here to see if you were all right," Dylan amended. "What's going on? Who was that guy they were putting in the ambulance?"

"Ellis Gardner. Another of Julian's 'muscle boys,' as you so politely put it. He fell down a flight of stairs." She could hear the anger in her own voice and it excited her, a dangerous thing, begging to be let free.

Dylan didn't respond directly. "I've been worried about you," he finally said. "This isn't like you." He took a step toward her; Truth raised a hand as if to ward him off.

"How do you know what's like me and what isn't, Dylan? I'm Thorne Blackburn's daughter—blood will out." Truth strode across the room to the fireplace, and stood with her back to Dylan. "And while I suppose I should appreciate your concern—for your equipment if not for anything else—now you've seen me, and Julian really doesn't want visitors right now so why don't you just be on your way?"

The silence stretched, and Truth turned to find that Dylan was staring at her. "What the hell's gotten into you?" he said bewilderedly. "What's going on here?"

"The Blackburn Work," Truth said harshly. "And no, I haven't gotten involved with it, if that's what you mean. I'm here because Julian has a useful collection of Blackburn memorabilia—that's all."

"And what about the haunting?" Dylan asked angrily. "Or am I supposed to just forget about that too?"

Truth shrugged, trying to back off from the building confrontation and not entirely sure she could do it. "I'm not . . . All the equipment runs on electricity, Dylan. It isn't working. The battery packs drain in hours; nothing holds a charge." She laughed shortly. "But see for yourself—Julian will be delighted to have the phenomena investigated by a complete staff—next week." Her words were a warning.

"Once he's done his Halloween ritual? Oh, don't look so surprised, Truth—I'd be a damn poor ghosthunter if I didn't know the beasties' high holy days. Samhain and Walpurgisnacht, those are the biggies. Just how far is Julian planning to take after Thorne? Who's going to die this time?" Dylan's fists were clenched—he was almost shouting now, as if something in Shadow's Gate that fed on emotions had realized it had a fresh victim.

"That's a filthy thing to say!" Truth cried, losing the battle for calm, her body trembling with the need to lash out at her enemy. "You don't know anything about Julian and what he's done, but you just charge in here making baseless accusations, when Julian is—" She stopped, reining herself in with the greatest effort she had ever had to make. Her nails made separate stars of pain as she dug them into her palms, fighting for control. "Julian is the kindest, sanest human being I've ever known, and I won't listen to your filthy slanders. He wants to help me with the book—"

"No book is worth this!" Dylan interrupted loudly. "Are you listening to yourself? Can't you see what they're *doing* to you? How can you be so blind—"

"Get out." All Truth's anger had collapsed inward on itself, until it was a cold hard unyielding thing burning like frostfire in her chest. "Irene Avalon was my mother's dearest friend. Light is my *sister*. Do you think they'd hurt me? We even have a rationalist who's sure Julian's the Antichrist—Julian isn't likely to be raising any devils with *him* around. Go away, Dylan, and save your mumbo-jumbo for the Late Late Show." She folded her arms around herself, chilled even in the bright sunlight that streamed through the parlor windows.

Dylan came and stood before her, his expression remorseful.

"I should never have let you stay here once you told me this place was haunted. Hauntings play upon the *mind*, Truth, that's why they're so insidious—you don't need walls dripping blood and headless nuns when the untapped power of the human mind can be far more dangerous," he said sadly. "Please—"

Truth regarded him coldly. Why wouldn't he give up and leave her alone? Her kind had no use for human emotion.

But Thorne had chosen otherwise—and the choice had destroyed him.

"This is my specialty, Truth. I *know*," Dylan said earnestly.

"I am not finished here," Truth said. The power was here for her to draw on; she could see it now that she'd used it against the house. She started forward, and Dylan was forced to retreat a few steps.

"I suppose I could drag you out of here by force, or blackmail you into leaving with me by threatening to go to the police, but I've always preferred the use of reason," Dylan said. His hands were spread in a soothing gesture. "If you're staying of your own free will—"

"I am," Truth interrupted.

"Then you're a grown woman and capable of making your own choices, even if I happen to think they're wrong ones. But for God's sake take care of yourself, Truth—the most dangerous place on Earth for an unprotected medium is a haunted house."

"I'm no medium," Truth said, momentarily startled out of her anger. She'd never tested out of the normal range in any of the tests the Institute ran; considering her father, she'd been *glad*. . . .

Dylan sighed, and ran a hand through his hair. "Maybe. Can you take the chance? Your aunt was one of the most powerful trance mediums that ever worked with Rhine. That's how Thorne became interested in her and her twin in the first place. Of course, it was his theory that they had *sidhe* blood in them, too, or something, but no matter how you slice it, ESP is hereditary."

"Oh, God." The icy fury that held her was loosening its grip. Truth put her hands to her face, backing up against the mantelpiece. She could dismiss Irene, and Michael, and even Thorne in his ghostly visitation, but when Dylan—calm, rational, credentialed Dylan—said the same thing, what was she supposed to think?

"Why didn't I know?"

"I thought you did. *Truth*—" Dylan moved forward.

"I'm so glad you're still here, Dr. Palmer," Julian said.

"I'd like to take the opportunity to apologize for your reception earlier—if I'm not interrupting?"

"No, Julian, of course not," Truth said gratefully. Julian crossed the room to stand beside her, and Truth leaned against him.

"Just as you arrived, Dr. Palmer, a valued associate and a very dear friend suffered a severe injury. They're taking him to Saint Francis Hospital in Poughkeepsie."

"So far?" Truth asked, startled.

"I'm afraid there isn't anything closer that would do poor Ellis any good, darling," Julian said, reaching down to take her hand. "Northern Dutchess doesn't handle trauma of that sort and Albany Medical is even farther away. So I'm afraid I was more than normally abrupt," he finished, speaking to Dylan. "I take it you are the psychic researcher I will be paying host to next month?" He offered his hand. "I hope I can convince you to be our guest for lunch?"

Dylan was courteous enough to shake it. And everything else that might have been between Truth and Dylan went unsaid.

Julian phoned the hospital during the meal—the phone service at Shadow's Gate having experienced one of its intermittent revivals—and came back to the table looking dourly amused.

"He's still in X-Ray, and they weren't sure they wanted to talk to me at all. I told them I'd be covering the bills, and it was amazing how forthcoming they suddenly became."

"You?" Dylan asked.

"Of course," Julian said. "Actors have no money—and less medical insurance. And as Ellis was, in a sense, working for me . . ."

"*Noblesse oblige,*" Dylan said, but that was as pointed a remark as he made the entire time.

The enforced civility of the situation also gave Truth time to rein in her emotions and *think*. She couldn't just go

to Julian demanding the return of *Venus Afflicted* without
admitting she'd had it in the first place, and that would
mean admitting that she'd brought it to Shadow's Gate and
kept it hidden while he'd practically begged her for it.

She just couldn't.

Cut your losses and leave, a Thorne-like voice whispered
inside her. *You didn't have the book two months ago; you
don't need it now. Cut your losses and run.*

*"The most dangerous place on earth for an unprotected
medium is a haunted house,"* Dylan had told her.

*"You're not like the others, baby. You're special—you're
my daughter,"* Thorne's voice repeated.

No. She could not simply confess. And the only reason
to do so would be to gain Julian's help in recovering *Venus
Afflicted*, something she was not sure that she could count
on.

Truth studied Julian through her lashes, but he was chatting amiably with Dylan and seemed not to notice. Could
she find the book herself?

Maybe. She'd have the house and the night to search,
after all—she knew exactly where all the house's inhabitants would be, and for how long too. Midnight to six in
the Temple, and you could drop a bomb outside the door
without disturbing anyone inside.

Except for Michael, but in her need to do *something* to
recover Thorne's book, Truth glossed over that problem to
herself. She'd take care of Michael when the time came.
She'd find the book, take it back, and leave. Tomorrow
morning she could try again to get Light to go with her—
perhaps the final ritual wouldn't take place at all.

But if, with Ellis injured, Julian wasn't planning to continue the actions of the Circle, how could she go looking
for her book?

Dylan left after lunch, driving his small brown Datsun
down the road to the gate. Truth and Julian stood together
on the steps, watching him go.

"I'm glad he's gone," Julian said. "I felt like a nervous freshman being interviewed by the Dean. I wonder if I passed?"

"I've never seen anyone who acted less like a nervous freshman," Truth said, leaning against him. Julian put his arm around her waist, in a proprietary way that Truth no longer questioned. It was remarkable how guiltless she felt, considering that she intended to burgle Julian's room that very night. Of course, she didn't intend to steal anything, but that didn't make any difference, did it?

"It's my years of practice," Julian said, turning her toward him. "For a while I was wondering if I had a rival in Dr. Palmer—do I?"

"Of course not," Truth said, turning faintly pink. Julian had no rival—and no peer. He took her arm and led her back inside.

"Then come away with me, fair Incomparable—we'll put a girdle round the globe in considerably more than half an hour, find out all of Thorne's little secrets, and—Who knows?" He smiled down at her as he closed the front door behind them.

"Julian, what about the Work? I mean, Ellis isn't going to be able to work with you tomorrow night, even if it's only a few bruises."

"Which it isn't," Julian said, walking with her back into the parlor. "A skull fracture at the very least. I'm going down there to straighten out the bill, and possibly they'll have more information for me."

He picked up a glass paperweight from the mantelpiece and stared into it as if the information about Ellis's condition might be there.

"But what about the Circle?" Truth persisted. Julian turned back to her.

"Oh, one of the others can take on Ellis's part—we've had to double so many roles already that everyone knows everyone else's. Gareth can do it. We'll manage. I'm not putting this off for another year just because of—" he broke off. "I must sound terribly callous," he said with a small, self-deprecating smile.

"No. Just dedicated." Truth felt indecently relieved—they *would* be in the Temple tonight after all.

"I'm afraid, though, that I must—oh, not withdraw, but defer our invitation to become one of us. There's no more time. But perhaps I can persuade you on our travels." Julian's smile grew warmer.

"I—" Truth faltered.

She'd meant to tell him plainly that she had no intention of going to England with him; that she didn't think a romance with him was something she could comfortably handle; that right now her duty was to her sister and her work.

"Who knows?" Truth said instead, and the warm thrill of possibility made her skin tingle in a rush of surging blood.

Julian drove down to Poughkeepsie to settle arrangements with the hospital. He did not ask Truth to accompany him, and she did not ask to go with him. She went looking for Light instead, although she'd changed her mind—she didn't intend to even try to convince Light to come away with her. If Ellis's removal was a strain on the Circle's workings, Light's defection would bring its activities to a screeching halt. She'd always known that—Light was their trance medium—but before Ellis's injury she'd hoped there was a chance of convincing Light otherwise. Now she knew that was impossible. The Circle's incompleteness was too nakedly exposed. To lose Light was to fail utterly.

And while Truth wasn't sure that was such a bad thing, she wasn't sure she could get Light to agree. Julian wanted this ritual to happen so desperately, and Light owed him so much—and so did Truth.

And what was he going to do Tuesday morning, when the world was still as it had been and he saw it had all been for nothing?

If it was . . .

Truth sighed, caught between rationality and the compelling beliefs of the reborn Circle of Truth. Light would go with her Tuesday morning. She was sure of it. She'd take her away from here, and then . . .

Truth shrugged. She'd worry about that on Tuesday.

The evening meal was tense and edgy, as fraught as the new storm boiling up over Storm King Mountain. Julian wasn't back, but he'd called from Poughkeepsie—Ellis was in guarded condition, and Julian would return in time for the evening's ritual. The next to last.

Michael was gone also, without explanation, though no one commented on it. Perhaps he made them as uneasy as he did Truth—though he and Irene had seemed to be close.

Truth closed her eyes wearily. Who could she believe—*what* could she believe? Everyone couldn't be telling the truth—their stories were too contradictory.

"Poor Ellis," Irene sighed again, "I told him those stairs were treacherous."

"They wouldn't have been, if he didn't drink like a fish," Fiona snarled. "I don't care if he's hurt; I'm glad he's gone—I never liked him anyway."

"Spoken like a true lady," Hereward drawled. Fiona glared poisonously at him.

"It's nice to see we're all getting on so well in the master's absence," Caradoc said. He was wearing a pale gold silk suit and an open shirt, almost as if, with Julian gone, the responsibility of high fashion devolved upon him. He toyed with the signet ring on his right hand and did not touch his food.

"What do you expect?" Donner said irritatedly. He was so quiet Truth was always surprised when he said anything. She got the impression his fellow Blackburnites did not impress him much. "We're all exhausted. Six hours of ritual every night, four hours minimum of prep, more damn Latin and Greek than any of us has ever seen, and Julian push-

ing—" he broke off, as if what he had been about to say
was too far from favorable.

And in fact, Truth thought, he *did* look tired. They all
looked tired, even Fiona. No, more than tired. *Drained*, as
if someone were building . . . something . . . out of their
very life force.

"And Julian pushing," Hereward agreed. "Sometimes I
think he'd do it all by himself if he could."

"But he can't, so he doesn't," Caradoc said, and that
seemed to dispose of the matter.

Truth had set her travel alarm for midnight, just in case she
fell asleep. It was key wound, and did not seem to be afflicted with the troubles that beset other clocks at Shadow's
Gate, although her wristwatch had stopped long since. But
in any case there was no need—she sat bolt upright and
wide awake as the minute hand swept the hours away.

She used the time to review her working notes. She could
have sent them away with Dylan, but what was the point
if the grimoire wasn't going with them?

The truth was, Truth admitted to herself, that she hadn't
wanted to give her notes to Dylan—not now. He'd only
use them as a further excuse to meddle, to involve himself
in what was happening here at Shadow's Gate.

She didn't know if she wanted to protect him, or punish
him, or keep all the glory for herself—but she knew she
didn't want him here. Not until tomorrow night had come
and gone.

Outside her windows, rain drummed on the glass and the
out-thrust roofs below. The storm had broken after she'd
gone upstairs, but electrical power seemed to be holding
for now, and she had a candlestick and candles ready to
hand, just in case. The rain was a steady accompaniment
to her reading, and far-off thunder prowled the Hudson
River hills.

It had rained that night too: The 1872 fire had been so
easily contained because it had been raining all day, soak-

ing the earth and trees and protecting them from the sparks and flames. Otherwise the fire might have spread and devoured acres.

It had rained in 1969, for Thorne's final ritual. Irene had told her how the storm had blown open every door in the house.

It had been clear all week. Clear . . . and quiet.

And now it was raining again. Storming.

Truth looked at her key-wound travel clock, the most dependable timepiece remaining to her. Eleven forty-five. She'd wait another half hour to be sure, and then she'd search their rooms one by one for what had been taken from her.

She wiped damp palms on the legs of her chinos, nervous now. It had been so much easier when the possibility of meeting Elijah Cheddow in these halls simply hadn't existed. And though it was only a small possibility, it was enough to make her uneasy—and if Thorne showed up again she'd probably just die of fright.

If Thorne showed up, she could just ask him who had the book—and the necklace and the ring. They'd been gone too, when, after Dylan had left, she'd finally thought of checking on them, but by then she'd been too whipsawed by events to be properly angry. Let Thorne worry about them—he said they were his.

But the book—*that* she had to have. *That* wasn't Thorne's—not any longer.

At twelve-fourteen there was a crack of thunder right overhead and all the lights went out. Truth merely snorted and lit her candles. But the clinical rationalistic bravery she felt inside the room was harder to maintain once she got out into the hall with her wavering candle. She'd seen things that could not be—and talked to them too. It was harder to be brave knowing what could happen.

Or maybe bravery consisted of going on even when you knew *exactly* what could happen.

*   *   *

She wasn't sure where Michael slept—or even if he'd come back yet. If she did enter his room by mistake, she'd just tell him she was lost. Let him call her a liar if he chose—it was a plausible enough story, given what they both knew about Shadow's Gate.

And perhaps . . . But no. She shook her head. She could expect no help from Michael Archangel, for whatever reason.

She started with Irene's room. She'd come to love Irene, and didn't believe Irene would steal from her, but a perverse need to be fair made Truth feel that *everyone's* room must be searched, likely candidates for thief or not.

She found nothing—only clothes and makeup and earrings, a handwritten herbal that looked nothing like the book she sought, personal things. A picture of Thorne with Katherine and Caroline Jourdemayne, kept lovingly in a little leather case. A silver pendant of the same symbol as the gold one on Thorne's amber necklace.

She did Light's room next, on the same principle, and found even less, though confirming once more that Light had an outrageous sweet tooth.

She came back to the second floor. She'd search the rooms that were occupied first, the empty ones last. Then the rest of the house. If she had time.

And hope she didn't run into Michael.

But she didn't. Perhaps he wasn't back, though Truth knew too little about him to speculate where he might have gone. The room she thought was his was empty, though often she wasn't sure whose room she was in until she found something to identify the occupant.

Fiona's was easily guessed. Fiona had wads of currency snuggled away in odd locations, and at the bottom of a drawer Truth found one of Julian's charge slips and a sheet of paper covered with Fiona's careful copies of his signature. But Fiona didn't have the book, much as Truth longed for her to.

Ellis's room was a sad clutter, liquor bottles neatly tucked out of sight in every possible place. What had he been trying to tell her, there at the end? Truth searched his room especially carefully, but there was nothing to find.

Four more rooms. Caradoc and Hereward and Donner and Gareth's, but it was hard to tell what belonged to whom. Whose was the suitcase full of books on magick, and whose the gun and box of ammunition? Was Gareth the one with the can of gasoline in his room? Or was his the stack of porno magazines, shocking in their rawness?

The room she thought was Michael's was nearly empty; at first Truth had thought it *was* empty. But there were Michael's dark suits hanging in the closet—and in the back of the closet, a narrow black leather case six feet long and two feet wide but only six or eight inches deep; a case of the sort that could contain nearly anything from an electric guitar to a high-powered rifle, heavy and locked. *Venus Afflicted* might be in there, but Truth doubted it.

Which meant none of them had the book.

Her head ached—with the tension, the stress, the glittering candle flame. The scent of incense was chokingly strong everywhere she went, and the entire house seemed to throb to the beat of the ritual being conducted at its heart. If she only closed her eyes she could *see* it: the ring of unwinking candles; the blaze of power around Light; Julian crowned with the sun and the moon, his flaring aura blunt testimony to his inheritance of Thorne's power.

Power that was strong enough to do just what it promised. Power that could open the gate to the world beyond.

A spill of hot wax jarred her to consciousness. Truth's eyes flew open; she steadied the candle and realized that she'd been asleep on her feet.

It had been a dream.

Of course it had.

Unfortunately the headache was real. Truth rubbed her eyes with her free hand, and imagined that even now she could hear the chanting. She was standing in front of the door to Julian's suite. She'd saved him for last; perhaps unconsciously she did not want to uncover what she already suspected was true—that Julian had taken *Venus Afflicted*.

She opened the door gingerly, but of course there was no one there—Julian was in the Temple with the others. The nagging delusion that she could feel what was going on in the Temple was hard to push away; whenever she relaxed her concentration she could feel the power building like the current of the sounding sea. She could even smell the incense . . .

Truth brought herself back to reality with a start. That much at least was no hallucination; Julian's room reeked of incense—and why not? His clothes were probably saturated with it.

She pushed unreality from her mind and began to search.

The others were only visiting, but Shadow's Gate was Julian's home, this room held more of personal possessions than any of the other rooms had. But the file drawers of papers didn't interest her, nor did any other thing that was not *Venus Afflicted*.

In the drawer of Julian's nightstand she found a curl of paper torn from a photograph lying atop a manila envelope. She smoothed it out—a picture of a child, a thin, intense boy in a tie-dyed T-shirt, his long hair pulled back. It looked familiar; she knew she ought to recognize something about it, but there wasn't time. She picked up the envelope and shook out a clutch of photographs. They were old and yellowed and curled, and all of them were of the boy in the torn photo.

She leafed through them quickly by the light of the candle, and found one with Thorne in it. Pilgrim. The boy must be Thorne's son Pilgrim, the one who had run away.

Now she knew why the picture had looked familiar. The scrap had been torn from the edge of the group photo of Thorne's Circle in front of Shadow's Gate—as if someone had wanted to eliminate Pilgrim from the group.

But why were these pictures here instead of in the album downstairs?

There was no time to think of that. She had to hurry. She pulled the travel alarm out of her pocket and glanced at it. It still seemed to be working. Three A.M., and miles to go before she slept. She put the photos back in the drawer.

Venus Afflicted wasn't in Julian's rooms.

Truth went downstairs to his office, moving through the ritual's radiating current of power as if through a blood-hot ocean. There were unlit candles waiting in Julian's office; recklessly she lit them all. As the power hammered at her she tore through the files, the bookshelves, the drawers of Julian's desk with a reckless disregard for covering her tracks.

Nothing. Julian didn't have it.

Truth got slowly to her feet and stepped away from the desk.

No. *No.* Her hands trembled; she felt as if at any moment she might start screaming. She blew out all the candles but her own, quivering with exhaustion. She'd been positive Julian had it, she realized now; so damned certain that now she couldn't think of what to do next.

Her candle glittered off the decanter on the chinoiserie liquor cabinet in the corner; leaving the lone candle burning on the desk, she strode over to it, slopping the glass beside it full of a liquid that looked almost black in the dimness. She sniffed it before she drank—one of the sweet wines that Julian seemed to favor.

I hope it's amontillado. For the love of God, Montresor? Yes, Fortunato; for the love of God. She slugged the drink back as if it were Kool-Aid and poured another. She drank it more slowly; the first one hit when she was halfway through it—the world gave a violent subjective wrench and her feeling of agonizing sensitivity to the ongoing ritual snapped. What was it Julian had said when he was feeling the brandy to Light? Something about alcohol blunting the *chakras*, whatever they were.

No wonder Ellis drinks—I mean drank—if it was to shut this out. Julian would call it occult sensitivity, and Dylan the emergence of an hereditary psychic gift. Truth didn't care what they called it—she just wanted it to go away.

The wine made her flushed and lazy, but it didn't eliminate the need to *do* something.

But there was nothing she could do. Only go to Julian tomorrow and let him laugh at her or cry with her. Or say and do nothing, and let the book simply vanish. She sat down behind the desk again and stared at the candle mournfully.

Now that it was too late she saw all the things she should have done. Why hadn't she told Dylan everything while he was here? She'd been willing enough for him to read her journals. She'd been going to send him a copy of *Venus Afflicted*—why had she been so unwilling to tell him it existed?

She'd been . . .

She wasn't sure now *what* she'd been. But it was four o'clock in the morning and she was out of choices. She sipped at her wine. After a long moment she picked up the phone.

The dial tone sounded reassuringly, and she dialed Dylan's home number from memory.

Nothing. She let it ring long enough that even the most determined sleeper would know it was an emergency. He wasn't there. She got the dial tone again and phoned the office. The voice mail picked up at Dylan's extension. Truth hung up.

She phoned the lab on the direct line. Someone answered there, but it wasn't Dylan and he wasn't there, and who else could she talk to? Who else could she tell—and tell what, exactly?

That I'm losing my mind? That the old rules don't apply? That I'm sitting here in the modern day trying to make up my mind not even if magick exists, but whether some particular magick is white or black? I haven't been trained for this!

She put down the phone, defeated. There was no point in looking any further. She'd been outmaneuvered even before she'd known the game had begun. She filled her glass one more time, and took her candle and went to bed.

* * *

"Maybe I'm wasting my breath—maybe you're suicidal. Or just hard of hearing. But I come all this way—and you have *no* idea what that took—out of simple family feeling; I show you enough signs and wonders to incite feelings of self-preservation in most people, and *you're still here*. Now *why* is that, do you suppose?"

The (by now) half-familiar scolding tones dragged Truth up out of a heavy sleep. She sat up, feeling queasy—she'd had *far* too much to drink and still didn't feel entirely sober. The room was filled with a faint, predawn grayness, through which a pacing Thorne Blackburn was clearly silhouetted.

"Thorne," Truth said with a sense of groggy unreality.

"Right," Thorne shot back, and the tranquillity with which she accepted this convinced Truth she must still be asleep and dreaming. "Now pack your bags and get your hat and you can be home by breakfast time."

Truth sat up. As the light grew stronger she could see Thorne more clearly—he was wearing his necklace once again, and the lapis scarab was a dark oval on his hand.

"You've got your jewelry," she pointed out.

"And you've been drinking. This is a fine time to embrace the rites of Bacchus, but you always did have a great sense of timing. Get up. Get dressed. Get out."

"I can't go without Light," Truth protested, feeling more confused by .the moment. "And I can't—don't you want the Gate opened? If I take Light away now they can't do the ritual, and Julian's worked so hard—think of his feelings—I can't do that to—"

"*Julian's* feelings?" Thorne exploded. Truth winced. He stopped at the foot of the bed and glared at her, real beyond debate, and fear began to penetrate the alcohol-induced fuzziness in Truth's mind.

"You're worried about hurting *Julian's* feelings?" Thorne roared. "Wake up and smell the brimstone, baby— *there is no Julian*! That's your half-brother Pilgrim down there in the Temple—and you're just not up to his weight, darling girl. You haven't got the guts to be a hero," Thorne sneered.

Blood will out. She must have suspected this truth from the first moment—why else her strange reluctance in the face of Julian's seductions? She felt a peculiar sensation— half revulsion, half attraction—at how nearly she'd succumbed to Julian's advances.

To her half-brother's advances.

"But he loves . . ." she faltered.

"Himself," Thorne finished. "Anything else is just an act."

"Like yours? Did you ever really care about anyone but yourself?" Truth demanded. But she was talking to empty air.

Truth blinked, and drew a long shuddering breath. No one there. Of course there wasn't—Thorne's presence had merely been a vivid dream brought on by nerves, exhaustion, and too much sherry.

No. She was tired of lying to herself, of denigrating Thorne's memory and the evidence of her senses. If it was a dream, it had been a true one.

There was no Julian Pilgrim, and that changed everything. Julian had told her that no one knew where Pilgrim really was. Thorne told her Julian *was* Pilgrim. Which man was lying—the living, or the dead?

Thorne would never lie to her.

But why would Julian?

So I haven't got the guts to be a hero? We'll see about that!

Truth dressed quickly, stuffing her keys into her pocket as a sop to her conscience. She was going to get the truth out of Julian right now.

They were just leaving the Temple when she reached it. The door was open and the lights were on, making everything inside look false and garishly artificial. The members of the Circle of Truth looked like actors after a draining performance; moving like automatons, obviously interested only in reaching their beds. Truth stepped inside.

The sour smell of snuffed candles vied with the salt-sweet smell of the incense they used. Smoke still hung in a flat blue cloud halfway to the ceiling. There was an oblong altar in the center of the room; it was draped with animal skins, and Truth could see that it was on casters.

Some of the others looked up when they saw her, but most concentrated on their tasks—taking things from the tables around the edge of the room and packing them away. The men and Irene were in green robes, while Light's was red and Fiona was wearing a decidedly nonmagickal blue cotton kimono. She was sitting on one of the wooden stools, smoking a cigarette and staring at nothing, looking drained. Truth didn't see Julian anywhere.

Light's red robe made her look even more bloodless; her eyelids fluttered half-closed as she saw Truth, and Hereward, who was standing closest, put a steadying arm around her. His skin held the ash undertone of fatigue, and there were dark hollows under his eyes. He said something to Light, and she nodded, and Hereward began to lead her toward the door. He did not seem surprised to see Truth, only brushed past with a mutter of what might be apology, carrying Light with him.

The others followed in a ragged mass. She stood aside to let them pass her, and finally there was no one there.

"Julian?" Truth said hesitantly.

Julian came out through the curtains at the back of the Temple. Like Fiona he was not robed; he wore a black silk dressing gown and it was abundantly clear that he had nothing on underneath. Unlike the others, Julian showed no sign of fatigue; his cheeks were flushed and his eyes glittered with febrile vitality. A chokingly strong perfume radiated from his painted and glistening skin, and his hair was oiled until it fell in sharp black spikes. Sexuality radiated from him like a command, and Truth felt her body flush in automatic animal response to that. Yesterday she would have simply surrendered to this need that Julian woke in her—but she had come a long way in twenty-four hours, and other needs were stronger.

"I have to talk to you. Now," Truth said.

"Of course," Julian answered. A smile he could not quite repress tugged at the corner of his mouth—as if he knew something she did not. "I'll be with you in just a moment."

He turned away, leaving Truth standing in the open doorway feeling jittery and unsatisfied. The altar with its covering of furs was still in place in the center of the Temple. She saw Julian lift one of the furs and pull out a small bundle wrapped in embroidered violet silk.

"Here we are," Julian said. "Why don't we got up to my sitting room?"

"Julian . . ." Truth said, but he was already padding away, and she had no choice but to follow him.

"Now. Here we are, all comfy. My, I must say you're up early this morning." Julian sat on the gray velvet sofa in his private parlor, a towel draped around his neck. He'd used it to wipe away the last of the ritual paint and oils, but even without them he looked like some glittering half-wild creature of sorcery. The silk-wrapped bundle lay on the table before him.

Now that she was here, the clear cold light of day made her imaginings and might-be dreams ridiculous. Her head still ached, and she wanted nothing more than to go back to bed.

"Maybe a glass of wine? It may be early for you, but it's late for me, darling, so we'll call this a nightcap of sorts." Julian got up and went over to the liquor cabinet, selected two tiny, slender-stemmed glasses, and poured them full of a deep ruby liquid that held the light as if it were crystal itself.

"Port wine—it feeds the blood, or so they used to believe, and it's still one of life's pleasures, whatever they suppose now." He brought both glasses back and set them down on the table beside the bundle. "Sit down," Julian urged, taking his own suggestion. Truth shook her head mutely.

"Well? I don't want to rush you, my darling girl, but tonight's our big night and my current plans are for a shower and bed. Of course, if you're planning to join me . . ." He smiled.

Say it, Truth told herself. *Just say it.*

"You are Thorne Blackburn's son Pilgrim," Truth said. Each word was a separate struggle that left her feeling sick.

Animation did not fade from Julian's face—it vanished as if someone had flipped a switch, and when it went it took all humanity with it. The turquoise eyes blazed at her mutely, and Julian's face was a still, inhuman mask.

After a long moment vitality returned, but it was as if that skin held some new inhabitant—as if Truth's naming had been not only that, but a summoning as well. Julian was gone as if he had never been.

"Quite true," Pilgrim said. His smile widened. "How did you guess?"

Even at the last she had hoped it wasn't true; that Thorne was an illusion—or lying. But now that she looked for it she could see the blurred echo of Thorne's features in Julian's—in *Pilgrim's*—face.

Her brother—who even now was flaunting himself before her as if their shared blood didn't matter. And to her shame, the desire she had felt for him before was still there.

"Thorne told me," Truth said dully. Pilgrim tilted his head back and regarded her through his lashes, unsurprised.

"Ah. He's here, then. I thought he would be. What a happy family reunion this is—the quick and the dead gathered here together this side of Judgment Day, whereafter we will all go forward through the Gate of Life arm in arm—singing, no doubt, though Thorne will sing a different tune after tomorrow evening."

"Pilgrim," Truth said, trying to understand.

"Yes. Pilgrim. Your long-lost brother. Aren't you happy to see me? You should be. I was happy to see you." Pilgrim stretched, catlike. "I knew exactly where you were all along, of course. I'd been keeping tabs on you for years, but somehow I didn't feel that you'd be content to work toward the New Aeon with my happy band. Imagine my unalloyed delight when you turned up on my very doorstep making tenuous attempts to embrace your true heritage. And it *is* your true heritage, sister mine—the blood of the *sidhe*, the Bright Lords, flows in our veins, just as it did in Thorne's, and we are the natural rulers of Mankind.

"Thorne was too cowardly to take up his legacy; or— let's be charitable—perhaps the time was not so ripe for a leader. But these aren't the 'sixties, Truth, and the world is ready for . . . new heroes." Pilgrim smiled up at her sunnily and sipped his wine.

Truth was suddenly much too sober, and she had no desire to stay even a moment longer here at Shadow's Gate. She would try to persuade Light and Irene to go with her, but if she couldn't she would go alone—Dylan was right, you couldn't live other people's lives for them, and if the others would not go with her she would find some other way to rescue Light.

But she could not stay.

"Why didn't you tell me?" Truth asked. "I would have—"

"Lectured me, sister dear, with your tedious rationality— and morality. Would you have been as *nice* to me as you were, if you'd known who I was? I don't think so—but you're so pretty, so very pretty. . . ." Pilgrim murmured, his meaning unmistakable.

"You're my brother," Truth protested, fighting back the chill nausea of shock. All desire for him was gone now, drowned in fear of the man she faced. How could she have thought she ever knew Julian?—there *was* no Julian; Thorne had been right; there was only this smiling, feral-eyed demon.

"Incest, sister dear, is not a crime among the *sidhe*—in fact, it's encouraged, and in the ancient temples of Egypt and Atlantis they followed the custom of the Bright Lords.

But I see that the very thought disgusts you. How could I expect you to be ready to live in the New Aeon?—you wouldn't even give me the book, and I asked you *very* nicely."

"You knew?" Somehow it wasn't a surprise, as if part of her had known the hidden truths of Shadow's Gate from the very first.

"When you are willing to use more than your five brute senses it's *amazing* how much information you can acquire. I even waited—very patiently, *I* thought—for you to give it to me. It's not too late, you know," Pilgrim told her helpfully.

He was *enjoying* himself, Truth realized with the faint beginnings of anger. He should be guilty, humiliated, and instead he was lounging there at his ease, *laughing* at her.

"Where is *Venus Afflicted*?" Truth asked hoarsely.

"Right here." Pilgrim flipped back a fold of the silk to reveal the familiar binding. "Of course I copied the whole thing days ago—I told you there was a copier here the first day we met; did you think I'd forgotten about it, even if you did? I even put it back once I'd copied it; it only took me a few hours, and you were so sure it was safe under the laundry. But then it looked as if you were planning on getting rid of it—and we couldn't have that, now, could we? It doesn't belong to you. You were too timid to use it—but I'm not. The power of the Gate can be used for far more than our mutual father ever dreamed—I'll ride at the head of the Wild Hunt and the human race will once again acknowledge itself the slave race of the *sidhe*!"

"That isn't what Thorne was trying to accomplish!" Truth burst out.

"Sticking up for our father at last?" Pilgrim purred. "Blood will out, won't it? It's a pity you seem to have inherited all his timidity—and only I, his vision!"

"All right. You've inherited his vision. You've even got his book. And you can do his silly little ritual from here until the cows come home and see where it gets you!" Truth snapped crossly. She'd been made a fool of and she didn't like it, and all she wanted was to end this unpleasant, frightening interview and leave. She'd even apologize to Dylan.

"Such self-deception is a disgrace to our blood," Pilgrim said chidingly. "You know it will work—you've felt it. You, my love, are the key for this particular lock; your power, not mine, rends the Veil."

Truth stared at him. "You're nuts," she said simply.

Pilgrim sighed. "I suppose this is my cue to rant, but it's been a long night and I'm tired. But what you forget, my crack-brained obsessive little rationalist, is that *magick is a science*. Thorne said it, I said it—dear gods, I suppose even pretty Michael said it—and you ignored all of us. Still, I might as well say it one more time."

Pilgrim paused, and stretched luxuriously, and regarded her with an expression of infuriating innocence. Each moment he seemed younger, boyish in a way that Julian had not.

But Pilgrim and Julian were the same man—weren't they?

"The scientific method: that actions have consequences, procedures have results, and the same procedure will always have the same result. In layman's terms, the Gate cannot be opened except under precise conditions. One: The complete ritual with all its nithling details, now in my possession. Two: You can only open a Gate where there *is* one to begin with—and, as according to your fascinating notes you know full well, there's one here. Old Elkanah Scheidow propped it open just a crack, and now we'll rip it off its hinges. Three: The Gate responds to its Gatekeeper."

"That's Ellis," Truth said. Ellis was the Gatekeeper for the Circle of Truth—he'd said so the first night she'd been here.

"No, my dear. That's you." Pilgrim smiled, and despite herself Truth felt a sick chill of acknowledgment. No matter how crazy Pilgrim was, he was also right. The power here was hers: There was a bond between Truth and the magick that walked Shadow's Gate—she'd felt it herself, the first moment she'd seen the house. But she'd been too blind, too stupid, too *stubborn* to understand what her senses were telling her—until now.

When it was too late.

"Oh, you would have found it out eventually—in fact, if you'd bothered to read a few things while you were searching my room you'd have found it out last night. Did you actually think I needed your pitiful help to trace Thorne's history when I could call on the best detectives that money could buy? I found out everything there was to know about our mutual parent long ago—more than you could even begin to imagine. For example, the Thornes and the Jourdemaynes were cousins, did you know? And both families were cousins to the Scheidows—I admit that's several generations back, but it's there if you look.

"I did. Thorne did. Thorne came to Shadow's Gate because he already knew there was a Gate here. He sought out your mother to mingle his *sidhe* power with her human heritage—Thorne wasn't Edward Blackburn's child at all, though he was conceived and born in wedlock. Thorne's mother was *wicce*, as his grandfather had been Magus—his mother danced to keep Hitler's armies from England and Thorne was conceived in the ritual, by that which had been called forth in the ritual. Thorne's father was a Bright Lord—but his mother was human—and of the line that could command the power here."

"Why are you telling me all this?" Truth said.

"It's a relief to tell someone. Drink your wine," Pilgrim said. "As I was saying, Thorne was of the right lineage but the wrong sex—the Gates only answer to women; they have since the beginning of the world; it was old Elkanah's Taghkanic bride who brought the Gate as her dowry. So Thorne found Katherine and brought her to Shadow's Gate—their child would have been the logical Gatekeeper, but Thorne was impatient. He tried to open the Gate in his own generation, only to find that the power that poured through the Gate in the absence of its Gatekeeper—remember, Katherine was dead and you were a child—was more than he could handle. I won't have that problem." Pilgrim finished his wine and stood up.

His story, Truth realized, had the flawlessly self-consistent and totally comprehensive explanation of classical paranoid delusion—but which of the two of them was Pilgrim trying to delude?

"You won't?" Truth said, trying to be polite. Pilgrim paced restlessly around the room.

"No. Because you'll be there tomorrow, won't you? On the altar? You'll be my Hierolator, and together we will open the Gate Between The Worlds."

"*No!*" Her refusal was abrupt and instinctive. "You have Fiona," she added, trying to soften her words.

"That thieving slut," Pilgrim's voice was flat and deadly. "You can *not* imagine what rutting with her has been like. She can't give me what I need. You can."

"No, Pilgrim," Truth said. "I can't do that for you."

I've got to leave now. She could wonder later if Pilgrim had always been mad or if Shadow's Gate had driven him crazy. Now she had to get out of here—she could call the police from Shadowkill; they'd believe her.

"You mean you *won't*!" Pilgrim shouted, suddenly furious. He moved quickly, and abruptly he was between Truth and the door. There was an ornate key in the old-fashioned lock, and Pilgrim turned it. He put the key in his pocket.

"You!" he snarled. "Leading your *soft* life with your loving aunt to make everything *nice* for you—while I was punished—punished for being *his* son, by all the petty-minded little moralists who tried to remold me in *their* image! Do you have any idea what a child without parents goes through in this society? The foster-care system if he is lucky—institutions if he is not—and any one of those so-loving caretakers more suitable to a brothel in Hell than to anyplace upon this Earth!

"Shall I fill your ears with horror, sister dear? Shall I show you my scars the way I showed you Light's? Will that incline you to me? You have *no idea* what I've suffered to reach this place—and now I ask you for *one little thing* and *you won't do it!*"

He was raving now, shrieking, but no one would hear through the thick walls of Shadow's Gate.

Oh, Daddy, you were right. Please help me. . . .

"I—" Truth began, but the lie dried in her throat.

Pilgrim laughed softly, his mood undergoing another one of those jarring unsane shifts. "Oh, don't worry, little sister. I've dealt with rebellion before. I am, you might say, an expert in the field.

"Take Ellis, for example. Ellis, you see, found out who I am—and that raises so many awkward questions. How did a poor orphan boy get his hands on all those millions— and at such a youthful age? Well, never mind; it's a long story and boring in spots. But he was going to tell you— which is why he took his little unscheduled flight. I *don't* think he'll be coming back to us, either—insulin is usually fatal to nondiabetics, and poor Ellis was so badly hurt. . . .

"Michael, of course, knew all along," Pilgrim continued, while Truth watched him with the frozen terrified fascination of a bird watching a cobra.

"I thought he'd want money, but no—and after all, what could he prove? Being Thorne's son isn't a crime, is it?" Pilgrim circled around again, until he reached his original position, and leaned against the arm of the couch. He smiled at Truth; and his eyes were alive with a malicious knowledge of her fear.

"I thought pretty Michael would have to go, though it would have been *very* inconvenient for me just at that moment, but all he wanted to do was live here. Our Michael, you see, preaches repentance, and he thought he could convince me to—not do what I intended. I let him try, of course, until I found out . . . Well, I won't tax your credulity; suffice it to say that the Archangel Michael has had— *car* trouble, and I don't think we'll see him again." Pilgrim smiled; a smile of sharp, white teeth.

"Pilgrim, please open the door." It took every ounce of control Truth possessed, but she kept her voice even and steady; free from the sick fear she felt. This reality was far more terrifying than any ghost—the reality of a madman who had killed and would kill again.

"Soon," Pilgrim said, almost crooning now. "I promise. I won't hurt you—you're my sister. I want you to love me. When I found Light and got her out of that filthy *prison* they called a hospital I wanted her to love me, and she did, but it wasn't enough. I want you to love me too," he said, his voice caressing.

Truth's mouth was dry; every nerve in her body ached with terror. Pilgrim wanted an answer, and she didn't dare lie.

"I want to love you, Pilgrim. So does Thorne."

But that wasn't the right answer.

"Thorne!" Pilgrim shrieked, furious again. "He doesn't love me—he ran out on us—out on *me*! And I don't care if he's sorry now—it's too *late* for him to be sorry!" he paused, panting.

"He shouldn't have done that, Pilgrim," Truth said. She concentrated on the key in Pilgrim's pocket. She needed to get it—and get out of here. She didn't think the others *could* know what sort of monster Pilgrim was, and the only way to save any of them was by going to the police.

"No." For a brief moment Truth saw tears glittering in Pilgrim's eyes as his mood made another maniacal shift. "I loved him—I believed in him—and then he was gone, and everyone . . ." Pilgrim drew a deep breath and rubbed his eyes.

"Won't you help me? Please, won't you help me, little sister? I didn't really hurt Ellis, you know," he said, and Truth could see him trying to pull the shred of the Julian-mask around himself. "Or Michael. Michael had to go down to New York. He'll be back tomorrow. We're old friends—we went to seminary together. I'm sorry I scared you. The others understand. Magick is the redirection of reality by the exercise of the will. Sometimes we all get caught up in our own illusions. The rituals excite me, and we're so close. . . . Just twenty-four more hours." Pilgrim bowed his head, the picture of contrition.

It would be so easy to believe him, and Truth wished she could. Inside herself she wept for the lover who had only been an illusion and for the brother she'd never known, but she was through lying to herself or letting others lie to her. She would do everything she could to help Pilgrim but she would begin by making herself and the others safe.

She waited for the next outburst, hardly daring to breathe, but Pilgrim did not move. Finally he seemed to shake himself awake, and sighed.

"Oh, well. We can always try again some other time. I don't suppose you'd agree to stay and say nothing if I gave you your book back?" Pilgrim laughed lightly, and by now the illusion of normalcy was almost complete.

Truth said nothing, not knowing what was safe, and what would trigger another shift toward violence. Finally Pilgrim seemed to give up trying to bend her to his will.

"Okay. I guess I deserve this. But before you go I need you to forgive me," Pilgrim said. "Not for what I've done to anyone else—I know I can't ask that—but for what I've done to you. Please, can't I ask that much? You're my sister. . . ." Pilgrim held out Truth's untouched glass. "Please."

Truth took it. Even then she might not have drunk it, but she saw Pilgrim watching her. To refuse would be to give him the excuse to do . . . what?

It would be safe enough. The glass held hardly more than a tablespoonful. Truth had seen both drinks poured from the same decanter, and Pilgrim had emptied his own glass. He placed the key to the door on the table in front of her and watched her through lowered lashes. Truth felt tears of pity gather in her eyes for the little boy who had suffered so much that he had become the man here with her now.

"I forgive you, Pilgrim," Truth said, and drank.

She reached for the key.

Pilgrim smiled.

The wine had a bitter aftertaste. She felt the numbness on her tongue. And she tried to get up—to run, to fight him, to *scream*—but the wine was already turning her blood heavy and cold.

"Sucker."

CHAPTER FOURTEEN

THE SPIRIT OF TRUTH

*Who ever knew Truth put to the worse, in a free
and open encounter?*

—JOHN MILTON

"I MUST SAY," THORNE BLACKBURN SAID, "WHEN ONE OF
my offspring renounces common sense, there are no half
measures involved."

The voice penetrated her uncomfortable sleep. Truth tried
to sit up and found herself unable to move.

The attempt brought full consciousness, and with it an
awareness of her body. Aching shoulders, aching wrists,
aching head, aching throat—everything hurt. And she
wasn't lying down at all.

She pried her gummy eyes open with an effort and
looked around.

She was sitting on a rough wooden bench somewhere
that smelled of moist earth and old rot. There was a low
wooden door directly opposite her, its wood the dusty gray
of age and neglect. The beams of the low wooden ceiling
began almost directly above it, and Truth could see cobwebs clustered in their angles. The walls were old rough
handmade brick, their grayish mortar crumbling away from

between them. The floor was pounded earth, and the room itself was far from square.

At first she didn't see Thorne. She found that her hands were held level with the top of her head, and this time when she tried to move them she could hear a clinking and feel the cold unyielding metal of shackles about her wrists. She craned upward, staring. There was a shiny metal plate mortared into the wall. The ring in its center allowed the chain to pass through it freely; its three-foot length was attached to the shackles on her wrists. She yanked.

"Don't do that. You'll probably bring the wall down on top of you."

"Huh—?" Truth said. She turned toward the voice and saw Thorne, standing in the far corner of the room as if he'd just come through the wall. The beams of the ceiling nearly brushed the crown of his head; the light she was seeing by came from the utterly prosaic Coleman lantern sitting on top of the ice chest at his feet. Thorne was wearing a fringed leather vest over an embroidered chambray shirt, and the bells of his jeans were so wide they hid his feet. He held up a key.

She'd never been so glad to see a ghost in her life.

"What—"

"The old wine cellar under the house. Or did you mean, 'How did he drug you'? Simple enough. The drug was in the glass, not in the wine. It's an old trick, really," Thorne said apologetically.

Truth shook her head, and was rewarded with a sharp jolt of pain and a reeling nausea. She lay back against the wall, panting.

"I'm going to let you out of those, but I need your help," Thorne said. "I want you to stay here and go with them when they come back. That little bastard has to be stopped, and I don't want anyone else hurt."

Truth nodded cautiously, though the effort made every tendon in her neck throb. She took a careful breath, and felt the nausea recede. "I guess I really blew it, didn't it? I'm not a very good hero."

Thorne smiled at her fondly and shook his head. "Oh, I don't doubt your bravery, baby—but I do wonder about your brains. What on earth possessed you to confront Pilgrim that way? He's nuts, you know," Thorne told her.

"So I've heard," Truth commented dryly.

Thorne crossed the little distance between them and reached for the cuff on her wrist. The cellar was cold; Truth could feel the heat radiating from Thorne's body—

—feel the grip of his hands as he steadied her wrist—

—see the makeup, carefully blended to cover the lines of age on his face; the hair, still long but now unnaturally golden—

One cuff sprang open, then the other.

"You're alive!" Truth yelped. She jumped up and grabbed his hands before he could pull back. They were hard and warm and real in hers—calloused and worn and marked with age: the hands of a man in his fifties. Thorne's hands.

"You're alive," Truth repeated.

"Surprise," Thorne said, grinning.

Now that she looked for it, the mask of youth fell away—all it was was pancake and Clairol and expectation; antique clothes and careful lighting. This was no ghost. This was a living man, as real as she was.

"Oh, my God," Truth said, sitting down slowly. Her head reeled, and she closed her eyes tightly.

"Want a beer?" Thorne said, dragging the ice chest out of the corner. There was a blanket on top of it; he shook it loose and draped it around her shoulders.

"I've been here since 'sixty-nine," Thorne said. He was sitting beside her on the bench, his arm around her. Truth held a bottle of apple juice between her hands, and at intervals in his story Thorne would bully her into taking sips from it. "And with the muddle everything was left in at my, ah, 'death,' I expected I'd be able to stay here undisturbed until the end of my days."

Truth sipped at the juice. Thorne's tale, delivered in simple, matter-of-fact tones, was almost more unbelievable than anything else she'd heard at Shadow's Gate.

"I admit that Pilgrim's arrival was a shock, but not half as much of one as I got when I found out what he was up to. I was sure he didn't stand a chance—I didn't know where *Venus Afflicted* was any more than he did, and at first I had no idea who he was or how much he'd found out. And later—Well, that was later."

Truth reached out and patted his knee. "But how—? But why—? I mean, all these years, everyone was *looking* for you. . . ." She closed her eyes, stunned and exhausted with the aftermath of her drugging and these new revelations.

"Wake up. Drink your juice," Thorne chided. "Well, to begin with, you may have noticed my rather unorthodox entrances and exists?"

Truth giggled, mostly with relief. "You scared me to *death*!"

"Hardly. You're like your mother—she'd walk up to Satan himself and spit in his eye to see him flinch. But playing ghost was easy—this place used to be a stop on the Underground Railroad that smuggled slaves into Canada. The place is riddled with tunnels."

"But Hereward said they'd all been filled in—or something," Truth protested, although by now she wasn't sure just *what* Hereward had said.

"What? Do you think they showed up on the architect's blueprints filed in the town hall? Nobody but the people who dug them ever knew they were there; the maze was built right over one of the main exits in eighteen ninety-something and nobody ever even noticed. Very convenient, those tunnels—I lived down there for quite some time while the heat died down."

She wasn't crazy. Relief coursed through Truth like strong medicine, warming and steadying her even more than a thick, woolen blanket and her father's presence. She wasn't crazy, she wasn't having a breakdown—Thorne was alive and *here*.

"After awhile I started venturing out—scavenging, doing odd jobs for the locals as a means of barter, that sort of thing. I don't know whether they thought I was a draft dodger, a radical on the run, or what—and mostly they didn't care. Drink your juice."

Truth sipped at it again—she was thirsty, but swallowing hurt. She was lucky, she supposed, that Pilgrim hadn't simply poisoned her.

"Pilgrim," she said, trying to get up.

Thorne shoved her back down without effort. "You're in no shape to take on Pilgrim just now."

Truth sat back, feeling the weakness in her body that told her Thorne was right. And there was so much she wanted to know; so many questions to ask.

"What about my mother?" she said.

Thorne sighed, and for a moment looked every day of his more than fifty years. "Grant me . . . a little more time before we talk about Katherine. I've stolen so much from you, daughter, but—just give me a little time."

Truth nodded. "I hated you, you know," she confessed, embarrassed. "I thought you were some kind of monster, stringing everyone along with your lies for what you could get out of them. But—"

"Oh, I was sincere," Thorne said heavily. "God help me, that was the worst of my sins—that I *believed*. And I have sown dragon's teeth. Pilgrim—dear heaven, that my work could be so warped—what we did, we did in love and innocence, but all Pilgrim wants is *power*—the power that is bought with blood and lies and endless, endless pain. When I think of what he will do with it if he gets his way . . . I'm frightened."

"But can't you—?" Truth said.

"Call the police? Oh, sure—and Pilgrim would have my ass on toast and some fascist-pig lawyers to swear black was white and he'd be right back here next year with a new Circle ready to believe anything he told them. No, we have to close the Gate," Thorne said solemnly. "And I need your help to do it."

There was no Closing of the Gate in *Venus Afflicted*, but Truth supposed that Thorne could invent one if anybody could. "I'd almost forgotten you believed in all that nonsense," Truth said before she thought. Thorne laughed.

"Humor your old dad, sweetheart. Once I've got Pilgrim out of the way you and I should be able to shut the whole thing down without any trouble. I've learned a lot in the last twenty years. You'd be surprised—that is, you would if you knew anything about magick to begin with," Thorne amended wickedly.

"Don't worry—I won't ask you to do anything you can't stand up and confess to in church," he added, grinning as if he guessed her worries. Then the smile faded. "But it's . . . the only way I can make it right, don't you see?" His voice was almost plaintive.

Truth squeezed his hand. She knew what he wanted, and it would have been easy to agree without thinking, but she was determined this time to make the *right* choice, not just the logical one. She was stronger now, her head clear—she could ask Thorne to lead her out of here, call the police as she'd originally planned, stop the ritual and stop Pilgrim.

But Thorne was right about the lawyers. And while it was true that she could accuse Pilgrim of murder . . . *which* time had he been lying about Michael and Ellis's fates? If she did accuse him of their murder, and they turned up alive and well . . . Truth shuddered at the thought of the media circus *that* would be.

And Thorne Blackburn was still wanted for murder, a crime for which there was no statute of limitations. There would be no way to keep him out of this, no matter what, and in the frenzy surrounding Thorne's reappearance, any case against Pilgrim could simply disappear.

But suppose she and Thorne stopped Pilgrim's ritual first? If anything she'd been told was true, closing the Gate should shut down the paranormal activity at Shadow's Gate, just as she'd hoped. And then Pilgrim would not have the Circle's power to draw on—or the house's.

A month ago she would have called this line of thinking

deluded raving—but she'd seen the members of the Circle, gray and drained, while Pilgrim bubbled with unwholesome vitality. She'd felt the power they raised, with the paranormal locus of Shadow's Gate to draw on.

Stop the ritual. Close the Gate. Seal the seeping psychic wound that tainted everything here, then settle the mundane matters.

That was the right thing to do.

"If I go along with you," Truth said, "you won't hurt anyone, will you?"

Thorne grimaced. "I won't kill Pilgrim, if that's what you're hinting at—I've never killed anyone and I'm too old to start now. But I think I can get Irene to slip him a mickey, and failing that, I can always hit him over the head." He smiled. "I think he at least deserves a headache."

"So do I," Truth said darkly, rubbing her own throbbing temples. "Okay, what do you want me to do?"

Thorne stayed with her a while longer. They talked of inconsequential things—books and movies, daily life at Taghkanic College. Truth found that Thorne's knowledge of popular culture stopped short in 1969—well, if he'd been living a fugitive's existence all these years, that was only to be expected. But toward the end he looked more and more uneasy, and finally admitted he ought to leave.

"There's not much I can do to pull the wool over their eyes if they walk in and catch me here," Thorne said apologetically.

"Go on, then. I'm not afraid of the dark."

"Oh, I'll leave you the lantern and the rest of the stuff. Let them explain *that* as a 'conflation of mystic energies,' " Thorne snorted. He stood to go.

Truth stood, too, and hugged him. He was only a few inches taller than she was, and what had once been the slenderness of youth was now the painful thinness of undernourished age.

"You're so thin!" Truth said. "Are you sure you're eating enough?"

"Worry about yourself." Thorne laughed. "You don't believe in magick yet—not quite. But before the night is out we're going to put on a show here that I guarantee you'll never forget."

"I'm looking forward to it," Truth said, and this time it was the truth.

Thorne raised his hand, the first two fingers spread. "Peace," he said. He walked around a crook in the cellar wall and was gone.

Truth sat back down, pulling the blanket around her again. Now all she had to do was wait.

There were sandwiches in the cooler and after a while Truth ate one, but it was boring sitting in the cellar with nothing to read except an apple juice bottle, and after some unmeasurable time Truth dozed off. She was awakened some unknown time later by the rattle of keys against a padlock, and a moment later the door across from her opened and Fiona stepped in.

"Well," Fiona sneered, looking around at the lantern and the ice chest. "All the comforts of home. Was this your idea, Gareth?"

"Uh, no." Gareth entered the cellar behind Fiona. They were both in green robes, and Gareth looked uncomfortable.

"Well, come on—since you've managed to get out of those cuffs already," Fiona snapped. Truth stood up, stretching.

"Shouldn't we—?" Gareth began.

"Oh, Jesus Christ—what do you want me to do, read her her rights? Okay, bitch—you have the right to do just what I tell you or get your face rearranged. And if Gareth won't do it, Julian will."

"There is no Julian," Truth said.

"Oh yeah? That's sure going to come as a big shock to

the guy upstairs in the antlers. Move your ass." Fiona grabbed Truth's arm and yanked.

Truth staggered forward, and would have fallen if Gareth hadn't caught and steadied her.

"Gareth," Truth said. "Why are you going along with this? You know it isn't right."

"I—" Gareth said.

"He's doing it for *me*," Fiona said mockingly. "Because I love him. Isn't that right, Gareth?" She grabbed Truth's arm, digging in with sharp nails, and between them, the two members of the Circle of Truth hustled Truth out of the cellar and up the stairs.

As soon as they reached the first floor Truth knew that things had gone somehow horribly wrong. Power radiated from the Temple as from the open mouth of a blast furnace, and everything in her vision seemed to have acquired multi-colored haloes, making phosphorescent trails through the trembling air.

It was raining outside, a hard driving downpour that Truth could hear clearly, but over the sound of the storm she could hear the chanting, as certainly as if she were already in the room with it. The sharp smoke of the incense was in her nose, her throat, choking her.

They reached the door to the Temple, and at last Truth understood. This was not the start of the ritual, when she and Thorne could easily seize control and change things. The ritual had already been going on for hours.

Where was Thorne? Why hadn't he come and gotten her?

Gareth opened the doors.

As if the mere physical barrier could hold back intangible psychic power, a new wave of force rolled over Truth—a black sucking whirlpool that nourished as it devoured. The energy dragged at her, pulling her into the past, into the other night, the other death . . . and the baby girl, barely two, whose frantic attempts to follow her into the courts of Death had caused her agony enough to seal off her psychic powers forever . . . until now.

As if she had suddenly been released from a too-tight

garment, Truth felt her perceptions flower and change, until with newfound confidence she could sense the rhythm of Being and Becoming as it flowed though her. *This* was the real world, to which she had been awakened perhaps too late.

Inside the Temple, the perimeter of the circle was a blaze of candles, the sound of drumming—the rain, magnified a thousand times by the room's acoustics—and Light's chanting pounding at her with a force that made her shudder—a force far beyond the power of the Temple's inhabitants to produce. Truth strained to see, though her vision was filled with a galaxy of sparks and blazing rainbows, and her entire body vibrated to the beat of the house's power.

Light stood at the head of the altar, head thrown back. She was deep in trance: Her eyes were closed; she cried out line after line of speech in some unknown tongue and her body was a pillar of viridian flame in Truth's new sight. Each word seemed to hang upon the air, as if the sound waves had suddenly become visible, and Light trembled with the power pouring through her, oblivious to the others. Light's will and that of what spoke through her held the ritual in focus—having come this far, Pilgrim no longer needed the others.

Irene stood frozen, her face a paint-streaked mask of incredulous tears. Beside her, Hereward knelt upon the floor, his hands folded tightly against his stomach. His face was ghastly pale and there was blood on his mouth, and more blood oozing between his clutching fingers. Blue light pooled about him on the floor—his life force, slowly draining away.

As Truth entered he looked toward her. *Sorry*, he mouthed and shook his head, trying to get to his feet.

Caradoc stood beside the altar. He held a censer of incense, and his face was perfectly blank. Was this sort of thing what he'd had in mind? He gave no indication that he'd noticed that anything out of the ordinary was going on at all. Truth looked at Caradoc and saw nothing, only a howling silence, the leading edge of a gale upon which some soaring inhumanity spread its wings.

Where was Donner? She looked for him and found him at last. He was standing very still, his entire strained attention focused on Pilgrim.

"Looking for your white knight?" Pilgrim said to Truth. His cheeks were flushed, and he wore an elaborate antlered headdress and a wolfskin about his shoulders. He was naked, and held an enormous ritual sword in one hand and a small black pistol in the other, pointed at the only other person in the room who was likely to do him harm. The gun glowed like a burning coal in Pilgrim's hand, scarlet with recent use to Truth's otherworldly sight. He'd already shot Hereward—was Donner next? Were these the deaths that Pilgrim was counting on to fuel his sorcery and open the Gate?

Or was the death to be hers?

Truth began to struggle. She tore loose from Fiona's grip, but Gareth's hand was locked around her arm like an iron vise.

"Let me go! Gareth—for God's sake!" Truth cried. She felt the power Pilgrim had called drawing her forward, sucking her irresistibly into the pattern Pilgrim had created, the pattern that would end in the horror of Chaos come again.

"I'm afraid your god and his messengers won't be coming tonight—and neither will Thorne Blackburn!" Pilgrim shouted over the sound of her voice and Light's. "Really, Truth—did you think one feeble old man who has rejected the gift of the gods could defeat *me*? Now come here—I'm going to cut your heart out, you stupid bitch—once the Gate is open I don't need you! Come on, Gareth—it is expedient that one woman should die for the good of the people!"

Pilgrim laughed crazily, but the gun never wavered from Donner's chest.

Incredibly, Gareth began to drag her forward—out of weakness, of being lost in the ritual, in the desire to give

himself to anything outside himself. Truth fought him, and
even then she might have broken free, but Fiona hit her in
the stomach with one of the heavy candlesticks and when
Truth gagged at the blow Gareth wrenched both of her arms
up behind her back.

He brought her in front of Pilgrim. Heat radiated off
Pilgrim, and power—she could see it with her new senses;
a dull violet glow gathering on the surface of his skin, as
if some astral double inside him were soon about to burst
this mortal chrysalis.

"Now we chain her to the altar, violate and mutilate her,
and cut her heart out. Oh come *on*, Irene, stop sniveling—
these aren't the sixties any more! Donner, be a good boy
and come over here and help," Pilgrim said, his face a
maniacal mask of glee.

Oh how could any of them think he'd let them live after
what they'd seen here tonight? How many of them were
here like Irene—secretly, illegally, with no one to notice
them when they were gone?

"Donner! Don't do it!" Truth screamed. "He'll kill you!"

Pilgrim brandished the gun and laughed again, the sound
high and jagged against Light's chanting. Even if you
didn't believe in magick, couldn't feel the power raging
here, there was still the gun. Truth felt Gareth lift her toward the altar, and she began to kick.

*"In the name of the White Christ and Yod-He-Vau-He,
the Tetragrammaton all powerful!"* a voice roared from the
doorway.

Light's voice cut off as if she'd been slapped. Gareth
swung around, dragging Truth with him.

Michael Archangel stood in the doorway. His hair was
wet with blood; beads of red formed a spiky decoration
along his brow. He wore a priest's long robes, and in his
bleeding hands he carried a sword like nothing Truth had
ever seen. A white radiance blazed from it, as if it were
bathed in a spotlight that fell upon it alone.

"I charge you to cast off these errors of darkness and
surrender yourself to the judgment of the Lord!" Michael

shouted, and Truth felt the power in Whose name he acted
reach out, burning and implacable.

Pilgrim swung his sword, and Gareth jumped back out
of the way, dragging her with him. Truth felt the opposing
forces come together, and for one moment the Veils of
Time and Birth were rent, and everyone in the room stood
in the presence of Eternity.

"*Domaris!*" screamed Light. "*Help me!*" She fell to her
knees and screamed again, in purely human fright and pain.

"Deoris!" The ancient, the eternal name was on Truth's
two lips—two sisters who had sworn before a shrine at the
beginning of the world never to be parted until Time itself
would end. For one moment Truth saw the whole uncoiling
of their shared lives through birth after birth, back to the
moment of this ancient sin that had bound them to the
Wheel forever.

Then the moment was gone. She struggled loose from
Gareth without difficulty now, and headed for her sister,
half-blind in the vortex of powers swirling through the
room.

"I bow to no creature—god or devil!" Pilgrim shouted.
The ritual sword he carried was darkness visible, its black
blade a hole in the fabric of Creation itself as he raised it.
"It is you, slave-god's pawn, who will bow to me—and
worship!"

Michael stepped forward, his bare feet leaving bloody
prints upon the Temple floor, his own blade raised to meet
Pilgrim's attack. A shimmering fog seemed to cut the two
men off from the others in the Temple, as if their bodies
were no longer wholly upon the mortal plane.

Truth reached Light and knelt beside her. The screaming
had stopped—her sister lay, limp and unconscious, upon
the floor. Her skin was icy. Truth felt for a pulse, terrified,
and finally found it, faint but strong. She clutched her sister
to her chest, watching the battle.

Michael's voice was raised in sonorous, deep-pitched
Latin, and each syllable seemed to claw at the fabric of
reality. Pilgrim swung his sword, but it was not from its

blade that his attack came. With his other hand, he sketched a shape in the air, and Truth seemed to see the glyph he had drawn hanging there, as if drawn in some dark and bloody fog.

"Adonai!" Michael cried, and the swirling symbol began to fade.

"Come on," Thorne said, grabbing Truth by the shoulders. She screamed at his touch, nearly dropping Light, and saw the curtains of the alcove swinging where Thorne had pushed through them. She could barely see; the whole Temple was choked with blazing sound, and Truth felt as though she were drowning in the intangible made real.

"No! Light—"

"There is no time!" Thorne shouted in her ear. "It's gone too far! It isn't going to stop—we have to shut it down!"

He was right—Truth could feel it; the imbalance created here was feeding on Michael and Pilgrim's struggle. It did not matter now if the ritual were ever finished—the Gate would open, unless the two of them could stop it.

Reluctantly she let Light slip to the floor and got to her feet. "Will she be all right?"

"Not if we don't win," Thorne said grimly. He reached out and plucked *Venus Afflicted* from the altar, and Truth snatched it away from him. Its hardness was burning and icy at once beneath her hands and it burned like a captive star.

Thorne grabbed her wrist and dragged her through the curtains of the archway. It was pitch black behind the curtain, but Thorne moved unerringly in the darkness, opening a door and revealing a set of stairs that curved downward. A faint glow, almost phosphorescent, radiated up from below; enough to navigate by, at least if you were desperate.

"The old cistern," he said briefly.

Truth followed him down the stair into a room every bit as large as the Temple above, a great drum-shaped room made of brick and stone centuries old. The chaos within the Temple retreated from her senses till she could see the physical world once more and, staring at one curving wall,

Truth realized that she was looking at part of the original foundation of the 1648 house.

"Come on," Thorne said.

The staircase was wrought iron; it creaked and shook as Thorne and Truth ran down it, Truth clutching the book tightly against her chest. When they reached the bottom, Truth saw that the illumination was coming from a glass-chimneyed hurricane lamp, vintage unknown, that was set into a niche in the wall.

"The spring's down there." Thorne's mouth quirked as he gestured toward the floor. "Scheidow convinced the Taghkanics that he was a great *manitou* by diverting it to his own purposes. It's how he got them to cooperate in his fur trade."

"I guess this area just attracts con men," Truth shot back, and Thorne laughed.

"Come on. There's a tunnel to the outside off this way."

She was too afraid of other things to be frightened at the time, but for the rest of her life that escape from Shadow's Gate would return as the stuff of her nightmares. The old network of brick and marl tunnels had not been kept in repair; the walls bowed inward with the weight of spring rain and winter ice, and roots had plunged through the roof, their lowering tangle sometimes making it necessary to go on hands and knees in order to get through. There was the constant fear that the tunnel would collapse and bury both of them alive; each time the thunder shook the valley Truth's hands jerked faintly, but at the time her mind was worlds away from the purely animal terror.

She could feel the power of the open Gate loose all around her, its pulsations unbound from the rhythm of the interrupted ritual, building and growing to the summons of a pattern all its own. Everything she saw glowed with a spectral light, as if Shadow's Gate was no longer wholly of this world.

At last she and Thorne came to a place where timbers

reinforced the roof, and the door before them was timber-framed, set in a lime-washed wall.

"The old ice house," Thorne explained, opening the door.

The ice house was even filthier than the tunnel, if possible, but its outer door—half-rotting, falling off its hinges—led to the outside. The night was a pale silver, as if lit by a full moon, although the witchstorm still raged over the valley. Truth brushed dirt and cobwebs from her skirt with her free hand; through the door she could smell the sharp sweetness of the night air, electric with the power of the storm.

"Out there?" she said dubiously. A gust of rain blew through the doorway, spangling her skirt with drops and making her shiver.

"Next time I rescue you I'll bring an umbrella," Thorne promised.

Truth stuffed the book under her sweater and pushed past Thorne. The rain was icy and sweet, sluicing the dirt and taint from her even as it drenched her to the skin. Above her peal after peal of thunder sounded, as lightning stitched the sky like the flash of far-off artillery fire.

Thorne came to stand beside her on the brambled hillside. Truth heard him swear as the rain soaked him. She looked around. Shadow's Gate was nowhere in sight.

"Hurry," Thorne said. "There isn't much time." Taking her hand once more, he began to run through the mud and the pounding storm.

They were both covered in mud and bleeding from a hundred bramble scratches by the time they reached Thorne's destination, and each of them had fallen at least once. Truth had nearly lost the book half-a-dozen times—only her stubbornness had allowed her to retain her hold upon it at all, and that at the cost of bruises and broken fingernails.

Thorne stepped slowly into the clearing, pulling Truth after him. She scrubbed rain and hair out of her eyes and stared around herself.

They were deep in the forest behind Shadow's Gate now, where old-growth trees stood like the pillars of a temple among lesser vegetation. Here the force of the rain was broken somewhat by the branches of the trees, though it was late autumn and the trees had few leaves left.

The clearing was surrounded by a horseshoe-shape of pale granite pillars, rough-hewn like the bones of Stonehenge itself and sunk deep into the earth. The stones were set fairly close together, no more than four feet apart, and there were twelve of them. The earth they surrounded had been raked and smoothed, but that had been many years ago, and now the short, deer-cropped grass was drifted with fallen leaves.

"We worked on this all that first summer. Carl broke his wrist and Irene got the worst case of poison ivy you ever saw," Thorne said. He was gasping for breath from the run, his hair plastered to his skull, but even now he was grinning, as if no matter what the outcome, it was the fight that mattered to Thorne Blackburn.

Truth reached out and touched the nearest pillar. She'd thought it would be cold, but it was as warm as if the sun had been shining on it for hours, and it vibrated faintly beneath her fingers. After everything else that had happened to her tonight, Truth wasn't even frightened by this new strangeness.

"What do we do? Why are we here?" Truth said. She shook her dripping hair out of her eyes again, resisting the temptation to cuddle the pillar for warmth. Whatever the source of its heat was, it would not serve her body's needs.

Thorne walked to the head of the sarsen crescent, where a distinct gap separated the two tallest stones. He hesitated, as if what he was about to do next would cause him pain.

"Pilgrim found this place, but Irene never told him the truth about it—I made sure of that much. Evil is oddly gullible—he knew as little of me as you did—but he chose to believe a different part of my legend. It's true that the house was your mother's magick—but mine was here."

Then Thorne took a step backward, placing himself directly between the two columns. They vibrated, a high sweet singing that cut through the roar of the storm, and suddenly all the stones seemed to glow with an ice blue radiance like starlight.

His body jerked—as if electricity were coursing through it, completing some powerful circuit. Truth could see the gleam of his bared teeth in the eldritch blue glow of the stones.

"*Daddy!*" Truth screamed, lunging forward.

She slipped in the mud and went sprawling, the grimoire a hard uncompromising weight beneath her sodden sweater. She struggled to her knees and knelt in the mud, staring up at her father—he wasn't hurt, as she'd thought, but in some way Thorne's body *completed* the circuit of power here.

Slowly, he held his hands out to her, coronaed in blue-white power. She knew what he wanted her to do.

Still kneeling, Truth pulled *Venus Afflicted* out from under her sweater. Its cover was damp and slimy with rain, and some last shred of mundane pragmatism grieved at its soaked and mud-spattered state. She reached up from where she knelt, holding the book out to Thorne.

He said something, but she could not hear it over the hiss of the rain and shook her head. Then he touched the book.

The power of the Circle poured through her body, seeking escape into the earth, and Truth's body spasmed as Thorne's had done, even as the power held her rigid. There was no escape—she felt it as the power flowed into the earth and met an even greater power, a river flowing to a measureless ocean that returned its power to the river again. The power cascaded back through her body, through Thorne, through the stones, and down into the earth again and again, onward without end. Truth's eyes closed; here was the peace she had sought; here at last, asking only her surrender to its eternal tidal call.

"No!" Thorne's shout roused her. She stared up into his blazing blue eyes, and knew this surrender was not what he had brought her here for. The power must be ruled, the

Gate must be closed. She must take the tide of power that flowed through her and impose her will upon it—she was the Gatekeeper, and here was the Gate.

But how?

Thorne's chest rose as he inhaled, drawing in both breath and strength. Then he began to chant, the strange short phrases that had haunted Truth's dreams since her first night at Shadow's Gate—the words that in this world were only that, but in another place were living things, real and solid and aware.

The night, the storm, the forest and the ring of stones, all fell away from Truth's senses as an outmoded garment from the body. She passed beyond the Gate, and stood with Thorne upon a high hill where fantastic armies gathered all about them awaiting the signal to ride. The ocean roared on the cliffs below, and above the heads of the host Truth could see a Wheel spinning among the stars—a Wheel of blinding silver, and every spoke was a double-edged sword.

Into the earth; up from the earth; the endless sacrament of gift and gift . . . Thorne had never ceased his chanting, but now Truth could understand the words which were not words, but Reality.

"I am a hawk/Above the cliff—"

And now her voice joined with his. Each phrase was a rune, a word, a spell woven with living breath. . . .

"I am a thorn/Beneath the nail—"

And now she saw the shape of it all. She could see what she must do; saw the task that Thorne had meant her for and how to accomplish it; saw the price and the pain and measured her strength against the task, and now her voice went on alone:

"I am a lure/From Paradise—"

And somewhere upon the horizon of her sight she could see the shape of Pilgrim's twisted working, saw it and knew she must deal with it too. Thorne's voice joined with her own again, and the book burned between their hands like forging iron, but neither of them would release it.

"I am a wizard, who but I/Shall know the Gate Between The Worlds?"

Pilgrim's tangled creation fell away, and now the Gate burned before her inward eyes, argent and gleaming, its blades the perils the seeker must pass through to reach Paradise.

She knew what she had to do. The words kindled clearly in her mind, but to speak them would commit her to a path that she must walk the rest of her days.

She must. There was no one else.

"I am the birth of every hope—"

Her hands burned. Her will and her honor bound her; the passion to know and to make that had brought her to this moment.

"I am the door for every wall—"

And she could feel it rushing toward her; the massive weight of intention, as if on some plane far beyond her own some great balance shifted, and the Gate Between The Worlds swung closed again, righting a balance that had long been wrong. The moment at which she could stop what she had begun came and vanished, and Truth felt the terror of any wild thing standing in the path of an onrushing train as the power she had invoked peaked and exploded through her, gathering momentum, seeking its release; she screamed with the sensation of it and on her hands the blisters broke; the liquid spilled over her fingers like tears, but the Gate was closed at last; she had closed it, and now there was only one last thing she must do.

"I am the key for every lock—"

And the key was her body, her soul, wrenched and twisted from its living shape, and now Thorne could no longer help her.

"I am the lock for every gate—"

Her voice failed; her tongue was bleeding with the words she had forced from it, but if she stopped now the damage would not be undone, and all the sorrow and pain they had suffered would be for nothing.

"I am a wizard, who but I/Shall seal the Gate Between The Worlds?"

And it was done. The hill was gone, and the armies. The Gate was gone from among the stars, and so was the light.

She was lying in the mud. Truth opened her eyes, but the ghostly sight that had sustained her was gone; everything was black. All that was left was the dazzling scraps of her vision, already fading like a dream.

Except for the choice she had made, that she must now learn to live with.

She was freezing, numb and wet and cold and sick. The rain was a far-off pattering; the fury of the storm was past, and the storm was moving away. Truth pulled herself to her knees with a sucking sound. She was covered in a thick sheet of mud from her chin to her ankles.

"Daddy?" Truth said hoarsely. There was mud in her mouth; she spat.

"Here," Thorne said. She could see him only faintly; he was standing between the pillars, his arms crossed over his chest, and she could see that he held *Venus Afflicted* in his hands.

"You—I—" She sat back on her heels, shoving her hair out of her face with muddy hands. "It worked. We did it. It's real." The words were only shadows of what true speech might be—this was how she would see the world from now on; how the world was for those who had seen Paradise and must live out their days among shadows.

"I've always said so." Thorne's voice was amused. "And now—I'm sorry, sweetheart, but I haven't been quite truthful with you tonight. I hope someday you'll forgive me, but now . . . I can't stay. That part was a lie. I have to go now."

She knew. The part of her that had stood upon the hill before the Gate of the Silver Wheel understood, but the charade must be played out to the end.

"Go *where*?" Truth demanded. "*Why* do you have to go? Daddy, I've just found you again—"

"And I will always love you, Truth. But the night your mother died I came here to get her back—with the power of my blood I forced the Gate, and for that overweening folly I was awarded a fitting penance. Good-bye, baby."

"*No!*" Truth flung herself to her feet and ran toward him, but she was too late.

The lightning flashed. And in the gap between the pillars where Thorne Blackburn had stood he stood no longer— only a great gray oak with the symbol of the Circle of Truth carved deep into its bark.

And *Venus Afflicted* was gone at last from the human world.

CHAPTER FIFTEEN

TO THINE OWN SELF BE TRUE

Thou that stupendous truth believ'd,
And now the matchless deed's achiev'd,
Determined, dared, and done.
—CHRISTOPHER SMART

IT TOOK TRUTH ALMOST AN HOUR TO MAKE HER WAY down from the hillside, and when she finally reached Shadow's Gate everything was in chaos. The smell of burning hung heavily in the air, and there seemed to be police and ambulances and fire engines everywhere, and even a few gawkers from Shadowkill, drawn by the sirens and the noise. She arrived just in time to see Hereward loaded into an ambulance, a white-coated attendant standing along beside him, holding the bottle of saline solution over his head.

What had happened? Surely Pilgrim had not won if there were all these people here—but what had happened? She ran through the tangle of parked vehicles looking for Light, for Irene, for anyone else from the Circle.

"Wait a minute, miss; you can't go in there." A fireman grabbed her at the front door of the house, his heavy coat smelling of smoke. The doors were open; Truth could see thick, white hoses snaking into the building's interior, and pools of water standing on the wooden floors. The electric lights were still on, lending the scene an odd, surreal aspect.

"My sister's in there!" Truth said, trying to pull away.

"There's nobody still in there," the fireman said. "Hey! John! Looking for her sister!" he shouted to someone standing a few feet away.

A man wearing the wide-brimmed hat of the State Police came over to where Truth stood. The walkie-talkie on his belt emitted random blurts of garbled speech. "Go with him, miss, he'll help you find her," the fireman told her.

"Your name?" The policeman said. He put a hand under her arm and began to walk her back toward his car. "You live in there?"

"Truth Jourdemayne. I've been staying here for the past few days working on some research. My sister was in there! Do you know—"

"Everyone got out, ma'am," the policeman said reassuringly. "If you'll just—"

"Truth!" Light barreled into Truth, nearly knocking her down again.

"Oh, God, you're all right—but you'll get wet!" Truth added almost instantly.

The young medium was still wearing her red robe, but over that was wrapped what looked like one of the banners from the Temple. Her long, silver hair was damp and tangled, and there were soot marks on her pale skin.

"I don't care!" Light said fiercely. She hugged Truth tighter, squeezing the water out of Truth's sodden clothes and into her own garish satins. Truth hugged her back, feeling a painful sense of relief. Light was safe.

The policeman, seeing he was not needed now, moved away, but Truth knew it was only temporary. There would be questions that had to be answered—and what would she say when the time came?

But now there was only one other thing that was important. "Pilgrim—where's Pilgrim?" Truth demanded.

"He's there," Michael said, stepping away from one of the trucks to stand beside Light. There was a blanket draped around his shoulders; he looked tired, but worlds away from the bleeding apparition with the flaming sword that Truth had seen earlier tonight.

Had that been real at all? She looked where Michael gestured, and saw Pilgrim.

He was stumbling across the grass, being led toward one of the waiting police cars by two of the EMTs. They were holding his arms; his hands were cuffed behind his back, and he was babbling:

"—kings in the darkness the citadels of the earth and ocean towering castles in the candles and the rain singing in the dark and rocks over stones in the ocean—" His words rambled on; there was no intelligence behind them, and seeing-without-seeing Truth could look and recognize the chains that bound him, stronger than any she or Thorne could have forged, binding Pilgrim tightly and ensuring that never again would his madness harm anyone but himself.

Michael had done this—or what Michael served—when Julian had lost the power of the Gate, and Truth could not find it in her to be sorry. She looked into Michael's eyes, and saw at last what he had been trying to save her from: the knowledge of what she was and the responsibility that came with walking the path her feet had now been set upon.

Truth felt a desolate sense of loss; now that she finally understood the truth she could have hoped to count Michael her friend. But no. She and Michael had chosen different paths a very long time ago.

The Christian Church held that Man was not strong enough to endure the experience of the Higher Knowledge, and so its teachings held that all such knowledge must be withheld. Julian Pilgrim had sworn that all knowledge belonged to Man, no matter that he was not ready for it.

"You're soaking wet," Michael said chidingly. "You'll freeze." He took the blanket from around his shoulders and wrapped her in it. It was warm from his body, and Truth smiled at him sadly. Tonight she and Michael had been on the same side against a greater evil, but the next time they met it might be as enemies.

Michael held out his arm, and Light went back to his side.

"I will care for Light, and see that her gifts bring her no further pain. I can . . . There is still time for you to choose, Truth. Will you come with us?"

"No, Michael," Truth said gently. "I've made my choice."

There was a middle ground between Michael's way and Pilgrim's—a path neither black nor white, but gray as mist: Thorne's path, and now hers. A path that Pilgrim had rejected, and that Light was not strong enough to follow.

Truth blinked back tears of loss, knowing already that time would lead her path and Light's farther apart, until in the end no common ground would remain to them. But Michael could give her the protection that Truth could not. And Light loved him. If what Truth and Thorne—and Michael—had done here tonight was for anything, it was for the freedom to make such choices. She turned away. "I'd better go see if I can find the others," she said.

"Go with God, then, Truth," Michael said quietly and she knew that the words were not empty—that they were a prayer she could not answer. Truth turned away.

Unlike the last time the house had burned, the devastation of Shadow's Gate this time was not total, though the Temple at the core of the house was destroyed—if not by fire, then by the water the arriving firemen had poured into it to save the house.

The fire trucks were pulling away and going back to the town, so the danger must be over. Truth wondered selfishly if any of the house could still be inhabited—she desperately wanted a hot shower. The cold was settling into her bones, and her fingers were already numb.

She found Donner and Irene together. He had his arm around her; Irene was sitting on a camp stool someone had brought her. Both of them were wrapped in blankets. Tears furrowed Irene's cheeks, and she looked terribly old.

" 'Who is my brother or sister in the Art, that is my brother or sister in all things,' " Donner said with a crooked smile, seeing Truth. "How are you?" he added cautiously.

Like Light, Donner was still wearing his ritual robe and was marked by soot; he looked as if he had aged ten years in the past few hours and his brown eyes were wary.

"I'm okay," Truth said, equally guardedly. "Aunt Irene, are you all right?" She knelt before the older woman, clutching the blanket around herself.

"It was wrong—all wrong," Irene said, weeping quietly. "He destroyed it all—everything! He made it ugly—"

"No," Truth said strongly. "Pilgrim didn't destroy anything we can't fix. We'll fix it together. I need you, Aunt Irene. I need you to teach me. Will you?" She had not known what she was about to say, but she did not doubt its truth. The art of magick was innate power bound to discipline and training—training that Truth still lacked.

Slowly Irene Avalon's gaze turned from her own inward grief and focused upon Truth's upturned face. With trembling fingers she reached out and caressed Truth's cheek.

"Yes," she said, her voice growing stronger. "Yes, I will."

Truth stood up and looked at Donner. "Where are the others?"

He shrugged. "They took Hereward off in an ambulance, and Julian . . ." his voice trailed off. "Michael and Light are around here somewhere, and I saw Gareth and Fiona—"

Who, Truth was sure, were already well away from here. Of all of them who had stood in the Circle tonight, only Pilgrim and perhaps Fiona had known fully what they were doing. She only hoped Gareth wouldn't suffer too much at Fiona's hands—but whatever happened to Gareth, in some sense he had chosen it.

"Donner, what happened in there tonight?" Truth asked him. It was not to confirm her own perceptions—she knew what she had seen—but to test the perceptions of others, now that she must live in two worlds.

Donner's gaze flicked away from her and back, but he could not meet her eyes. "I don't know," he said, and then, incredibly, "We were all pretty drunk."

"*Drunk?*" Truth said, stunned.

"Of course," Irene said firmly, though not as if she believed it. "That's how the fire started. The candles were knocked over by some of the boys' horseplay. If we hadn't all been so occupied with the fire, I'm sure we would have heard Julian shoot Hereward."

"Yes," said Donner, with relief, rejecting the reality in favor of the soothing lie. "That was it."

Truth shook her head. She wondered what the others had really seen, and how much any of them had truly been responsible for their own actions once the ritual had begun.

"I'll be back," she told Donner and Irene. "I'm going to go see if I can find anyone who can tell us if it's safe to go back inside."

She cast around until she found the Fire Marshal standing by his car.

"I'm Truth Jourdemayne," she said, introducing herself, "and I'd really like a hot shower. Is there any chance of going back inside the house yet?"

"Well, offhand I'd say it would be okay," the Fire Marshal said, pushing his cap back on his head. "It looks pretty bad in there but I wouldn't say there's any real structural damage. Just stay out of the room where the fire was until the insurance people've gone over it."

"Not a problem," Truth said. "And—thank you for coming."

"That's our job, Ms. Jourdemayne," he said, smiling. "It's been a heckuva night, hasn't it?"

Brother, you don't know the half of it, Truth told him silently.

As she was turning back to tell the others that they could all go inside, she heard a horn beeping. She turned in the direction of the sound and saw a brown Datsun swerving up the drive, headlights flaring as the driver cut the wheel from side to side.

Dylan.

Truth ran toward the car, which was already sliding to a stop. Dylan issued from behind the wheel almost without opening the door, worry radiating from his entire body.

"Dylan—it's okay—none of the equipment's damaged, and—" Truth began.

"To hell with the boxes!" Dylan said, grabbing her and all but shaking her. "What about you?"

What about *her?* Truth wondered that herself. She had made a long journey to reach this place, a longer journey than miles and hours could tell. And in making it, she'd found not only her father, but herself.

"Are you all right?" Dylan demanded, all but shaking her. "I came back to Shadowkill—I wanted to be here, if— And then I saw the fire—"

She pulled away just enough to link her arm through Dylan's.

"Oh, I'm all right. Come on inside; we'll find you a place to sleep for what's left of the night, but I don't think you'll have any luck finding any ghosts now, somehow. And do you know, speaking of ghosts, I think I have an entirely new slant on that biography of Daddy I'm going to write," Truth said, leading Dylan back toward the others.

Not as the world wanted him to be, but as he was—a man who had found in the end that perfection is sometimes the wrong choice.

And she would call it *Venus Afflicted*.

· *it's a* GOD *thing* ·

other books by luis palau

GOD IS RELEVANT

WHERE IS GOD WHEN BAD THINGS HAPPEN?

· *it's a* GOD *thing* ·

PICTURES AND PORTRAITS
OF GOD'S GRACE

LUIS PALAU

WITH MIKE YORKEY

doubleday

NEW YORK   LONDON   TORONTO

SYDNEY   AUCKLAND

PUBLISHED BY DOUBLEDAY
a division of Random House, Inc.
1540 Broadway, New York, New York 10036

DOUBLEDAY and the portrayal of an anchor with a dolphin are
trademarks of Doubleday, a division of Random House, Inc.

Unless otherwise noted, all Scripture quotations are taken from the *Holy Bible,*
New Living Translation, copyright © 1996. Used by permission of Tyndale
House Publishers, Inc., Wheaton, Illinois 60189. All rights reserved.

Library of Congress Cataloging-in-Publication Data

Palau, Luis, 1934–
It's a God thing : pictures and portraits of God's grace /
by Luis Palau, with Mike Yorkey.—1st ed.
p.   cm.
1. Christian life—Anecdotes.   I. Yorkey, Mike.   II. Title.

BV4517.P25 2001
242—dc21
2001017421

Chapter 10 features stories from Joseph Stowell, author of
Far from Home (Moody Press), and from the CoMission newsletter,
The Chariot. Used by permission.

ISBN 0-385-49800-4

Printed in the United States of America

October 2001

First Edition

3   5   7   9   10   8   6   4   2

Book design by Jennifer Ann Daddio

· contents ·

· *it's a* GOD *thing* ·

· introduction ·

God moves in a mysterious way
His wonders to perform.
  —*William Cowper, English poet (1731–1800)*

I love meeting people because, sooner or later, they want to tell me a story.

"Luis, you won't believe what happened to me," they begin, and what unfolds is a story of a gripping, personal, and often miraculous series of circumstances that only the Creator of the Universe could orchestrate.

What you're about to read are stories of how God has worked in the lives of dozens of individuals. Each of these true accounts illustrates something about God's grace, His greatness, His goodness, and His faithfulness.

You will find three types of stories in this book.

First, you will find *pictures*. Snapshots might be a better word. They are short and powerful word sketches, intended to show that God is intimately concerned with the short-term details of His special and unique creation . . . you! They show how God intervened in the normal stuff of life. Since that's where you and I live most of the time, you'll be inspired to see God's concern for the details.

Second, you will find *portraits*. If you've ever seen one of the large paintings of individuals by DaVinci or Rembrandt, you know that they contain incredible amounts of detail. You can tell by looking at one that it likely took months or even years to complete, and the result was a masterpiece. Likewise, God is creating a masterpiece out of my life, as well as yours. And a masterpiece means effort in the detail.

Third, you will find *pictures in a portrait*. This means that the events of the story shared, though perhaps a small part in someone's life, contributed to its overall course.

I believe you'll find this particular collection of stories to be a lot like life—the mundane combined with the heart-wrenching instances that mark a life forever.

Before I tell you more, let me ask two questions.

First, are you patient with God, or do you like fast-food answers to the deeper issues of life?

When I'm at the end of my rope—and I've been there many times—there's nothing I want more from God than an immediate answer. Sometimes He has sent it . . . and many times He hasn't. I'll tell you plainly: one purpose of this book is to help you be patient with God. I've discovered that His timetable for answering your most difficult circumstances will rarely fit yours. The reason? It takes time—and trial—to build you into the person you are meant to be—a masterpiece. As many people in this book will quickly admit, the miracle of answered prayer is savored most when God is given time to do His work. At the time of their deepest trial, did they want a positive resolution that was more immediate? Absolutely! But many on the other side of their unique yet common dilemmas of life—some who waited one, two, five, or twenty years for the answer they longed for—would not trade God's timing for the cheap and easy out they thought was the ultimate answer. They learned too much that added richness to their life, and too many of life's deepest questions were answered. Thus they could teach their loved ones the best lesson of all: that God is *always* great, *always* good, and *always* faithful.

Second, do you really believe God cares about you? In this book, you'll discover the answer should be an unequivocal yes!

I've seen clear evidence of God at work in my own life since I made the choice to trust my todays and tomorrows to God's Son, Jesus Christ, at a Christian camp in the Argentine Hills when I was twelve years old. From my earliest memories, I can see how He was making of me . . . a masterpiece. Not a portrait to be pointed at and admired as hundreds of tourists do in art museums, but one that causes someone to point back to the One who is the Master, the One who patiently and lovingly painted the portrait of what you see today.

Sadly, many people do not believe God is in the business of making a masterpiece of them. And why not? They hear stories of angels and miracles—the sudden recovery of a terminally ill child or the unexpected check arriving in the mail—and wonder why those events always happen to *other* people. If God doesn't perform an instant miracle at a person's time of need, does it mean He *isn't* working? That He doesn't love him or her? That He doesn't care?

If you are not sure whether God is near or far away, this book is for you. Whether you're in church more often than the church custodian or the road to your Sunday attendance is paved with good intentions, I pray that these true stories will boost your confidence that God doesn't take coffee breaks. He's painting tens, hundreds, if not thousands of brushstrokes to make your life's masterpiece.

I have reserved two stories at the end that to me represent brush strokes that have made my life what it is today. But for now, let me get right into the stories of real people who have experienced "God things" themselves.

A PORTRAIT

1.

· *seizing an opportunity* ·

Worry and deep concern for a loved one does not demonstrate a lack of faith in God. They are actually the very emotions that can serve to draw us to Him at critical hours of need. Have you ever been worried sick you were about to lose someone close? If so, you know, as Phil Callaway's story demonstrates, that when you're at the end of answers, love—and faith—sometimes find a way.

"Daddy, is Mama going to die?"

Five-year-old Stephen asked the question that Phil Callaway for years had dismissed far too casually. The woman he loved deeply had warned him of the trouble that could lie ahead.

When Phil and Ramona were in the "serious dating mode," they talked about marriage and kids and where they were going to live and what they wanted to do with their lives. At one point, Ramona had stood and paced the floor.

"What's wrong?" Phil asked.

"There's something you should know," Ramona replied anxiously. "I may have a rare disease called Huntington's. My dad had it, and I've been told that I have a fifty-fifty chance of getting it. Huntington's causes mental and physical deterioration and seizures, and if you get it, you usually die young. I just thought before we get too much further along . . ."

"I'd like to marry you someday, Ramona. I love you."

Phil never gave Huntington's disease much more thought. They were young. Invincible. And fertile. Three children were born in thirty-six months, which caused Phil to quip one day:

"Ramona, sure, we have three kids, but do you know why we're far more satisfied than the guy who has three million dollars?"

"No, why?"

"Well, the guy with three million wants more!"

Before long, however, life wasn't so funny. Ramona began waking up and pacing the floor in the middle of the night.

"What's wrong?" Phil asked through half-open eyes.

"I'm fine. I just can't sleep."

By that time, three of Ramona's six siblings had been diagnosed with Huntington's, and she was convinced she was next. The symptoms were there: lack of sleep, irritability, occasional clumsiness, even a craving for sweets.

A few weeks later Phil, the editor of *Servant* magazine in Alberta, Canada, took a phone call at his desk.

"Hello?"

Silence for five seconds.

"Hello?"

"H-h-h-elp me, please help me," Ramona cried. "I don't know what's happening."

Phil drove home in record time and burst through the door. He found his preschool children sitting on the kitchen floor, pouring cereal into bowls. "Is Mama going to die?" asked Stephen, the oldest.

Ramona lay on the living room sofa, an ugly gash on her left leg—the result of her sudden fall against a wooden bed frame—dripping blood on the carpet.

Staring with vacant eyes, she asked, "What day is it? Monday."

It's Friday, Phil thought.

"She's making funny noises," Stephen said. "She thinks I'm her dad."

Phil gathered the three children and held them close. "Maybe we should tell Jesus," said Rachael, who was three. "Maybe He can do something."

Squeezing them tightly, Phil prayed out loud: "Dear God,

help Mommy to be okay. And thank you that you're right here with us all the time."

After Phil wrapped his wife's leg and called his parents, he was searching for the doctor's phone number when Ramona let out an agonized moan. Phil watched in horror as her back arched and her head snapped back. Her face turned gray, and she slumped to the floor.

Ramona's arms and legs thrashed as Phil tried to calm her and keep her from biting her tongue. Ramona's mother, who had just arrived, called for paramedics. While Phil rode in the ambulance and held his wife's hand, he recalled reading an interview with singer Linda Ronstadt, in which she said, "I'll never get married. There's too much potential for pain."

I guess I finally understand what she meant.

The battery of tests began. CAT scans. EEGs. No clear diagnosis could be given, and Ramona returned home as doctors sorted out the conflicting signals. Meanwhile, over the next eighteen months, Ramona experienced dozens of seizures. Then some good news: doctors said a test had been developed to isolate the Huntington's gene.

On February 14, 1994, Phil and Ramona stood in the doctor's office while a doctor opened an envelope that held the test results.

"Ramona, you have the normal gene."

"We don't have Huntington's?" Phil asked.

"You don't have it."

The Callaways hugged the doctor. Ramona was clear. The disease would not be passed on to their children.

As the months dragged on, however, the seizures worsened. Ramona's weight slipped to ninety pounds, and people barely recognized her. Phil wondered if she would make it past her thirtieth birthday.

One day as they drove to visit Ramona's sister, another seizure laid Ramona out in the front seat. The children cowered in the back seat, crying.

"Is Mama going to die?" asked Rachael.

"I don't know," her father said. "But you know what? God says He'll always be with us. And He's never broken a promise. We can tell Him we're scared."

Yet late at night, it was Phil who could not sleep. A sense of panic built within him. "What do I do now, Lord? Where do we go from here?"

Bible verses memorized long ago offered comfort. "God is our refuge and strength, an ever-present help in trouble. Therefore we will not fear . . ." (Psalm 46:1–2).

By the fall of 1996, the seizures were occurring daily, sometimes hourly. Phil rarely left Ramona's side. Once, when she was finally asleep, he paced their dark backyard, then fell to his knees. "God!" he cried out. "I can't take it anymore. Please do something!"

As he stood, a doctor's name came to mind. Although this man attended the same church as the Callaways, Phil had never thought to ask him his opinion. Within minutes, Phil had him on the phone and was describing Ramona's symptoms.

"It sounds like something I've seen before," the doctor said. "Bring her first thing in the morning."

Phil hadn't really believed in miracles before. But within a week, Ramona was a different person. The doctor diagnosed a rare chemical deficiency and prescribed an antiseizure medication. The seizures ended. Ramona's eyes lit up with the sparkle that had first attracted him to her. Their children don't have to worry anymore that their mom will black out; that she could die at any moment. Instead, there is normalcy. So much normalcy, it brings tears to Phil's eyes to realize where they'd been . . . and where they are. Miracles do happen.

"God gave me back my wife."

Praise the Lord, [who] heals all my diseases.
He ransoms me from death and surrounds me
with love and tender mercies (Psalm 103:2–4).

A PICTURE

2.

· *the water filter* ·

If you look for them, you'll find that "love letters" come in all shapes and sizes. A picture drawn by a preschooler, a surprise check in the mail, and a clean house after a long day at work all say the same thing: I love you. The time after a loved one leaves—for whatever reason—is often the time when we need a love note the most; something tangible to hold on to. Be ready for that note, because such "God things" are everywhere!

This is not shaping up to be a cheery holiday season, Susan Wilkinson thought as she flipped through a thick stack of mail. Three months earlier, her husband, Marty, had lost a valiant fight against cancerous melanoma. He drew his final breath on August 2, 1995, at the age of forty-nine; an obituary in the *Houston Chronicle* noted that he was survived by his wife, Susan, and three children under the age of eleven.

Susan continued to sort through the mail. Nothing stopped the reminder of the crowning blow of the last three months: just five weeks after Marty's death, her mother had succumbed to lung cancer.

Lord, how am I going to get through this holiday season without Marty and Mom? Susan felt sick to her stomach as she contemplated seeing the empty seats on Thanksgiving Day and Christmas morning.

Susan opened a few bills, then held up a notice from Sterling Springs, a water filtration company. Like many Texas families, the Wilkinsons used a canister that filtered impurities from their kitchen tap water—and improved its taste. "It's time to change your filter!" said the notice, listing a phone number customers could call to order one.

The thought of ordering a simple filter was almost too much for Susan to bear. Marty had been the do-it-yourself guy around the house, the man's man who mowed the lawn, changed the sprinkler heads, fixed leaky plumbing, and had even made their son's wooden cradle in his workshop in the garage.

The thought of her "honey-do" list falling on her own shoulders greatly discouraged Susan. With a sigh, she ordered the new water filter. Three weeks after it arrived, she still had no idea what to do with it. One Saturday morning, however,

Susan decided to tackle the project. Their water was tasting pretty bad.

She turned the canister over and saw a label. Something was written in her husband's script: "November 4, 1994." *Hmm. Marty had changed that filter.* But right after the date was another inscription: "I love you."

When Susan saw the message, she stepped back and blinked hard, then drew a large breath. Such a simple message felt like a kiss from heaven, a tangible reminder of Marty's love for her months after he was gone.

Susan thought it through. Marty had learned on October 28, 1994, that his melanoma was malignant and incurable. "Two percent live five years," one of his doctors said. "But you're young, and we'll give it everything we've got."

It wouldn't be enough. Both Marty and Susan knew that his chances for surviving another year were slim, because the October biopsy revealed that the cancer was "very aggressive."

Two weeks after learning his condition was terminal, Marty changed the water filter. Knowing that the odds were poor that he would be around to change the filter again, he penned a short missive of love to his wife, knowing that she would find it.

Susan peeled off the label and tucked it into her prayer journal. After drying her eyes, she thanked God for giving Marty the idea to make a profound yet bittersweet expression of love after his death.

> . . . the sorrows of widowhood will be remembered no more, for your Creator is your husband. The Lord Almighty is his name! (Isaiah 54:4–5).

A PICTURE

3.

· *letters to a stranger* ·

Many think God wants to do only "big things" through them, that the "little things" don't matter all that much. In God's economy, the littlest things often become big things. Availability is like yeast in the hand of God. He makes your smallest bit of concern grow to make an impact in this life . . . and often for eternity. Do you want to see "God things" around you? Then tell Him you're available.

"Lord, I have so little to give back to you," Susan Morin prayed one Sunday at church. "It seems like I'm always asking you to meet my needs or answer my prayers. But Lord, what can I do for you?"

Susan, a single mom of three teenagers, was finding it hard to cope with her children's emotional needs and her precarious financial situation. Nevertheless, she longed to serve God in a way that made a difference for eternity, even though she had so little spare time to give.

The answer seemed so simple. She could pray. Susan committed to pray during her forty-five-minute commute from New Hampshire to her workplace in Vermont.

"Lord, will you give me some people to pray for?" she asked the next day as she drove to work. "I don't even have to know their needs. Just let me know who they are."

Susan arrived at the Mary Meyer Corporation, a company that makes stuffed animals. She was in charge of accounts receivable, a job that included opening the mail and preparing the bank deposits. She opened an envelope and found a note attached to a check. "I'm sorry this payment is late. I have been seriously ill. Thank you, Beverly Thompson."*

You want me to pray for her, don't you, Lord?

So began Susan's journey of praying for Beverly Thompson. At first she found it awkward to pray for someone she didn't know. She knew that Beverly owned a bookstore in Presque Isle, Maine, from where she ordered the company's plush animals to sell. But how old was she? Was she married? Did she have any children? Was her illness terminal?

Sometimes, as Susan prayed for Beverly, she found herself in tears. She prayed that Jesus would give Beverly comfort for what-

*Beverly Thompson is a pseudonym.

ever she had to endure. She pleaded for Beverly to find strength and courage to accept things that she might find hard to face.

A month or two passed, and Susan considered sending Beverly a card. This was risky—she could lose her job if Beverly was offended and complained to the company.

"Lord, I've grown to love Beverly Thompson," Susan prayed one morning. "I know you'll take care of me no matter what happens."

In her first card, Susan told Beverly a little about herself and how she had asked the Lord for specific people to pray for. Then she mentioned how she came across her name. She also said that God knew what Beverly was going through and loved her deeply.

Beverly never answered that letter, nor did she respond to the subsequent notes and cards Susan mailed that summer. But Susan never stopped praying for Beverly and even told her Tuesday night Bible study group about her.

Susan really was hoping Beverly would respond. She was curious what Beverly thought about this stranger and her stream of notes. Did Beverly think she was completely crazy? Did she hope that Susan would stop?

Six months passed. On a bitterly cold January evening, the phone rang. "Mom, it's for you!" fifteen-year-old Tajin hollered.

"Who is it?" Susan asked. She was tired after a long day. Actually, it had been a long month. Her car had died five days before Christmas, and she had lost a week's pay because of illness.

"It's someone named Bob Thompson," Tajin said.

Bob Thompson . . . ?

At first the name didn't register, but then Susan remembered, *Yes, Beverly Thompson. It must be her husband.*

She took the phone from her son; her hands became clammy. *I know why he's calling. He's calling to tell me to stop bothering his wife. They probably think I'm a religious kook.*

"Hello, Mr. Thompson," she squeaked.

"Hello, Susan," he replied. "My daughter and I have just been going through my wife's things, and we found your cards and notes, along with your phone number. We wanted to call and let you know how much they meant to Beverly before she died."

"Oh, I'm so sorry."

"We found your cards and notes tied up with a red ribbon," he said. "I know she must have read them, because they looked very worn."

"That's very nice, Mr. Thompson. Can you tell me more about your wife?"

"At the age of forty-eight, Beverly was diagnosed with lung cancer, which spread to her brain. She never suffered any pain at all. I know that this was the result of your prayers."

Then Mr. Thompson answered the question in Susan's heart.

"You may be wondering about this," he said, "but our relationship with God amounted to going to church once in a while. Church was nothing that had much effect on our lives. But that changed after Beverly began receiving your notes. I want you to know that she asked to be baptized two weeks before she passed away. The night before Beverly died she told me it was okay for her to die, because she was going home to be with her Lord."

Because Susan made herself available to God, she had made an eternal difference to a woman she never knew.

The earnest prayer of a righteous person has great
power and wonderful results (James 5:16b).

A PICTURE

4.

· *beyond the norm* ·

Many Christians believe the Bible when it says to go "to the ends of the earth" to share their faith. Oftentimes, when faith in God meets obedience to His Word, the path ahead is dimly lit. Reliance upon God to direct your steps is the best—and only—course. Has God ever told you to go, however, without giving you directions? He did so with the two women in this story.

Before the December 1989 revolution and execution of dictator Nicolae Ceausescu, Romanian Christians risked their lives by making any expression of faith. That didn't stop Norm Miller, CEO of Interstate Battery System of America, and his wife, Anne. The couple made several trips behind the Iron Curtain.

On one trip without her husband, Anne teamed up with a friend, Sherry, in Vienna. They entered Romania as tourists but intended to lead women's Bible studies. In their purses was the address of a pastor and his family. After knocking on the door, they were greeted warmly and shown inside.

"Did anyone see you?" the pastor inquired.

"No, we don't think so," Anne replied.

"Good. It will be less risky if you stay inside."

For two days, the cloistered American women observed how their counterparts lived in Romania. All women worked outside the home. They began the day at five-thirty A.M. by standing in bread lines, arrived at work at seven, left at four, went home to household chores, and then fell into bed exhausted.

Every meal except one followed the same menu: a plate lined with fatty summer sausages and goat cheese, filled in the middle with tomatoes and cucumbers. Anne and Sherry ate sparingly, wondering if they were taking food from the mouths of their hosts, who had two small children. They did not butter their bread, because they knew the monthly ration was just one kilo.

Each night, the pastor's home filled with women who came to hear Anne and Sherry teach biblical concepts regarding child rearing and building a marriage. The women eagerly took notes and asked questions. Meetings closed with fervent prayers and quiet singing.

Romanian law prohibited religious meetings. Conversing with Westerners was also illegal, as was religious literature. So the meetings were secret, and the women diligently hand-copied all the materials.

The time came for Anne and Sherry to travel by train to the next city. They were told to wear dark clothing, eschew makeup and jewelry, avoid eye contact, and try to blend in as best they could.

Because their train trip involved several tricky changes, Anne and Sherry worried whether they would find the right city and the people expecting them. They boarded their train at five-thirty A.M. and looked for an empty compartment where they could munch on granola bars and drink orange juice—a "luxurious" Western breakfast. They found a compartment, took their seats, and started to open their overnight bags containing their food. Before they could begin eating, however, four more people piled into the compartment. That meant no talking (a dead giveaway that they were Americans), no reading, and no eating their foreign food.

Two hours into the journey the train stopped at a station. The conductor bellowed out the name of the town as he walked through the train. Sherry, who was responsible for the travel arrangements, glanced at Anne and shook her head, but in the back of her mind, she wondered if they had missed the right town. She silently prayed, asking not to make the wrong turns . . . or the wrong moves.

A few minutes later, the conductor yelled out the name of the next stop. A young woman sitting across from Anne had been sleeping, but she suddenly awakened and stopped the conductor. She seemed to be asking questions about the next stop.

When the train rolled into the station, the young woman stood up, grabbed her belongings, and nodded at Anne as if to say, "Follow me." Sherry and Anne shot each other panicked looks, yet they somehow knew they should follow.

They stood behind the woman as she took her place among waiting passengers on the station platform. Ten minutes passed. Another train pulled in. The young woman glanced at the Americans and said one word in English: "Accident."

Anne and Sherry wondered why this young woman had picked them out as Americans when they had not uttered a word in English or done anything to draw attention to themselves. When she boarded the train, the two Americans dutifully followed.

No backing out now! Anne thought.

The train was a "local," stopping in every town and city along its route. After three hours of traveling, the young woman looked over at Sherry, caught her eye, and nodded. The train braked to a stop, and they saw the name of the town they were supposed to go to on the sign above the platform. Anne and Sherry stood and left, while the train transporting "their angel" disappeared down the track, leaving the Americans alone again in a strange city.

"What do you think is going to happen next?" Anne asked.

"With God there is always another surprise around the corner," Sherry replied. "Plan A was for someone to meet us, but I don't see anyone."

"Well, what's Plan B?"

"Don't you remember?" asked Sherry. "We were supposed to stand in the waiting area with a newspaper under one arm."

"Is there a Plan C?"

"If all else fails, we're to walk out of the station and turn right."

Anne prayed for guidance. She had been praying for three years to take this trip to teach Romanian Christians. Couldn't God be trusted to shine a light on the path they were supposed to take to the next pastor's house?

They left the train station and started walking down the street.

"Where are we going?" asked Sherry.

"God is going to lead us where we need to go," said Anne.

After a block, Anne said, "Let's turn right here." Two blocks later, she sensed she was to turn right again.

"There it is!" she exclaimed. God had led them straight to the pastor's front door.

Trust in the Lord with all your heart; do not depend on
your own understanding. Seek his will in all you do, and
he will direct your paths (Proverbs 3:5–6).

5.

· *busing their way to history* ·

One of the most important prayers is asking for God's direction. While there are always mid-course corrections throughout life, you never know how God will answer that prayer. Have you ever asked God to direct your steps? A man named Cliff did. Fifty years later he's on the same path, and he's never looked back.

Married all of three days to Cliff, Billie Barrows was worried about where they were going to spend the night. Brides have a way of wanting to know those things.

"We could go to Wisconsin Dells," Cliff offered.

"Wisconsin? What about that resort hotel at Lake Lure?"

"Yes, we could go there, and it's not too far from here," Cliff said.

They agreed their next bus destination would be North Carolina's Blue Ridge Mountains. Just before the young couple left their motel room on that June day in 1945, they asked the Lord to give them a safe trip to Lake Lure, a few hours away.

Cliff and Billie, who was still a student at Bob Jones College in Greenville, South Carolina, a year after Cliff had graduated, were on their honeymoon.

With two suitcases, the couple set out on their next adventure. The bus dropped them off in a nearby town, and some kind strangers picked them up and dropped them off at Lake Lure, where they discovered the military had taken over the hotel. World War II, finally winding down in Europe, was still raging in the Pacific.

A Christian couple invited Cliff and Billie to stay with them. For the next few days, they swam in Lake Lure and climbed to the top of Chimney Rock.

"Well, we need to be moving along," Cliff told his hosts.

"Where are you going?"

"I don't know. Where are we going, Billie?"

Before she could respond, one of their hosts said, "We know a family in Asheville, less than an hour from here. The Browns would enjoy having you stay with them. Let me call and ask. The Browns have a daughter you might know—Hortense. She's a student at Bob Jones College."

"We know Hortense," Cliff said. "It will be nice to meet her family."

So it was off to Asheville. At the city's municipal pool, Cliff and Billie bumped into a man named Jim Adair, whom Cliff also had met at Bob Jones.

"What are you doing here?" Cliff asked.

"Working. I'm a reporter at the *Asheville Times,*" said Jim. Although they hadn't known each other well at college, Jim had admired Cliff's energetic song leading.

The next day, Jim's pastor, Reverend Julian Bandy, called. "A young evangelist is in town," he said. "He wants to play some golf this afternoon. Care to join us?"

"Sure," said the cub reporter.

On the first tee, the tall, lanky evangelist, wearing a red golf cap, introduced himself. "Hi," he said. "I'm Billy Graham."

"Jim Adair."

The loop around the golf course went quickly, as Billy played "ready golf" and rarely took much time to make his shots. Reverend Bandy had honors for most of the eighteen holes.

At dinnertime, Jim received a phone call from his new golfing buddy. "Do you know someone who could lead singing for me tonight?" asked the earnest evangelist, who was scheduled to preach that night. "My song leader was unexpectedly called back to Chicago."

Jim suggested a friend of his, and Billy said, "Sounds fine to me."

As soon as he hung up, Jim thought about Cliff Barrows and his enthusiastic singing in college, and he remembered that Billy said he was speaking at a youth event. Maybe a younger man would be better, and besides, he played a mean trombone . . .

Jim called Billy back. "I think I know someone, a younger fellow, who would be a better fit. His name is Cliff Barrows, and he happens to be in town on his honeymoon."

"Well, if he can lead the singing, then send him out."

"I'll get on it."

Jim phoned the Brown residence and asked for Cliff. Then he looked at his watch. The event was only hours away.

After relaying Billy Graham's request, Jim asked Cliff if he was available.

"Sounds good," said Cliff, "but let me check with Billie."

After a minute, Cliff returned to the phone. "She says it's fine, and she plays a good piano. We'll ride out to the auditorium with the Browns."

That evening, the auditorium pulsated with enthusiastic singing as Cliff directed and Billie played the piano. Afterward, Billy Frank, as some people called the young evangelist from Charlotte, preached with vigor.

That was the start of a long friendship between Cliff Barrows and Billy Graham. A year later, Billy asked the couple to join his crusade team. For more than a half century, Cliff was the world-renowned evangelist's song leader and right-hand man, helping bring the good news of Jesus Christ to millions.

We can make our plans, but the Lord
determines our steps (Proverbs 16:9).

A PICTURE

6.

· *"trust me"* ·

Whether you're faithful or faithless, there are times when it is truly difficult to believe God can provide. While many of us have never had to worry about where the next day's food would come from, or next month's rent, there have been days in our history when such worry was the norm. Along with this constant unknown came a deep dependence upon the Unseen Guest. If you knew the resources—and the character—of this Guest, any doubts about God's power would disappear . . . as they did for Susan and Andrew . . .

Susan Warren's breath crystallized and sparkled in the rays of dawn creeping into the bedroom. The freezing temperature that January morning encouraged her to tug the comforter up to her nose. Then she snuggled closer to her sleeping husband, Andrew. That movement awakened her unborn baby, who stretched and kicked inside her abdomen.

A few moments later, sunlight trumpeted through the flimsy curtains. Susan tapped Andrew lightly.

"It's time to get up," she said. "Please go light the heater."

Their one-bedroom cinder-block home was a mere five hundred square feet, and the old kerosene heater struggled like a mighty warrior against the drafts that assaulted the cracks in the fifty-year-old house. During the day, with sunlight as an ally, the heater kept their house toasty warm and comfortable. At night they let the old soldier flicker out, preferring instead the brisk Tennessee air.

Andrew groaned and rolled out of bed. Susan heard him shuffle to the family room, then strike a match. The crackle of the wick warmed Andrew's hands as it heated to a cherry-red glow.

As quickly as the wick came to life, it died. That could mean only one thing.

"We're low on fuel!" Andrew hollered. "I'm going to fill up the tank."

Susan heard the back door slam. A fifty-gallon barrel in the backyard held their winter supply of kerosene. Andrew knew it was more than half full—plenty to get them through the winter.

Susan slipped out of bed and tiptoed to check on their son, sleeping in his crib. His blond hair curled against his face, and a slight sweat glistened on his brow from the heat of the double layer of pajamas he wore. Susan leaned on the door frame, her hand on the life growing within her, and thanked God for providing for their needs during their lean college years.

Andrew was a full-time student in his final year of aviation school; Susan had opted to stay home with their son. Andrew's sideline, auto-repair jobs helped keep food on their table and pay their rent, but they rarely had anything left in the bank at month's end. Their last forty dollars had just paid the electric bill.

The back door slammed again. When Susan turned and looked at Andrew, her mouth went dry. He had carried in a load of worry and despair. "Our barrel has a leak. The kerosene is gone."

They stood there in silence, listening to fear keep the beat with their hearts. They had no money in the cookie jar; they were eating corn bread left over from the Wednesday night church supper. What were they going to do?

"We'd better pray," Andrew said quietly. As he asked the Lord to rescue them, Susan's heart stormed. Dismay buffeted her faith. Through the rain she heard a voice thunder in her soul, "Trust me," but she could not see past the dark clouds to hold on to her Savior.

Andrew left for school while Susan started on the housework. A chill invaded the house. Susan bundled her son in another layer and tried to pray again, but all she could feel were waves of despair, tossing her about in an ocean of doubt.

Shortly after lunch, a friend stopped by and asked if Andrew could repair his pickup. He handed Susan the keys and said something about leaving town for the weekend. "I'll come for the truck Monday."

Well, that will help us buy some groceries, Susan thought.

When Andrew arrived home two hours later, the house was cold, but a warm smile flickered on his face.

"Guess what we got in our mailbox at school?" he said. He handed Susan an envelope. Inside were two crisp twenty-dollar bills. "Money for the kerosene."

"From whom?"

Andrew shrugged and shook his head. "I don't know." Then his smile faded. "But how are we going to fit the barrel into our hatchback?"

It was Susan's turn to smile. She dangled the pickup keys in front of his wide eyes.

While Andrew loaded the barrel into the truck, Susan searched the envelope for evidence of the identity of their bene-factor. A slip of paper was folded between the twenties. She pulled it out, and a chill rippled through her. The note said, "Proverbs 3:5—Trust in the Lord with all your heart."

> And this same God who takes care of me
> will supply all your needs from his
> glorious riches (Philippians 4:19a).

7.

· *choosing a different road* ·

You've heard the phrase "you've made your bed, now lie in it."
Perhaps you've also heard "what you sow, you'll reap." Both
speak of facing consequences for reckless behavior. Yes, there
are physical consequences of poor decisions, and sometimes
those consequences are tough to swallow. But the emotional re-
sults—no matter how debilitating or long-lasting—can serve to
point you toward choosing one of two alternatives: prison or
freedom. A mill worker in Washington State faced choosing one
of those alternatives after a terrible accident.

They called it the "green chain" at the Aloha Cedar Products
sawmill outside Hoquiam, Washington. For five days a week,
eight hours a day, Bob Mortimer pulled freshly sawn 2 by 4 boards
and 6 by 6 beams off the roller belt and stacked them for shipping.

At twenty-one years old, Bob didn't mind the physically demanding work. It fit well with the blue-collar lifestyle of drinking

Rainier longnecks and getting stoned with his buddies after quitting time.

Bob was sixteen when he tried to wake up his father in their single-wide trailer home—and couldn't. He had died from a drug overdose, and when the family moved to the Pacific Northwest to start over, Bob found himself drinking and doping with a new group of friends.

Some of those friends worked at the sawmill and, after partying one night in Olympia, Bob and his brother, Tom, started the drive back home to Hoquiam, fifty miles away. Tom took a curve wrong, overcorrected, and struck a power pole before sliding down an embankment.

The brothers were lucky this time; they emerged from the car unscathed.

"You okay?" Tom asked.

"Believe so," said Bob, stepping out of the car. "Where's the road?"

"Dunno."

"Did we hit a tree?"

"I don't know what we hit," Tom said.

Bob saw a path to the highway through the knocked-down brush.

When he climbed the embankment and reached the road, Bob didn't realize that waiting for him were five downed power lines. In the darkness his left arm touched a line, causing 12,500 volts of electricity to surge through his body. He fell to his knees, which grounded him. The electrical charge, looking for somewhere to go, exploded out of his knees. He fell forward across the other wires, which burned the front of his body.

When Tom came upon his brother, Bob wasn't moving. Tom figured Bob was dead, so he sat on the side of the road and wondered what to do next. Then Bob moaned. Tom pulled him free and kept him alive until help arrived.

The next morning Bob woke up at Harbor View Medical Center in Seattle and signed a release to amputate his left arm. Two weeks later doctors took his right leg. He kept his left leg several months before surrendering it.

Bob endured six months of recuperation and rehabilitation at the Seattle hospital while doctors grafted skin over his burns. Following his release, Bob returned to the only world he knew— drinking and drugs. This time around, he drank beer and smoked marijuana to blunt the pain of being a triple amputee.

He was twenty-five when he met Darla Hollis, who was baby-sitting his sister's children. They were chatting one day when Darla said, "Would you like to go to church with me sometime?"

Hey, my life's so messed up. Why not? Bob thought.

That Sunday in church, Bob heard the good news of Jesus Christ for the first time. When the pastor invited listeners to allow God to take control of their lives, Bob thought back to the decisions that had framed his life. When he chose his own way, he lost his limbs and burned his body. When he allowed others to choose his path, he lost his dignity and pride. *What more can I lose? Why don't I let God lead the way?*

Bob didn't think twice. He rolled his wheelchair to the front of the church. That morning Bob repented of his party lifestyle and hard heart, and he surrendered his life to Jesus Christ.

Six months later Bob rolled his wheelchair down the church aisle once more, this time waiting for Darla, dressed in a white wedding gown.

Nearly twenty years later, Bob can't speak about Darla without smiling. They live in Gig Harbor, Washington, with their twelve-year-old daughter, Nicole, eight-year-old son, Grant, and toddler, Chanel.

Bob travels around the country, speaking several hundred times a year to school assemblies, community organizations, and churches, ministering with a message of hope borne out of horrible tragedy.

To all who mourn . . . he will give beauty for ashes,
joy instead of mourning, praise instead of despair.
For the Lord has planted them like strong and graceful
oaks for his own glory (Isaiah 61:3).

A PORTRAIT

8.

· the three storks ·

God speaks the way He wants to speak. A burning bush, a donkey, an angel . . . Cover to cover, God shares His wisdom and will throughout the Bible. Some people believe God also speaks through the audible voice of another believer. If you have ever wished God could show you what to do next, then this story will open your eyes to one fact: God can be very creative when He wants to be!

Friends had warned Mary and Rolf Benirschke that a Russian adoption would be fraught with peril and meters of red tape. Sure enough, ten months passed before the Russian government notified the couple they could return to Moscow to finalize Valery's adoption.

Mary's heart had melted when she first met the shy four-year-old at a Russian orphanage. As her brother-in-law held a camcorder, Mary lifted Valery into her arms and kissed him. She bonded with him immediately.

Rolf made the trip from California this time. An interpreter and guide met him and other anxious parents-to-be at Moscow's Sheremetyevo Airport on an Easter morning in 1996 and drove to an imposing government building. Finally, Rolf's name was called.

"Did you have a pleasant flight?" asked the ministry official as he ruffled through the Benirschke file.

"Yes, I did," Rolf replied.

"Hmm, yes. Before we can proceed, Mr. Benirschke, there is one small problem."

"And what would that be?"

"It seems that Valery has a brother named Viktor. We found him in another orphanage about three hours from here. You may not be aware of this, but it's our policy not to break up families. If you want to complete the adoption of Valery, you will also have to take Viktor."

Even with jet lag, Rolf quickly figured out he was at a disadvantage. This Russian had an American on the hook—here was a way to dispatch two kids from overcrowded orphanages instead of only one.

Two children? This was not part of the plan. Rolf and Mary

already were parents of a special-needs three-year-old, Kari, who had a mild form of cerebral palsy.

"Can I meet him first?"

"By all means."

The next day, Rolf was driven to Sovietsk in a ramshackle Lada that couldn't top 40 mph. At the orphanage he was led to a community room, where two dozen pale and malnourished boys, ranging in age from two to four, were playing.

"That's him," said the orphanage director, pointing toward a corner. Rolf saw a pallid, listless boy staring into space.

"How old is he?"

"Two years, three months. He weighs eight kilos."

Seventeen, eighteen pounds, Rolf calculated, way under the chart. He also had a cleft lip that had been poorly repaired.

Most of the boys seemed happy, eager to receive gifts their visitor had brought. Viktor? He stood by himself, unresponsive. Rolf walked over and blew up a balloon. Nothing. He tickled him, tried to get him to laugh. He waved a hand in front of his face. The eyes didn't follow.

"What are you going to do?" asked Sergei, his interpreter.

"How long do I have to decide?"

"Until tomorrow."

Back at his hotel, Rolf fell to his knees and asked God for guidance. He opened the Bible and read several psalms about relying on the Lord. As much as he wanted to, he couldn't call Mary—the national phone system wasn't working.

"Father, please give me a sign one way or the other," Rolf prayed. "Show me what I should do."

When Rolf woke up the next morning, he still wasn't sure what course he would take. He continued to pray for a sign as the Lada rumbled through the countryside. Riding with Rolf were an American couple who also were receiving a child that day.

"Look, storks," said Sergei, pointing to the regal birds alongside the road.

Rolf had grown up in a bird-watching family in New Hampshire. Sergei was right, those were beautiful storks.

"We have a saying in Russia that storks bring babies," Sergei continued. "Perhaps a good omen for today, *da?*"

Rolf counted three storks walking through the marshy land. Three? *That's it,* he thought. *Three storks means three babies—one for the American couple and two for me.*

At the orphanage, he gathered up little Viktor and hugged him, tears freely flowing. "Yes, I'll take him," Rolf said. They gathered up his belongings and returned to Moscow for Valery.

Two days later, they boarded a flight for London and then New York. Once on American soil, Rolf called Mary in California.

"Honey, you know how you said you always wanted a larger family? Well, I have a little surprise for you . . ."

Renamed Erik and Timmy, the boys are thriving. Timmy (Viktor) has gained weight and has begun school.

Children are a gift from the Lord; they are
a reward from him (Psalm 127:3).

A PICTURE

9.

· *the andes mechanic* ·

Many people think prayer is complicated. They have to be in a certain place, pray in a certain position, and say just the right words for the Almighty to listen and act. The story below illustrates how the simplest prayer can bring you the miracle you need, when you need it.

The weekend getaway in Huancayo had been the perfect tonic for Esteban and Carmela Tosoni and their children, Vanessa and Marco.

Situated at a breathtaking elevation of eleven thousand feet, Huancayo is one hundred miles east of Lima, Peru's capital city. Picturesque colonial architecture draws hundreds of thousands of tourists annually to its cobblestone streets. The Tosonis had enjoyed ambling through the city's outdoor market looking at Indian textiles.

Most families began driving back to Lima by four P.M. Sunday afternoon, but the Tosonis lingered an extra hour before loading their white Nissan station wagon. Then they set off to cross the lofty Andes.

"Look, the train!" ten-year-old Vanessa exclaimed.

"That's the Centrale, built by the French and considered one of the most remarkable railroad constructions in the world," Carmela said proudly. "The Centrale is the highest railroad in the world. I remember from my school days that the train goes up to 15,800 feet. Esteban, how high will we be going today?"

"I think the top of the pass is just below that," he said. "This time of year, there's sure to be some ice."

The car suddenly lurched, and the engine coughed twice before quitting. Esteban pulled onto the shoulder of the narrow two-lane highway.

Esteban rolled up his sleeves and opened the hood. He wasn't a mechanic, but he could do a few perfunctory things—check the spark plugs or see if any hoses were broken. "I don't know what's wrong with her," he said. "She's not overheating."

The sun was starting to drop behind the mountains, and few cars were passing by. Every now and then a truck rumbled past them.

"What are we going to do?" Carmela asked.

"We are a family that believes in prayer, so I think the answer is obvious," said Esteban.

"Yes, Daddy, let's pray," Vanessa said.

"Me, too," said Marco.

The family members took turns praying aloud that God would send someone to help them.

"Look," said Marco, moments after they all opened their eyes. "Someone is coming."

"I don't see anyone," Esteban said, looking in each direction. He looked again and spotted a lonely figure walking toward them in the middle of the highway.

"See, I told you someone was out there," Marco said.

"What's he carrying?" Carmela asked.

"It looks like a box of some sort," Esteban offered.

"Maybe he works around here," said Vanessa.

"I doubt it, Vane. I don't see any houses or stores nearby," said her father.

The man walked up to their car. He looked to be in his early thirties with straight black hair but no mustache. He wore faded work pants and a shirt, along with dusty leather shoes. His right hand held a small, wooden box.

"Are you a mechanic?" Esteban asked.

"Yes, I am."

"Could you help me?"

"You want me to help you? I can do that."

The man looked under the hood of the car for a few minutes.

"You are not getting gas from the gas filter into the engine, but I can fix it for you," he said as he pulled several tools from his box and began the necessary repairs.

"See if it starts," he said to Esteban.

The engine roared to life.

"Let me help you get over that pass, because your car might quit again," said the man. "Can I drive?"

"Sure," said Esteban, who wasn't wary at all. The man seemed so kind-hearted.

The full station wagon labored but crossed the Andes over the next twenty miles. Once the car started downhill, with Lima visible in the distance, the man pulled the Nissan into a gas station.

"I will stay here," he said.

"But can't we take you home or someplace you have to go?" asked Esteban. "We don't want to leave you out here in the middle of nowhere."

"No, I will be fine."

"But let us pay you something. Surely, you are hungry and need something to eat."

"No, I will stay here," he said.

The Tosoni family waved good-bye, then started driving on toward Lima.

"Do you think he was an angel?" Carmela asked.

"I don't know for sure," Esteban said, "but now I do know God really does take care of His children."

My help comes from the Lord, who made the heavens and the earth. He will not let you stumble or fall; the one who watches over you will not sleep. The Lord keeps watch over you as you come and go (Psalm 121:2–3, 8).

10.

· *open doors once more* ·

God is never limited by time or space in answering a prayer or accomplishing His will. That's what being omniscient means. Have you wondered if your life and faith will make a difference in succeeding generations . . . if your silent pleas for family and friends will be heeded by the hand of God? The following story is so remarkable it can only be described as a "God thing."

When Mikhail Gorbachev liberalized Russia's strict thought-control policies, no one could have guessed that two lives would intersect in a most unusual way. Dimitri, a Russian citizen, knew nothing of God and existed from day to day trying to stay alive. Silently, he blamed the Russian system for failing to bring about abundance of food and family cohesion. As a boy, he learned that many in his extended family had not escaped the brutal side of Communism.

Paul Eshleman, director of the *Jesus* Film Project for Campus

Crusade for Christ, was invited to screen the film at a Moscow film festival. Paul ended up signing a contract to show the film throughout the former Soviet republics—but for theater release only. To protect the financial investment made to bring the film to the silver screen, the contract stated that *Jesus* would not be shown on television while the film circulated in theaters.

Paul soon learned, however, that a Russian producer had sold the TV rights on the side—and pocketed the rubles. A distressing development for sure, but without it a high-ranking bureaucrat in the Soviet Ministry of Education might have missed a divine appointment.

Alexei Brudenov happened to catch the last ten minutes of *Jesus* at home on television one evening. Curious to learn more about this man named Jesus, he purchased a ticket a couple of days later at a theater whose marquee advertised the film. When he saw the Roman soldiers nail Jesus' hands to the cross, Alexei broke down and wept. He cried again at the close of the movie when he trusted Jesus Christ as his Savior.

Alexei ordered sweeping changes in the educational system. He allowed ministries and schoolteachers to come to Russia and instruct elementary and high school teachers on how to teach Christian principles and ethics to their students. Since 1991, millions of Russian children have heard the good news of Jesus Christ in the state-run schools.

When *Jesus* arrived in the city of Stavropol, Doug and Kyle Clarkson worked with a team of schoolteachers who wanted to teach a curriculum based on the Bible and show *Jesus* to their students. The team soon ran out of its supply of New Testaments. One of the teachers mentioned that a warehouse outside of town once stored Bibles confiscated from Christians in the 1930s. Multitudes of believers were sent to the gulags, where most died for being "enemies of the state."

A team member drove to the warehouse to check it out. Sure enough, the Bibles were still there. "Can we have them to distribute to the people of Stavropol?"

The next day the team returned with a truck to load Bibles. A laborer named Dimitri, an agnostic college student, had come only for the day's wages. Midway through the job the young man disappeared.

"Have you seen Dimitri?" someone asked.

"No, I haven't," replied one of the Americans. "I'll look around."

Dimitri was found weeping in a corner of the warehouse. He explained he had picked up a Bible to steal it, but what he found inside shook him to the core.

"Here," he said, pointing to the first page. "That's my grandmother's signature."

The odds of Dimitri reaching for his grandmother's Bible

were astronomical but not beyond the reach of God. Though decades separated a grandmother and her grandson, the most important message she could bring—perhaps a message she had specifically prayed for—was finally delivered in God's time and in God's way.

The results will echo in eternity.

Forever, O Lord, your word stands firm in heaven.
Your faithfulness extends to every generation, as
enduring as the earth you created. Your laws remain
true today, for everything serves your plans
(Psalm 119:89–91).

A PICTURE

11.

· *believe it or not* ·

When catastrophe strikes, as it has for millions upon millions from the beginning of recorded history, there is a natural tendency to place blame . . . usually on a higher power. But is that the correct response? Although our culture has adopted the phrase "act of God" to describe an unpredictable disaster, I believe the true "acts of God" are found in the aftermath of catastrophe in the acts of those who respond to save and comfort individuals who have been devastated. The debate will always be with us as to what—or who—causes catastrophe, but this story shows a silver lining in the inevitable clouds of trouble.

"Oh, Jesus, have mercy!" said a nameless rescuer. Then finally, "Somebody is alive!"

For the moment, Mike Redlick had survived the Loma Prieta earthquake.

It was October 17, 1989. A festive atmosphere had permeated Safeway's corporate headquarters in Oakland, California, where Mike worked as a logistics analyst. Radios had been tuned to the pre-game show of game three of the World Series between Oakland and San Francisco. The first pitch was scheduled for 5:25 P.M.

Mike looked at his watch: 4:25. Normally, he left work at 4:30 for the drive home: northbound on Interstate 880, west across the San Francisco Bay Bridge, and then south to San Bruno, where his pregnant wife, Lynn, was caring for their two preschoolers, Matt and Sean. If he left now, however, he'd get caught in the baseball traffic around Candlestick Park. *Better wait fifteen, twenty minutes,* he thought.

At 4:50, Mike walked out to his 1984 Sunbird, a root-beer-colored four-door with plenty of commuting miles on the odometer. Almost by rote, he buckled his seat belt and drove to the Cypress Freeway, Interstate 880.

The expressway was a double-decked structure elevated over the east-west grids of the streets below. Mike stepped on the gas and easily merged into lane two of the northbound lower deck. Commuter traffic usually clogged the four lanes, but on this afternoon Mike saw nothing but clear sailing. *Everyone left work early to watch the World Series,* he thought. *I've timed the drive home perfectly.*

Suddenly a vehicle bumped his car from behind. Then all

four tires flattened. In the instant his mind struggled to process what this meant, he was flung sideways and crashed through the passenger-side window.

Dazed, Mike took a few moments to focus his eyes. When he did, he realized a lot more than tire blowouts had happened. Slabs of concrete entombed his car. One huge chunk had nailed the hood, but his engine was still running. He could hear a frantic voice on the radio, announcing that a major earthquake had struck the Bay area.

Blood dripped down Mike's face from a cut on his forehead, but he didn't feel any broken bones. Pinned precariously under tons of concrete, he was unable to budge from his half-in, half-out-of-the-car position.

"God, You're in control here," he prayed. "If You want to take me, it's in Your hands. You know that I have a beautiful wife, two kids, another on the way, but if it's Your will that I not survive, I give myself to You."

Mike coughed several times from the acrid dust swirling through the air. He began screaming for help.

Minutes after the earthquake struck, residents from a nearby housing project ran to the wrecked freeway—the top deck had "pancaked" onto the lower deck, crushing cars and their occupants. Several people climbed shattered support columns, holding on to curled steel reinforcement rods that had been bent and exposed. An aftershock threatened to drop the entire freeway onto the streets below.

Mike continued to call out for help as he heard rescuers working their way toward him. Three men finally reached him.

"I can't get out," he said. "You're going to have to get the door open."

"I'll be right back," said one, who returned a few minutes later with a crowbar.

They worked the door until finally it sprang open. Mike was able to walk to safety. Sitting on a nearby sidewalk, he felt soreness in his chest. Several teeth had been chipped, but he was going to be okay. Looking north, he saw what resembled a Hollywood set for a disaster film. Flames licked the sky as emergency vehicles responded to a five-mile stretch of concrete rubble that had been the Cypress Freeway. Later, Mike would learn about the forty-one deaths and the scores of injured—some whose legs were amputated to free them.

At eight P.M., Mike phoned Lynn from the hospital where he was treated and released. A cousin from the East Bay offered to drive him home. As their car sped across the undamaged San Mateo Bridge, Mike realized he had been given a special gift— life. Why was he thrown sideways, not forward, when the car came to a sudden halt? And why wasn't the Sunbird totally crushed by tons of concrete that landed on its hood and roof?

Great questions, and ones that Mike can't answer. All he knows is that God spared his life.

> For you have rescued me from death; you have kept my feet from slipping. So now I can walk in your presence, O God, in your life-giving light (Psalm 56:13).

A PORTRAIT

12.

· *moving mountains* ·

Few have the courage to "pray big." Yet some people have an earnest desire to see God do something extraordinary in a hopeless situation. Prayers for the healing of the common cold or for a more respectful teenager—as valuable as these prayers are— simply aren't what excites them. Have you ever tried to pray a prayer that was too big for God to answer? As you'll discover— through time, persistence, and effort—there is no prayer too big for God.

What could be more foolish? Two Americans deciding to pray for twenty-five years for a continent they knew nothing about.

"We have to pray for something bigger than ourselves," Doug Coe told Bob Hunter, a new Christian who asked his friend how to pray. "Pick a city like Washington, or a state like Virginia, or a country like Russia, or even a continent like Africa. If you pray and stick with it for twenty-five years, you will see God move mountains."

For some reason, the thought of praying for Africa stuck with Bob. Several days later Bob and one of the other men in his prayer group began meeting to pray for this vast continent. First they looked at a map to learn the names of new countries that had been formed since they were in high school. Then they prayed. A couple of other men soon joined them.

Back in the 1970s Uganda was in the news. Idi Amin was executing thousands of people. So the first country the group prayed for in earnest was Uganda. Following Jesus' instruction to ask God "to send out workers into his harvest field" (Matthew 9:38), the men asked God to raise up a worker from Kampala, Uganda's capital, whom they could support.

A few days later Bob attended a retreat at a hotel near Washington. That morning it was announced a group was gathering to pray for Africa after lunch. A missionary nurse who was not attending the retreat came to pray with them. It turned out she worked at Mengo Hospital in Kampala!

Bob invited her to visit his family and go to church with them. It happened to be "Missions Sunday," and when the scheduled missionary speaker failed to show, Bob suggested that the nurse from Kampala take his place.

A few weeks later the church missions committee chairman asked Bob to find out what single monetary gift might help

Mengo Hospital most. Try as he might, Bob could not reach the Ugandan hospital via telephone, so he prayed.

The next morning Bob joined a group for breakfast. The host asked if Bob would like to meet his guest, a man from Uganda. It turned out his wife worked at Mengo Hospital, too!

Instead of giving a single gift of about $1,000, however, the missions committee decided to make Mengo Hospital an ongoing project. (In the last two decades, the church has sent about $3 million worth of supplies.)

Bob took his first trip to Uganda to visit the hospital just as Idi Amin was being pushed out as president. Convinced that helping the hospital was futile without working on reconciliation in the ravaged country, Bob met with parliamentary leaders friendly to the new president, Milton Obote, and those who opposed him. He found each side willing to meet with him but not with each other.

"Lord, how can we get these guys to sit together and heal their land?" he prayed.

The answer came quickly. During a layover at the Nairobi airport, Bob sat next to an American missionary as he waited for his plane. She was the daughter of Andrew Young, then mayor of Atlanta. She suggested that Bob call her father and ask him to visit Uganda. Bob called. Andrew Young agreed. And back to Uganda Bob went.

It worked. Bob and Andrew Young met and started a process of reconciliation. Then Bob returned to Uganda with a team that included several U.S. senators and members of the German Bundestag.

The German ambassador in Kampala asked the Bundestag members why they were wasting their time on this hopeless situation. They replied that a U.S. senator had asked them to come.

The ambassador turned to the senator and asked, "Why are you here?" The senator replied that Bob Hunter asked him to come.

"And why did you come?" Bob was asked.

"Because we are here to build a bridge of reconciliation among divided people," he said.

"Just who are the men who will be the pillars for this bridge?"

"I don't know, but God does."

Both the U.S. senators and the German ambassador rolled their eyes. "Well," Bob said, "you have all the money, all the diplomatic skill, all the power, and look at the mess in this country. Can we make it any worse?"

The reconciliation effort included opposition rebels, one of whom, Yoweri Museveni, became president in due course. A Museveni adviser who believed in Jesus Christ met with Bob, and they talked about forgiveness, reconciliation, and love for one's enemies.

President Museveni was persuaded to attend the National Prayer Breakfast in Washington, where he spoke about his relationship with Jesus Christ—"I left the official church, but never Jesus," he said. His wife's prayer brought tears to business leaders, politicians, and diplomats.

President Museveni authorized Bob to help organize a prayer breakfast for Uganda. People of every tribe, color, religion, and station attended. Speaker after speaker talked of the hate they had held for others in the country, and how much they had been changed by God.

Prior to the prayer breakfast, the president called Bob to his office and asked what he thought about the situation in South Africa. Bob replied that he thought the country was heading in the right direction after releasing Nelson Mandela from prison. President Museveni agreed.

"I am now the chairman of the Organization of African Unity," he said. "It can't be official just yet, but I want to send a delegation to South Africa to tell the leaders that love and reconciliation are the answer to the bloodshed that everyone predicts for their country. What do you think?"

"That sounds like a great idea," said Bob.

"Can you go? We need a white in the delegation to make the point we want to make."

Bob went and met with Mandela, de Klerk, Buthelezi, and

other South African leaders. He read 1 Corinthians 13, the Bible's love chapter, and Christians from Kenya, Zambia, and Uganda spoke of how forgiveness was critical to South Africa's success, and emphasized that South Africa's success was critical to the continent's prosperity. This message proved pivotal in the bloodless transition from white rule to majority rule in South Africa.

To say the least, Bob Hunter's little group is still meeting to pray for Africa. And mountains keep moving!

"I assure you, even if you had faith as small as a mustard seed you could say to this mountain, 'Move from here to there,' and it would move. Nothing would be impossible" (Matthew 17:20).

A PICTURE

13.

· *the guardian* ·

God sends His protection in hundreds of different ways. Sometimes, that heavenly guard seems almost angelic. I don't pretend to understand why protection is given to one and not another, but I've learned not to miss the hand of God in my life when the outcome of circumstances is obviously a "God thing." The woman in the story below has learned that lesson, as well.

"You really shouldn't stand around in places like this without watching your back."

Holly Hudson froze, then slowly turned to her right. A man had silently walked up behind her and stood just inches away. His dark clothing matched his short black hair; his steady brown eyes seemed to pierce her soul. She stared at the horizontal scar that scored his left cheek.

"You don't know where you are, do you?" he asked, breaking the silence. His tone made the comment more of a statement than a question. "People get killed here all the time," he said, gesturing to the area underneath the west end of Portland's Burnside Bridge. Holly had sought refuge under the bridge during an Oregon rainstorm while she waited for a ride home. "There's all kinds of heroin addicts around. Just last week, somebody got stabbed here."

Holly shivered. "I had no idea," she said. "I figured it's safe enough. They have outdoor markets here on the weekends. And it's still light out."

"On the *weekends* it's safe," he corrected her. *"Not* during the week!"

Holly's heart began racing as the man continued his rebuke. "You should be standing at the light-rail station over there. You stick out like a sore thumb."

"I was going to take the MAX all the way home, but it's not running," she explained. "They closed it down because of some kind of police action on the other side of the river. We had to get off. So I called my boyfriend and asked him to come get me."

"How long will that be?"

"About twenty minutes. It's been ten minutes already. Should I move over that way?" Holly glanced toward some nearby shops.

"No, you should be okay," the man replied. "They know me around here, and they see me talking to you. But I'll keep an eye on you just in case." The man turned and strode across the street toward the Willamette River, instantly blending with the scattered people loitering in the area.

Holly swallowed, watching his every move. Who were "they" who knew this man? Then she looked—really looked—at the area where she had chosen to wait for her ride.

He was right. She didn't know where she was.

The people wandering under the bridge where she stood and those hanging around across the street wore ripped, disheveled clothing and had unkempt hair. Some had sunken, hungry eyes. And as soon as the man in black walked away from her, several of the "locals" drifted in her direction.

Trying to appear casual, Holly wandered away from the bridge and further down the street. Almost instantly, three people gathered where she had been standing, as if to point out that she had invaded their turf.

Adrenaline pumped through Holly's veins as she realized she had naively put herself in a bad position. "Lord," she whispered, "I'm scared. I can't believe I did something so foolish. Please take care of me!"

Holly felt safer in her new location, but she longed for the security of her unexpected champion. She spotted him across the street, and he came over and stood next to her again. "Did you see how they came out of the woodwork as soon as I left?" he asked.

"Oh, yes," Holly agreed. "They sure did."

"I tell you what. I'll wait with you until your friend comes," the man said. Then he grinned and stuck out his hand. "I'm Dallas. My real name is Leroy Brown, but you can call me Dallas."

"Nice to meet you, Dallas. I'm Holly," she replied, smiling as she shook his hand. "I guess the Lord sent you to be my guardian angel today."

His eyes met Holly's again. "I've heard people say that before."

Startled, Holly looked closely at Dallas. "Oh, really? When?"

"Oh, you know . . . when people get lost in this area and ask me for directions. I seem to be sort of an unofficial Portland guide."

"Well," said Holly, "I'm glad you were here today to guide me!"

She looked hard at Dallas again. The scar on his cheek—was it an old knife wound, she wondered. "Who are you?"

"That's a good question," he said. "I haven't figured that out yet."

"Do you have a job around here?"

"I've had a hundred jobs in my lifetime," he said smoothly, evading her question. "I do like to restore classic cars. If I don't get some temp work in the next week, I have a job lined up to do that."

Suddenly, Dallas gestured to a station wagon that had just passed by. "You see that station wagon?"

"Yes," she said, wondering why he had changed the subject.

"That car is going to turn right at the corner and pick up that prostitute," he said, nodding toward a young woman walking down the street in jeans and a sweatshirt. The car turned right and the girl turned left, moving to intercept the car.

Dallas's perception amazed Holly. He did know this area!

She glanced toward the bridge once more and saw Sean, her boyfriend, waiting there at last, his car pulled over to the side of the road. Dallas followed her gaze. "Oh, is your friend here?"

"That's him," she said, relieved.

"Well, let me walk you over."

They reached the car in a few seconds, but Dallas didn't stop or say good-bye. He just looked at Holly and said, "Take care." Then he walked toward the closed light-rail station.

Holly watched him for a second. Then she jumped into the car, locked the door, and looked at Sean. "That was my guardian angel!"

"What happened?" he asked, concerned.

They pulled onto the street and as Holly began her story, she looked for Dallas. He was gone.

For weeks afterward, Holly would look out the window of the

light-rail car to see if Dallas was among the street people gathered under the Burnside Bridge. She never saw him again.

If you make the Lord your refuge, if you make the Most High your shelter, no evil will conquer you . . . For he orders his angels to protect you wherever you go (Psalm 91:9–11).

A PICTURE

14.

· *armed and ready* ·

Why is one person spared physical catastrophe and another is not? Close calls are all around us. Most of the time we're oblivious to the Hand that protected us from danger. And while anxious prayers for protection are not always answered . . . sometimes they are! There is a police officer in the Bay Area who certainly believes this today.

A dozen jocular and animated police officers filed into the briefing room at eleven P.M. The graveyard shift of the Newark Police Department—located in a San Francisco Bay Area working-class suburb midway between Oakland and San Jose—was about to begin.

"Listen up, guys," the staff sergeant began. "Earlier this evening an Oakland police officer made a routine stop. As he walked up to the car, a perpetrator stepped up and shot him to death with an AK-47 . . . We've got a cop killer on the loose. He fled the scene, but we were able to get a physical description and make on his car. It's all in this briefing paper," he said, as he passed copies around the room.

Newark patrolman Patrick Hunt glanced at the suspect's description.

"He is armed and dangerous," the sergeant continued. "We've been told that the perp may be in our area. Be careful out there."

The subsequent East Bay manhunt failed to locate the gunman over the next week. Seven days after their comrade had been killed in the line of duty, Patrick attended a men's Bible study with three friends from church and his younger brother, Tim, a police officer in neighboring Fremont.

Patrick was struggling with the cop killing. When the group took prayer requests, he said, "I know God exists, but I can't comprehend how He can know the thoughts and deeds of everyone. I was at an Athletic's baseball game recently and, as I looked around the Coliseum, I wondered how God could know the thoughts of all fifty thousand people. And when that officer got ambushed . . ."

Patrick didn't have to finish. His buddies knew he was wrestling with his emotions, so they prayed God would help him understand His all-powerful nature.

Several hours later Patrick reported for his graveyard shift. A light rain was falling.

At 12:40 A.M., the 911 board at the dispatch center lit up like a Christmas tree. "There's a man shooting at everyone in sight!" screamed one caller.

"A van got hit in the motel parking lot!" cried another. "Now it's trying to get out of here!"

Patrolling alone in his cruiser, Patrick was dispatched as a backup officer to the motel, located in the center of Newark. Up ahead, he spotted the disabled van—parked on the wrong side of the road. Its headlights beamed brightly through the windshield, blinding him.

Patrick slowed as he approached the van, wary that a gunman could be hiding in the shadows.

Ka-blam!

The window on the driver's side of Patrick's patrol car exploded in his face, scraping his exposed skin like a wire brush. More shots rang out. Lead fragments and door shrapnel exploded all around him. His leg suddenly burned with pain.

Instinct and police training took over. Patrick slammed the car into reverse. The windshield exploded. Bullets whizzed by as Patrick continued to floor the damaged vehicle. Then he heard two tires pop.

"God, please don't let me die!" he screamed, as the crippled car rolled on two tire rims. He backed up the bullet-riddled cruiser a quarter mile before another officer came to his aid.

The shooting stopped. Patrick pulled himself out of the car and began shaking uncontrollably.

"My God, you've been hit!" said the other officer.

Patrick looked down. Blood was seeping through his ripped pants. Within minutes, paramedics arrived on the scene. They quickly cut off Patrick's pant legs and assessed his injuries. Then they put him on a gurney and carted him off to the hospital.

Patrick's wife, Lynette, five months pregnant with their third child, met Patrick at the hospital. In the early morning hours, doctors cleaned his legs of the visible bullet fragments and lead shrapnel. Then his brother Tim arrived.

"It's the same perp who killed the Oakland officer last week," Tim reported. "He just started shooting people in the motel parking lot. One guy was on his bicycle. He survived, but it looks like he'll be paralyzed. You know the driver of that van? The van got hit, and when someone came to his aid, the suspect opened fire on the Good Samaritan and nearly tore his leg off. He played dead as the gunman stood over him and said, 'Sorry I had to shoot you, man.' "

"Did we catch him?"

"Not yet. He's running through streets, pounding on doors with the butt of his AK-47. A perimeter has been established. Anyway, if you're up to it, you're wanted down at the office. Reports have to be filed."

At the police station, Patrick and Tim heard that the suspect had carjacked a BMW. The driver and her children fled for their lives.

The perimeter tightened, and when officers surrounded the stolen car, they ordered the gunman to give up peacefully. When the suspect reached for his rifle, a hail of police gunfire brought the night of terror to an end.

Patrick realized how terrifying the previous night had been when he visited the crime scene later that morning. He stepped out and surveyed the area where his patrol car was first hit. He found ten bullet casings. The first pile of spent casings lay no farther than twenty feet from where his car had been, and other casings moved closer with each shot.

"He had a flash suppresser on the gun," said another officer. "That's why you never saw him. It's amazing that you weren't killed at such close range."

Then Patrick inspected his damaged patrol car. Two bullet holes had punched right through the center of the driver's door. Had they not been deflected, or if one bullet had traveled an inch and a half higher, he would have been struck in the opening between the front and back of his bullet-proof vest. One round was lodged in the portable radio on his left hip.

As for the flying bullets that never found their mark—Patrick realized he should have been dead. Any doubts of God's almighty power were erased. God had answered his hasty prayer and protected him.

> Though I am surrounded by troubles, you will
> preserve me against the anger of
> my enemies (Psalm 138:7).

15.

· *down to the wire* ·

Immediate answers to prayer. You want them. I want them. But God simply does not always work that way. And to get His best, we must be patient. In some cases, we must wait until the last minute for His answer to come. And when the clock shows 11:59, get ready to be amazed. The woman below certainly was.

The infant arrived at the door in a gunny sack, carried by a Madras (now Chennai), India, utility worker who found her on the street, abandoned, naked, and near death. Colleen Redit took her in, notwithstanding the fact there already were thirteen girls in her legally adopted family. When the baby, whom Colleen named Judith, miraculously survived through prayer, intravenous feedings, and blood transfusions, she became number fourteen.

Since her arrival in India more than thirty-five years ago, Colleen has given her heart and opened her home to thousands of girls and young women. First, she longed to tell them about Jesus, but the missionary from New Zealand also searched for a way to lift their self-esteem and build a measure of independence.

Most of the teenagers Colleen met on the hard streets of Madras had finished school but had virtually no chance to escape dire poverty apart from an arranged marriage, which might tie a girl to a man as old as her father.

One day, Colleen moved the car out of the garage of her rented home, wiped the oil off the floor, and invited girls to learn how to cross-stitch, knit, and type. Girls flocked to the garage, and Colleen looked for larger premises. In the meantime, she registered her work with the government, calling it the Christian Mission Charitable Trust.

Colleen and the girls were invited to sell their handicrafts at various churches in the region. Colleen found a larger building to rent—one with enough room to start a hostel and orphanage for girls like Judith. By day, the girls used every available inch to produce crafts; at night, they moved furniture and equipment to open a place to sleep. Colleen wondered how much longer they would be able to stay at 18 Khader Nawaz Khan Road in Madras.

One evening in 1994, Colleen received a phone call from an acquaintance who offered to sell her a piece of land.

"But I don't have any money to pay for it," she said.

"I still want you to come look it over," the vendor replied. "Can you join me at the property this Sunday afternoon?"

Colleen shrugged her shoulders and agreed. What she saw was a ramshackle two-story building ready for the demolition ball.

"What I'm offering you is the land," said the man. "The building will have to be torn down."

"But where am I going to put my girls?" Colleen asked.

"Tell me a little about your work."

Colleen described the work of the Christian Mission Charitable Trust, but the man also wanted to know where the financial support came from and who paid Colleen's salary.

"I have been called by God to His work," she said. "I look to Him day by day, and He has never failed me."

"Yes, I see. Well, here's my offer. My original asking price was thirty-eight lakhs per ground," he said, using an Indian form of measurement, "but for you, I am happy to reduce the price to twenty-eight lakhs per ground."

"I was thinking of something along the lines of twenty-seven lakhs per ground," Colleen replied.

"Okay," he said. "We have a deal."

"Before we have a deal, I must pray and seek the mind of the Lord, and I will need a month for an answer."

"A month? Sure, that's okay. I will take the property off the market until you decide. You have my word."

During the month, a friend from Singapore called and asked Colleen if he could bring a small team of men to visit the mission. The men were impressed with the impact being made in the lives of young women. When they commented on the overcrowded living conditions, Colleen asked if they would like to see a derelict building that the mission was thinking of purchasing.

That evening, they gathered around the building and prayed for the Lord's guidance. Then the men boarded a return flight to Singapore.

Meanwhile, Colleen continued to pray. Monday was the last day of the one-month deadline, and Colleen knew she had to phone the vendor and tell him that she could not complete the purchase.

Colleen was sitting at her desk Monday morning when the fax machine gushed paper. She leaned over and began reading. The men in Singapore had discussed the mission's need with church elders, who decided to allot $40,000 (in Singapore dollars) to the Christian Mission Charitable Trust.

Colleen stared at the fax, wondering if she could believe her eyes. Then she locked her office door, turned off the light, and thanked God for this clear and direct answer to her prayers.

She called the vendor to tell him she could proceed with the property purchase.

"Good," he replied. "I almost called you last night to inquire about the status of our transaction, but something held me back."

"If you had called, I would have told you to go ahead without us, because I had no leading from the Lord," Colleen said.

"It's good you didn't—I have been inundated with offers at the original asking price!"

A gleaming, six-story structure opened its doors in Chennai (formerly Madras) in 1999. Today, the structure educates and feeds more than 600 destitute children and young people.

"Keep on asking, and you will be given what you ask for.
Keep on looking, and you will find. Keep on knocking,
and the door will be opened" (Matthew 7:7).

A PORTRAIT

16.

· back home at last ·

Some people have experienced so much pain—both physical and emotional—that it makes it hard for them to see God. The Bible verse they most relate to is Jesus' statement, "Here on earth you will have many trials . . ." Though they may not know the verse, they know trials! Yet our lot in life is not to be a pawn in the hand of a fickle "God" who doles out trouble on unsuspecting victims. Jesus' statement is simply a fact. The second half to that verse, however, is a promise: ". . . but be of good cheer. I have overcome the world." If there ever was a story that illustrates this passage, this one is it!

William George Loney, a harsh man who ruled his family with an iron fist as his Irish forefathers had before him, never gave his blessing when his daughter was courted by the eligible young men of Portadown. *Nobody will ever be good enough for my Sarah,* he thought.

Sarah chafed at his restrictions, but what options did a lass have in the late 1930s, when war clouds were darkening skies over Europe? She and her father had terrible rows, pushing Sarah to search for love in the arms of other men. One of those liaisons resulted in the birth of a daughter, May, when Sarah was twenty years old. May was handed to "aunties" to rear.

Sarah fell in love with another bloke, and while Nazi Messerschmidts pummeled England in 1940, a son, named Jim, was born.

Scorned by the Portadown townspeople, Sarah went "in service"—walking to people's houses early in the morning to scrub floors, wash clothes and dishes, change beds, and perform other menial tasks. Though Sarah had grown up in a Protestant family, a big-hearted Catholic lady offered to look after Jim during the day.

But Sarah could not soldier on. Working her fingers to the bone for a pound note or two and trying to raise a toddler—and visit May as often as possible—proved too formidable a task. With great sorrow, Sarah decided to give up Jim for adoption.

The Patterson family lived thirty-five miles away in Ballygawley. They knew Sarah and offered to adopt Jim. William and Edith Patterson drove to Portadown and brought Jim back to their home.

Three-year-old Jim loved his new father and imitated everything he did on the farm, from mucking stalls to milking cows.

Twice a year, relatives looked in on him, including Aunt Sally, who walked peculiarly, swaying left and right.

"Why does Aunt Sally walk like a penguin?" Jim asked one day.

"She has rheumatism," his adoptive mother said.

William Patterson died suddenly when Jim was twelve, the cause of death listed as septic poisoning that started with a finger cut. Edith would not allow Jim to see his father at the hospital or attend the funeral. She was angry at God, angry at the world, and angry at Jim, her nearest target. For nearly a year, she stripped Jim and whipped him with a sally rod.

"Your mother was nothing but a whore," she screamed, as the rod came down. "You are nothing but a little bastard."

As Jim reached his teen years, Edith verbally abused him. "I give up!" she yelled one afternoon. "Your father's gone, and I can't do anything with you. I should just take you to the police station and let them lock you up."

Jim, seventeen at the time, thought she meant it. He hatched a plan to run away from home and live with one of his adoptive sisters, Mary Barnett, who was living in the Midlands north of London. Jim had never been out of Tyrone County, let alone Ireland. Somehow, he managed to take a train and find his sister.

After working for a time in a biscuit factory, Jim joined the British Army—the Royal Engineer's Regiment at Aldershot in Hampshire. He met a young woman, fell in love, and became engaged. Then he learned that she had been unfaithful, which stirred up all the old feelings of abandonment and betrayal.

Jim had once read that a man could live forty days without food, eight days without water, and up to six minutes without oxygen—but only seconds without hope. He made plans to take his life. After pouring a tall whiskey, he washed down one hundred sleeping tablets, and then lay down to die.

Jim awakened the next morning in the army sick bay. A few days after his suicide attempt, he was nursing a drink at a bar when John, a member of the parachute regiment, took a seat next to him.

They began talking, and Jim poured out his woeful story. "Do I have any hope?" he asked.

"Yes, you do," John said, "the hope of Jesus Christ."

John laid out the story of the gospel, and Jim said he wanted to give his life to Christ.

"Do you want to pray with me?" John asked.

"Right here in the bar? Are you kidding?"

"Okay," said John. "I know a church nearby."

At eleven P.M., they walked into an empty Anglican church, and Jim found the hope, peace, and joy he had been searching so long for. "Oh, God, if you can heal my broken heart and dry my tears and give me hope, I'll go to the nations of the world to tell them of the hope you have given me."

Life improved in a hurry. Jim met Christine, and they married on August 27, 1960.

During their honeymoon, the couple returned to Northern Ireland to visit relatives, including Jim's older adoptive sister, Jean Davidson, who lived in Portadown.

During their visit, Jean asked, "Have you ever thought about your real mother?"

"Yes, I have," Jim answered. "But I don't know my mother. I don't know whether she is dead or alive."

"Oh, your mum is very much alive, and you know her."

"What are you talking about?"

"Do you remember Aunt Sally?" Jean said, as she showed him an old black-and-white photo of the woman who used to visit the farm when he was a boy.

"You mean the one who walked like a penguin?"

"Yes. That's your mum."

The world stopped for Jim.

"She knows you're married," Jean continued. "You can see her if you like, but it's up to you."

"When?"

"Today at three o'clock."

"That's less than an hour! Where is she?"

Jean stood and walked over to the large picture window. "See the second house just past the corner? That's where your mum lives."

A few minutes before three, Jim and Christine began their walk down the street. Jim immediately recognized the woman walking toward them—her stiff-legged penguin gait gave her away.

They met at a crossroads and fell into each other's arms. Sarah Loney was crying hysterically.

"It's okay, Mum," Jim said, holding her as tight as he could.

Sarah stepped back and attempted to speak. "On this very spot on the road seventeen years ago, I handed you to the Pattersons. To be reunited at the very place . . ." Sarah composed herself. "I thank God for this day."

Jim learned that his mother had become a Christian and had eventually married, and all that time she was praying that God would save her son and use him in the ministry. Three years after being reunited with his mother, Jim entered seminary.

A decade later, Jim returned to Northern Ireland to pastor a church fifteen miles from Portadown. Today, he is pastor of Elim Church in East Finchley, North London, confident that God had a special plan for his life all along.

And we know that God causes everything to work
together for the good of those who love God and are
called according to his purpose for them (Romans 8:28).

A PICTURE

17.

· *a heart to save* ·

*Do you ever wonder if you should ask God for a miracle? Stop
wondering! The God of the Bible loves to perform miracles if
they are in line with His perfect will. But first we must ask.
Second, we must not doubt that He is able. Why? Because He
IS able!*

"Dr. Meeker, please report immediately to the ICU."

Meg Meeker, senior pediatric resident at Children's Hospital
in Milwaukee, Wisconsin, had a feeling that the monotonic summons over the intercom was not good news. Then again, if she
had learned anything about the medical profession, it was that
being paged to the pediatric intensive care unit was never good
news.

Dr. Meeker strode into the ICU and saw a half-dozen gowned
colleagues gathered around a small bed.

"It's Katie," said a nurse. "We have a code blue. She's not responding."

Meg looked at the cardiac monitor. The rapidly sinking blood pressure told her what everyone else in the room already knew about the six-month-old infant: Katie's heart was giving out. She was dying.

Dr. Meeker's colleagues stood aside so that she could begin efforts to restart the heart. She took two small electric pads in her hands and attempted to restart the life-giving muscle. The baby's body heaved with the first jolt of electricity, but the heart failed to start beating.

"Dr. Meeker, her father is here."

Meg turned around and saw a distraught father standing in the doorway. "We can't let him see this," she whispered to another resident. "Too traumatic. Ask him to take a seat in the waiting room."

Meg turned her attention back to Katie. She went by the book as she fought to bring Katie back to life, but the infant did not respond to her ministrations. Katie was at death's door as her pallor turned from blue to white to a brownish gray. Meg knew that if the blood flow to the brain stopped for much longer, the girl would be severely brain damaged.

Lord, what should I do? Meg was the senior medical technician in the room, and everyone was looking for her to come up with an answer.

"Listen up, everybody. Our only hope is internal cardiac massage, but before we begin, we need to pray. Lord," she began, "we ask that you spare the life of this girl. Please help us to start her heart again."

There wasn't much time. She picked up a pair of oversized cutting shears and cut into Katie's chest to split it open. Then she reached under the chest cavity with her left hand and found Katie's heart. She began squeezing it, causing the muscle to send much-needed blood to and from the heart. As Meg continued pinching the heart, the monitor reported that Katie's blood pressure was mounting. Pink color returned to her skin.

"She's alive!" Dr. Meeker cried out.

Katie was stabilized, and a pediatric cardiac surgeon was called in to attend to further cardiac complications. While Katie was being attended to, Meg walked into the waiting room.

Hospital protocol did not allow Meg to speak to the parents; that duty was reserved for the primary care physician. Meg noticed the couple was sobbing, and it took every ounce of strength not to walk over and tell them that their daughter was going to make it.

When she turned a corner, Meg stopped and leaned against the wall. *Lord, thank you for guiding my hand, but I pray that you would somehow make it known to those parents that you intervened and saved that little girl's life.*

Meg found a phone to call her husband, Walt. After telling him what happened, she said, "God literally walked into the room and held my hand as I opened that baby's chest."

"No, you're wrong," Walt replied. "Jesus was in that room before you came in."

> If you need wisdom—if you want to know what
> God wants you to do—ask him, and he will
> gladly tell you (James 1:5).

A PORTRAIT

18.

· *nothing was wasted* ·

The death of a loved one rarely seems to make sense, no matter what the age or circumstances. And for the first few years after a death, the nerves of loved ones are often too raw to find purpose amid the pain. Sometimes on this earth, however, we get a glimpse of what God has done. His big portrait comes into view, and all we can say is "Now I see."

"Come give Daddy a hug."

Seven-year-old Diane Morris put on her bravest face and then wrapped her tiny arms around the hunched-over frame of her father, Bernard. Dressed in a well-creased brown U.S. Army uniform topped with a hard-bill cap, Bernard tousled Diane's hair as they both fought back tears. The car horn beeped a second time. With a sweep of his hand, Bernard waved good-bye to Diane, her ten-year-old sister, Charlene, and her little brother, Tommy, who was four.

The year was 1944, and Uncle Sam's draft notice had informed Bernard he was now the property of the U.S. Army. The timing couldn't have been worse. His wife, Alene, was quarantined in a tuberculosis hospital. The only way to keep the three kids together under the same roof was to place them with foster parents who lived twenty-five miles from their home in Oxnard, California.

"What if he doesn't come back?" Diane asked Charlene as their father disappeared down the street.

"Oh, he will."

"But what if he doesn't?"

Her question hung in the air. Over the next few months, their father wrote as often as he could, but censors stripped out any pertinent information. One sentence was particularly revealing, however: *Tell Aunt Phyllis that I'll be seeing her soon.*

Diane knew she didn't have an "Aunt Phyllis" in the family. Then she heard adults say her father was trying to tell them he was on his way to the Philippines. All she knew was that her father went somewhere overseas to fight in a terrible war.

One afternoon, Diane was summoned from class at school. When she saw her mother, Diane knew something was wrong. Alene's face was ashen gray. Her hand clutched a telegram: THE SECRETARY OF WAR DESIRES ME TO EXPRESS HIS DEEP REGRET THAT YOUR HUSBAND, PRIVATE BERNARD L. MORRIS, HAS BEEN REPORTED

MISSING IN ACTION SINCE 11 FEBRUARY IN SOUTHWEST PACIFIC AREA. J. A. ULIO, ADJUTANT GENERAL.

"What does it mean, Mommy?"

"It means Daddy's probably dead."

Alene Morris had learned from other service families that the armed forces followed a two-step protocol when a body was not found. Six torturous months passed before the second telegram arrived in September 1945—more than a month after war in the Pacific ended. The telegram stated that Private Morris had been killed in action and UNAVOIDABLE CIRCUMSTANCES MADE NECESSARY THE UNUSUAL LAPSE OF TIME IN REPORTING YOUR HUSBAND'S DEATH TO YOU. A followup letter to Mrs. Morris filled in the details:

On 6 February 1945, your husband sailed from Hollandia, Dutch New Guinea, for the Philippine Islands. On the morning of 11 February at approximately nine o'clock, his ship was attacked by an enemy submarine and received two torpedo hits amidships. The explosion broke the vessel in half and the entire stern section sank in a matter of minutes, trapping everyone inside.

During an extensive search, all survivors were rescued by two Navy ships in the convoy. I deeply regret that your husband was not among the survivors. Death would have come

very quickly, and I am sure he could have suffered very little, if
any, pain.

   Private Morris died that our people might continue to live
in freedom and, in that great ideal, may you find solace.
   Ralph C. Moor
   Major, U.S. Army

With Alene quarantined again in a tuberculosis hospital, the
family decided not to arrange a funeral or memorial service. Besides, the body was never recovered. Not having had a chance to
say good-bye to her father left a gaping hole in Diane's heart.

Alene Morris's health eventually improved to the point that she
was able to move back to Oxnard with the three children. Diane
suddenly became very ill with acute nephritis, a kidney infection.
She spent the next three months in the hospital.

   Meanwhile, life presented one challenge after another for Diane's mother. Raising three children on a pension was proving to
be more than she could handle. Alene turned to drink when
Charlene and Diane were old enough to care for Tommy.

   Aware of the difficulties, the pastor of a neighborhood church
where the children had attended Sunday school offered Charlene and Diane a scholarship to attend summer camp. There Di-

ane, thirteen years old, made the decision to trust Jesus Christ with her life.

GI Bill benefits and a scholarship for "war orphans" enabled Diane to attend the University of California at Santa Barbara. She had no trouble declaring a major. Diane had wanted to teach primary school since she was a little girl. At her college graduation, her junior high music teacher, Marge Brown, appeared with her husband, Larry.

"What are you doing here?" Diane exclaimed after the cap-and-gown ceremony.

"To watch you graduate," Marge replied. "We wouldn't miss this day for the world."

Marge and Larry Brown had taken Diane under their wings years ago, but now they had important news.

"We're leaving soon," Marge began.

"Where are you going?"

"To Taiwan to teach at a school for missionary kids. That's where we believe the Lord is leading us. We're going with a mission called Overseas Crusades."

A seed was planted in her heart that afternoon. Diane spent the next two years teaching in the Los Angeles County public school system, but newsletters from the Browns in Taiwan and prayer for their ministry nurtured a desire to teach at a mission school. At a holiday Christian conference, Diane prayerfully considered what she felt God wanted her to do with her life.

Lord, I'm willing to go anywhere for you.

Certain of her calling to teach mission kids, she told her school district she would not be returning in the fall. Then she wrote to Overseas Crusades (now known as OC International) and asked what she should do next. It was suggested that Diane attend a one-year graduate program at Multnomah Biblical Seminary in Portland, Oregon. With no money in savings, Diane saw God working again when she learned that the same GI Bill that provided for her college education would also pay for graduate school.

That year at Multnomah, a man came on campus, asking to see Diane. His wife had been Diane's Pioneer Girls leader. During their visit in the dining hall, he said that if Diane wanted to go overseas, then he and his wife would like to help in her financial support.

Finally, Diane was ready for the field. She thought she was headed for Taiwan, but at the last minute, she was placed at Faith Academy, a missionary school on the outskirts of Manila.

Shortly after her arrival in the Philippines, Diane went with missionary friends on a Sunday drive. They stopped at the Filipino-American War Memorial for those killed in World War II.

"My father was killed in the war," she told her hosts. Terrible memories came rushing back to her. The constant fear of not knowing, the fateful letters, and the years longing for a daddy to hold, all rushed back into her heart like a flood.

The memorial consisted of well-tended lawns dotted with tens of thousands of white crosses. Diane and her friends strolled over to a large, semicircular wall with inscribed panels whose heading was: COMRADES IN ARMS WHOSE EARTHLY RESTING PLACE IS KNOWN ONLY TO GOD.

Under the then-forty-eight states, the names were arranged alphabetically and by rank and date of service.

Was his name there?

"California," she said as she scanned the list, her hands trembling. There it was: MORRIS, BERNARD LEE, PRIVATE.

Diane nearly collapsed in tears as friends wrapped their arms around her. "There was no body, no funeral, no ceremony," she said. "All we got was a telegram and a Purple Heart. For years, my sister and I discussed the stories we heard about people who were thought to be dead in the war, who suddenly appeared on the doorstep . . ."

God had worked nearly twenty years in her life to bring her to this place outside Manila, on this day, to provide closure for her father's death. Living in a foster home had prepared her for what the mission kids who boarded at Faith Academy were going through. Her father's tragic death had funded her college education. Then God sent her to the very part of the world where her father had died. A perfect circle!

Then Diane remembered a line from missionary Amy Carmichael's biography: "God never wastes his servant's time."

Diane Morris taught twenty-eight years at Faith Academy in the Philippines. She now serves as the Coordinator for Missionary Kids and Families at OC International's headquarters in Colorado Springs, Colorado.

Pure and lasting religion in the sight of God our Father means that we must care for orphans and widows in their troubles, and refuse to let the world corrupt us (James 1:27).

19.

· *the teddy bear* ·

Sometimes, for God to break through the hard heart of a certain person, He must reveal Himself in remarkable ways known only to that person. As He does that, He will typically ask His followers to do things that don't appear to make sense. God is not limited to our human, finite wisdom in healing deep emotional wounds as an angry bear of a man discovered . . .

Earl's crossed arms and permanent grimace told everyone in the room he didn't want to be there. Meanwhile, Kim wiped tears away as she expressed her desire for a happy marriage with a husband who managed his anger.

The couple was attending a Cleansing Stream seminar, led by Church on the Way in Van Nuys, California. Earl, sporting a two-day stubble on his chin, was a bear of a guy—an angry, burly man with an intimidating scowl. His demure wife, Kim, radiated warmth.

During a portion of the seminar held at a hotel, Earl and Kim joined three other couples, including Mike and Judith Hayes, for informal counseling and prayer. Judith, part of Cleansing Stream's leadership team, began with routine questions: "Where did you meet? How long have you been married? What do you do for a living?"

Earl grunted a few answers in between complaints about this "inquisition," but Judith, who believes the Lord has given her the biblical spiritual gift of discernment, could see right through his bravado. Something was bothering this guy.

Kim said that if Earl did not get help soon, she saw no way the marriage could continue. Years of belligerence and yelling had taken their toll.

The session concluded with a time of prayer. With her eyes closed, Judith kept seeing a fuzzy brown teddy bear with a plaid bow around its neck. She wondered if she hadn't received enough sleep the previous night. What did a teddy bear have to do with this guy?

As the meeting broke up for lunch, a leader asked if Earl felt any differently. "I never believed in any of this anyway, so the answer is no," he replied. "I only did this for my wife."

Judith leaned to Mike and said, "I know this sounds crazy, but the Lord wants me to buy Earl a teddy bear."

Mike rolled his eyes, but after twenty-nine years of marriage, he had learned his wife's spiritual antennae usually captured the right signal. "Okay, let's go find one."

At a nearby market, which happened to be having a sale on teddy bears, Judith found the exact one she envisioned: a furry brown bear with a plaid bow. She purchased one and wrote a note explaining that God had told her to give Earl this bear, although she didn't know why.

When the seminar regrouped in the hotel ballroom, Judith found Earl and Kim sitting toward the back. She walked over and handed him a brown paper bag. When he lifted the bear out of the bag, Earl clutched it to his chest and his shoulders began heaving uncontrollably. Tears rolled down his cheeks. People couldn't help looking his way.

After pulling him aside for a few minutes, seminar leaders asked Earl to approach the front of the room, which he did, clutching Kim and his teddy bear.

"I would like to thank the group for praying for me," he stammered. "Something happened here today, and it happened because a lady brought me this teddy bear.

"You see, no one in the whole wide world knows what this teddy bear means to me. When I was a little boy, I had a very authoritarian father, and he regularly beat me. One day I disobeyed him and, for my punishment, he took me and my favorite teddy bear to the backyard incinerator, where he burned my teddy bear right before my eyes. I was so crushed, so hurt, that I never forgave him. I realize today that God knew my unforgivingness caused great anger in my marriage. Now that God gave me back my teddy bear, I can start healing."

Dabbing at tears, Judith sat in awe of God's tender grace and unfailing love.

The unfailing love of the Lord never ends! By his
mercies we have been kept from complete destruction.
Great is his faithfulness; his mercies begin afresh
each day (Lamentations 3:22–23).

A PICTURE

20.

· *on the heels of an angel* ·

While accidents and bad things happen to innocent people, there is no doubting the fact that God holds children in high regard. His angels protect our loved ones in countless ways through miracles we never see. After raising four boys, I can honestly say it's amazing that any child arrives at adulthood without trauma and harm. The story below illustrates why children are so well protected.

Doris ran straight toward the McKenzie River, hoping and praying Roger hadn't reached it yet. A three-year-old would be no match for the cold, roaring water.

The Smallings lived in a log cabin deep in the woods behind a relative's riverfront property near Springfield, Oregon. Doris arrived home to find Roger's baby-sitter, Jennie, asleep on the sofa.

"Where's Roger?"

Startled, Jennie jumped up.

"Uh-oh, I must have dozed. He was here a minute ago, play-ing right beside me."

"How do you know how long it was if you were asleep?" Doris said. "We've got to find him. Run over to your house and see if he's with your little brother Ned. I'll head toward the river. If you find him, come yelling."

Doris ran to the yard to check Puppy's enclosure. Roger loved the German shepherd his grandfather had given him and promptly named him Puppy. Long after the ball of fur had grown larger than the boy, the name stuck.

Puppy wasn't there. Knowing how much Roger loved to show the "ribber" to Puppy, Doris ran straight toward the McKenzie, dodging pine branches.

God, I worried when Auntie offered this log cabin next to the river . . . Dear God, you love that little boy, too, and you know he's my life. Put your protecting arms around him. Please!

Like giant cymbals that crashed without pause, the sound of the cold and wild McKenzie cascading over the rocks swallowed Doris's frantic calls for "Ro-ger! Ro-ger!" She didn't see the tree root that stretched across the path and caught her foot, slam-ming her face down in the dirt.

Please don't let my ankle be broken. I've got to find my little boy. Please, God, help us.

Doris grabbed an overhanging branch. After pulling herself to a standing position, she shifted her weight to the injured foot. A twinge flashed through her ankle, but she could walk.

Point me in the right direction, God.

Doris staggered toward the water's edge. "Ro-ger!" she frantically yelled ever louder above the river's roar.

Was that a dog's bark? It seemed to come from the river straight ahead. *Please let it be Puppy. Let my son be okay.*

A bright shaft of sunlight spotlighted Roger's golden curls. The toddler was standing on a fallen tree jutting out into the river, about ten feet from shore, with Puppy beside him. If her son lost his balance and tumbled into the river, Doris doubted she could save him. She gasped when Puppy barked and Roger looked up, fixing his gaze straight ahead. The last thing she wanted was for Roger to see her and make any fast movements.

Suddenly, the boy hunched down on all fours and started crawling toward shore. Puppy hunched down as well, almost groveling as he crawled behind Roger.

Doris felt transfixed as she quietly watched Roger inch his way to the bank. She held her breath, wondering if the rough bark was cutting his knees.

Help him, Lord Jesus. Help him keep his mind only on the crawling. We can fix his knees. Bring him to me, Lord, please.

The boy and his dog didn't waver or change pace, creeping along the trunk. Just before they reached the bank, Puppy straightened and leaped over Roger, barking and running toward Doris. Roger stood and ran the last few feet into his mother's arms.

Doris hugged Roger so hard he squealed.

"Rogie, I was so scared. I prayed Jesus would take care of you, and he did. Now I want to hold you while I thank him."

"Mommy," he interrupted, wiggling out of her grasp, "that man was so nice. He told me and Puppy to get down on our knees."

"What man?"

"Didn't you see him? He told me to crawl like you're smelling the log. 'Don't look at anything but my heels and don't stop till I tell you to stand up.' And you know what, Mommy? Even Puppy knew what he said."

Who was that man? Doris wondered. Roger had a great imagination, but this was something else.

When Doris examined Roger's knees—not a blemish on either one—she finally understood. God had sent a guardian angel to protect her son.

For the angel of the Lord guards all who fear him,
and he rescues them (Psalm 34:7).

21.

· *father's day* ·

A hole in the heart is never quite so big as when a father's love is missed. Like our innate need to know the God who loves us, our need for a father never goes away. Though death and divorce have made many children "fatherless," God promises that He will be especially close to these hurting souls. The key: recognizing that God is the loving father you always needed.

Single-parent families were not common in the 1950s, especially in the predominantly Catholic community of Niles, Ohio, where Velma Meares grew up. Kids as well as adults often inquired where her dad worked or where he was.

"He's dead," Velma replied, never getting used to saying those words. When people reacted with shock, Velma felt even more uncomfortable.

In Velma's first-grader's mind, every problem was linked to her father's death—he had had a heart attack when she was four years old. *If only I had a dad, everything would be all right,* she thought. Every night in bed she would lie in the dark and pretend that her dad was sitting next to her. Velma would tell him how much she missed him and whatever else was on her mind. She knew her father wasn't there, but, after a while, she began to feel that Someone really was listening.

Velma's mother had been an alcoholic like her father, and, about a year before he died, she persuaded him to go with her to Alcoholics Anonymous. In this particular group, members acknowledged that to stop drinking, they totally depended on God, not just on AA or their own willpower. After the first meeting, Velma's mother never touched alcohol again.

To make ends meet, the widow with four children worked two or three jobs, sometimes on Sundays. One of her co-workers offered to take the children to church. There Velma realized God was the one overhearing her bedtime conversations. She stopped pretending to talk to her dad and began praying to her *heavenly* Father. As time went by, her mother went to church with the kids on the Sundays she wasn't working.

When she was seven years old, Velma experienced bouts of insomnia and began praying that she would be able to go right to sleep. After several nights, God spoke gently to her heart. "Don't you trust me? I love you. I know you're afraid. You don't need to ask me over and over every night."

During summer camp meetings when she was eleven, Velma trusted Jesus as her Savior. As the evangelist spoke, Velma's heart pounded. She wanted to be sure she would go to heaven, because she had learned that her dad had given his heart to the Lord in the hospital before he died. She wanted to make sure she saw him again.

After graduating from high school, when Velma was asked to teach a preschool Sunday school class, she realized she had just been going through the motions of being a Christian for quite a while. To teach children about Jesus, she knew she needed to be closer to Him herself. So Velma made a new commitment to Christ. This gave her a hunger to spend much more time reading the Bible and praying.

College followed when Velma was twenty-one. During her sophomore year at Southern California College, Velma met Dan Meares. When she married Dan, Velma was given not only a husband but also a father—Bob Meares, her father-in-law. Finally Velma could celebrate Father's Day and talk about "my dad" as her friends had for all those years.

Shortly after their honeymoon, Dan and Velma invited Dad to spend a long weekend with them—he lived a few hours away in California's Central Valley. When Bob appeared on the doorstep, Velma hugged him tightly and kissed his cheek. She could tell from the look on his face that her father-in-law was not used to hugs and kisses. Dan later told her that his grandmother died when Bob was thirteen, leaving him to be shuttled from relative to relative.

After learning more about Bob's background, Velma decided just to go for it whenever she saw him. It wasn't long before he was initiating the hugs, telling everyone within earshot that he was as pleased to have a daughter as Velma was to have a father. She had to be careful whenever walking through a mall with him. If she casually mentioned she liked "that blouse in the window," he would return later and purchase it as a gift. He loved surprising her.

During his last visit for Christmas in 1992, he had a cold. The cold developed into pneumonia. Before anyone was aware of how sick he was, he died.

Velma felt an emptiness worse than before. Once again, all she could think was *I don't have a dad.* But in the midst of her grief, once again, her *heavenly Father* heard her cry and spoke to her heart, this time during a choir rehearsal.

The choir director's family, including his daughter, was visiting the rehearsal. Watching the father/daughter relationship reminded Velma all over again of her loss.

Then the choir began singing "He Is the Same":

He is the same yesterday, today and forever
His unchanging love is forever

God used the song to remind her that He was her heavenly Father when she was a little girl and was still her Father today.

Father to the fatherless, defender of widows—this
is God, whose dwelling is holy. God sets the
lonely in families (Psalm 68:5–6).

22.

· *waiting in the wings* ·

"One person's garbage is another person's treasure." This is a true statement but tough to swallow when it refers to children. Yet we all know of couples who would like to have kids and can't—and couples who shouldn't have kids but do. Where's the justice? Well, sometimes it's in the loving, the praying, and the all-out attempt to fulfill the heart's desire to love a child and be a family.

David Clausen hadn't yet popped the question, but he was making no effort to hide his intentions.

"I want to grow old and gray with you," he said, and then he broke out in a song: "Will you still need me . . . when I'm sixty-four?"

Ginger laughed—the Beatles' Paul McCartney had nothing to worry about.

"I see a future for us, a future with a lot of kids running around," David continued, getting mushier by the minute.

Ginger loved David and knew he was serious. Should she tell him?

"David, there's just one thing."

"What would that be?"

Ginger looked away, and then said, "My system doesn't work right."

"Your system?"

"I don't get periods," she explained. "I can't have kids."

If that news bothered David, his face didn't betray him. He took a deep breath. "That's okay, Ginger. If God wants us to have kids, He'll let us. If not, then we can adopt."

Within a year, the couple stood before family and friends and pledged their love for each other. A month after the honeymoon, Ginger's mother knocked on their apartment door. "Here," she grinned, handing over a bag of baby clothes. "When are you going to make me a grandmother?"

"Oh, Mother, you know I'm not sure I can even have kids."

"You think I'm kidding? Sure, you'll have kids. Doctors have all sorts of ways to help couples these days."

"Mom, we're still on our honeymoon."

A year into the marriage, the Clausens started down a path of doctor visits, fertility drugs, and monthly pregnancy tests—all negative.

One evening, Ginger saw a television special about a couple who adopted a dozen kids, including some who had been foster kids in their home.

Adoption was out of the question—friends had told them that adoptions cost $5,000 to $10,000 or more. They didn't have that kind of money. But what about foster care? Could caring for youngsters who needed a home ease the ache in her heart?

After two years of futility with fertility drugs, Ginger carefully broached the subject with David. "What would you think about becoming foster parents?" she asked one evening. "If we can't have children, at least we could love some kids who desperately need love."

"I think we should check into it," David said, speaking without hesitation. "My only concern is that you could have your heart broken when the kids leave us."

The Clausens filled out applications, welcomed social workers into their home, and endured comprehensive interviews. They were told that they could probably expect to care for toddlers and preschoolers—kids two to five years old.

A month later Ginger received a phone call.

"Would you be willing to pick up a little boy tomorrow at the hospital?"

"What did they do to him?" Ginger asked, fearing that the child had been abused.

"He was just born," said the social worker. "You can pick him up tomorrow at ten A.M."

Ginger called her parents and several friends in their couples' Bible study. David borrowed a truck and picked up a crib, bassinet, swing, huge bag of clothing, crib sheets, and blankets. By eleven P.M., they had a bona fide nursery!

The next day, Ginger and David drove to the hospital. "We have to give him a name," she said. "I'm not going to call him Baby Boy for the rest of his life."

They finally settled on Joey—a compromise between Joseph and Joel.

"Here you go," said the social worker, handing over a six-day-old baby boy. "Good luck. He's a drug baby, you know."

"Oh, really?"

"Yes. His mother was high when she came here. Right after she gave birth, she split."

For the first week, Ginger felt she was baby-sitting a poor child all alone in the world. When her case worker failed to call for a month, she thought, *Nobody cares about this baby except us.*

As they raised Joey, the Clausens began thinking about adopting him, even though everyone had told them it would be a miracle. Young, childless parents rarely received a newborn in the first place, because they easily bonded with the infant, which complicated matters if the birth mother got her life together and asked for custody.

As Ginger rocked the baby to sleep, tears rolled down her cheeks. She asked God to give him good health and parents who loved him and honored the Lord, and finally, with every ounce of her being, she humbly asked the Lord to allow her and David to adopt Joey.

Case workers were skeptical at first, but they allowed the adoption application to proceed. The Clausens' hopes were raised when they learned they could adopt Joey before his first birthday, but red tape slowed things for more than a year. Their patience and steadfastness were rewarded when just after his second birthday their little boy officially became Joseph Albert Clausen.

Since then the Clausens have adopted two girls, Kimarie and Carolyn, who originally came to them as foster children. God has granted the desire of their hearts.

I asked the Lord to give me this child, and he
has given me my request (1 Samuel 1:27).

23.

· *wheels up* ·

God's grace for mothers is not limited to whether they are "stay-at-home" moms or "working" moms (since they're all working moms!) But when a true "God thing" occurs, you'll often see it affect the big picture. It confirms an important decision that weighs on your heart and needs God's hand of guidance. The following story about Shelley's struggle illustrates this truth perfectly.

Shelley Shrader struggled with the question millions of working mothers have asked: "Is my career worth it?"

Married at twenty-one, with another year awaiting her at the University of Texas at Arlington, Shelley wanted to enjoy life with her husband, Greg—just the two of them—before kids changed their lives forever.

After college, the couple moved to Fort Worth, where Shelley joined American Airlines as a flight reservationist. Greg began working in the data processing department at DynCorp, a defense contractor. Shelley didn't like being desk-bound, so she applied to become a flight attendant. She received her wings in 1990, four years into her marriage.

Flight attendant work, she discovered, was more difficult than it looked, and less glamorous than it was made out to be. Serving 125 people dinner in one hour was a trick. Work hours and layovers were long, and passengers took out their travel frustrations on their nearest targets—flight attendants. Shelley often felt like a doormat at thirty thousand feet.

One evening, Greg and Shelley discussed their future. "Remember how one of my goals was to have children before I was thirty?" Greg began. "Well, I'm nearly twenty-nine, so if now is a good time . . ."

Shelley, two years younger, nodded her agreement. "I wasn't mature enough to have kids when we married, but I'm ready now."

Lauren arrived in 1994. Eric joined the family three years later. Shelley juggled flight and day-care schedules. She wanted to enroll Lauren in her church's preschool program, which met from nine A.M. to two P.M. on Tuesdays, Wednesdays, and Thursdays, but she couldn't guarantee that those would be her off days. Flight attendants generally crossed the country three to four days a week.

When Lauren turned four in August 1998, Shelley tried to "give up" her scheduled trip to a co-worker wanting a few extra hours, but she had no takers. Then she offered extra money for anyone to take her trip. Still no takers.

Her new work schedule for September and October showed Shelley working three out of every four weekends. The holiday season was just around the corner, and Shelley didn't want to be away from the family on Christmas morning again. What would be best for her family? She began to pray in earnest.

Shelley worried that if she quit work, frustrations would billow and she would be a worse mom. She kept thinking, *Don't I need the stimulation of the business world? Wouldn't I be a better mom if I got a break?*

She sought out the advice of a friend, Linda Eslick. "I'm so confused about what I'm supposed to do," Shelley said. "I just saw the doctor for my tension headaches, which he attributed to stress."

"Tension headaches are not a good sign," said Linda sympathetically. "One thing I've learned is that God has always provided. It might not be the way I hoped things would turn out, but He has provided."

Shelley was heartened. She took Linda's words to mean that if she put all her faith and trust in the Lord, He would not fail her. *Perhaps God is using this situation to increase my faith in him,* she thought.

For two weeks, Shelley agonized over the decision. "Lord, please let me have peace. Please let me be assured that this is the right thing."

She decided to quit and worked her last day on December 1, 1998. Leaving American wasn't all that bad: Shelley's seniority qualified her for an "early retirement" plan that allowed two flights a year for her and her family anywhere the airline flew.

The money? The Shraders would have to tighten their belts, but having Mom home was the best thing to happen for Lauren and Eric.

Early in January, Greg came home from work and enthusiastically invited Shelley out for dinner. At the restaurant he handed her an envelope. "I got this at work today," he said.

The letter, marked "Private, Confidential," noted that Greg's salary had been frozen for two years, but now, based on his excellent work performance, he was receiving an annual increase of $17,000.

"That's what I was making with American!" Shelley exclaimed.

Shelley had followed God's leading to leave American Airlines, and when she and Greg least expected it, the Lord made up the shortfall to help her stay home with her children. Her new career as a full-time mom was cleared for take-off.

> Even strong lions sometimes go hungry, but those who trust in the Lord will never lack any good thing (Psalm 34:9).

A PORTRAIT

24.

· *peggie's place* ·

Few things are more important to pray for than a sign of God's will as it relates to a lifetime spouse. The potential joy and the potential heartache are so strong that no one should settle for a second-best, rushed decision. Sadly, many are in too much of a hurry to wait. But when God is asked to take the reins, I've discovered that the loneliness of waiting never compares to the joy of giving Him time to send His very best.

"When God puts a hesitancy in your heart, it's usually because He wants to do something different with your life."

Standing on the doorstep of adulthood, Peggie Coletti thanked her father for his advice, then retreated with a mixed bag of emotions to her bedroom. Her parents didn't have the money to send her to the Christian college of her dreams, and now uncertainty about the future troubled her.

Alone in her bedroom, she opened *Streams in the Desert*, a

book of daily inspirational readings by Lettie Cowman. On the page for that day, February 5, her eyes fell on a poem based on the story of Ruth and Boaz in the Old Testament. (Ruth was a destitute widow who left her own country to care for her mother-in-law in a foreign land. There, God blessed her with marriage to Boaz, a godly, wealthy landowner.)

What she read succinctly demonstrated how God can and does support His people in times of crisis, trial, and tragedy. One short verse from the Book of Ruth made a lifelong impression: "Sit still, my daughter."

Okay, Lord, I'm going to sit still.

Peggie stayed home and worked as a legal secretary while helping her father, a pastor of a small church in Pennsylvania. She led the church youth group, visited the sick, and directed the choir. Romances blossomed several times during her twenties, but quickly withered.

I'm going to sit still, Lord.

By the time she rounded her thirtieth birthday and then hit her mid-thirties, Peggie wondered if she would ever meet the man that the Lord wanted her to marry.

After another romantic relationship soured, Peggie turned to the Book of Ruth for more comforting words. "Lie down until the morning," she read in chapter 3, verse 13. It seemed God was telling her to rest during this period of discouragement. He was promising that joy was coming "in the morning."

On another occasion, after Peggie had received a "this-isn't-working" missive in the mail, a retired missionary wrote her a friendly letter that finished with this statement: "My prayer for you is Ruth 1:9." The verse said, "May the Lord grant that each of you [Ruth and her sister-in-law] will find rest in the home of another husband."

Okay, Lord, I'll lie down until the morning.

A matchmaking friend tried to introduce Peggie to Joe Bohanon, a thirty-seven-year-old professor at a Christian college, but they never went out for one reason or another. Eventually, however, Peggie attended a conference where she saw Dr. Bohanon. They introduced themselves and, after chatting, took seats next to each other.

At the close of the session, the speaker asked those with prayer requests to stand. Peggie had a sinus problem, but most of all, a "special unspoken need."

The speaker then inquired if those nearby could pray for their neighbor. Joe quietly prayed for Peggie, not knowing the personal nature of her "need."

Three days later, Joe called. Over the next few weeks, their friendship flourished under a parade of flowers, presents, and dinners. Within three months, Joe asked Peggie to marry him.

During their engagement, Joe and Peggie attended a breakfast meeting. The master of ceremonies, who knew Joe and had just learned of his engagement, asked Joe and Peggie to stand in the crowded conference room.

"The Lord has a word for you," he began, "and he has showed me that you, Joe, are her Boaz, and Peggie is the one prepared from the foundation of the earth to be your helpmate. A blessing will come out of this union."

At that moment, fifteen years of promises from the Book of Ruth came together in Peggie's mind. Joe, at six feet, seven inches tall, was her "tower of strength." He was sensitive to those in need, and showed a keen sense of responsibility.

Completing the "Ruth and Boaz" theme on their wedding day, Joe and Peggie decorated the church with sheaves of wheat to symbolize how God had brought them together.

Peggie is creator of the very popular www.peggiesplace.com Web site.

Weeping may go on all night, but joy comes
in the morning (Psalm 30:5).

A PICTURE

25.

· *turning a corner* ·

Have you ever wondered if there has to be more to life than what you are currently experiencing? I have. I get caught in that proverbial forest, and I can't seem to find the trees. If you ever wonder whether life has meaning beyond the mundane, and purpose above the inner pain, look for something. Look for God to speak, tell Him you're listening, then get ready to experience your own "God thing."

Duane Brannon had a great job, a wonderful wife, four beautiful children. Why was this middle-aged dentist feeling so restless and dissatisfied? On the outside, he "had it all," but on the inside, he needed . . . something more. To identify what it could be was beyond him.

One Saturday, Duane thought it would be a nice change of pace to invite the entire family out for lunch following church the next day on the Memorial Day weekend. "We can drive down to Old Town and eat at the Casa De Bandini," he said, referring to a classic Mexican restaurant in San Diego's restored Old Town quarter.

"It's too far," one child complained.

"I don't want to go either," chimed in his teenager.

"Let's make this a special occasion," Duane persisted. "We can get all dressed up and have a special meal out."

The next day, the children still registered mild protests as the family Suburban headed south for the thirty-minute drive. On this holiday weekend, however, it seemed as if *everyone* had the same idea—eat authentic Mexican food at one of the restaurants ringing the pioneer square at Old Town. Nearing Casa De Bandini, they found no place to park.

"Why don't you take the kids and put our name in," Duane said to Becky. "I'll try to find a place to park this beast."

For ten minutes, Duane drove up and down the narrow streets. Finally, he gave up and headed several blocks northeast of the restaurant, a good ten-minute walk. Duane parked the Suburban and began walking briskly in what he thought was the direction of the restaurant.

Walking up one block, he realized that he had passed the right street. Should he turn around? *No,* he thought. *I'll just make a right at the next corner and work my way over.* He stepped up his pace, knowing Becky and the kids were waiting for him.

Up ahead someone was making a scene—*another one of those crazy homeless men,* Duane thought. As he approached, however, he saw that the man was dressed in combat fatigues. He pegged him at fifty years old, with his gray beard. *A Vietnam veteran?*

Maybe twenty-five people sat on the sidewalk or stood listening to the veteran as he implored the crowd, "Don't forget the veterans this Memorial Day weekend! This is not the time to forget our comrades who made the ultimate sacrifice on behalf of our country."

Duane noticed a small memorial statue and plaque—and very little space to walk through. He decided to stride quickly in front of the veteran, who was calling out names of San Diego County men killed in Southeast Asia.

Just as Duane passed directly in front, his ear twelve inches from the veteran's mouth, the former soldier loudly proclaimed, "Jack Davis."

Jack Davis?

Duane stopped in his tracks and looked at the veteran. Jack Davis had been Duane's good friend at Fallbrook High School in San Diego. Jack was killed in Vietnam when his helicopter went down. Instantly, Duane recalled Jack's big smile and what a good buddy he had been. Losing him had been devastating.

Then Duane was jerked back from the reverie. What were the odds that Jack's name would be called out at the moment

Duane passed directly in front of this veteran? Had God orchestrated this event on a Sunday afternoon?

Duane knew the answer. God had wanted to remind him of Jack, who died so young without ever experiencing the love and closeness of a wife and children.

What did Duane have to complain about? So what if he was down in the dumps!

God had made an appointment for Duane to learn an invaluable lesson. From that "chance" moment, he understood that life was God's gift to be appreciated every day.

Jesus said, "Come to me, all you who are weary and carry heavy burdens, and I will give you rest. Take my yoke upon you. Let me teach you, because I am humble and gentle, and you will find rest for your souls" (Matthew 11:28–29).

26.

· listening to God ·

Have you ever had an emptiness come over you in response to a prayer? When God senses an earnestness to your prayers, He is very serious about answering . . . but not always in the way you expect. If you were to pray for new ways to become intimate with God, you might expect to get more out of the Bible, see rainbows through the thunderstorms of life, or witness God do a miracle through you. What happened to Diane no one could have predicted . . .

Strangely, people were mumbling more. No matter how hard she listened, Diane could pick up only bits and pieces of phone conversations or friendly chatter. A hearing specialist finally confirmed her fears: "Young lady, you are going deaf."

Until then, Diane Comer's life seemed close to perfect. Raised in a loving home, she married a pastor and had three healthy children by the age of twenty-six.

Diane had become a Christian while a teenager, followed the faith, and lived what appeared to be an exemplary life. But still, an emptiness nagged at the edges of her heart.

Laurie Keyes and Alice Wilhelm, fresh from overseas missionary assignments, reached out to Diane in their women's Bible study at church. Their mentoring prompted Diane to begin praying that God would lead her to a deeper intimacy with him. She asked God to do "whatever it takes."

Soon afterward, Diane heard the doctor's diagnosis loud and clear. *Deaf? With three young children? How will I be what my family needs me to be?*

As days and weeks passed, Diane's hearing slowly declined. Doctors could find no cause, no cure. For reasons unknown, the cochlear nerves in both ears were disintegrating.

At first, it was the little things. She couldn't hear the telephone ring if she was in another part of the house. And if she answered the phone, she couldn't be sure with whom she was talking. All voices began to sound the same. Once she carried on a fifteen-minute conversation with Stacey, only to discover she was talking with Lucy.

Diane could hear—she just couldn't understand what she heard. With a group of people at church or a restaurant, she had to work hard to wring out every intelligible bit of sound from the roar that met her ears. She often went home exhausted by the effort, or embarrassed.

Well-meaning individuals told her, "But you do so well—nobody would ever know!" What they didn't know was how much she missed, how often she bluffed, how tense she felt in conversation, how many people she avoided for fear of having to say, "I'm sorry, but I can't hear what you're saying . . ." She felt stupid every time she saw that look in their eyes that meant she had blundered.

But Diane's home was no refuge, either. There she felt the worst pain. When her baby cried at night, she couldn't hear the need. When her toddler wrapped her dimpled arms around Diane's neck and whispered sweet secrets, she couldn't hear the love. When her son told her all about his first stay away from home at church camp, chattering away in the car, she couldn't hear the excitement.

Of course, not hearing birds or crickets or alarm clocks wasn't so bad. But those lovely, intimate, important words . . . she longed to hear. She had to hear!

Diane began to sink into depression. She had never experienced such sadness before. Difficulties before this she had handled almost cheerfully, but this was darkness. She couldn't "just cheer up." Fear, anger, and most of all self-pity overwhelmed her.

Why had God turned his back on her? How could He allow this to happen?

She prayed, and felt only silence. She read her Bible, and wept. She wrapped herself in a cloak of despair, and firmly shut everyone out.

Finally, Diane asked the elders of her church to pray for healing. As these men surrounded her with prayer and anointed her with oil (a practice that the Book of James in the Bible recommends), the darkness that seemed to cloud her vision lifted. Brilliant light broke through the despair. She sensed clearly the voice of God speaking to her heart. And in that instant of illumination, she knew that His answer was no—no miraculous healing of her ears, but an instantaneous healing of her heart. God's peace invaded her life; her heavenly Father was by her side.

Early the next morning Diane woke up and began reading her Bible. This time God spoke to her through Scripture:

I waited patiently for the LORD;
he turned to me and heard my cry.
He lifted me out of the slimy pit,
out of the mud and mire;
he set my feet on a rock
and gave me a firm place to stand.
He put a new song in my mouth,

a hymn of praise to our God.
Many will see and fear
and put their trust in the Lord.
           —Psalm 40:1–3 (NIV)

Diane had heard from God. His "no" left her filled with more peace and joy than she had ever experienced before.

Several years later, Diane retains only 15 percent of her hearing. But as the voices of those she loves grow dimmer, the voice of the One who will never leave her or forsake her grows clearer with each day. The intimacy with God she once craved is hers now—Diane knows she's never alone.

God has said, "I will never leave you. I will never
forsake you." That is why we can say with confidence,
"The Lord is my helper, so I will not be afraid"
(Hebrews 13:5–6).

A PICTURE

27.

· *cartoon character* ·

After speaking at large festivals and conferences for more than thirty years, I can attest—a million times over—that God sweats the details. In the following story, a man needed a practical miracle to use his God-given gifts. Guess what? God knew what he needed, when he needed it.

"Ralph" was a cartoon character antihero who poked fun at the school administration and tweaked Establishment noses—perfect for the mid-1970s at the University of Nebraska, where Ron Wheeler had persuaded the student newspaper to publish his first comic strip.

Fellow students told Ron there was a lot of truth in his cartoons, but deep down he wondered if they were right. He decided to set off on a course to find out "What Really Matters." He scaled mountain peaks, jumped out of airplanes, and attended Mind Dynamics seminars. He purchased a hot sports car and found willing women to fill the passenger seat.

None of these pursuits satisfied his hunger for truth.

Ron had wrapped his persona into that of a cartoonist, which was a tough way to make a living. After years of rejection, he discovered that what he was missing was Jesus Christ—not his own syndicated Sunday newspaper comic strip.

Hearing a presentation of the Christian message to make peace with God using the bridge of Jesus Christ, Ron trusted Christ as his Savior and began reading the Bible. When he fathomed that his pride and selfishness had kept him from experiencing God's love, he stopped trying so hard to become a cartoonist. In fact, he was willing to give up the dream altogether.

By "coincidence," the very next day, Ron got his first full-time job, drawing cartoons for a slide show production company right across the street from his apartment.

Ron is now a freelance cartoonist. One of his first clients was the American Tract Society, which in the early 1980s found his humor in comic-book-like tracts effective. Tracts are small booklets handed out to people to explain something about the Christian faith when a long conversation isn't possible. People will read tracts, especially tracts with cartoons in them, when they won't take time to read anything else.

After several years, however, the ministry had a change of leadership, and Ron's tract work abruptly halted. He shrugged and returned to the drawing board. Though his job changed, one thing never changed over the years for Ron: tight finances. When he later began creating CDs containing his cartoons in a clip art format, this entrepreneurial effort stretched him to his financial limits.

Then his balky computer, which Ron uses to manipulate images and even "draw," began showing signs of permanently crashing. Ron's three-year-old Macintosh operated behind the curve: the processing speed was too slow and the hard drive storage unable to meet the demands placed on it.

With a huge poster assignment deadline looming on the horizon, Ron wondered if he should charge a new computer on his Visa card and worry about paying for it later. If he decided to pull the trigger, Ron figured he needed to buy an Apple Macintosh G3 with 266 MHz and a 6 gigabyte hard drive.

Ron began to pray about the situation. Two weeks later, he got a call from Rob Moritz, whose one-man drama ministry as "the apostle Paul" takes him around the country reciting the apostle's New Testament writings.

"Did I tell you I have a new Apple computer?" Rob asked out of the blue.

"Yeah, do you want to give it to me?" Ron joked.

"As a matter of fact I do."

"No, you can't be serious."

"But I am."

"What's it got on it?"

"It's a G3 with 266 MHz and a 6 gig hard drive."

Ron looked down the MacWarehouse mail-order catalog. The same model was staring him in the face.

"No, let me buy it from you."

"I insist on giving it to you. We don't need it anymore, and I know you can put it to good use," Rob said.

Ron drove to Rob's house to pick up the computer. "There it is," Rob said with a sweep of his hand. "You know something? You're going to be amazed when you get to heaven and see how many people were helped in their salvation because of the cartooning gift God has given you."

"I'm overwhelmed, Rob, but I haven't done any gospel tracts in years."

Shortly after setting up the new Mac at his home office, Ron took a call from the American Tract Society. With the new leadership in place, they told Ron they were ready to revise and update their cartoon tract line. Could he revise or create eleven new tracts in two months?

"I sure can," he replied. He had never been asked to do more than four tracts in a year, but with his new computer the assignment was doable.

Then a new client called. Good News Publishers wanted Ron to create five more gospel tracts. God clearly had a plan and His own timetable for getting the message out.

Ron has nearly fifty cartoon gospel tracts in print, and more than 35 million have been handed out all over the world. To learn more about Ron's cartooning, visit his Web site at www.cartoonworks.com.

Whatever is good and perfect comes to us from God above, who created all heaven's lights. Unlike them, he never changes or casts shifting shadows. In his goodness he chose to make us his own children by giving us his true word (James 1:17–18).

A PICTURE

28.

· *the wake-up call* ·

Have you ever awakened in the middle of the night and wondered why? If so, you have likely been prompted by God to do something supernatural: pray. If instead you roll over and fall back asleep, does it mean that something bad will happen in the world? I don't know for sure, but I do know that something good can happen if we are sensitive to God's supernatural nudges in the night.

Suddenly awakened at one A.M., Elaine Cunningham couldn't shake the feeling that something terrible was about to happen. Not to Elaine in her comfortable home in the Pacific Northwest, but to her son, John, and his family in Africa.

Pray! The command was urgent. Now wide awake, Elaine sent fervent pleas to heaven. "Please, God, help John and Sandy and the girls. Protect them if they are in danger."

At that very moment, John and Sandy, with five-year-old Sara and three-year-old Jessica, were driving through the *bushveld,* looking for elephants. Sandy was behind the wheel, so that John could take photos.

"It's so hot, Mommy," one of the girls complained. The temperature had already reached triple digits by midmorning.

"I'm sorry, honey, but there's nothing we can do about it," said Sandy. Dust billowed behind the Toyota sedan as the car bumped along the dirt road. John asked the occupants of the few cars they met, "Have you seen any elephants today?"

Finally a positive response: "Go one kilometer and turn left. You'll see some elephants in the river."

Sandy drove down an embankment toward a clearing, veld grass scratching the car's undercarriage. John wondered about snakes. He knew that deadly cobras, black mambas, green mambas, and puff adders inhabited the area. Sandy parked the sedan in a clearing above the muddy river.

"Look, elephants!" Sara spotted them first. John climbed onto the window ledge and looked over the car's roof to get a better view. Even with a telephoto lens, however, he was too far away to snap good pictures.

"I'm going to walk down toward the river," he announced.

"Go ahead, but please be careful. The girls and I will stay in the car," Sandy said.

Stepping onto what looked like a trail, John watched carefully for snakes as he picked his way toward the river. He stopped about a hundred feet from the car and gazed at a small group of cow elephants sucking brown water into their trunks and spraying it over their backs, their huge ears fanning back and forth. Bulls on the riverbank flung red sand high overhead. Calves frolicked in the river, standing with their forefeet on each other's backs. A huge old bull, his tusks nearly touching the ground, stood guard as he moved his head slowly back and forth across the horizon. The view was stunning.

John raised his camera and shot away, wishing that Sandy and his daughters could see this "greatest show on Earth" from his ringside position. That's when he heard an ominous low rumbling like rolling thunder. Looking up and down the river, John saw nothing unusual, but feeling uneasy, he placed the cap on the camera lens and turned toward the car. He stopped dead in his tracks as he realized the source of the noise: a herd of elephants, perhaps more than two hundred! The rumbling was the sound of their running across the dry grasslands.

John's mind raced with pictures of uprooted trees and overturned automobiles. He recalled a missionary's warning never to stand between elephants and their source of water. They become violent if their access is threatened.

Standing between these hot, thirsty animals and their cooling bath and refreshing drink were John and the car holding his family.

Dust swirled in great clouds as the elephants halted momentarily on the crest overlooking the water hole. The herd and John were about equal distances from the car. He faced a quick decision: stay where he was and be trampled, or run for the car and die with his family. Three panic-stricken loved ones screaming from inside his tin can of a car were telling him to run.

Sprinting as fast as he could and ignoring the trail, John raced through the grass and its deadly snakes. He was halfway to the car when the elephants charged.

The first elephants were closing in at full speed as John reached the tiny auto. Jumping in, he slammed the door as the car was engulfed in blinding dust and bellowing elephants. The beasts passed on both sides, rocking the car as they scraped against it. Sara and Jessica screamed in terror as they looked up through the windows and saw nothing but massive pachyderms bearing down on them. John gasped for breath, and Sandy was too frightened to speak. The car jolted back and forth from the thundering vibrations of hundreds of massive feet.

When the last of the herd passed and the dust settled, the car still vibrated from the shaking ground. Every blade of grass and small bush on the hillside was flattened.

Sandy and John tried to calm the girls, then with one voice they thanked God for saving their lives.

"Someone must have been praying for us," John said.

"Only a miracle kept us from being crushed," Sandy agreed. "Let's get out of here!"

Meanwhile, back in America's Pacific Northwest, the hour turned to two A.M. Elaine relaxed as the burden to pray lifted. "Thank you, Father. I know they're in your hands."

Great is the Lord! Your awe-inspiring deeds will
be on every tongue; I will proclaim your greatness
(Psalm 145:3a, 6).

A PICTURE IN A PORTRAIT

29.

· *living in God's economy* ·

Perhaps you've heard the phrase "you can't outgive God." I've found this to be more than true in my own life, especially when what you have to give doesn't appear to be much. When we give cheerfully to God, there is always a reward. Sometimes it's immediate, sometimes it comes back to you in a roundabout way. And sometimes, as this story shows, God makes things happen in an immediate roundabout way!

Australian David Smallbone could make flowers bloom in rocky soil. The Christian concert promoter made a living in a country where Christianity had taken root among only 5 percent of the people.

Then disaster struck. Too few fans filled the seats of a major tour David was promoting throughout Australia. When ticket sales fall short, artists still get their guaranteed money, and the promoter eats the loss. David took a $250,000 bath in red ink.

Creditors swiftly repossessed his house, and the father of six looked for work elsewhere. A top artist asked him to become his manager, with just one catch: he had to move to Nashville, Tennessee, hub of the Christian music industry. Moving without his pregnant wife, Helen, and the children, who ranged in age from one to fourteen, was unthinkable. So, in the fall of 1991, the Smallbones sold their furniture and other possessions and purchased tickets to America.

The fresh start in a new world almost immediately turned sour. The house they had planned to rent was no longer available, so the family bunked together in two motel rooms and survived on fast-food hamburgers until a new rental could be found. Worse, after a couple of months of work, David was informed that his position was "no longer available." He had brought his family halfway across the world for nothing.

David literally could not get out of bed for several days. He and Helen had a "no secrets" policy with the children, and they carefully explained everything that happened. Then they got on their knees as a family and asked God to help them.

All they had was God and one another, plus a roof over their heads. They furnished the house they rented with no more than a few cushions, a table, and a single mattress for Helen, who was now seven months pregnant. Everyone else slept on the floor on beds made out of clothes.

Then the most interesting things happened. Bags of groceries were left at the front door. Acquaintances from the music world took the family out for dinner. Sunday school classes donated furniture. And a Nashville songwriter named Jon Mohr gave the Smallbones—no strings attached—a three-month-old Toyota Previa van with six thousand miles on the odometer.

"It's all yours," Jon said, handing Helen the keys.

Meanwhile, family members took on odd jobs in the neighborhood. Rebecca, the oldest, and two brothers raked leaves and mowed lawns. She also baby-sat and helped her mom clean houses, rarely complaining about disinfecting toilet bowls.

Then came the big break so fitting for Nashville: Forefront Records heard a demo tape of Rebecca singing and offered the fifteen-year-old a recording contract.

Taking on an old family name for the stage, Rebecca recorded her first album as Rebecca St. James, and the family made plans for her concert tour. Jon Mohr knew they needed bigger wheels, so he traded the Previa for a Chevy 15-passenger van. Awestruck by his generosity, David offered Jon 50 percent of Rebecca's "publishing rights"—the money she earned from writing songs.

Flash forward to today. Rebecca St. James has become one of the hottest Christian artists in America. *Christianity Today* magazine has named her one of the top fifty up-and-coming evangelical leaders under the age of forty.

Meanwhile, Jon Mohr and his wife left the music industry to become missionaries in the Ukraine, where they live with their six children. The Smallbones' twice-a-year royalty checks sent directly to the Mohrs' missions account significantly helps support their ministry.

All along—no surprise—God knew what he was doing!

"For I know the plans I have for you," says the Lord. "They are plans for good and not for disaster, to give you a future and a hope" (Jeremiah 29:11).

A PICTURE

30.

· *october sky* ·

Like an orchestra conductor who knows the smallest details of a complicated symphony, God has the performance of history— and your life—well in mind. At the right moment, the experienced conductor motions to a section to play louder and a moment later, he signals the cymbals to clash their notes of exclamation. Throughout our lives, God works just like this. Through the high notes and low notes of our particular symphony, God remains firmly in control of the baton.

In the middle of her senior year at Seattle Pacific College, Pat Scofield was called into the business office. She sat down while a school accountant thumbed through her file.

"I'm afraid we can't go on," he announced. "You owe the college too much money. It's not good for us, and it's not good for you."

Pat was dumbfounded. Tight finances had played a role in

her college education all along, but why had money suddenly become an insurmountable barrier to a diploma?

In high school in Oregon, Pat had the grades and the desire to attend Wheaton College, one of the top Christian colleges in the country, but the private school was too expensive for her parents. In fact, her father said family finances precluded much help from them at all.

Pat wanted to become a schoolteacher, so she enrolled in nearby Portland State University. After her freshman year, she transferred to Seattle Pacific College (now University), a private Christian school with a fine academic reputation. Pat's part-time job didn't come close to covering tuition and room and board, but the school's business office allowed her to sign up for a "borrow as you go" loan program.

With graduation now in sight, "borrow as you go" became "you can't go on." Why hadn't something been said before?

"I'm afraid you're going to have to bite the bullet and start paying us back some of what you owe," the school accountant continued.

"But how am I going to do that?" Pat asked.

"Ask your parents for the money."

"But you already know that they are not able to help me financially."

"Perhaps someone in your church can loan you the money."

The conversation was going nowhere.

"What happens if I can't borrow the money?"

"Then you'll have to drop out for a while," he said.

Pat had never felt so dejected in her life. If she dropped out now, she might never return to college and earn her teaching degree. But the more she thought about it, the more she resigned herself to moving back home to Portland and finding a job to pay off her college bills.

A week passed. Pat studied for her finals, sure that her future lay behind some Smith-Corona typewriter in a downtown office pool. Then she was asked to report to the business office again.

"You're probably wondering why you're here," said the man behind the desk.

Pat nodded.

"Have you ever heard of *Sputnik*?"

"Of course," Pat replied. Everyone had. When the Soviet Union launched the world's first satellite, called *Sputnik*, into space on October 4, 1957, the U.S. government and national media reacted hysterically. Something had to be done, or the Soviets would beat us to the moon.

"One of the things that Congress did in response to Sputnik was to pass the National Defense Student Loan Act last summer," the school official said. "Basically, the act calls for more and better elementary school teachers."

"What does that have to do with me?"

"We've decided to make you one of the first recipients of the National Defense Student Loan program. The government will pay for your education, and for each year you teach, the government will forgive ten percent of your debt. Not a bad deal, is it?"

God had used a complicated international situation, the space race, to pave a way for Pat to earn her teaching degree. Following graduation in June 1959, she started teaching the primary grades at Buckman Elementary, a Portland inner-city school.

The story doesn't end there. Pat soon desired to teach at a mission school in Taiwan or the Philippines. Before she could go overseas, however, she was required to take a year of graduate courses at Multnomah Biblical Seminary, where she met a dashing young student from Argentina *(the author of this book!)*.

I must have charmed the socks off Pat in our Survey of the Old Testament class, because we married the following summer, in August 1961. After we joined Overseas Crusades, we finished paying Pat's outstanding college education debt. In every detail of Pat's college education, big and small, God was there.

Yours, O Lord, is the greatness, the power, the glory, the victory, and the majesty. Everything in the heavens and on earth is yours, O Lord, and this is your kingdom. We adore you as the one who is over all things (1 Chronicles 29:11).

A PICTURE IN A PORTRAIT

31.

· *the hiding place* ·

The Holocaust is a tragic mystery I will never understand. I know there are millions alive today who would agree. Was it the natural consequence of a madman given freedom of choice like the rest of us? Could it have been prevented if courageous people—including God's people—had spoken up in the early stages of Nazism? Any answer would be trite and incomplete. The courage of the few who were good did not always outweigh the consequences caused by the many who were evil, but within the darkness there were many lights. This chapter points to a light the world will never forget.

The Weil family was the first to ask the ten Booms to save them from the Gestapo. The ten Booms fixed up several spare rooms—one built with unexpected corners and spaces. A false wall provided a hiding place, allowing the Jews to scramble to safety if the house were suddenly raided. Everyone lived in fear . . .

Corrie ten Boom was born in the Netherlands in 1892, the youngest of four children in a *gzellig* family—Dutch for a pleasant, cozy home in which the family works and plays together. Her father, Caspar, a respected watchmaker in the town of Haarlem, had been raised in a devout Christian home. His father, Willem, was particularly interested in the biblical prophecies that the Jews would one day return to their homeland. Willem passed on his love for the Jewish people to his children and grandchildren.

Corrie, who learned her father's trade, was content to live in her parents' home and work in their first-floor watch shop.

Life changed overnight in the spring of 1940, when the Nazi war machine blitzed through Europe's Low Countries. No one could buy food without ration cards. Dutch newspapers were shut down. Bikes were confiscated and radios turned in, although the ten Booms hid theirs.

All Dutch people fifteen years of age and older were issued identity cards; Jews received a yellow J across theirs. German soldiers smashed the windows of Jewish shopkeepers and pilfered their goods. Jews began disappearing. Rumors swept through villages and towns that the Nazis were carting off Jews to death camps. Aided by sympathizers like the ten Booms, many Jewish families went into hiding.

The day of reckoning came in February 1944.

"Where are the Jews?" screamed the Gestapo major.

"There aren't any Jews here," Corrie answered, lying to save lives.

The Gestapo major belted Corrie, then fifty-two years old, across the mouth. She tasted blood.

"Where is the secret room?"

Corrie didn't answer, except to say, "Lord Jesus, help me."

"If you use that name again, I'll kill you!"

Corrie, her father, and her sister Betsie were arrested, but the Jews who had been hiding in the secret room escaped. Within weeks, her father died in custody, but Corrie and Betsie were dispatched to Ravensbruck, a notorious concentration camp that was home—usually a temporary one because many died there— to 35,000 women.

The roll call siren sounded at four-thirty A.M. In subfreezing temperatures, the shivering inmates often stood in the *Lagerstrasse* until daylight while lines were counted and recounted. Anyone who fell to the ground was pummeled with truncheons and brutalized with kicks. The work was extremely physical: the ten Boom sisters loaded heavy steel sheets onto carts, pushed them the required distance, then unloaded them.

With only a bowl of thin soup, a scrap of dark bread, and maybe a potato to sustain them, the sisters became weaker each day. They knew that if they were committed to the camp hospital, a one-way trip to the gas chambers would soon follow. Everyone could see the tall chimney belching gray smoke from the crematorium.

Corrie had been stripped of every possession except for one item she smuggled into Ravensbruck—a small Dutch Bible. After an exhausting day's work, Corrie and Betsie invited everyone in the barracks to join them for a Bible study.

The guards never intruded. Why? The inmates' beds were crawling with fleas, so the guards kept their distance. Corrie and Betsie thanked God for the fleas.

Corrie managed to keep up with the physical labor demands—nothing short of miraculous given the malnutrition and ill treatment. Whipped by a guard for not working hard enough one day, Betsie was carried off to the infirmary on a stretcher. Two days later, Corrie found Betsie's body dumped in a washroom with other decaying corpses. When she looked into her sister's face, Corrie saw a youthful-looking woman filled with peace and happiness.

Four days after Betsie's death, Corrie's number was called. She was ordered to report to the main office. For what? A trip to the gas chamber? Transport to another camp?

Corrie stood in line. She watched another disheveled woman stand in front of a large desk. The officer stamped a paper and handed it to her.

Entlassen! he barked.

Released? Why was this woman going free?

Each prisoner received the same stamped paper and command. *Could it be true?*

Corrie ten Boom was released from Ravensbruck on the first day of January 1945. It took days to reach occupied Holland by train. Her first real food was tea and a dry crust at a Christian hospital called Deaconess Home.

A young nurse dropped by and asked her where she came from.

"Haarlem," Corrie replied.

"Do you know Corrie ten Boom?"

The nurse, Truus Benes, hadn't recognized the emaciated, hollow-eyed woman as the robust leader of her Girl's Club, which Corrie had organized in Haarlem years ago.

"I am Corrie ten Boom."

Millions of people have read Corrie's biography, *The Hiding Place,* and viewed the movie by the same title, but not many know that Corrie was released from Ravensbruck by mistake, a "clerical error." A few days after Corrie walked through Ravensbruck's iron doors, the order was given to kill all women her age and older.

For the next four decades, Corrie ten Boom crisscrossed the globe, speaking to millions of people about her faith in God that kept her strong under depraved conditions. The nation of Israel also honored Corrie for aiding Jewish people, inviting her to plant a tree in the Avenue of the Righteous Gentiles near Jerusalem.

> Those who live in the shelter of the Most High will find rest in the shadow of the Almighty. This I declare of the Lord: He alone is my refuge, my place of safety; he is my God, and I am trusting in him (Psalm 91:1–2).

32.

· *total turnaround* ·

The most amazing "God thing" I've witnessed is God entering the heart of a hurting soul through the healing, forgiving power of His Son, Jesus Christ. I have had the privilege of witnessing this miracle thousands upon thousands of times. When someone makes the choice to open the door of their heart from the inside, unexpected miracles start to occur. Like the one Mike Rogers experienced after one of our events.

Mike Rogers never missed a chance to party at the University of Oklahoma. The only time he felt a pang of guilt was when a fraternity brother, John O'Neal, asked him to join his Bible study. Everyone looked up to John, a defensive back on the Sooner football team, but whenever John asked, Mike averted his eyes and mumbled some excuse about having to study.

Little changed even after graduation, as Mike settled into a career in the insurance business. He dated every woman in sight—and slept with them as well. Although he knew casual sex was dangerous, Mike didn't regard it as sinful behavior. Then again, he wondered why it didn't feel right. He sought advice from his oldest brother, Jim.

"The answers are right here," Jim said, handing Mike a Bible. "Why don't you start reading this a bit?"

Books are usually meant to be read from page one, so Mike started with Genesis. By the time he reached Leviticus, he was totally lost. He put down the Bible, though he occasionally dropped by his brother's church.

Meanwhile, Mike continued to love 'em and leave 'em. On a ski trip in 1997, he met Melissa. They clicked and quickly began spending all of their free time with each other. Melissa was still living with her parents, so Mike usually had dinner at their house, followed by some tennis, a movie, or just watching TV. When Mike and Melissa had the house to themselves, they retreated to her bedroom.

Mike had been down this road many times, and the emptiness in his heart drove him crazy. Then he heard about a coming citywide Christian event. Mike thought that was something he and Melissa needed to check out. Sitting together in the bleachers that night, Mike listened closely while the speaker outlined the steps to becoming a Christian. When an invitation was given to respond to the Christian message, Mike wanted to go forward but couldn't, as if he were paralyzed by the Holy Spirit. He did, however, pray to receive Jesus Christ right there in the bleachers, while Melissa remained standing and singing with her father.

Not much was said during the car ride home, but the next evening, Mike said, "Melissa, I gave my life to Jesus Christ last night, and I'm going to be making some changes, which include not sleeping together."

Melissa nodded, but she remained skeptical. The next Saturday night, when Mike said he didn't want to take her to Erin's Bar to throw darts and shoot pool, she thought he was going overboard.

"Come on, Goody Two-shoes. You gotta have some fun in life."

"No, sweetheart, I don't want to do that anymore."

"Then we could do some other things," she said, drawing close to him.

"No, we're not doing that, either."

Mike never thought he would turn down an invitation to go to bed with a beautiful woman.

Melissa couldn't handle this Christian stuff anymore. While in the car one afternoon, Mike popped a Michael W. Smith CD in the player (he's a Christian recording artist). Midway through the album, Melissa turned down the volume. "We're not going to have to listen to this the whole way, are we?"

"I'd like to, Melissa."

"But I'm tired of this music. I'm tired of the way our relationship is going. All you want to do is study your Bible and go to church. I want to listen to Celine Dion."

Mike and Melissa broke up three times over the next few months. She continued to call him until Mike said, "Melissa, you've got to stop hounding me. It's over, and I'm comfortable with that. You need to make God your number-one priority."

The next day, Melissa called again. "We need to talk," she said.

"Melissa . . ."

"This time it's different. I promise. Can you meet me at the park?"

Melissa was sitting at a picnic table with a Bible when Mike arrived. She didn't turn around as he walked up behind her.

"Mike, I gave my life to the Lord this afternoon," she said, looking up with tears in her eyes.

Mike hugged her and couldn't stop the tears from flowing either. "Tell me what happened."

Melissa recounted a conversation with her dad. When he said she needed to get her life right with God, something in her heart opened up and she asked Jesus to come into her life.

Now, most readers probably expect to read that Mike and Melissa fell into each other's arms, pledged their undying love for each other, and got married. Actually, that has not happened. They don't know what is ahead. But they're confident God is writing the "rest of the story."

> What this means is that those who become Christians become new persons. They are not the same anymore, for the old life is gone. A new life has begun!
> (2 Corinthians 5:17).

A PICTURE

33.

· *the house on the hill* ·

If God gave you something undeserved yet magnificent, what would you do with it? In our society, where many people make more money than 85 percent of the world's population, something undeserved yet magnificent applies to nearly all of us. So . . . what do you do to return God's blessing? The answer, of course, is between you and God. I know what one couple did in Ireland, however, that showed their thanks to God for the miracle He sent.

Robin and Olive Boles met at a youth congress in Belfast in the early 1950s and married in 1959. One of the couple's entertaining pastimes was looking at houses and speculating where they might put down roots and start a family.

Robin first spotted Carrigoona, a large house for sale on two acres of landscaped gardens among the Wicklow mountains, known locally as the "Garden of Ireland," when she took a holiday job.

"Do you think it's too big?" Olive asked.

"Probably, and certainly it's too dear for us," Robin said. "But the house is going on the auction block next month. Why don't we go along, if only to see what price it goes for."

The couple was surprised when Carrigoona did not receive one realistic bid and was withdrawn from auction. Olive knew the vendor's solicitor (attorney) and gave him a call.

"Want to take a look?" he asked.

Why not? Robin and Olive inspected the house and fell in love with it. Like most young couples, they had very few savings, but they felt the Lord was driving them to purchase the property. They put together an offer of $3,685.

"I'll tell you what I'm going to do," said the solicitor. "I'll forward your offer with the recommendation that it be accepted in the absence of any other bids."

Family and friends thought they were crazy to contemplate the purchase of Carrigoona, but the couple was confident that if the Lord did not want them to have it, their small offer would not go through.

Three weeks later the solicitor phoned with the good news that their offer had been accepted.

That same afternoon the directors of a nearby film studio toured the property and informed their agent they wished to purchase the house, making it clear that "money is no problem." When the agent phoned the solicitor to present an offer, however, he was told Carrigoona had just been sold!

Over the next three decades, the Boleses opened their home for the Lord's work. Wanting to help young people who lived in nearby Bray, Olive started a Girls' Club on Thursday evenings. The first week six girls came, and Olive taught them to make an apple tart, gave them a Coke and a sticky bun to eat, told them a Bible story, and encouraged them to bring a friend the next week.

Seven days later, twelve girls were waiting for their ride to Carrigoona. The club quickly grew to thirty-six, the most Olive thought she could handle. She told the girls that if they missed for three weeks, their place would be given to someone else. Very few missed!

Their mothers lobbied for a Boys' Club, too, and thirty-six boys soon were gathering on Wednesday nights.

"When are we going to get our own club going?" one mum asked, and the Ladies' Club began meeting monthly. Later, a monthly Bible study was begun. Olive brought some of her friends to hear a Christian speaker at the Point Theatre in Dublin. At least two of them trusted Jesus Christ as their Savior.

Today there is an active church in Bray called Christians at

No. 5. They meet in a house at 5 Eglinton Road. Many of the original members first heard the good news of Jesus Christ at Carrigoona, the lovely home on the hill that God provided for Robin and Olive Boles.

"You are the light of the world—like a city on a mountain, glowing in the night for all to see. Don't hide your light under a basket! Instead, put it on a stand and let it shine for all. In the same way, let your good deeds shine out for all to see, so that everyone will praise your heavenly Father" (Matthew 5:14–16).

34.

· *not in vain* ·

Five men were killed. Widows, orphans, and extended family members were left to cope. A tragic and senseless event, right? If God had loved these people he would have prevented it from happening, right? Since it did happen, all those touched by it would grow up to be angry and bitter at God, right? All three questions can be answered in the negative. Read on and you will see that because God is the Great Redeemer—even in this life—He is able to make something good out of anything, if people ask and expect it to happen.

In 1997, thirty-four university students from Washington State embarked on a summer trip of a lifetime: an anthropological trek to visit the Huaodani (pronounced wow-DAH-nee) people deep in the Amazon jungles of South America.

When they left for the jungle, the students weren't aware of three very important facts. First, the Huaodani had come to the world's attention more than forty years earlier when several of their tribesmen speared to death five young missionaries. Second, being from state universities and not young men and women of faith, they had never heard the names of the five who were killed: Jim Elliot, Nate Saint, Pete Fleming, Ed McCulley, and Roger Youderian. Third, following that horrific event, many Huaodani came to know Jesus Christ through the efforts of Nate Saint's sister, Rachel.

To reach the Huaodani encampment, the students followed Steve Saint, the son of one of the five martyrs. Steve had spent time living with his aunt Rachel and the Huaodani while growing up and could communicate in their language. Several Huaodani acted as guides to walk the group along the eastern flanks of the Andes mountains in Ecuador and down into the virgin Amazon basin. Their three-day trek along a jungle trail included several downstream stretches in dugout canoes. Steve saw rapport building between the students and their guides.

Finally, the students unloaded their bags at the Huaodani campsite. As they settled around a campfire that evening, a student asked Steve about the "savage Huaodani" they had read about before leaving the United States. Sitting on a log under a star-studded sky, Steve calmly explained, "The very people you have been traveling, eating, and sleeping with—your guides—are, in fact, those 'savages.' "

"That can't be true!" one student exclaimed, as others murmured their agreement.

"But it is," Steve replied. "If you don't believe me, why don't we ask some of these Huaodani where their fathers are."

Taking up the challenge, one student nodded toward a Huaodani woman. Steve translated.

"Boto meampo doobae wendapa," she replied. "Having been speared, he died a long time ago." Her tone of voice suggested that any other cause would have been unusual.

Overhearing the conversation, four more Huaodani volunteered that their fathers had also been speared and killed. One woman, Ompodae, nodded toward an older man a few feet away who was listening to their conversation. His name was Dabo.

"See him?" said Ompodae. "He killed my father and nearly the rest of my family, too."

The students couldn't believe that a woman could talk so calmly about a person—someone sitting a few feet away—who had killed most of her family.

Dawa, another Huaodani woman, spoke up. Pointing to her aging husband, Kimo, she said, "Hating us, Kimo speared my father, my brothers, my mother, and my baby sister, whom my mother was nursing in her hammock. Then he took me and made me his wife."

The visitors were stunned. "How could she live with a man who murdered her family?" one young woman asked.

Realizing that the students did not know about the missionary slayings, he put his arm around Kimo's shoulders and informed them, "Kimo killed my father, too."

This was too much to comprehend. "What changed these people?" a student asked.

Steve knew the answer but wanted the group to hear it from the lips of Dawa, Kimo, and the other Huaodani. They explained how they used to kill inconvenient babies, and how mothers strangled daughters to meet the demands of dying husbands, who wanted their children to keep them company in the hereafter.

The Huaodani explained that evil spirits and witch doctors' curses could kill as effectively as their warriors' spears. They spoke of living in constant fear of being ambushed, even while working in the gardens. Then they explained to these highly educated young people how they learned that the "Man Maker" sent His Son to die for people full of hate, fear, and desire for revenge.

"We now follow God's trail," said Dawa. Then she asked Steve to translate a question for the audience. "All people die, but if you are following God's trail, then dying will lead you to heaven. But only one trail leads there. Have you heard me well? Which one of you wants to follow God's trail?"

There was silence again. A lone hand rose into the night air. Dawa joyously clapped her hands and said, "We will see each other in God's place some day."

Around a campfire in the Amazon, the dawn of the twenty-first century came face to face with the Stone Age—and came up short. In a fleeting but eternal moment, Steve Saint saw the Great Commission of Jesus Christ—"tell people about me everywhere [even] to the ends of the earth" (Acts 1:8)—come full circle. Dawa's witness to the gospel was living proof that his father's blood truly had not been shed in vain.

Go into all the world and preach the Good News
to everyone, everywhere (Mark 16:15).

A PICTURE

35.

· *dutch treat* ·

What would it take for God to get your attention today? Did you know that the God of the Bible is in the "restoration business"? He wants to restore hearts to Himself. I have found He is lovingly persistent in reminding a human soul of His deep affection. Is He in a hurry? Sometimes, perhaps. But I have more often seen Him take His time to get the message across. What is that message? That today is the day of salvation . . . as an elderly couple discovered not long ago.

Clara loved both new things . . . and surprises. Within a week's time, she would get both.

Luke Mulder's idea was to install two skylights in their home outside of Bothell, Washington, while Clara, his wife of thirty years, visited her sister in California. Luke prided himself on his handyman skills. The first skylight went in without a hitch. He moved his aluminum ladder to the living room hallway to tackle the second.

Luke positioned the ladder just so, then decided he should throw a rug underneath it so that he wouldn't scratch the tile floor. *Clara wouldn't like that.* He was standing on the ladder, trying to yank a nail from the ceiling, when it slipped out from underneath him. Luke crumpled in a heap, and his head broke through the drywall.

Dazed and in pain, he considered calling 911, but then they would see how stupid he had been to put a rug under a ladder. They'd probably whisk him off to the hospital, and that would be the end of his skylight surprise.

Luke rolled over, pulled himself up, and hobbled to the kitchen. He filled a bag with ice and shuffled upstairs to bed, where he lay on his stomach and let the ice bag rest on his aching back. *I could have broken my neck . . . I could have killed myself,* he thought. *And if I had died, what would have happened to me?* He pondered that question . . .

Nearly one thousand miles due south, Clara was receiving some well-deserved rest. She had worked herself to exhaustion preparing the food and hosting her youngest son's wedding in their wooded backyard just a week earlier. That made two sons married in her home in seven months, and Clara needed a break. Luke suggested she visit her sister Mieke in California.

All Mieke wanted to talk about was how she had "found Jesus" and become a Christian. "It's been the best thing that ever happened to me," she told Clara, who could tell by the excitement in Mieke's voice that her sister had experienced something special.

Clara was born in 1926 in the Netherlands East Indies, a Dutch colony known today as Indonesia. Her parents called themselves Protestants, but they never entered a church, never had a Bible in the home, and never mentioned the name of Jesus.

In 1942, the East Indies fell to the Imperial Japanese Army, and Westerners were imprisoned in concentration camps. Clara, then sixteen, soon learned what hunger was all about. Daily rations amounted to a slice of dry bread and local greens such as water lily leaves. The women exchanged recipes so they could at least think about meat, mashed potatoes, and raspberry pies.

Two hundred kilometers away at another concentration camp, Luke Mulder was thankful to be alive. A Japanese submarine had torpedoed the Dutch freighter he was aboard. After managing to escape the burning hulk before it sank, Luke survived ten days on the open sea in a crowded lifeboat. They landed on an uninhabited island near Sumatra, Indonesia, but were later captured by the Japanese.

Luke also experienced hunger. One day he caught a handful of frogs, which he and others turned into frog soup. If the Japanese guards had ever found out, he would have been beaten within an inch of his life.

After the war, Clara returned to Holland, where she taught school, and Luke took a job with Dutch Shell on the island of Curaçao in the Caribbean. Feeling adventurous, Clara accepted a position in Curaçao teaching children of Dutch employees. That's when she met Luke, and they married in 1952. After Luke retired in 1970, they returned to Holland, but they found the Dutch people had changed in ways they didn't like. They moved to America because Mieke said it was a nice place to live.

Moaning in agony, Luke knew that if he had died from the fall off the ladder, he would not have gone to heaven. Years ago he had rejected the God of heaven and rebelled against his Christian parents' strict but loving upbringing. Now it was time to come back to Jesus.

"Lord, please forgive me," he prayed as he got on his knees. "I have not followed You, but please have mercy on me. I want to change my life. I want to find a church. I want to study Your Bible."

Though the years had made some things fuzzy, Luke remembered that coming to God in humility and repentance was all that was required to rekindle a dormant faith. After his prayer, he knew he was a Christian.

At the same moment in California, Clara sat in the church classroom with mixed emotions. She had been invited to a women's prayer meeting—an experience all new to her. The women seated around her began to pray one by one for Clara, and as they did, she became drawn to Jesus Christ. That's when Clara realized that her only hope was in God, who loved her unconditionally and was ready to accept her. She opened her heart to Christ and received Him.

On the plane ride home, Clara wondered what she would say to Luke. He wasn't going to understand that from now on she wanted to worship God each Sunday and study the Bible.

On the way to the airport, Luke—sore but okay—carried on a similar conversation in his mind. How could he ever explain what had happened to him?

They fell into each other's arms.

"Honey, I have something to tell you," Luke said.

"No, I have something I must tell you first . . ."

The Lord . . . does not want anyone to perish,
so he is giving more time for
everyone to repent (2 Peter 3:9).

A PICTURE

36.

· *in the rough* ·

Sometimes God chooses the "easy" way to get someone's attention, sometimes the "hard" way. It all depends on how a person learns best. Whether we're a consistent follower or haven't thought about God in years, I'm convinced that God is always there, reminding us to give Him the attention needed to make a difference in our life hour by hour. How do you learn best? There is a golf instructor in Georgia who admits he's had to learn the hard way.

Charlie Sorrell didn't pick up a golf club until he was twenty-one years old. Yet within four years, his splendid hand-eye coordination led him to seek a career as a professional.

After becoming the head pro at Lake Spivey Golf Club in Jonesboro, Georgia, Charlie thought his game was good enough for him to give the Professional Golfers' Association tour a shot. He followed the pro circuit for two years before deciding to stay closer to home with his wife, Joyce, and two daughters.

One Friday morning in 1980, as the head pro at Fairfield Plantation in Carrollton, Georgia, Charlie accompanied several of the club's top amateur players to Moultrie, Georgia, to play in a two-day team competition.

In a motel room that night, Charlie woke and had to use the bathroom. When he tried to roll out of bed, however, his body would not respond. He tried to move his legs. Nothing.

"Guys, I think I'm in trouble," he said in the dark.

His playing partners turned on the lights. "Something wrong, Charlie?"

"Yeah. I can't move."

"Let's take a look."

They tried to roll Charlie onto his side, but the motion caused him to scream in pain. Paramedics were called, and they rushed Charlie to a nearby emergency room, where the attending doctor examined him. "I'm afraid we're going to have to operate on your back right now," he said. "We've got to do something about this."

Something told Charlie, dazed from the horrific pain he was experiencing, that letting a stranger mess around with his spinal cord was not a good idea.

"No, I have to go home."

"I don't recommend it, Mr. Sorrell."

"I don't care what it takes. Get me home."

"Okay, whatever you want."

Charlie was strapped onto a board and lifted into an ambulance for the three-and-a-half-hour journey home. Joyce had called a lumberyard and ordered a four-by-eight sheet of three-quarter-inch plywood for him to lie on.

His doctor came and examined him and talked in ominous tones of "fusing" two spinal disks. Charlie feared the delicate surgery, so he decided to follow a wait-and-see course.

Lying on his back twenty-four hours a day gave Charlie plenty of time to assess his situation. *My goodness,* he thought, *I can't even get up to go to the bathroom. Is my golf career over?*

For the next two weeks, Charlie seriously evaluated his life. He was a forty-one-year-old golf pro with no other job skills. If he couldn't fulfill his duties at the club, he didn't know what he would do.

Charlie prayed. As he did so, he realized that golf, not Jesus Christ, had been number one in his life. He went to church on Sundays, but he didn't have much of a commitment to church, let alone the Lord.

"Lord, if You will let me get up, I promise I will be there for You. Any time I can share this story with people, I will. I confess that I haven't been there for You in the past. But if You will allow me to get up and walk, You will see changes in me."

The next day, Charlie was able to pull himself up and then gradually, with the aid of a walker, take a few faltering steps. Day by day, he walked a little farther—even as far as the Fairfield Plantation pro shop in an attempt to perform his duties. Placing one foot in front of the other, he doggedly pursued the resumption of his career.

After another month of rehabilitation, he felt well enough to start hitting balls again. He was healed! No surgery was ever needed.

Twenty years later, Charlie is running his own twenty-five-acre private teaching facility behind his home in Stockbridge, Georgia. People come from all over the world to spend several days working with Charlie, who was selected National Teacher of the Year by the PGA and named as one of the "Top 100 Teachers in America" by *Golf* magazine.

Doctors who have examined his back can't explain why the two damaged disks healed themselves. But Charlie knows, which is why his story has become part of his daily lesson plan when he teaches golf to friends and strangers alike.

And whatever you do or say, let it be as a representative
of the Lord Jesus, all the while giving thanks through
him to God the Father (Colossians 3:17).

A PICTURE IN A PORTRAIT

37.

· *one untimely born* ·

Is it ever too late to start over? Some people may think so. They may think that if they've lived their whole life separated from God, He somehow doesn't like them anymore. Nothing could be further from the truth. There's a story in the Bible about some workers who were hired at different times of the day. When their pay was given out at the end of work, they all received the same wage— even those hired one hour before quitting time. God has a bigger view of time than you or I. He doesn't grade on a curve, either.

Clara Ruffin knew only this about her father: George Franklin Lewis was the only child of a schoolteacher and a florist. After schooling, he began an aimless existence marked by recklessness and irresponsibility. What else could explain why Clara and an older brother were born only two months apart to mothers who never married George Franklin?

Clara didn't see her father more than a half dozen times during her childhood. He eventually married Helen, a rival of Clara's mother, who later bore him four more children.

When Clara began attending Tougaloo College in Tougaloo, Mississippi, she joined the college choir. Since they traveled to nice places to perform, she desperately needed a nice pair of shoes. Her mama didn't have the money, so Clara decided to ask the father she barely knew.

"George Frank," she said over the phone, using the familiar form of his first and middle names (Clara refused to call him "Daddy" because he had never been a father to her), "I'm going to be in a concert next Friday, and I need some shoes. Can you wire me some money?"

She listened to his promise to help out. He was earning some money for a change, working a new job at the state hospital, and Clara dared to believe him. She had never asked him for anything before. No matter how poor the family had been, they were not beggars.

But the money never came. The ache of disappointment stayed with her for many years.

A decade passed, and Clara moved to Connecticut with her husband, Richard, and two sons. One day she was visiting her sister, Anne, who lived in Brooklyn.

"Did you know that George Franklin is in the hospital?" Anne said.

"No, I didn't," Clara said. "Let's go visit him," she suggested, curious to know if the years had changed her father.

They found St. Mary's Hospital and were directed to his room. Clara watched her father's eyes narrow in concentration as she approached his bed.

"Hi, George Frank," she said.

"Hi," he returned.

Clara noticed a puzzlement in his eyes. "So, how are you doing?" she asked.

"Fine," he answered. The puzzlement was real. He was straining to remember who his visitor was.

"Do you know who I am?" Clara asked.

"Well," he began, rubbing his chin, "you're some of my people. I can tell by your eyes."

"George Frank, I'm Clara!"

"Clara. Oh, yeah."

Clara wondered if perhaps her new hairstyle, a short Afro, threw him off. But she left the hospital that afternoon knowing her father had forgotten her.

More years passed, and George Franklin landed in the hospital once more. The years of carousing had caught up with him in the form of high blood pressure and diabetes. He lost a leg to amputation, and an infection kept him in the hospital.

Since her last visit with her father, Clara had become a

Christian, and her spiritual awakening prompted her to see him again. This time his eyes were filled with fear and loneliness, and Clara was moved with compassion.

"George Frank, do you know me?" she said, inching closer to his bed.

"Yes," he replied softly.

"Then who am I, George Frank?"

"You're Clara."

"Are you scared, George Frank? Do you feel alone?"

A slight nod gave Clara the answer she expected. His eyes were locked on her.

"Oh, George Frank! You don't have to be scared or alone. If you accept Jesus Christ as your Savior, you won't be alone." Clara paused. "Do you want to accept Him?"

Again he nodded.

"I mean really, because if you do I can lead you in a prayer that sinners like me have prayed. Right here, right now."

"Yes, I want you to do that."

"All right. Then repeat after me."

George Franklin followed Clara in prayer, acknowledging that Jesus was the Son of God, that He died on a cross for our sins, that He rose from the dead, that He would come again to judge and reign in splendor.

"Since God is life, George Frank, you don't have to fear

death," Clara said. "Jesus has said that He will never leave you or forsake you."

Clara wasn't surprised when she learned the next day her father had slipped into a coma. Two nights later, as Clara drifted in and out of sleep, she found herself praying earnestly—as hard as she'd ever prayed in her life—asking God to be with George Frank, until suddenly she sat up in bed.

"It's over," she said to her husband, shaking him awake. The alarm clock read 4:16 A.M. "George Frank is dead."

He had died at 4:14. A new, much better chapter in George Frank's life had just started in glory.

> God showed how much he loved us by sending his only
> Son into the world so that we might have eternal life
> through him. This is real love. It is not that we loved
> God, but that he loved us and sent his Son as a
> sacrifice to take away our sins (1 John 4:9–10).

A PICTURE

38.

· *pennies from heaven* ·

When I hear stories like the next two you are about to read, I picture God up in heaven saying to the angels, "Watch this!" The angels, of course, have seen it all many times. The loving God of the Bible coming through—to the penny—for a follower who stays faithful to Him and His Word.

Their schoolteacher salaries never left Bill and Eleanor Schlegl with a fat bank account or paid for Hawaiian vacations, but they were thankful for always having food on the table for their growing family. As the years passed and college arrived for their son, Bill, Jr., they needed another car.

"I'll make a deal with you," Bill told his son one night. "I'll pay your insurance premiums if you can handle other car expenses."

A couple of weeks later, Bill was sitting at his desk, working the calculator as he wrote checks to pay bills.

"Bill, dinner is ready," Eleanor said, wiping her hands on her apron.

"I'll be right there, honey."

"What's wrong, Bill?" She couldn't help noticing the frown on his face.

"I don't think we can pay all the bills this month. Billy's car insurance put us over the limit—by my calculations, two hundred and fifty-two dollars over the limit."

"What are we going to do?"

"I'm not sure, El. I don't know what to do."

Eleanor glanced at the pile of bills and checks and envelopes scattered across his desk. She noticed a check sitting off by itself.

"What's that?" she asked.

"Our church contribution."

Eleanor patted him on the back. "Bill, you've always paid our offering to God first, and still do. He won't forget us. He's taken care of us all these years, and He's not about to stop now. Something will happen to help us pay these bills."

Bill tried to force a smile. "Let's eat," he said.

The next day in the classroom, as Bill diagrammed a math problem on the chalkboard, the assistant principal walked into the room. This wasn't unusual, because he visited classrooms regularly, but on this occasion he didn't stand in the back and observe. Instead, he walked over to Bill's desk, placed an envelope on his lesson plan, smiled, waved, and walked out.

Bill's curiosity got the best of him. "Okay, class, I want you to do the even-numbered problems on pages twenty-four and twenty-five," he said. Bill sat at his desk and opened the envelope. To his utter disbelief and sheer delight, he found a check from the school district for $252.

The attached note said that after the last teachers' union contract, some faculty had been accidentally omitted from a special raise. The assistant superintendent had discovered the mistake and asked the school board to correct the error.

Some people might label the event pure coincidence, but Bill and Eleanor insist God answered their prayers. More than ever, they know that whatever they give to Him, He always gives back many, many times over.

But as for me and my family, we will serve
the Lord (Joshua 24:15d).

A PICTURE

39.

· *the last-minute enrollment* ·

On the road of life, there are speed bumps. Everything is running smoothly until, seemingly out of nowhere, there's a bump. It's during these bumps in life that "God things" tend to happen. What may look like God's answer to prayer . . . isn't. What may feel like a right decision . . . isn't. But when we hang in there long enough, and trust God to work it out, we find that "God things" happen in ways we never could have predicted.

Everyone told Rick Myatt that God wanted him at Claremont McKenna. *If so,* Rick thought, *God would need to provide.*

In the spring of 1968, Rick was going to *some* school. It was either college or a draft notice—an invitation to Vietnam—in the mailbox.

"What about Claremont McKenna College?" Rick's dad, Cal, suggested. "I did some graduate work there years ago." Claremont McKenna is one of the Claremont colleges located thirty miles east of downtown Los Angeles and one hundred miles south of the Myatts' home in Bakersfield.

"Isn't it expensive?" asked Rick.

"Yes, but it's top notch. You can apply for grant money from the state."

Rick's dad was right—he qualified for a Cal-Grant scholarship, which covered 80 percent of the $5,000 annual fee for tuition and room and board.

A month before the start of classes, Rick attended a Campus Crusade for Christ (a college parachurch ministry) conference and received the names of two other Claremont students who professed faith in Christ. Rick quickly looked them up on campus, but as the school year wore on, the two guys didn't seem all that interested in a ministry to students.

"I feel like I'm the only Christian on campus," Rick told his father during Christmas break.

"Hang in there," Cal replied. "The Lord has you there for a reason."

That spring, several Campus Crusade staff members got in touch with Rick, who arranged appointments for them with friends and classmates. Four students put their faith in Christ.

"Dad, I think we have some positive things happening here," Rick said.

Back home for the summer, he worked as an engineer's aide at

Occidental Petroleum Corporation. Not only did the job pay well, considering he was a college kid, but his office was air conditioned, much to the chagrin of his older brother, Jerry, who worked on a "traffic crew," painting crosswalks in the torrid Bakersfield heat.

During his sophomore year, Rick organized Bible studies in his dorm room and helped stage events where a large number of people could hear the Christian message, including a performance by a Christian illusionist named Andre Kole.

Jerry graduated from UCLA at the end of that school year, and Cal-Grant administrators figured the Myatt family didn't need as much scholarship money. Rick's grant was cut by $1,500—enough to keep Rick from returning to Claremont McKenna.

"We just can't swing it financially," his dad said that summer. "I'm just a high school social studies teacher."

Rick returned to the air-conditioned comfort of Occidental Petroleum and prayed that somehow God would provide the money for his junior year at Claremont McKenna.

Two things happened that caused him to wonder if the Lord was opening other doors: Occidental Petroleum offered Rick a permanent position, and California State University opened its campus in Bakersfield. Rick could work full time with Occidental and take night classes at Cal State.

This looked like God's answer to prayer. Besides, the more Rick thought about it, Claremont was a rich kids' school. His classmates were from the tony environs of South Pasadena, San Marino, and Atherton. Hadn't the scholarship rug been pulled out from underneath him? Maybe it was time to move on.

Or was it?

His heart was still in Claremont, where he was having an impact for God's Kingdom in classmates' lives. So why was God closing the door?

Several Claremont friends called. "I'm not coming back," Rick said.

"Not coming back? Rick, God wants you at Claremont. You *can't* leave."

"Sorry, but I can't go. I don't have the money."

Decision day was September 7, a week before the start of classes. On that day, Claremont McKenna needed to know whether he was returning; if not, they would give his place to a student on the waiting list. Occidental Petroleum was pressing for an answer as well.

Rick decided that if nothing fell out of the sky by September 6, he would accept the Occidental Petroleum position and enroll at Cal State Bakersfield. He pinned his hopes on an unexpected check in the mail. No letter came.

Well, that's it. I guess I'm staying home and working. It doesn't feel right, but that's God's answer.

At eight-thirty that evening, the phone rang for Rick. "This is

Richard Montgomery from the admissions office at Claremont McKenna."

"Good evening, Mr. Montgomery. What can I do for you?" Rick wondered why he was working so late.

"I understand that you're thinking about leaving Claremont."

"That's correct."

"Is money part of the reason?"

"Yes, it is."

"Well, if that is the reason, I've found a scholarship for you. Will that enable you to stay in school with us?"

"It depends on the amount of the scholarship," said Rick, his hopes rising.

"Let's see. Yes, it's for $1,500."

"I'll be there!"

His final two years at Claremont McKenna left no doubt God had good reasons for providing the scholarship money. The continuation of Rick's on-campus ministry not only led students to Jesus Christ but also changed career plans. After graduating with a math degree, Rick entered seminary. He's now the pastor of a thriving church in San Diego.

But I am trusting you, O Lord, saying, "You are my God!" My future is in your hands (Psalm 31:14–15a).

A PICTURE IN A PORTRAIT

40.

· *the unexpected trade* ·

In Acts 7, a disciple named Stephen was brutally martyred while others watched. Was it something about Stephen's death, however, that helped make a Jewish zealot named Saul into the beloved apostle known as Paul?

I wish following God and obeying His will sometimes had different earthly consequences. For Stephen, it meant death. But for Saul, Stephen's death may have played a critical role in leading him closer to a new life in Christ. What man meant for harm, God turned for good. The story on the next few pages shows how God allows a faithful follower to impact thousands in the midst of trial and adversity.

National Football League running back Sherman Smith, the "Sherman Tank," stood six feet four inches tall and packed two hundred twenty-five pounds of the most solid muscle you'd ever want to tackle. His reputation for bowling over defensive linemen raised his celebrity to near-cult status in the Pacific Northwest, where he played for the Seattle Seahawks. Sherman couldn't cross a Seattle street without being stopped, patted on the back, or asked for an autograph. He was treated like royalty.

Without warning, the Seahawks traded their most popular player to the San Diego Chargers. Everything changed for this running back whose Christian faith was as rock solid as his rib cage. Sherman arrived in a city where nobody knew him and nobody cared. He wasn't with the Chargers for more than a few weeks when he blew out his knee. While in rehabilitation, he wondered, *Lord, why did you ship me to San Diego?*

While his knee mended, Sherman participated in team meetings and joined the club on road trips. He also spoke boldly about his faith—fellow Chargers knew exactly where he stood.

Once while flying back to San Diego after a game, Sherman stood in the aisle with a Bible the size of the Ten Commandments tablets in one hand while leading a Bible study for several players. A defensive back named Miles McPherson asked Sherman to move so he could use the rest room.

Sherman didn't know that Miles had a line of cocaine in his pocket and was planning to get high, but he knew his teammate did not have a personal relationship with God. A good-looking party guy, Miles was a single who knew how to mingle.

"Can I get by?" Miles asked.

"What's up, little brother?" Sherman responded.

"Who are you calling little?"

"You!"

"Okay, okay," Miles laughed. They both knew who the big guy was on the plane.

Before he let Miles pass, Sherman asked him point-blank, "If you were to die today, what would happen to you?"

"I would go to heaven."

"How do you know?"

"Look, man, I went to Catholic school for eight years. I wore a green suit every day. I'm going to heaven for that."

"Nah, you ain't going to heaven for that."

"Look, man, we used to have nuns in our school who were five-foot-two, two hundred and sixty pounds, and they used to smack us in the head. I'm going to heaven for that."

"Nah, you ain't going to heaven for that."

"Why not?" Miles asked.

"Let me tell you a story, little brother."

Sherman proceeded to tell Miles about Nicodemus from the third chapter of the Gospel of John. Nicodemus was well educated in Jewish culture and the Old Testament. He had watched Jesus Christ heal lepers, raise a little girl from the dead, and restore the sight of a blind man.

Nicodemus said to Jesus, "Rabbi, we know you are a teacher who has come from God. For no one could perform the miraculous signs you are doing if God were not with him."

And Jesus said to him, "I tell you the truth, no one can see the kingdom of God unless he is born again."

"How can a man be born when he is old?" Nicodemus asked. "Surely he cannot enter a second time into his mother's womb to be born!"

Miles thought about Sherman's message for a long time. On April 12, 1984, after doing cocaine all night, Miles got on his knees and surrendered his life to Christ. He prayed, "Jesus, I ask you to be my Savior today, and I will surrender my whole life to you. I don't want to live for myself anymore. I will do whatever you want me to do. I will be whatever you want me to be."

When Christ became his Savior, Miles stopped doing cocaine, stopped smoking marijuana, stopped cursing, and stopped picking up girls. He also told Sherman what happened. Sherman and two other players began meeting with Miles to study the Bible, helping him learn from the Word of God. When Miles said he wanted to share his faith with others, they said, "Go for it."

Today, Miles McPherson is an outstanding youth communicator who preaches to tens of thousands each year at Miles Ahead crusades.

Miles and Sherman both know now why the "Sherman Tank" was traded from Seattle to San Diego. God had a plan.

Seek the Lord while you can find him. Call on him now while he is near. Let the people turn from their wicked deeds. Let them banish from their minds the very thought of doing wrong! Let them turn to the Lord that he may have mercy on them. Yes, turn to our God, for he will abundantly pardon (Isaiah 55:6–7).

A PICTURE

41.

· *hitchhiking to a safe place* ·

"With God, all things are possible." Is that a trite phrase or the truth? A witness can only testify to what he has seen. As one witness for God, I can say—without reservation—that there are few six-word phrases with more truth in them. I have heard the stories of thousands of people at the end of their rope who reached out for God. And when they did, they quickly discovered that God was already reaching out for them. God's grace works in many ways, but never more powerfully than when someone finally reaches out to firmly grasp the hand of the Savior.

"Why don't you just kill yourself?" Kristi Dougherty muttered as she stumbled out of yet another bar.

Her teenage daughter had walked out on her and went to live with her father. Another man Kristi was living with abused her and told her she was worthless. *Maybe you are worthless,* she thought. *In fact, you have no reason to be alive.*

Kristi had begun drinking heavily in high school. She bragged that she drank a case of beer a day. Then she met a guy, had a child, and tried to deal with life as best she could. Her best coping mechanism was getting drunk or high enough to fall asleep quickly.

In the summer of 1998, Kristi drifted from Seattle to Pasco, Washington, with a few bucks in her pocket . . . and a death wish. Along the way, she visited her mother and then her brother, a crack addict who frequently lived on the streets.

"You can always find clothes and something to eat in the city," he said. "Just ask for the worst part of town and look for a mission."

Kristi didn't want to be homeless; there was no future in that. She needed money to pay for a hotel room, so she took to the streets and prostituted herself—*a first for me,* she grimaced. Then she checked into a threadbare motel with a six-pack of beer and three dollars to her name. Her plan, she decided, was to drink the beer and then slash her wrists with a broken bottle.

When she walked into the bathroom and broke off the top of a brown bottle, she decided it was too early in the evening. *I need to write those suicide notes first,* she thought.

She set down the piece of glass and walked outside, where she spied a tavern down the street. Inside, the bartender gave her three sheets of paper, a pencil, and an ice-cold draft. She made small talk with the bouncer, and before she knew it, she had invited him to her room to drink a few more beers.

Early in the morning, Kristi was awakened by a hard knock on the door.

"Who is it?"

"Hotel manager. You're going to have to go."

"Wait, I got money. I promise."

"If you can't pay me now, you gotta go."

Kristi didn't have the money so she shuffled out the door with a broken beer bottle in her hand. Up ahead, she saw the Blue Bridge spanning the Columbia River between Pasco and Kennewick. She found a place under the bridge, sat down, rolled up her left sleeve, and jabbed the jagged glass at her wrist, causing it to bleed, but not profusely. Apparently she had missed the main artery, so she tried the other arm. Same result.

You can't even kill yourself, she thought.

Wearing black dungarees and a blood-stained white shirt, Kristi stumbled onto the bridge. She looked over the edge and contemplated leaping into the Columbia. *No, I'd probably survive the fall.* She could see the newspaper headline: SUICIDE ATTEMPT FAILS. She kept walking.

Ahead a green eighteen-wheel truck was parked on the shoulder. The driver, an old man, was sleeping.

"Mister, I need a ride to California," she said.

The trucker rubbed his eyes as he pulled himself out of the sleeper behind the seat.

"I can lose my job if someone catches you riding with me," he said.

Kristi shrugged her shoulders.

"Okay, get in," he said. "I have to sleep some more, but you can lie down here." He pointed to the bench seat in the cab and then handed her a blanket.

Several hours later, he fired up the rig and drove west toward Portland. Just outside the city, he pulled off at a truck stop.

"I'm afraid this is the end of the line. You're going to have to catch a ride with someone else," he said. "If you hitch a ride with another trucker, you're going to have to sleep with him, so be forewarned."

He pulled out his wallet and handed Kristi three dollars. "Here. You may be needing this."

Kristi decided to take her chances hitchhiking on the freeway. A man about her age, in his thirties, pulled over.

"Where you headed?"

"I don't know," replied Kristi. "Portland? I want to go to the worst part of town. That's where the missions are."

Kristi soon found herself at the Harbor Light Salvation Army, a women's facility, working in the kitchen. Two days later, someone handed her a gospel tract.

Kristi stuffed it in her pocket, and when her shift was over, she returned to Room 210 and read the tract. In tears and on her knees she prayed, "If there is a God, I ask You to come into my heart. Please do that right now. I need You. If You can forgive me for what I've done and take away all my guilt and shame, I will walk with You the rest of my life."

Kristi repeated that prayer three more times and felt that God had heard her. But what to do next? The following day, Pastor Jeff at the mission invited her to a Bible study and promised to get help for her at a domestic violence shelter.

What put her on the road that turned her life around, Kristi decided, was God sending two unlikely yet kind male drivers who took her to the very place she needed to go, so that she could get her life—and eternity—together. An elderly truck driver who never picked up hitchhikers, and a gentleman who didn't try to take advantage of her. Why did they give her a ride? Kristi only knows that if they hadn't, she never would have reached her appointment with God.

But then God our Savior showed us his kindness and love. He saved us, not because of the good things we did, but because of his mercy. He washed away our sins and gave us a new life (Titus 3:4–5).

A PORTRAIT

42.

· *a better sense* ·

Those reading these pages who appreciate the fact that God places a "call" on specific individuals may also know that He won't place that call without giving an extra measure of grace and skill to accomplish the task at hand. The story that follows shows how creative God is in portioning out His boundless grace to those who have devoted their lives to Him.

When Lillian Doerksen boarded the ship in September 1950, she had no doubts God was leading her to India.

"Dear Lord, if I am to serve you here in India as I believe you want me to," she prayed, "I need you."

A friend at school had told her about the Pandita Ramabai Mukti Mission in Maharashtra, where eight hundred orphans were in need of care. The mission was founded by Pandita Ramabai in 1868. She had been a Hindu before she found the Lord Jesus Christ and devoted her life's work to caring for thousands of starving, destitute girls, many of them abandoned by their families.

When Lillian disembarked the ship in Bombay, a mass of humanity and poverty assaulted her senses. Walking through the dusty streets, she saw desperate mothers lying on the sidewalk with their children, hands outstretched for alms; rail-thin men straining to pull carts through the crowded thoroughfares; and bony cows, aimlessly walking through the fetid streets. Hindu strictures against the killing of cows allowed them to roam at will.

And the smells! The spicy smells of cumin and coriander in the marketplace made Lillian's stomach turn. Then smoky-scented waves of curry-spiced food simmering on street carts blew across her face, causing her to nearly double over.

Fighting nausea, Lillian bowed her head in prayer. "Lord, please sanctify my smeller. I need you to take away my sense of smell, or otherwise I will have to go back on the same ship to Canada."

Lillian opened her eyes and breathed deeply through her nostrils. The smells were gone! She inhaled again. She couldn't smell! As she continued to walk through the packed marketplace, Lillian bent over a bag of curry spice. Again, nothing.

Lillian devoted herself to the orphaned girls of the Mukti mission until her retirement thirty-seven years later. Although her taste buds can savor the food she eats, she still has no sense of smell. None of her doctors has ever been able to explain why. Other than a miracle.

As for God, his way is perfect. All the Lord's promises come true. He is a shield for all who look to him for protection (Psalm 18:30).

A PORTRAIT

43.

· a child shall lead them ·

Do all things truly work together for good? As you have seen throughout this book, the answer is "If you wait long enough, they usually do." And although it is difficult to wait, without waiting comes anger, resentment, bitterness, and faithlessness. Is it possible to notice things working together for good without faith? Unlikely. So . . . God simply asks us to be patient and depend on Him to keep His promises.

Three-year-old Brandon was a fussy eater, but this was ridiculous. He loved eggs, pancakes, and sausage for breakfast, but for lunch and dinner as well? If his mother, Karen LeMaster, didn't cook breakfast three times a day, Brandon threw head-banging fits and tried to dismantle every toy in the house.

The LeMaster home had to be "Brandon-proofed," so Karen's husband, Steve, put locks on everything and even installed motion detectors to catch Brandon during his middle-of-the-night mischief prowls.

The parents sought medical help. Tests revealed that Brandon was autistic. Autism, the LeMasters learned, is a developmental disability, the result of a neurological disorder.

Because Karen worked full time outside the home, Brandon's autism presented a problem when she searched for adequate day care for her son. The last day-care director informed Karen that they no longer could handle Brandon and his penchant for pulling the fire alarm.

Karen looked at eight day-care centers in one day, three of them church-based. Although she and Steve didn't attend church, they were open to sending Brandon to a church-based day-care center because of the "good values" and loving discipline he was likely to receive.

During her interview at St. Matthew's Lutheran Church, Karen was brutally honest about Brandon's behavioral problems. "He is hyper, he needs to be watched constantly, and he's autistic," Karen told Rhonda, the day care director.

"Let's give Brandon a try," Rhonda replied.

Although Brandon was still a handful, his parents were amazed at the subtle changes they noticed. On the drive home, Brandon sang choruses he had learned that day. At dinnertime, while his parents and twelve-year-old brother, Christopher, were poised with forks ready, Brandon said, "Wait, Mom. We have to say grace." Then he would bow his head and pray, "God is good, God is great. Thank you for the food on our plate. Amen."

Brandon also insisted on praying before bedtime, putting his hands together while reciting, "Now I lay me down to sleep; I pray the Lord my soul to keep. Guide me safely through the day; wake me in your care I pray."

Karen and Steve were touched by their son's sensitive heart, as was Christopher. One time after picking up Brandon, Christopher said, "You know, Mom, I'd like to go to church."

The LeMasters had never gone to church together as a family. It wasn't that they didn't believe in God; there was just never enough time. But with Christopher's desire and Brandon's budding spirituality, the LeMasters began attending the church where Brandon went to daycare. After a few months, they found Sunshine Community Church, a growing congregation.

Steve's mom was ecstatic that the family had hooked up with a church. When she heard about the Luis Palau crusade coming to El Paso in May 1997, she encouraged Steve and Karen to attend one night.

They didn't seem interested and made no plans to attend, but on the spur of the moment they decided to come to the Wednesday night rally at the Convention Center, along with their boys.

The LeMasters were going to sit near the front, but Brandon's ears were too sensitive to the loud music. Instead, they found seats at the rear of the auditorium, which was packed with more than six thousand people.

When they sat down, Brandon tugged at his mother and pointed to Grandma LeMaster sitting in the row in front of them!

"Grandma, what are you doing here?" Brandon asked.

When Steve's mother turned, the surprise on her face became a huge smile.

Later that evening, the LeMasters stood as a family and walked forward to publicly state their commitment to Jesus Christ. Grandma LeMaster didn't know if she could keep her heart from bursting, she was so happy.

Brandon's behavior has improved considerably since then, but that isn't the biggest miracle, of course. God used Brandon's autism to steer Steve and Karen to church and an interest in spiritual matters. Without Brandon, the LeMasters might have never found a true relationship with God.

But Jesus said, "Let the children come to me. Don't stop them! For the Kingdom of Heaven belongs to such as these" (Matthew 19:14).

A PORTRAIT

44.

· *to latvia with love* ·

Have you ever wondered if you're worthy of God's rich love? Many people do. A life of either ignorance of God's character or intentionally ignoring what you know to be true can make you believe you are somehow unworthy to receive the great love of God. Did you know that God never thinks anyone is unworthy? I can't say that strongly enough! If this book or the story that follows doesn't illustrate this truth well enough, would you do me a favor? Please call, write, or e-mail my ministry (see page 227) and give us a chance—without any pressure—to convince you that God loves you today, tomorrow, and forever. I pray you will.

Like her childhood friends, Kristine Strele, seven years old, was a Child of October. She proudly wore a star bearing the image of Vladimir Lenin, leader of the revolution. She didn't know what it meant. "I just thought Lenin was a great man who loved children," she said.* "That's what we were taught."

When she was a little older, Kristine joined Pioneers—not that she had a choice. Her friends also were members of the Communist student organization. "There was a certain pride to wear the red scarf around my neck," she said, even if everyone else did, too.

But by the time Kristine was sixteen and a student in art school, the sameness of the Soviet system in Latvia left her feeling caged in and insignificant. She discovered not everyone in the world lived such austere, rigid lives. She was a teenager with opinions she couldn't express, a unique person whose identity couldn't stand out. Kristine wanted to be special, to be important, to have friends who admired her.

"We were all potential artists, so no one was any more special than anyone else," she said. "I was looking for friends who would understand me outside of school and the artists' society. And I met people who weren't good friends for me . . ."

Even in Communist-controlled Latvia, a teenager can get in trouble running with the wrong crowd. Kristine's compulsion to

*To receive a VHS copy of Kristine's full testimony, please write to the address on page 227.

be special hit another feeling head on: guilt. The voice of conscience was telling her she wasn't doing "good" things; she wasn't with the "right" people.

Kristine's grandparents were Christians, and although they didn't talk much about their faith, occasionally they took their little granddaughter to church with them. As a result, Kristine grew up believing in God.

"I knew there was somebody more powerful we can pray to when we have a need, and that's all," she said. "When I needed help, I prayed to God, but I didn't know who He was. But the feeling was growing quite strong that I should do something more worthy of believing in God."

That's when Kristine decided it would be a good thing to sing in a "spiritual choir," and she ended up in her grandparents' church, Saint Matthew's Baptist Church, Sunday morning, September 10, 1989. Gorbachev's *glasnost* had opened doors for Christian speakers in five cities of the Soviet Union, including Riga, the capital of Latvia.

"When I asked my mom which choir I should go to, she suggested Saint Matthew's," Kristine said. "Interesting thing, when my mom was a teenager, she was singing in the choir because of her parents. Later, when she got married, she walked away from God. But the choir was still in her memory as something special."

Kristine had been in the choir only a couple of weeks when it was announced a special service was coming. "We will have this evangelist—everyone please wear white blouses or white shirts."

"I'm glad it happened soon, because I was desperate," Kristine said. "There wasn't peace in my heart. As he was preaching, it seemed as if he knew exactly what was happening in my life. I understood one thing: I needed forgiveness. My life hadn't been right, not the way it should be, and I finally heard that I could say no to my past and start a new life with God.

"As he invited people to come forward who wanted to have Jesus in their life, my heart was starting to beat really fast. I thought, if I stay in my seat I'm going to explode. My knowledge of things was very small, but it was so powerful that one thing I understood: I need Christ."

Fluent in English, Kristine began serving as a translator for Western missionaries who came to Latvia when the Iron Curtain lifted. One young man about to graduate from Bible college in Canada needed someone to translate the Bible studies he was teaching out in Latvia's countryside. Dustin Peterson asked for Kristine.

Kristine had a hunch this was more than a ministry opportunity. She prayed a long time before she accepted the job. Dustin and Kristine eventually married and are teaching the Bible and translating Bible study literature in Latvia as missionaries with Greater Europe Mission.

"I feel very special," Kristine said. "I'm special because I have the Lord, because I can talk with him and He lives within me. And I feel very special that I can serve God."

So now we can rejoice in our wonderful new relationship
with God—all because of what our Lord Jesus
Christ has done for us in making us friends
of God (Romans 5:11).

A PICTURE AND A PORTRAIT

45.

· *over the years* ·

And finally, two stories from my own life; two of many I could tell of how God is intimately aware of the pictures of my life, yet just as aware of the portrait He is creating.

After my father died when I was only ten years old, my family plunged into poverty, and eventually I became the breadwinner, responsible for my mom and five younger sisters. I was still a teenager when the Bank of London in Buenos Aires gave me a trainee's position. Everything I earned went to the family to pay bills—it seemed we owed money to everyone.

On a day when I didn't even have money for the bus ride downtown, I prayed, "Lord, I'm going to trust You to get me to work. I want to test whether You will answer my prayer." I figured the Lord would answer by providing the money—somewhere from my home to the bus stop I would find ten pesos.

On that dark, foggy morning, I walked slowly all the way to

the bus stop, searching the pavement for money. When I didn't find any, I decided to walk a little farther into town to the next bus stop. Not a peso.

I was getting discouraged and thought, *I don't have enough faith, that's all. I'll keep walking.*

Just then I saw a fellow trying to get an old car out of a garage to start it. "Would you like a hand?" I called out.

"Yes, please," he said.

I helped him push the car out of the garage and down the hill. The car started and disappeared into the fog. I kept walking, still looking for my ten pesos.

A few minutes later I heard an idling car. "I'm really embarrassed," the driver said. "You helped me push my car and then I left you. Where are you going?"

"Right into the heart of town. I work at the Bank of London."

"I work at the bank across the street," he said. "Come on, hop in."

There was my answer to prayer! Today that seems an awfully simple answer, but it was the first time that God clearly answered my prayer. Different from what I expected, but He answered.

A much more dramatic story took place a few years ago. I had accepted an invitation to conduct a speaking tour in Peru, South

America, during what ended up becoming a very precarious time in that nation's history. Maoist *Sendero Luminoso* (Shining Path) guerrillas pushed the country to the brink of anarchy, wiping out entire villages, executing military and civil authorities, and martyring religious leaders by the score.

In Shining Path's bloody attempt to overturn the Peruvian government and create a "new society," the terrorists turned their attention to the capital city of Lima, a teeming metropolis of seven million people. The guerrillas targeted American symbols to gain Washington's attention, invading United Press International offices, blowing up an American-owned department store, and even attacking the American Embassy.

I found myself in a panic-stricken country with speaking engagements booked solid for two weeks.

My meetings in Peru's second-largest city, Arequipa, concluded without incident. As I walked out of the last meeting, several envelopes were pressed into my hands. I put them in my pocket for later reading. Later in my hotel room I remembered the envelopes and pulled them out, expecting to read letters of thanks from individuals whose lives had been changed in some way. A colleague noticed when I suddenly tensed up. "What's the matter?" he asked. One of the notes I had just opened was a death threat from the Shining Path. I was warned to leave the country within twenty-four hours or "die like a dog." I didn't know exactly what it meant to "die like a dog," but I wasn't eager to find out.

After much discussion, my colleagues and I decided to proceed anyway. Security was tightened, but there's only so much you can do to guard against terrorists.

The first night at Lima's Alianza Stadium, thirty thousand packed the stands to hear how God still changes lives today. The crowd gasped when they heard a series of explosions in the distance. The stadium lights flickered, yet—thank God—remained on. The rest of Lima, however, was suddenly plunged into darkness. Shining Path guerrillas had blown up electrical power stations throughout the city in an attempt to shut off our power supply, but the only place the lights remained on was the neighborhood surrounding Alianza Stadium!

Grateful that we didn't have thirty thousand people panicking to reach for the exits, I breathed deeply and continued speaking with an extra sense of urgency, thankful that God had miraculously kept the lights on. I told those assembled that this was a time when a decision for God could *not* wait.

[R]emember the former things of old; for I am God, and there is no other; I am God, and there is none like me, declaring the end from the beginning and from ancient times things not yet done, saying, "My counsel shall stand, and I will accomplish all my purpose," calling a bird of prey from the east, the man of my counsel from a far country, I have spoken, and I will bring it to pass; I have purposed, and I will do it (Isaiah 46:9–11 RSV).

· *acknowledgments* ·

All praise to God, for whom "everything is possible" (Matthew 19:26).

Thanks to my editor, Trace Murphy, and to my agents, Greg Johnson and David Sanford, who believed in this book and encouraged me to tell these stories.

Thanks to Mike Yorkey for talking at length with scores of individuals and working so hard on many of the chapters in this book. Thanks also to Greg Johnson, Mike Umlandt, Holly Hudson, and Christine Skultety for their invaluable editorial assistance. Additional thanks to Steve Halliday, Debbie Hedstrom, Diane McDougall, and Stephen and Amanda Sorenson.

Thanks to the thousands of people around the world who have shared their stories with me in recent years.

Special thanks to my son Keith and my wife, Patricia, for helping me select the stories to feature in this book.

· *we'd love to hear from you!* ·

Do you have an amazing story to tell? Did God work a miracle in your life or the life of a close friend or family member? If so, we'd love to hear about it! Tell us your story in your own words and send it to:

Luis Palau
P.O. Box 1173
Portland, OR 97207
Fax (503) 614–1599
E-mail palau@palau.org
Web www.lpea.org

· *more true stories!* ·

To receive more true "God thing" stories via e-mail, please sign up for our new electronic newsletter. Once or twice a month, you'll receive a new inspirational "Look at what God did!" story via e-mail.

To request your free e-zine subscription, simply send an e-mail note to Godthing-subscribe@lists.gospelcom.net with only the words "subscribe Godthing" in the body of the e-mail. Or use the handy subscription form at http://www.lpea.org/sub-scription.shtml.

And while you're online, be sure to look for more stories at http://www.lpea.org/Godthing.shtml.